LOVE
FROM THE
Shadows

L. J. WEDE

ISBNs:

978-1-965706-08-4 (Digital)

978-1-965706-07-7 (Paperback)

978-1-965706-06-0 (Hardcover)

CONTENT EXPECTATIONS

Certain scenes in this book may be upsetting for some readers. A non-exhaustive list of potentially upsetting content may be reviewed at https://ljwede.com/content-warnings/.

To the Italian Mafia.
Without you, I wouldn't have my favorite book genre.
Thanks.

CONTENTS

AUTHOR'S NOTE

Each time I sit down to write an author's note, I get the unique opportunity to reflect on the journey I took from ideation to publishing. It's both rewarding and a bit surreal.

On one hand, this is the third book I'm publishing, so it's nothing crazy or new. On the other, this project is the first step into the largest undertaking I've ever committed myself to — writing a six-book series, which is quite crazy and intimidating.

But as I stop to reflect on *Love From the Shadows,* I get an incredibly warm feeling all throughout my body. I often joke that I read each book five or so times before it gets published due to the sheer amount of editing involved, but I think I've read *Love From the Shadows* genuinely fifteen times or more. Likely more.

Somehow, I have written my favorite book, and that is a breathtaking realization.

Truly, I'll return to this book to check a detail as I'm working on the rest of the series, and several hours later, I'll look up to realize that I've finished reading the book *again* and I've forgotten what I was fact-checking in the first place. It's a joy and a privilege I try not to take for granted.

You know what's even crazier?

There's five more books to follow.

-L. J. Wede

PROLOGUE
VIVIANNA

My entire life, one thing has been true. The Palazzos protect the Maranos. One statement. One fact. As undeniable as gravity or the moon. Grass is green. Two plus two equals four. Garlic doesn't belong in carbonara. The Palazzos protect the Maranos, and I'm a Palazzo.

It's been this way for generations. Our families have been linked together long before we emigrated to Bridgeport City. The details of this arrangement have been lost to time. Vague family legends speak of a life debt owed from when a Marano saved a Palazzo centuries ago, but the truth of the story is, the origin doesn't matter. My ancestors created the Ombra, the protective shadow always a step behind, silently standing guard over the one we shield. Grass is green. Two plus two equals four. Garlic doesn't belong in carbonara. My life's purpose is to join the Ombra and protect the Maranos.

Or, it should be. It would be if I was a man. Instead, the role falls to my twin, Vincenzo. From a young age, he trained with firearms, blades, fists. Instead of geometry and physics, his education consisted of first aid and defense training.

They didn't know what to do with me. My mother tried to entice me with cooking and housekeeping lessons, teaching me to be the perfect wife for a good Italian husband, but it didn't fit. Then, much to my mother's chagrin, my father pulled me into Vinny's lessons.

"Enzo needs a training partner," he said. "Someone his age to push him to improve. Let Anna help him."

She protested with excuse after excuse, wanting to raise me as a proper woman to be wed off, much like her own life. But she married into the Palazzo family. She doesn't understand. The Palazzos protect the Maranos. And I'm not a woman, I'm a machine.

It didn't take long for me to catch up to Vinny, and even less time to surpass him. I excelled, spending all of my free time in the shooting range or the gym, pushing myself harder and harder. Meanwhile, Vinny seemed to withdraw, begrudgingly going through the motions of training. I still don't understand how he doesn't want this, to fulfill the Palazzo legacy and become a member of the Ombra, especially when it comes to Damian Marano.

Dad is responsible for protecting his father, but Damian, he is our duty. No, my brother's duty. Born just a few months apart, Vinny and Damian were sent on playdates since before they could talk. I have always been kept away from Damian, though I sneak glances through the kitchen window to catch glimpses of his black hair, carefully combed out of his face. Our interactions come in small moments. His voice as he says my name. His smile as I deliver biscotti to Vinny's room. His eyes catching mine as someone closes his car door. Then he is gone again, ushered back to the compound of his father's mafia, where he waits until Vinny is old enough to protect him. Turns out, the magic age is sixteen.

My mother has never been more restless in her life — fluffing pillows and picking lint off of Vinny's suit jacket. Dad walks into the living room and wraps his hands around her waist, lightly kissing her neck. She relaxes into him and just for a moment, she smiles. Dad tousles my hair as he moves to sit next to Vinny.

"I'm so proud of you, Enzo." Dad beams, nudging Vinny's shoulder. "Finally joining the Ombra, becoming a man."

"Thanks, Dad." His voice is quiet, submissive. He doesn't lift his eyes from the black material of his suit sleeves, a perfect match to Dad's. Each member of the Marano syndicate wears the same black suit. Vinny got his today. I'll never have one. Maybe that's why today I'm wearing a black dress, trying to pretend in some way that this isn't the day my dreams finally wither and I am left behind, trying to pretend that today I am also pledging my life in service to Damian.

But I'm not.

Instead, I'm summoned to the kitchen to help Mom put the finishing touches on the tiramisu. The doorbell rings and I hear Mr. Marano excitedly greet my father. The two are practically inseparable, both physically and emotionally. Best friends. Companions. Confidantes. The ideal Ombra and protectee.

I take our finest china to the table, meticulously arranging each place setting as I try to duck the melancholia floating aside me. Napkin. Fork. Knife. Spoon. Napkin. Fork—

"Hi, Viv."

Only one person calls me by that nickname.

"Damian." I glance up to see him casually standing in the entryway. It seems Damian also got his suit today, crisply pressed and tailored to his frame. A sleek tie is carefully knotted around his neck, setting him apart from Dad and Vinny. The suit makes sense on him, befitting his smooth charm and suave confidence. "I like your suit."

"Thanks," Damian chuckles, smoothing his lapel. He steps into the dining room fully and grabs a few wine glasses from the hutch. "I can set these out for you."

"Oh, this isn't something you need to worry about." I reach out to take the crystal from him, but he takes a step back out of my grasp.

"I'm not worried," he counters, clutching the glasses to his chest defensively. "Let me help."

"Okay," I relent, returning to my napkins and silverware. Damian follows me to each place setting until we fully circle the table.

"What's next?" He asks. His gaze settles back onto me, awaiting instruction.

"Next you go back to the den and get ready." I lean over the table and adjust the centerpiece, spinning the vase so the prettiest flowers face the seat which I know will be Damian's later. We shouldn't be talking. I'm not supposed to interact with him. "My mother and I will finish up here, but my father is probably getting nervous that you're not spending time with Vincenzo before the ceremony."

"I would argue that I'm with the more interesting twin." He says that with such informality, though I'm acutely aware of every move he makes as he leans against the wall. "Besides, I'll see Enzo every day for the rest of my life. He can wait."

Before I can stop it, I frown ever so slightly. Vinny will be his Ombra, not me. I never had a chance. I shove my dismay down somewhere hidden inside and collect myself, but not fast enough for Damian to miss my reaction. His eyes stare into mine, a slight flicker of concern hidden carefully behind his composed expression.

"Enzo will visit often," Damian promises. "I'm not trying to separate you two."

"I know." I turn away from him, smoothing down the perfectly fine tablecloth.

"It must be hard watching your father and your brother risk their lives for my family." His voice is soft, sympathetic. "But I swear to you, that is not something either my father or I take lightly. I'll do everything I can to keep Enzo safe."

"They'll be fine." My expression is steeled, concealing my dejected thoughts from view. "Palazzos don't go down easily."

"Viv…" His hand brushes my shoulder, and I whip around to face him, startled by the sudden contact. Damian retreats a step, hands in the air nonthreateningly. After a breath, I relax while he cautiously moves closer. His brows furrow as he scrutinizes my face, unable to see my emotions through my practiced defenses. "Talk to me. What's wrong?"

"Damian!" Mr. Marano calls from the other room. "Where did you run off to?"

"Go," I urge softly, forcing a smile to my face. "I need to check on dinner anyway."

"We're not done," Damian protests weakly, but it's no use. I step around Damian to close the doors of the hutch as I leave the room. As I cross the threshold, I spare one final glance his direction. His head is bowed and his shoulders sag as he fiddles with his cufflinks.

"The suit really does look nice on you." I hesitate as Damian looks up at me, meeting my eyes one final time. "I'll see you at the ceremony."

With that, I leave him. My mother directs me around the kitchen, finishing this and that for dinner. She's acting as though we're cooking for the Queen, and I suppose in a sense, the Maranos are our royal family. Mr. Marano is our king, Damian is our prince, the Ombra is the guard, and I am no one. There's no place for women in the mafia. There's no place for me.

But now's not the time for my self-pity. Now's the time to celebrate Vinny.

The families gather in the den. The two sons face each other in the front of the room, with their respective fathers standing proudly behind them. My dad passes a small knife to Vinny, the polished metal reflecting the ceiling light.

Vinny slowly kneels before Damian. The blade shakes in his hand until Dad places a reassuring hand on my twin's shoulder.

A deep breath in. He closes his eyes and presses the edge into his palm until it draws a thin line of blood. Mr. Marano nudges Damian forward and he extends his hand down to Vinny, looking just as uncomfortable as my brother. Their hands join and Vinny recites the blood oath in Italian, the words stumbling from his mouth barely coherent.

Then it's done. Dad bandages Vinny's hand with proud tears in his eyes. Mr. Marano claps his son on the back as Damian stares at the blood smeared on his palm. My mother clenches her hands in her lap, but I just sit there.

Numb.

Vacant.

A forced composure masks any emotion I won't let myself feel as I watch my brother get everything I ever wanted. And I just… sit there.

As the fathers continue celebrating, my mother ushers me into the kitchen. I take trays of food to the dining table — osso buco, citrus gremolata, polenta, bread. No sooner than the last dish was laid on the tablecloth did the men stride in, glasses of whiskey in hand. Mr. Marano and my father take the head and foot of the table. Vinny and Damian sit on one side, and my mother and I sit on the other.

Mr. Marano doesn't visit often, and when he does, I never get so much as the time of day from him unless I'm doing something useful. He stops by occasionally to watch Vinny train, admonishing him when I win our spars. My successes are always viewed as my twin's failures. Even seated, his intimidating stature seems to swallow me in his shadow. The upside is, I am sitting across from Damian.

Food is passed around, and the adults launch into jovial conversation. Vinny pushes his veal around his plate with his fork. Damian's gaze keeps drifting to me, and I can see the gears turning in his head, still digesting our earlier conversation. But I was trained better than to let anything show.

Emotions make you vulnerable, my dad would always say. *Hide them or they will be used against you.*

So I don't let Damian see my disappointment. Instead, a fake smile brightens my face as I listen to Mr. Marano tell a story about my father hitting some thug over the head with a table lamp once upon a time. I chuckle absentmindedly at a joke my Dad quips and Damian quietly spreads butter onto a hunk of bread. Our eyes meet once again and linger there, his amber irises trapping me in their depth. It's no wonder I don't see the gunmen until it's too late.

BANG!

I leap over the table without a second thought, tackling Damian to the ground as a second bullet pierces the wall behind where he was sitting a second earlier. With my body shielding his, I turn and see eight pairs of boots storm into view. Who knows if there's more coming? We can't stay here.

"Dad!" Damian screams from below me, reaching for his father's crumpled form. Blood seeps from the wound in his forehead.

He's dead.

My mother's shrieks cut through the sound of the gunshots. I risk a glance up and see my father firing at the horde of men streaming into the doorway. Vinny is crouched under the table, eyes wide.

"We have to go!" I tug on Damian's arm, urging him to follow me, but instead he crawls to his father, shaking his shoulders as if he was only asleep.

"No, Dad!" Damian's voice cracks in desperation, but we can't stay here. There's no time for compassion as bullets continue to fly.

I yank Damian harder, and he slips in the growing pool, drenching his new suit in ruby blood. My cruelty persists as I drag him to his feet, forcing him to abandon his father's corpse to try and save his life. He staggers behind me still in shock as I lead him to the wine cellar, taking the stairs down two at a time. We sprint toward the back, and I pull on the sconce hiding the false wall, grunting at the exertion of moving the heavy bricks. Damian's hands wrap around mine, lending his strength, and the emergency exit is revealed. This was put in ages ago, originally meant for Mr. Marano, but it seems it will only benefit his son now.

"Get in." I wave frantically. "There's a kit at the end of the passage with a burner phone. Call someone you trust."

"You're not coming?" His eyes widen in alarm. "I can't just leave you!"

"They're not here for me." I glance over my shoulder as gunshots echo down the stairs. How much longer can my dad hold them off? "I can buy you time to escape, but you have to go *now!*"

"Viv," he pleads, his hands trembling at his sides. "They'll kill you."

For the first time, I don't see Damian as a god-like figure, as a Marano lifted onto a pedestal. Instead, I see a kid, barely sixteen, covered in the blood of his father. I wonder what he sees when he looks at me. I squeeze his hand in mine, the only reassurance I have to offer.

"Palazzos don't go down easily," I whisper. Footsteps pound down the staircase and Damian's breath catches in his throat. "Go! Now!"

He pulls me into an anguished hug, and for only a moment, I allow myself to absorb the slight comfort, but then I push him off into the corridor and close the wall behind him.

Focus, Vivianna. I might not be in the Ombra, but I can still protect Damian, if only for a few more seconds. I steel my nerves as I turn to face the approaching intruders.

Run, Damian. Run.

There's a pounding on the door an hour later. Piercing headlights glare through the windows. Help is here. Damian made it out safely. My family is sitting in the den. Silent. Dazed. Lost.

I wince as Vinny dabs my face with a wet cloth, cleaning the blood from my skin. Mom sits on a footstool, pale from shock. Dad is the only one not here. He is alone in the dining room. Well, kind of alone. He refuses to leave Mr. Marano's side, though his corpse has long grown cold.

Another knock at the door. Louder. More insistent. Voices yell. My mother shakily moves to the entryway, peering through the peephole. She steps aside as men in black suits force their way in. I recognize a few of the men, including the one currently barking orders at the rest of the crew. His disgust in us is evident, and I can't blame him. We failed.

A final gunshot rings through from deep within the house. The unit draws their weapons, but Vinny beats us all to the dining room. He gasps as he steps over the threshold, but then immediately turns to block the doorway, pushing my mother and me away. Mom sees though. She falls to the floor wailing as her heart breaks.

"What happened?" I claw at Vinny's arm, trying to get by. "Where's Dad?" Tears well in Vinny's eyes. I push through as I see the gun fall from my dad's fingertips. "No... No, Vinny, help him! No!"

My father is dead.

Two funerals on the same day. My mother covers my face with a veil, trying to pretend that she can still wed me off in a few years to a respectable family. It's not likely. No one will look or stand within ten feet of us. We're social pariahs. The only ones trusted with the lives of the Marano family, and we failed.

Vinny stands behind Damian during the funerals, the perfect shadow, the perfect Ombra. He blends in among the other upper-ranking mafia members with his matching suit, or he would if he were ten or twenty years older. Damian stands at the front of the group, watching his father's casket get lowered into the ground. He is poised, composed, stoic. The scared sixteen-year-old is gone, in his place is the new Don of the Italian mafia. I guess he's Mr. Marano now. He flinches as my mother sobs, watching the dirt fill her husband's grave, but he forces himself to keep his head up, shoulders back.

The priest says a final prayer and then dismisses the mourners, and for a moment, I had to admit that I was impressed by Damian. He didn't cry or show any emotion through the entire funeral, he was strong. That is, until he glances at me. Regret. Grief. Remorse. All of those feelings flicker through his face in a millisecond. He takes a step toward me, but Vinny grabs his arm in a vise, firmly whispering in Damian's ear. Damian looks at my brother and then back at me, torn by whatever my twin had to say. He stands there for a moment before mouthing two words.

I'm sorry.

That was the last time I saw Damian for ten years.

CHAPTER 1
VIVIANNA

There's no place for women in the mafia, but that life is all I've ever known. I guess that's not completely true. Women can be wives, keeping the house warm while the men are off gallivanting through dark alleyways. Women can also be "dancers," keeping the bed warm while the wives are away.

Despite my mother's best efforts, I seem to be unwedable. I don't know what she expected. Palazzo used to mean something, a surname that demanded respect. Now, we're avoided while rumors swirl in every shadowed corner like cigarette smoke. Combine that with the scar running down the side of my face, I don't exactly fit the mold of "bride." But something I can't place keeps me desperately tied to the world I've lost, so I took option two.

As soon as I turned eighteen, I reached out to an old family friend who was a manager at one of the grungier Marano strip clubs, the Deja Vu. He was able to pull some strings as a favor to my late father and get me a job. From there, I spent my nights working my way through the establishments, slowly getting promoted to nicer and nicer clubs. My days I spent dodging my mother, enjoying the occasional visit from Vinny, and training.

I don't know what I'm training for. But it's cathartic throwing knives at a mannequin, sprinting until my legs give out, shooting at a paper target until the silhouette disappears. And maybe there's a small piece of me still hoping for something I won't let myself say out loud.

Vinny notices but doesn't say anything. He just stands with his arms crossed and his lips pressed in a thin line of disapproval, occasionally commenting on my form. Even rarer, he'll step in the ring with me, and we'll go a few rounds. I'm still the better marksman, but he gives me a run for my money when we spar.

It was a steady routine for years. I made it to the top of my career, selected for a luxurious gentleman's club that only hired the best ladies to dance. The Masquerade was the classiest establishment the Maranos owned. I still remember stepping onto their stage for the first time. The dim house lighting, the subtle fog machines, the spotlights casting a soft glow on my skin. This club had all of the girls wear matching lingerie with a lacy mask to add to the ambiance. It wasn't a black suit, but it was the closest I could get.

I almost fell off my pole when I saw Damian walk in. His guards stood in a line by the door as he escorted another man to a private seating area. Damian was wearing the same pressed black suit with a crisp tie around his neck. The man at his side wore navy. Must have been a business meeting.

Damian came in a few times a month, rarely with the same person. He always ordered a whiskey and drank it slowly over the course of his meeting. Occasionally, a girl would be summoned for his associate, but he never requested one for himself. In fact, he was largely uninterested in the girls, ignoring us completely.

Except for me.

In moments when he thought no one was watching, his eyes would scan the club until he found my body. It didn't matter if I was on the stage or wandering around the floor to offer private dances, he always looked for me. Despite his interest, our interactions were kept only to stolen glances. If he recognized me, he didn't let on. I don't know which would be worse, if he did or didn't.

His guards always kept watch by the entrance to the club, leaving Damian to conduct his business in private. His entourage was formed of a few men. One I knew, a few I've come to recognize, and of course, the Ombra — my brother.

I should have been worried about Vinny recognizing me, but he completely zoned out every time he entered the club. I should chew him out for that. It's irresponsible, reckless. He needs to focus. But if I scolded him, he would ask questions, and my family doesn't need to know where I go most nights. Besides, the club is my territory. When Damian steps through those doors, I'm watching.

"Taking the stage now…" A sensual voice announces over the loudspeaker. I roll back my shoulders before I step into the light. "The Italian Jewel, Gemma."

I stride down the walkway, smiling as I notice one of my regulars sitting nearby. He winks at me and waves. I smirk to myself, knowing that we'll be going to a back room later. He tips well, so it's always a pleasure spending time with him.

I casually walk around my pole as the music starts, giving the audience ample time to view me from all angles. I lean back against the cold metal, sliding all the way down as I widen my legs. There are some other dancers on the side stages, but nobody pays them any mind. All eyes are on me. My chest. My thighs. And as I roll over onto my hands and knees, my ass.

I stand and wrap a leg around the pole before pushing off, slowly spinning as I slink up toward the ceiling. One benefit of my vigorous training routine, I'm strong enough to do some really fun pole tricks. If I'm going to dance for random strangers, I might as well enjoy it. I climb until I am nearly at the ceiling and grip the pole tightly between one thigh and knee. Carefully, the other leg extends, and once I feel secure, I arch my back until I am dangling upside-down, holding onto the pole with just the strength of my thigh. My hands run down my body, over my chest, tangling in my hair. Everyone in the audience has stopped what they're doing, transfixed by my sensuous movements, but there's only one pair of eyes I care about.

He's stopped mid-stride on his way to the private loft, amber irises locked onto the curves of my body. They follow my hands as I caress my stomach, my tits. His pupils dilate as I wrap my fingers around my throat, his hands clenched at his side. I shouldn't, I know I really shouldn't, but I wink at him. His lips part before he blinks rapidly, the spell broken. A small chuckle escapes me as I savor the feeling. For a moment, just a small moment, Damian Marano wanted me.

My thigh loosens on the pole, allowing me to slide down the shaft into a front walkover dismount. Once right-side-up again, I throw myself back onto the pole, enjoying the sensation of flying as the metal spins faster. By the time I glance up again, Damian is lounged in a velvet armchair, holding an untouched glass of whiskey in his lap. His associate gestures wildly with his hands as he speaks, but Damian doesn't spare him a glance as he responds. His eyes are locked firmly on me.

The club is packed, a patron in every chair. I should be flirting with them, trying to convince someone to hire me for a private dance or a special service later, but I just don't give a shit. Right now, I'm dancing for one person and one person only. Worse, I think he knows it.

A waitress walks into the room and Damian flags her down. His drink is still full. His gaze returns to me, and a ghost of a smile crosses his lips before he conceals it.

Oh fuck.

The rest of my set, I can feel my heart pounding in my chest. I poked the bear, and now I have his attention. Does he recognize me? Do I want him to? My trepidation stays buried beneath a calm, sensual exterior, perfected over eight years of dancing. Stay focused, Vivianna. Hook my ankle around the pole. Whip my hair as I lean back. Extend my arm just so. Graceful. Elegant. Sexy. Not at all nervous. But my set ends, and my manager is waiting for me with another girl as I step backstage.

"Gemma, VIP request," he rattles off a clipboard. "You're giving a lap dance to the gentleman in the black suit, while Crystal does the same to his guest in the navy. These are important men, ladies. Don't fuck this up."

Crystal practically skips to the side room, but I take my time, Damian's eyes trailing each step of my platform heels as I maneuver through the cocktail tables and booths to where he is waiting. He licks his lips as he takes a sip of his whiskey, trying and failing to hide his smirk. The door quietly latches shut behind me as Crystal and I enter the bear's den.

"Close the blinds." Damian's voice is just as smooth as I remember, like melted caramel.

My shoes click with each step as I continue my casual walk, covering the floor-to-ceiling window to isolate the four of us from outside eyes. Crystal eagerly runs her hands along the associate's chest, but I have a gut feeling, that's not what Damian wants. I've been in the business of pleasing men for years, I've learned to size them up, figure out their innermost desires. Loosely coiffed hair. Cleanly knotted tie. Precisely tailored suit. No, he doesn't want someone throwing themselves at him. He wants control.

I lower myself to my knees, look up at him through my lashes, and crawl to him across the floor. Damian adjusts himself in his seat, widening his legs as I kneel between them. My fingernails drag along his thighs, feeling his muscles through his dress pants. I rise to straddle him, perching on his lap.

"Good evening, Mr. Marano," I murmur, running my finger down his tie.

"You know who I am?" His eyebrow raises in pleasant surprise. He doesn't recognize me. I can't blame him, it's been a decade. We were just kids then.

"Every good employee knows who her boss is." I lean closer and nip his ear. "And I am very good at what I do."

"My apologies, Miss Gemma," he teases. "I'm sorry I called your expertise into question."

"You're forgiven." I smile as I rock my hips, brushing against the bulge in his pants.

Damian relaxes into his chair, taking a sip of his whiskey. A few drops of condensation fall from the glass, dripping onto my upper thigh. I gasp at the sudden cold in contrast to my heated skin. Damian moves to wipe away the spilt liquid, but I catch his hand.

"No touching, Mr. Marano," I tsk sensuously. "That costs extra." I worry for a moment that I overplayed my hand, but Damian just tilts his head amused, sizing me up.

"How much?"

"Depends." I hold his hand a hair's breadth away from my thigh, slowly running it along my body up to my neck without letting him touch. His eyes darken as he envisions what I'm offering. "Where do you want to touch?"

He sets his whiskey on the side table and reaches inside his jacket pocket, pulling out a money clip secured around a wad of hundreds. Damian licks his thumb and deliberately leafs through the bills, one at a time. My eyebrows furrow as I realize he's not rifling through for smaller bank notes. He only smirks at my concern. I completely drop the sultry act as he continues unfazed.

"Stop," I stammer. "That's too much."

"Is it?" Damian taunts with a wicked grin. "I've been told you are very good at what you do."

He adds a few more bills to the bunch and tucks it securely into my garter with a little pat. I can't breathe. This is more than I make in a whole week, maybe a month. After stowing his much thinner money clip back inside his jacket, he returns his attention back to me. He gently wipes the droplets off my thigh. Damian's eyes meet mine as he cautiously drags his fingers along the route I teased him with earlier. His hand moves slowly, as though he's waiting for me to snatch it again. But I don't. I let him caress my hip, my stomach, my breast.

Gradually, he climbs higher, his fingertips grazing the veins of my neck. My heartbeat flutters rapidly at his touch, my breathing shallows. Oh god. Damian hesitates, silently asking for permission as he feels the change in my body. I raise my chin, giving him more access.

"Please," I whisper.

A switch flips in him as he grips my neck, yanking my mouth down to his. This means nothing to him. I'm just a whore he overpaid for. But to me, this is everything.

His lips are softer than I could have imagined. Normally, I hate the taste of whiskey, yet I don't seem to mind the burn when he comes with it. The rough fabric of his suit might as well be silk against my thighs as I grind against his erection, pulling myself ever closer with my fists clutching his lapel.

Damian groans into my mouth, and I melt into his arms. His hand shifts, weaving in my hair. He yanks my head back with one hand and cradles my back with the other, pulling our bodies flush together. My chest heaves as I gasp for air, my nerves electrified by his touch. Damian buries his face in my neck, nipping at the sensitive skin exposed to the heat of his breath.

A growing knot tangles in my stomach. I desperately wish we were alone in this room so I could give Damian his full money's worth. The reasons are more selfish than I'd like to admit, but it doesn't matter. We're not alone, and I need to cling to any semblance of professionalism I have left in my quivering body.

I glance over at the pairing to my right. Crystal is bent over, shaking her ass in the air. The other man is reached over the table, dumping a vial of liquid into his drink.

Wait. No.

That's not his drink.

CHAPTER 2
DAMIAN

I don't visit the club often, but after tonight, I'll have to make it a habit. Usually, I only come here to entertain clients and potential business partners. Never pleasure, only professional. Occasionally hire them a girl, but never one for myself.

They call her the Italian Jewel. At first, I thought it was just a clever play on her stage name, Gemma. But then I saw her.

Whereas most of the girls here are thin sticks, she was muscular, toned, athletic. The lingerie hugged her tan curves, while her long, black hair tickled her shoulder blades. The lace mask seemed to be a part of her, hiding everything while hiding nothing at all. Something about her seemed familiar, almost nostalgic, like a song that I don't remember learning the words to, yet can recite by heart.

Months went by, casual glances her direction as I negotiated favorable deals with suppliers and distributors. But nothing could happen. Composure, control, competence. These were the ideals my father passed onto me. How would it look if the Don of the Italian mafia was brought to his knees by one of his whores? A sensual, alluring, flexible, titillating, sultry... Fuck!

I was fine. I had it under control.

But I walked in today and there she was, dangling from one leg, the spotlight casting a glow over her body as her hands trailed down her chest, getting lost in her hair. I forgot why I was there, the importance of this meeting with Landry. She caught me watching, and she smiled, a mischievous grin that told me she knew what she was doing as she played with the lace of her bra. Her fingers crept further, encircling her throat. My cock twitched in my pants, begging me to replace her hand with my own. Then, she winked.

She fucking winked at me.

A gasp was pulled from my lips before I forced myself to get my shit together. I was here for a reason. I needed Landry to agree to our proposition, and he wouldn't do that if I was fawning over Gemma. We walked to my private viewing room to discuss terms, but even as she spun on that pole, her eyes wouldn't leave mine. The words fell from my mouth before I could stop them.

"Landry, are you in the mood for some entertainment?"

A few minutes and a few grand later, Gemma is straddling my lap, grinding on my dick through the fabric of my pants. Her skin has a faint tinge of salt, and it's intoxicating. My hands roam her body, claiming every inch of skin as mine. Her ass. Mine. Her tits. Mine. Her throat. Mine. All mine.

Gemma tenses in my arms, and I pull back, searching her face to find what caused the reaction. There's a flash of worry in her eyes, but then it's gone, concealed beneath the lace mask all of the dancers wear. The feeling returns, a reminder of something or someone that I can't place.

I reach for my whiskey, but she snatches my hand away, placing it on her breast. Her mouth crashes into mine before I can react to her sudden shift in behavior, but as her nipple pebbles beneath my thumb, I can't remember what was bothering me a second earlier. She moans softly as I massage her chest. My other hand palms her ass, my fingernails digging into her round flesh. God, could this woman be any more perfect? I breathe in the scent of her hair as I extend my hand once again.

"No!" She hisses, so quietly I almost miss it. I freeze with my hand brushing my glass, confused by her command. What, is she some kind of prohibitionist? She leans in closer, her lips grazing my ear as she whispers, "Trust me, Damian."

"Who are you?" I stiffen beneath her, fully alert, my lust replaced by caution.

Gemma doesn't answer, instead she takes my drink from my hand, a faux laugh bubbling from her lips. She throws her head back and loses her balance. I catch her hips before she can fall, but the glass isn't so lucky. It hits the floor and shatters, the liquid splashing on the ground.

"I am so sorry!" She blurts, but her act isn't fooling me. That was intentional. I analyze her face, searching for clues. A faint memory tickles my subconscious. *Fresh biscotti, still warm from the oven.* I've met Gemma before, but where? Who is she?

"It's okay," I mumble, still trying to connect the dots. "I'll order another."

Landry stands, shoving aside the girl who was entertaining him. I sit up, annoyed with his treatment of my staff, but then I see the tension of his shoulders, the weight of his steps, the fists clenched by his sides. Gemma sees it too, adjusting herself on my lap to face away from me, her back pressed into my chest. I have to protect the girls.

"Get behind me," I order, my voice low. My hand reaches beneath my suit jacket, unclipping the leather holster of my pistol. But Gemma doesn't move. Her hand grips the edge of the chair, and I realize that I was mistaken when I thought she was afraid. No, she's primed, waiting, ready. Another memory fragment. *Wine glasses on a linen tablecloth.*

"Mr. Marano," Landry sighs. He flicks the lock on the door. "I really wish you would have drunk the poison. That would have made this much simpler."

Excuse me?

"Sorry to cause a hassle," I say dryly. "But I prefer my whiskey with notes of caramel or maple, not death."

Gemma creeps forward, her footsteps silent on the floor. I told her to get behind me, not get closer! What the fuck is she thinking? I pull my firearm free, quietly pulling back the slide.

"Goodbye, Mr. Marano."

Landry turns with a pistol outstretched, only to have it kicked out of his hand by a platform heel. It scatters across the floor, and Gemma pounces, knocking him to the ground.

He lashes out, catching her with his fist. The mask is dislodged from her face, but she is unfazed, grabbing his shoulders and slamming him into the ground. Landry tries to flip her over to gain leverage, but she is smarter than to let him. Instead, she presses her forearm into his throat.

He struggles as he gasps for air, but she is relentless, applying pressure until his movements cease. The woman pulls off his necktie and flips Landry onto his stomach, securing his wrists behind his back.

"He's still alive," she grunts, pulling the restraints tight. "Your men can interrogate him if you wish."

The other stripper finally gets over her shock and runs screaming from the room, but I don't care about her. Standing in front of me, a slight trickle of blood on her temple, is Vivianna Palazzo.

"Viv…" My pistol hangs loosely from my hand.

"Hi, Damian." Her familiar sad smile flickers across her face as she slowly walks back to me. She won't meet my eyes.

I haven't seen her in years, not since the funeral. Wait, that's not true. I've seen her — er, Gemma — several times now. How did I miss this? She saved my life. Twice now. I owe her everything, and I didn't even recognize her as she worked in my club, as I ran my fingers over her bare skin.

"Wait, what am I doing?" I stammer, shedding my jacket and draping it over her shoulders.

"Thanks," she mumbles. Viv slides her arms through the sleeves, pulling the material closed over her torso.

"Why are you here?"

"I work here." She bristles at my question.

"I understand that." I step forward, closing the space between us. "But what I'm struggling to understand is why. This isn't a place for someone like you."

"Because where else would I go?" Viv glares at me. "I spend my entire life training, only to get told that women don't belong in the mafia. I could be a wife or a whore, those are my options. And if I'm going to get fucked over, I might as well get paid for it."

"What the hell are you talking about?"

She doesn't get a chance to answer as the door bursts open and five men in suits storm in, firearms at the ready. Viv rips the pistol from my hand, shoving me behind her as she turns, gun raised.

"Don't shoot! Everybody stand down!" I yell over the sound of safeties disengaging. The men hesitantly lower their weapons, but Viv keeps hers held high, her spare arm corralling me behind her back. I slowly place my hand over hers, guiding the barrel toward the floor. "They're with me, Viv. It's okay."

She relaxes as I take the gun back, her shoulders drooping from the post-adrenaline rush.

"Anna?" Enzo elbows his way to the front of the group. He looks her up and down, seeing her tousled hair and the wad of cash in her garter. His voice lowers in anger. "You better not be here. I better be fucking hallucinating. What the hell! You're supposed to be home with Mom!"

"And you're supposed to be doing your job!" Viv bites back. "Not twiddling your thumbs in the corner with your head up your ass. If I wasn't here, Damian would be dead right now."

"That's Mr. Marano to you!" My second, Marco, interjects.

"Stay out of this, Marco!" I've never seen Enzo so furious. He's normally detached, indifferent. But now his face is turning red, and his shouts cover the bass of the club speakers. "Vivianna, you are going home right now!" His arm latches out and seizes her bicep, yanking her toward the door.

"Let go of me!" Viv rips herself free. If looks could kill, we'd need to call an ambulance for Enzo.

"You're making a scene," Enzo scolds in a hushed voice. "Stop embarrassing the family. You've done enough already."

"Our reputation is so shitty, I think dancing is actually improving it," Viv scoffs, throwing her hair over her shoulder. "My regulars tend to think highly of me."

Something in me stiffens at the thought of her kneeling between another man's legs. Enzo feels about as warmly about it as I do.

"Home. Now." His voice is ice, not open for debate.

"That won't be a problem, Enzo," I cut in. "Vivianna is no longer an employee of this establishment."

In my line of work, reading people is the most important skill you can have. It's the difference between having someone watch your back or stick a knife in it. Mafiosos don't survive long if they can't. This is what I was raised to do, but still, sometimes there's a bit of guesswork involved. Sometimes, I make a choice and pray I read the room right.

"You're firing me?" Viv's mouth hangs open. Betrayal, hurt, anger meld in her features. "I just saved your life, and you fire me?"

"Of course." I force myself to appear casual, though I scrutinize every inch of her face, trying to decipher the one person who I could never read. "Being part of the Ombra is a full-time position. Outside work simply isn't allowed."

"I don't understand," she says quietly. Her face turns into an impassive mask, barring any emotions — positive or negative — from being revealed.

"You're a Palazzo, yes?" I stare into her eyes, and the rest of the world fades away from us — Enzo, Marco, the rest of my crew. None of them matter in that moment.

"Yes," she breathes. She hesitates, then takes a step toward me.

"Then it is my understanding that you should be serving in my Ombra, no?" The air in the room grows heavy, woven with the grave seriousness of my question.

"Yes." Her voice is stronger this time. I search for any signs of fear but find nothing. No paling skin, no trembling limbs, no widening eyes. Though what worries me is that I don't see anything else. She's blank, devoid of tells. I worry I'm making the wrong call, forcing her into a role she doesn't want, but I don't want to stop.

"Why aren't you in my Ombra then?" I ask quietly.

"I'm not allowed." Was there a sliver of sorrow just before she blinked, or am I just seeing what I want to in her eyes?

"This is your out." My voice leaves my mouth as a whisper, low enough the others can't hear. "If you don't want this, then turn around and leave. No harm, no foul."

Her feet stay planted on the ground, but that's not enough for me. I have to be sure. I close the remaining distance between us in two steps, leaving barely a few inches between us.

"Understand that this isn't a game," I continue. "If you do this, I will ask everything of you. You will get hurt, you will feel pain, you could be killed."

"I'm not afraid to die." She holds my gaze, not backing down.

Part of me feels guilty for even considering my next question. To ask her to give up her life for mine? Who do I think I am? But she's saved my life twice now, and I've never felt safer than with her by my side. It's selfish and wrong, but I ask her anyway.

"Vivianna Palazzo, would you do me the honor of serving in my Ombra?"

"Damian, what are you doing?" Marco blurts. "She can't protect you! You're going to get yourself killed!"

I don't listen to him. All of my focus in on the woman in front of me, wearing little more than my jacket, but standing with her chin high. I extend my hand and she gives it a firm shake.

"The honor is mine, Mr. Marano."

"Please clean out your locker." I smile as I release her hand. "Movers will come to your residence on Monday. I look forward to working with you."

◇　◆　◆　◆　◇

"There's a reason why the Ombra is comprised of male descendants." I haven't received a lecture from Marco in a few years. I was beginning to think he was growing lax. Unfortunately, he's choosing to use the confines of the SUV to get on his soapbox, and it's getting old. "Women are more emotional, physically weaker, don't respond well to stress. This is a mistake. You need to release her immediately."

"Good to see I'm never too old for a scolding," I mutter, annoyed.

Marco was my dad's second before mine. After my dad died, he practically became my surrogate father, guiding me through lessons that were never finished, teaching me to run the mafia when I was much too young to be thinking about supply chains and turf wars.

"How well do you even know the girl?" Marco continues, unfazed by my offhanded remark. "You're putting your life in her hands."

"I know she didn't even hesitate." I rub my thumb along the edge of a cufflink, reflecting on the worst night of my life. She hurdled over the table in the blink of an eye. Her body shielded mine before my dad could even fall to the ground. I couldn't think, couldn't breathe, but Viv was there, towing me to safety. And tonight, when I was stupid enough to let down my guard, Viv saved my life again. "And she did it in platform heels."

"Reckless. Brash. Impulsive," Marco snaps. "You were raised better."

"Really?" I roll my eyes. "We're going there? Fine. Wasn't Vivianna 'raised' to be my bodyguard?"

"Don't twist my words."

"Then maybe you should stop worrying about my personnel decisions and start trying to figure out why Landry tried to kill me." I glare at my second. "Sebastian and Tony are taking him to the Pit, correct?"

"Yes," he grits through his teeth.

"Good." I nod. "Join them when we get back to headquarters. I want answers by morning."

Marco is silent the rest of the car ride, no doubt irked that I pulled rank. I understand his frustration. It must be tough having the full power of the mafia in his hands and relinquishing the authority to me as I grew into my role. That doesn't change the simple fact that it is *my* role and *my* authority, and I will remind him of such if need be.

The SUV pulls up to the mansion entrance and I walk through the front doors. Marco leaves to go assist with the interrogation, and Enzo falls into step behind me. I don't spare him a second glance as we walk through the common areas, but he gives me pause as he follows me through the kitchen, past the barracks, and up the stairs to my private floor of the estate.

Enzo might be in my Ombra, but he makes no secret of his indifference toward me. Childhood "playdates" were spent in silence as our fathers tried to force a match, but truth is, we can barely stand each other. Normally, I have to send someone to go track him down when I need him. Never once has he ever bothered to step foot in my wing. Our footsteps echo on the hardwood floors until I reach my bedroom, where I turn to face him.

"Can I help you, Enzo?"

"We need to talk." Thank you, Captain Obvious.

"My office is on the first floor." I try not to sound annoyed. "You could have stopped me—"

"Shut up!" He snaps, and my words cut off mid-sentence. Immediately, I start analyzing Enzo, unsettled by this version I've never seen before. His voice lowers to a cold anger, and I begin to wish we were having this conversation in a more public setting. "Am I not enough for you?"

"I'm sorry?"

"You have my life, you can't have hers too."

"Vivianna had the opportunity to walk away." I swallow a lump of nervousness in my throat. "I made her options clear, and this is the path she chose."

"Your family took our father from us." Enzo takes a step closer as his voice deepens. "Now you're selfish enough to try and take my sister too?"

"You've been in my Ombra for ten years now, Enzo. Name a time that I didn't take every reasonable action to keep the both of us safe." He narrows his eyes. I'm passing through uncharted territory, but I'm committed now. "I feel the weight of your life every time I step out that door, and I will feel the responsibility doubly so when Viv accompanies me. This relationship is a two-way street. I do my best to protect you too."

"If anything happens to Anna," he threatens, "I'll make you wish you were dead."

"Get out." My voice rumbles from within my chest. "Leave before you say something you'll regret."

"Trust me, *Mr. Marano*." He puts extra emphasis on my name, mocking my title. "I wouldn't lose any sleep over it."

With that he whirls around and storms down the stairs, leaving me alone with my swirling subconscious.

CHAPTER 3
VIVIANNA

My new room is plain, but comfortable. Thick rug, warm tan paint, plush mattress. A small nightstand with a lamp sits by the window and a chest lines the foot of the bed. The closet is already filled with several identical black suits. I run my fingers along the sleeves. It still doesn't seem real as I button up the silky dress shirt, fasten the belt over my slacks, and buckle my gun harness over my shoulders. I secure a 9mm pistol under each arm and slide my two knives into the sheath on the back of my belt.

After I slide on my blazer, I search for the Oxfords I've seen Vinny and my dad wear. Eventually, I find them in the bottom drawer of my dresser, tucked behind a pair of bedazzled stripper heels.

What. The. Fuck.

My cheeks flush with anger. I tug on the laces of my shoes and then grab the heels, storming into Damian's office. He's bent over a stack of papers, scribbling something with a pen.

"If you thought that you would bring me here to be your little sex toy, you are sadly mistaken." I slam the heels onto his desk, and he jumps in his chair, eyes whipping up to mine. "I've put my life on the line for you. The least you can do is treat me with respect and some common fucking decency."

The room is quiet as Damian takes a breath.

"I'm going to need you to explain your grievance with a few more details," he says slowly, carefully choosing every word as he responds to my outburst. "If you could start with why you are throwing shoes on my desk, that might make things more clear."

"The shoes left for me?" His attempt at tact does nothing to soothe my ire. "I think I'll stick to the Oxfords, thank you very much. If you wanted to take advantage of my sexual services, maybe you should have done it before you fired me from your club."

"These were in your room?" Damian gestures at the disparaging footwear as his eyebrows furrow.

"No shit!" I throw my hands in the air, exasperated.

"I see." He tosses them in a trash can. My breathing slows as it starts to occur to me that he was not the one responsible, and I just screamed at my new boss. "Are you armed right now?"

"Of course I am." What does that have to do with anything?

"Good." He stands. "Follow me."

Together, we walk out of his office into the common room. A few men mull around, sitting on couches or playing ping pong. Damian whistles sharply and all chatter ceases.

"Listen up!" He barks as other personnel flow in from surrounding rooms. "We might now have a female team member, but she will be treated like every other person in the squad. Scratch that, she will be treated *better* than every other person in the squad. Disrespect will not be tolerated. Insulting my Ombra is a direct insult to me. I was thinking you would all be capable of behaving like men, but since that has already been disproved, here is our new HR policy."

He pauses to ensure that he has everyone's full attention.

"If anyone is idiotic enough to harass Vivianna, she has my blessing to shoot a bullet anywhere she chooses. If a second offense occurs, the next bullet goes through your skull. Am I crystal fucking clear?"

"What if that ass is enough to make us shoot our load?" A man in the back sniggers. Damian's face goes stone cold at that comment.

"Vivianna." His voice is calm, but a turbulent fury lurks below the surface. "Demonstrate."

I nod, striding up to the now less-confident man. My hand slides beneath my jacket, pulling out my shiny new gun. The instigator takes a few steps back, but a kick square to his chest knocks him to the floor. He tries to scoot away, but I kneel on his chest, shoving the barrel of my gun between his legs.

"No, no! I'm sorry!" He stammers.

"Excuse me, I didn't hear you," I seethe. "What did you say?"

"I'm sorry!" He repeats. "It won't happen again."

"How sure are we?" I pull back the action, chambering a round. "If you're willing to disobey a direct order from Mr. Marano, maybe I should just skip to step two and kill you now. Save me a bullet."

"I promise, ma'am."

I yank his chest up by his shirt and lean in close to whisper in his ear. "I was trained to kill before I had my first kiss. However good you might think I am in bed, I promise that my aim is better."

He whimpers. I shove him back to the floor and stand, flicking the safety on and tucking my gun away. Damian raises an eyebrow as I walk to stand behind him.

"His apology was very convincing." I shrug nonchalantly. "I don't think we'll have any further issues."

"Glad to hear it." He nods, then addresses the crowd. "Dismissed. Sebastian, Marco, Vincenzo, Tony, circle up. I want us all to spend the day with Vivianna. Get used to her being here, you'll see a lot of her."

The small group stays back as the rest of the crew disperses. Marco looks down at me with clear distaste. Unfortunately, the two of us have met previously. Of course, I also already know Vinny. Sebastian and Tony are new to me though. Most of the men I see around us are easily in their upper forties, but these two are about my age.

"Nice to meet you, Vivianna." Tony towers over me as he steps forward to shake my hand. His muscles strain beneath his dress shirt, clearly defined beneath the fabric. While I don't think he intends it, his grip is strong enough to crush my fingers. "I'm the lead enforcer. Busting heads and breaking kneecaps, that's my typical day."

"Pleasure." I smile warmly, subtly massaging my hand as he pulls away.

"Hey." Sebastian gives a polite wave. His eyes quickly scan me beneath his strong brow, assessing me much the same way I'm assessing him. "I'm Mr. Marano's capo. Anything he needs done, I make sure it happens."

"Speaking of which," Damian interjects, "have we been able to officially tie Landry to the Russian Bratva?"

"Are you sure we should be discussing such matters in this company?" Marco side-eyes me, and I stand a bit straighter under his scrutiny.

"I'm confident Tony can keep up," Damian deflects, silently daring Marco to push the issue further. "He might have a few concussions under his belt, but Sebastian can speak slow enough for him to understand."

"Yes, sir." Sebastian smiles, elbowing Tony in the ribs. "We don't have much beside his confession. The phone number he provided leads to a burner and his payment was sent from an account in the Caymans, untraceable. It's his words versus those of the vodka-drinking motherfuckers."

"Fuck," Damian grumbles. "Have we disposed of him yet?"

"Waiting on your approval." Tony answers, cracking his knuckles.

"Have one of your underlings dispatch him today and get rid of the body," Damian instructs.

"Excuse me, Damian." I jump into the conversation, before I'm cut off by Marco.

"You will address him as Mr. Marano or you will not address him at all," he commands bitterly. "He is your Don and deserves your respect."

"Stand down, Marco," Damian warns. "She deserves your respect as well." Marco scoffs indignantly.

"No, he's right." I force myself to remain composed, though I want nothing more than to give Marco a piece of my mind. "Please accept my apologies, Mr. Marano. I was only curious if anyone had sourced the poison Mr. Landry attempted to use."

Damian's eyes flick up to Sebastian and Tony, who look at each other like deer in headlights.

"I'll have someone get right on it, boss." Sebastian frowns. "I don't know how we missed that."

With that matter sorted, Damian returns his attention to Marco, studying him quietly. Whereas most people would shift under his gaze, Marco seems used to it, unbothered by the scrutiny. An impish light flicks across Damian's face before he smiles.

"How long has it been since we've played hide and seek?" He asks. The question gets mixed results, with Vinny groaning and Sebastian and Tony high fiving.

"Is that really the best use of our time?" Marco rolls his eyes. "We should be focusing on the Russians."

"I think it's perfect." Damian crosses his arms over his chest. "Since you're so concerned about my well-being, it will give Viv a chance to demonstrate her skill set. The Russians will be there tomorrow."

"Besides, it's tradition." Tony grins. "It's a great way to get to know new recruits."

"More like hazing," Vinny grumbles.

"If you insist, I look forward to shooting you." The light doesn't reach Marco's eyes.

"I think I have to object to the notion of shooting Mr. Marano." I raise my hand. "Ombra and all."

"Don't worry," Damian chuckles, grabbing my hand and leading me to an elevator. "Your job is to not let that happen."

Twenty minutes later, Damian is driving us on an ATV to the edge of the property. I duck to avoid getting hit by low-hanging branches in the dense forest.

He explains the rules as we weave through the trees. It's typically a field training exercise for Vinny, but today my brother gets to be on the hunting team. All firearms are swapped out for paint guns, a nonlethal but painful deterrent. Once we get to the starting point, we will traverse on foot back to the mansion.

My goal is to get Damian back "alive," as the rest of the crew try to take us out. If that's not difficult enough, Damian doesn't get a weapon. He is literally a sitting duck. My sitting duck.

Damian pulls over at the fence line and cuts the ignition. "Okay Viv, you're in charge. Please don't let me get killed."

"This is such a macabre game." I pull out my paintball gun, checking to ensure it's loaded and ready.

"In this career, it's important to find reasons to laugh." Damian shrugs, stretching his arms above his head. I sigh, getting my bearings from the sun. The compound is straight north of our position. I start the trek to the northwest. "Um, Viv, that's the wrong way."

"I know. Humor me."

"Do you not understand the goal?" Damian points toward the north. "That's where base is."

"Which is the route they're expecting us to take," I explain. "I'd like to avoid them as much as possible. No reason to go towards trouble."

"Huh." He scrunches his eyebrows but says nothing, instead choosing to follow me. We walk in silence for a while, the only sound is that of sticks crunching beneath our feet.

"We didn't have a ceremony," I say casually, after about a mile had passed. "Like the one Vinny had. Is there a reason for that? Or have we just not put it on the calendar yet?"

"Wasn't planning on doing that again. The last time…" His voice trails off as he looks toward the horizon. My hand subconsciously brushes the left side of my face, feeling the secret I hide below a layer of makeup. "Besides, it doesn't really mean anything. How different is a bloody handshake compared to the one we had?"

"I guess." I lift my hand further to shield the sun from my eyes and scan the forest around us, looking for any sign that we aren't alone.

"I can't tell what you're thinking." He's staring at me, the same way he does to everyone, but his strained speech hints at his frustration.

"I'm thinking that you staked my reputation on us being hunted in the woods by your top underbosses," I grumble. "And I'm thinking that me failing is not an option. It's already hard enough for a woman to get respect around here."

"So it doesn't bother you that we're not doing a ceremony?" He probes, not letting me shift the conversation.

"Of course it does." I step over a fallen log, careful not to catch my pant leg on the wispy twigs protruding from the bark. "My whole life, Dad would boast about how beautiful the ceremony was. The weight of the vow. The significance of slicing your own palm to show the pain you are willing to suffer to protect the one you bind yourself to. It's fine though, we don't have to do it. Maybe it's best the tradition dies. Just… it might not mean much to you, but it means something to us."

"You know what means something to me?" Damian grabs my arm, stopping my march so I face him directly. "I replay that night over and over, and as I've grown older, two things became clear. One, Vincenzo will always protect himself first, which is fine, whatever. I can't blame him for that. When the gunshots went off, he dove under the table. It didn't matter that not even an hour earlier he swore his vows to me. His actions haven't changed in the past ten years, regardless of whatever oaths he took."

I want to protest and defend Vinny, but I know Damian's right. Vinny doesn't have the heart of an Ombra.

"The second thing I realized is that your first thought was of me," Damian continues, a bit softer. "You threw yourself over me before I had even registered what happened. If you hadn't, the second shot would have hit me. You saved my life. Not Enzo, you. That's what means something to me."

His intense gaze leaves me shaken. I slowly slide my arm free of his grasp. "It's my job."

"It wasn't then." That's where he's wrong. It always has been. The Palazzos protect the Maranos. "I don't need some ceremony to put my trust in you, Vivianna."

I blink a few times before turning away. "Let's keep moving."

More hiking.

More silence.

"Is there something in the Ombra code about not speaking?" Damian asks. "Enzo never wants to talk either."

"We can chat." I shrug. Honestly, conversation would be preferred over the awkward quiet we currently find ourselves in. "Anything on your mind?"

"What do you like to do in your free time?"

"Train." A strand of hair falls loose from my braid. I brush it out of my face, regretting that I didn't bring any bobby pins. "I'm especially fond of knife throwing, but it's important to stay well rounded. Firearms, sparring, improvised weaponry, the works."

"That's not free time, that's work." Damian nudges my arm. "Give me a real answer."

"That is my real answer!" I protest with a lighthearted smile. "Throwing knives is surprisingly cathartic. Repetitive muscle memory, steady breath control, pleasant thunks as the blade embeds in the target. It's nice."

"What about something unrelated to work?" He insists. I stare at the ground as we walk a few paces. "Really? Come on, Viv."

"I'm thinking, okay?"

"This is just sad," Damian teases, though there's a hint of concern in his voice.

"If it's such an easy question, you answer it," I challenge.

"It *is* an easy question," he laughs. A bubbly sound that I've never heard from him before. I feel my cheeks flush as warmth spreads through my chest. "I'm a wine enthusiast. Mostly Italian wines of course, but I do have an appreciation for Californian, Spanish, French... Actually, Greece has a surprisingly pleasant wine culture as well."

"What's the rarest bottle in your collection?" A faint rustle draws my attention, movement in a bush toward my left. I veer right behind a particularly thick oak, subtly positioning Damian behind the trunk.

"I don't believe in collecting wine." He leans against the tree, speaking idly as I stand still. "It's meant to be consumed, enjoyed. Too many collectors hoard bottles they will never get a chance to drink..." His voice trails off as I crouch down, raising my paintball gun.

"Tell me more," I urge, gesturing for him to continue. "Red, white, favorite notes?"

"Depends on the day," he rambles, though his eyes are locked on me. "I tend to enjoy whites in the spring and summer, reds in the fall and winter, but I can appreciate either at any time. Wine just helps take the edge off and—"

"Boo!" Tony jumps out from behind the bush. My paintball pelts him in the chest before he can fire a shot. Not that he could — Damian is shielded by the oak tree. "Motherfucker! Goddamn, I forgot how much these hurt."

"One down. Three to go." I stand and dust my hands on my pants. "You were saying?"

"How did you…" His eyes flick between me and Tony, who is now trying and failing to wipe the paint off his shirt. "The tree? The bush? Wait, were you using me as bait?"

"Of course not." I tug him along, leaving Tony to nurse his pride. "Bait implies you were in danger, you were just my cover. You wanted to chat, so I adjusted my strategy accordingly. Besides, I was listening to what you had to say. So keep going, tell me about wine and seasonality."

We chat about wine for the next ten minutes, then the conversation deviates toward food — best pasta shape and sauce combinations, whether pineapple belongs on pizza, important things like that.

I hold up my hand to quiet him a few miles later when I spot a man in black meandering through the trees, his back toward us.

After stowing Damian safely behind some light cover, I skulk through the woods until I get a clean shot, a bright pink splat knocking Sebastian to the ground before he even knows I'm there.

"Fucking hell, Vivianna!" He curses. "God, why don't we ever play laser tag?"

I whistle the all-clear to Damian, who trots over quickly.

"Nice snipe." He nods his approval and gives me a fist bump. "Two more."

As we hike closer and closer to the mansion, a sense of unease sinks under my skin. It's possible Vinny and Marco are searching for us in the wrong part of the forest, or that we've passed them, but it doesn't feel right in my gut. They're close by, I know it.

We crest a hill, and I can see the edge of the forest below, followed by a clearing roughly a quarter mile wide surrounding the house.

"I don't like this," I whisper as we crouch behind a shrub. "This feels like a trap."

"Or maybe, you're going to be the first person to win hide and seek." Damian is giddy, practically bouncing with excitement. "We could do this, Viv!"

"No one's won before?" The blood drains from my face. Definitely too easy.

"Nope, Vincenzo's never come close." Damian shifts eagerly. "What's the plan, Viv?"

"How fast can you run?" I do quick math in my head. A quarter mile clearing, we'd be exposed the whole time. One, maybe two minutes at a dead sprint. Too long. Maybe he could make it if I stay behind and provide cover fire, but if Vinny or Marco are waiting, he'd be an easy target.

"Fast." He grins. "Really fast."

"Anything happens," I check my gun, "and you take off like a bat outta hell."

"I can do that."

I mutter a few curses beneath my breath and stand, hypervigilant of every squirrel dashing up rough tree bark. Damian follows me, stepping as quietly as he can.

A twig snaps, and my body moves of its own accord, dropping my firearm to yank the paintball gun barrel poking out on my right. Blue paint drips off a tree branch onto my shoulder as my foot connects with the ribcage of the hidden assailant.

"Damian, run!" I shout, focused on the threat in front of me.

"It's Mr. Marano to you!" Marco grunts and jerks his gun back toward him, but I'm not letting go.

We both wrestle for control, and the weapon flies to the ground. Marco shoves me, but I grab his lapel, pulling him with me onto the forest floor. Unfortunately, he's in a prime position to straddle my waist, pinning me down with his weight. He grips my jaw, pressing my head into the ground.

"I expected more from you, Palazzo," he spits, saliva specks coating my cheek. I reach for something, anything.

"Go fuck yourself, Marco." My fingers curl around a thick branch and I swing, the makeshift club knocking him to the side.

Instantly, I dive for the gun. Marco's hand seizes my ankle tugging me back, but it's too late. I spin, forcing the nuzzle under his chin.

"Yield," I command.

"Fine." He raises his hands above his head. "I win either way."

An evilness glints in his eyes.

Vinny.

I jump to my feet, turning to face Damian who is nearing the edge of the clearing.

"Stop! It's a trap!" I'm sprinting, moving my legs as fast as I can though it feels like I'm running in slow motion.

Vinny drops down from a tree, raising his gun as Damian jumps to the side. I fire off a volley of shots. *Pyew. Pyew. Pyew.* Vinny falls to the ground, blue coating his chest.

But Damian falls too, a yellow splotch on his leg.

"Damn it!" He cradles his thigh as I catch up to him. "We lost. We were so close."

"Sorry, Anna." Vinny winces as he sits up. "I shot him."

I hear Marco laughing behind me. My fists clench at my sides as I kneel by Damian.

"You're not dead," I state. "We're not done. I'm getting you back to the compound."

"We have to treat this as if it was a real bullet wound," Damian sighs. "If we were in the field, I probably couldn't walk."

"Give me your tie." I grab a sturdy stick off the ground.

"What?" He doesn't move, so I reach out and angrily yank it off him, tying a loose interpretation of a tourniquet around his leg.

"There." I dust off my hands. "I treated your injury, you're not dead."

"Vivianna, it's okay." Damian grabs my arm. "You were incredible. No one's ever made it this far."

"Stand up without using your injured leg." I ignore him, tugging him to his feet. "I won't have anyone saying I cheated."

"Don't make me hop a quarter mile," he begs. "Please just accept that you lost."

"I haven't lost," I declare. "I'm going to carry you."

"No way," Marco cackles. "This I've got to see."

"Viv—"

"No, Damian— sorry, Mr. Marano." I cut him off. "If this was real, we couldn't sit on our ass and wait for help. So you're going to shut up and I'm going to prove to you and everyone else that I won't let you down in the field, that I can protect you. Do you want to win or not?"

I don't wait for him to answer as I grab one of his hands in mine and step between his legs. I press my shoulder against his hip, and he yelps as I heave him off his feet into a fireman's carry. I stagger at the weight on my back, but slowly trudge forward toward the mansion. Vinny and Marco stand at the edge of the forest, watching in disbelief as I struggle through the clearing.

God, this was such a bad idea.

Sweat soaks through my shirt, dripping down my forehead and into my eyes in thick drops. My legs tremble with each step, taking far longer than the two minutes I estimated Damian could sprint it.

It's too far. I'm not strong enough. I won't make it.

"You can do this, Viv," Damian whispers, feeling my step falter below him. "Don't give up now. You're so close."

A flood of men pours out from the house, their concern turning to shock as they see the paint dripping from our clothes. A few of them rush over to try and help.

"No!" I snap, through every word is strained. "He's mine."

"Don't waste your energy," Damian coaches. "Just keep walking. One foot after the other. Give me one more step, Viv."

I groan as we make it to the stairs of the front porch, but with more patient urging from Damian, I force my feet up all four steps, grunting as I push us both up to the elevated deck. Luckily, our audience left the door open, so I don't have to try and maneuver the doorknob. I step over the threshold and kick the door closed behind us.

I made it. I won.

Damian slides off my back and I collapse to the floor, barely catching myself on my hands and knees.

"Water, hurry!" Damian snaps his fingers at a random bystander and drags me to sit against a wall. I can't breathe, my ribs feel like they're collapsing in on me. My head falls limply against the wall, too drained to even pretend that I wasn't exhausted.

"You did so good, Viv," Damian murmurs as he pours the cold water over my hair and face. I gasp at the unexpected chill, but a small amount of vitality returns to my body. "Keep them coming! Let's go! And a towel!"

More water runs down my skin, cooling the flush of my cheeks. Though we quickly lose our audience, Damian stays kneeling by my side, whispering small comforts as my heartbeat settles in my chest. His gentle hands tilt my chin up, holding a glass to my lips. I take it from him, drinking about half of the contents before offering it back to him.

"All yours." Damian pushes my hand back. "Drink up."

"You need to drink something too." My voice falters, but he gives in and takes the glass.

I try not to give him a side-eye as he takes only a small sip before placing it back in my hand, but I down the rest anyway. It helps. My body relaxes and my lungs remember how to fill without spasming. God, I'm going to be so sore tomorrow. I moan as I rest my head back against the drywall.

"Unless you're in mortal danger, we're not doing that again," I groan, and Damian chuckles beside me.

"I think that's more than fair."

He grabs a towel and carefully wipes the water droplets from the side of my cheek, moving up to my temple. His eyebrows furrow as he examines something closer. There's a tan mark on the white towel.

I jerk away and bring my hand up to cover the left side of my face. The water is washing away my concealer, uncovering the secret I've kept for years.

"Can I see?" Damian grips the towel tightly in his hands, concerned.

I hesitate before lowering my hand, though I can't help but lean away as the towel reveals the scar I tried to keep hidden. The cotton traces the line from my brow, over my eyelid, ending on my cheek.

"When did this happen?" His eyes darken as his voice rumbles in his chest. "Who did this to you?"

"It was a lifetime ago." I wince as the memories force their way into my mind. The bricks digging into the back of my head as I was held against the wall. My scream as the blade snaked lower and lower. The way the blood blurred the world around me. "My eye is fine. It won't affect my work."

"Tell me what happened," he orders.

"Stop prying." I can't share. It would only hurt him. "I don't like to talk about it."

"Fine." Damian takes a deep breath, and I watch as his anger gets buried deep behind his internal wall. "But don't feel like you have to cover it up. You're in my Ombra. You never have to hide any part of yourself from me."

I nod as his gaze peers into my soul, and for a moment, I forget the fatigue in my limbs.

"How are you feeling?" He redirects his attention, reaching for my wrist to check my pulse. It flutters at his touch but passes his inspection.

"I'm fine. I'll feel it tomorrow, but such is life." I shrug, trying to pass for nonchalant. My shoulders scream out at the motion, but I push it down, ignoring the ache of my muscles.

"Let me walk you back to your room." Damian offers me his hand, which I take gladly. My legs buckle as I stand, and he steps forward to catch me. I'm mortified as I compose myself, internally cursing my body for betraying my dignity. Damian just chuckles as he sweeps his other arm beneath my legs, holding me against his chest. "Or I suppose I could return the favor and carry you."

"I can walk," I protest, but Damian just shushes me.

"It is my ethical obligation to attend to my Ombra," he chides. "Let me take care of you."

I groan and roll my eyes but relax into his arms for the short walk to the barracks. Damian stops just outside my door, slowly lowering me to my feet. Once he's satisfied I'm not about to fall over, he takes a step back.

"Get plenty of rest, Viv." He smiles as I turn the knob in my hand. "Congrats on your win today."

"Thanks, Mr. Marano." With that, I close the door behind me and flop onto my bed.

The next day passes slowly. I spend the afternoon training with Vinny like we used to when we were kids. We take it easy since my muscles ache from my overexertion yesterday. Vinny rubs out my knots, soothing the sore tissues in my back and shoulders.

"You need to lose the chip on your shoulder or you're going to burn yourself to the ground," he lectures as I lay on a yoga mat. The gym is empty except for the two of us. "I've been here for ten years, and most people still don't respect me. You can't let them get to you."

"I can take it," I protest, wincing as Vinny digs into a particularly stubborn knot. "I'll make Dad proud."

"Yeah, well, he's dead," Vinny grumbles. "He doesn't get to have a say anymore."

"Don't say that." I try to turn to face him, but my brother forces me back into the mat, not done kneading my shoulders.

"He killed himself, Anna," he sighs. "It's like you want him to kill you too."

"I miss him." Words I'd never say to anyone except my twin, the only one who gets to see past the walls I so carefully built around myself. "What do you think he'd say if he were still alive?"

I'm proud of you, Vivianna. You did it! You're in the Ombra. Remember my lessons and you'll do great things.

"He'd be disappointed that you didn't stay home with mom."

"What?" This time I shove him off, hurt clearly written on my face. "That's not true."

"How would you know?" Vinny counters. "He's dead!"

"So you keep reminding me," I snap.

I jump to my feet and leave the gym, not listening as my twin calls after me. After a quick shower, I return to my room and dress in my uniform, tightly weaving my hair into a braid.

I know my dad is dead. Vinny got to run away, hide out here while Mom and I had to live in that house. Clean the blood splatter off the walls, box up the clothes in his closet, walk by the pictures of him every day.

I slide the two knives free of the sheath on my belt, facing the mannequin across my room. The weight is comforting in my hands, a familiar extension of my limbs. My eyes close as I breathe deeply, filling every inch of my lungs with air, grounding myself in this room.

My arms move with a practiced precision as soon as my eyes reopen, launching the blades toward the target. *Thunk. Thunk.* They embed themselves precisely where intended — one in the eye, the other in the neck. I retrieve my projectiles, resetting. *Thunk. Thunk.* Two in the chest, lodged directly next to each other between a pair of ribs. Again. *Thunk. Thunk.*

I'm making Dad proud, I know it. This is what he wanted. *Thunk. Thunk.* I could never be a submissive housewife — waiting by the door to see if my husband was going to make it home, raising the kids alone, cleaning and primping whenever it was time to show off our oh-so-perfect household to his colleagues. *Thunk. Thunk.* No, it couldn't be me. Wouldn't be me. I wasn't made for embroidery and pot roasts, I was made to be a machine. I am a machine.

Knock, knock, knock!

The sudden disturbance startles me and my arm jerks as I hurl the knife, the blade sinking into the shoulder of the mannequin. *Thunk.* I scowl at the offending outcome as I whip open my door.

"What?" My greeting comes out a bit harsher than intended, but Tony doesn't seem to notice.

"Hey, Vivianna." Tony types on his phone before looking up, his eyes not making it further than the knife I was subconsciously playing with. He steps backward rapidly. "Whoa, whoa, whoa!"

"Relax, you just interrupted me." I roll my eyes at his overreaction. "What do you want?"

"What could you possibly have been doing with a knife in your bedroom?!"

I raise my eyebrow at him unimpressed before opening my door further and stepping aside. Tony peers inside but doesn't cross the threshold. When his confusion doesn't dissipate, I spin around, hurling the blade with enough intensity that my braid whips around my face. The knife sinks into the mannequin's forehead up to the hilt. The head is actually a shitty place to aim since skulls tend to get in the way, but it looks impressive at a glance.

"Ah." He doesn't seem reassured by my demonstration, but I'm through caring.

"How can I help you, Tony?" I tug both blades free of the target, replacing them in the sheath on the small of my back beneath my jacket.

"We're going out." Tony clears his throat as he refocuses. "Tactical operation. Mr. Marano's coming along so we need the Ombra as well."

"I guess I could practice my knifework on live targets instead of Gary over there," I joke, and Tony finally relaxes.

"Yeah, great idea." He smiles. "Meet us in the parking subfloor in five minutes?"

"I'll head over now."

Vinny and Sebastian are already there when I step off the elevator. Sebastian is shirtless, adjusting the Velcro straps of his body armor before redressing. Vinny waves me over to talk me through the new equipment. He pulls out a bulletproof vest and sets it in front of me as I slide off my jacket and unbutton my top.

"What are you doing?" Vinny asks, alarmed.

"Sebastian is wearing his body armor under his shirt." I jerk my chin his direction. "We're trying to hide that we're wearing these, right?"

"Yes, but you can't just undress in public," he whispers. "Sebastian will see."

"He wouldn't be the first person to see me in a bra." I roll my eyes. "And if he tries anything, I'll enforce the new HR policy."

"Not trying anything!" Sebastian pipes up.

"Appreciate it," I laugh as the silk fabric of my shirt slips off my arms, piling next to my jacket on the table. I pull on the thin paneling of the vest, covering my bra from any prying eyes. Vinny gets over himself and grabs the straps, tightening the ones around my waist with a jerk. "Back off, I can put it on myself."

"Did you know wearing body armor quadruples the chance of survival if someone is shot in the torso?" Vinny continues yanking until he is satisfied. "I won't apologize for making sure my sister is safe."

I sigh, redressing quickly as Vinny continues walking me through the rest of the equipment. A wireless earpiece. A watch with a microphone, already calibrated to transmit to the team. A locker full of firearms and ammunition. I check my two pistols, ensuring that each 9mm has a full magazine before reholstering them. Vinny does the same before drawing me into a worried hug.

"Be safe, Anna," he murmurs. "Don't do anything stupid, okay?"

"I'll be careful," I promise.

Vinny stiffens around me, and I glance up to see Damian watching. He nods when his eyes meet my twin's, and Vinny tightens his grip around me protectively. I shrug his arms off and smooth down the fabric of my jacket, not wanting to look weak as Tony and Marco walk in. As they prepare for whatever mission we're about to embark on, I sit on one of the tables, polishing a knife as a leg dangles freely.

"Do you know how to drive a motorcycle?" Damian stands next to me, buckling a watch on his wrist.

"It was part of my training."

"Good." He tosses me a pair of keys as I slide my knife back into its sheath. "We found the facility where they were producing the poison. It's one of their drug kitchens. There's going to be a small fire there tonight."

"What a shame." I stand and grab a helmet off the rack, holding it against my hip. "If only we had marshmallows."

A laugh escapes his lips, and Damian covers his mouth as if he surprised himself with the outburst. Amusement flickers behind his eyes. "Maybe we can scrounge for some when we get back."

"I might just hold you to that," I tease, flipping my braid over my shoulder. "We ready to go?"

"Ready." Seriousness dampens the smile on his face as he shifts into his role as Mr. Marano. I click the keys to find my bike as Damian straddles his, Vinny sulkily sliding on behind him.

"This doesn't make any sense," Sebastian blurts, gesturing at Vinny. "Why is he still your backpack?" I vaguely remember the term, a slang for pillion rider or motorcycle passenger.

"Why wouldn't he be?" Damian flips up his helmet visor. "Enzo's my Ombra. He rides with me. That's not new, Sebastian."

"Yeah, but he's so big," Sebastian shrugs. "The two of you don't fit well on the bike. I'm just saying I think you both would be more comfortable if Vivianna rides with you and Enzo drives himself."

Damian looks between Vinny and me and shrugs. Vinny practically jumps off the bike and I toss my keys to him before straddling the bike behind Damian. It's at this point I realize how close our bodies will be, and I hesitate as I place my hands on his shoulders.

"Nuh-uh," Damian says. He reaches behind himself and yanks my hips flush with his. "Get over whatever personal space issues you may have, because riding pillion is safest when I can feel you. When I lean, you lean. Forward, left, right, doesn't matter. Otherwise, I don't know how to compensate for your weight. Got it?"

"Yes, sir," I stammer.

"Arms around my waist," he orders. "Unless you are actively firing at someone, I expect you to hold on at all times."

The holster in the back of his waistband presses against my stomach as I wrap my arms around him. His hand finds my wrist, adjusting the position until he is satisfied. I can feel the heat radiating from his body, and I swear it spreads between my thighs. I'm thankful that my visor is down, preventing anyone from seeing the flush painting my cheeks. With that, Damian revs the engine, slowly guiding the bike up out of the garage and onto the driveway.

CHAPTER 4
DAMIAN

I hold her wrist securely against my abdomen until I veer onto the highway. Her pulse is racing so quickly. The guilt gnaws at me. It almost killed me to see Enzo comforting her earlier. Her first op with us, she must be scared. Maybe she should be. After all, I'm asking her to risk her life for mine. Again.

My bike weaves through traffic as I lead the team toward the Russian facility. Marco stays up front with me, Tony and Sebastian hang in the middle of the pack, and Enzo takes up the rear. The wind rips at my suit jacket as the road curves, and Viv holds on tightly as the bike cants to the side. Her thighs squeeze my legs as she leans. Her muscular thighs. Flashes of her body flicker in my mind. Spinning on the pole, crawling across the floor, sitting on my lap as she grinds against my—

Viv shifts behind me, and I am roused from my illicit fantasies. What was I thinking? Vivianna is part of my Ombra, off-limits. I owe her everything. She deserves more than adolescent daydreams, at the least, a focused driver. I shake my head, clearing my mind of any lingering lust.

The facility comes into view as the sun dips below the horizon. Blue fades into orange and red, before even those colors dissipate too, leaving only the inky black sky. The perfect cover.

From our recon, we know there's only a skeleton crew working the kitchen at night. A few chemists and a light security presence, nothing we can't handle. We stow the bikes behind some trees which makes them practically invisible from a distance.

"Remember, no firearms unless absolutely necessary," Sebastian warns, the mastermind behind this plan. "The element of surprise is our greatest strength tonight. Let's keep it as long as possible."

Nods all around. From there, we split into two groups. Marco, Tony, and Sebastian are in charge of setting up the explosives in the storeroom. Enzo and Viv will accompany me to the depths of the security wing so we can turn off the sprinklers and fire suppression systems. These motherfuckers are going to burn to the ground.

We lose sight of the other team quickly, and it's just me and my Ombra. Enzo leads the way down a sterile hallway, a baton drawn in his hands. Viv creeps just a step behind me, a knife deftly twirling in her fingers. My only weapon is my holstered pistol, tucked in the small of my back. It's too noisy for a mission like this, so my real weapons will have to be my Ombra.

The white walls seem to go on forever. It would be easy to get lost here if I hadn't memorized the floor plan. A guard turns the corner. Before he can even look up, Enzo swings his baton. A sharp crack sounds as the club connects with the guard's skull, and he crumples to the ground.

"Quick, stow the body here!" Viv pulls open the door to a janitorial closet. "It'll buy us time before someone sounds the alarm."

Enzo and I grab the man beneath his arms, undignifiedly shoving him atop a mop bucket. With his corpse tucked away, we continue down the hallway.

We made it to the storeroom. Sebastian's voice pants over the comms. *The chemicals we were going to use for accelerant are being stored in these heavy as shit barrels that need to be moved. We could use some extra manpower to speed things along, otherwise, we'll be here for a while.*

"Enzo, go help," I order. He looks at his twin, and I know the thoughts running through his head. I snake my hand behind my back, grabbing my pistol. "Do you think she'll be safer if I send her alone instead? I'll watch her back. Now go!"

After a final glance at his sister, Enzo takes off toward the others, radioing in his status. Then, it's just Viv and me versus the world.

"Put that away," Viv grumbles, looking at my 9mm. "I don't need you to look after me. Plus, Sebastian said no guns."

"We're a team, aren't we?" I counter, forcing an easy smile to my face.

"No, we're not." She stares into my eyes, devoid of emotion. "And you treating me different than you do Vinny is insulting. Now put your gun away and let me do my job."

"I didn't send Enzo away to protect you." I reholster my gun. "I did so because I feel safer keeping you next to me."

"You are." Viv smirks slightly, tightening her grip on her knife. "Let's go."

She leads the way, one hand extended behind her and placed on my forearm, allowing her to feel where I am without having to constantly look behind her.

I stare at her curiously. Enzo's never used this tactic before. Despite moving further into the lion's den, my body relaxes. Is this what having an Ombra is supposed to feel like?

We turn the corner and spot a guard making his rounds down the hallway. Alas, he sees us too. His face pales as he fumbles for his gun, but Viv moves with grace, hurling her knife down the passageway where it lodges in his throat. He claws at his wound as blood spills down his shirt.

Viv jogs up and kneels behind him, grimacing as she snaps his neck. The man goes limp in her arms, and she carefully lays him down on the floor. Her fingers wrap around the hilt of her knife as she jerks it free and wipes the blade on his pant leg. She lingers by his side until I approach, resting a hand on her shoulder.

"First kill?" I ask, empathy tugging at my chest.

"Third," she whispers. Her hand grazes the scar on her face before she snaps back to reality. "I'm fine. Let's move."

"Do you want to talk about it?" I offer as her hand wraps back around my forearm.

"We are balls deep in hostile territory," she hisses. "What part of this situation makes you think it's a great time to chat? Do you want me to braid your hair too?"

"Damn, okay." I'm taken aback at her abrupt hostility. Viv digs the butt of her hilt into her thigh, her knuckles turning white from her grip. She takes a breath and rolls her shoulders back as she relaxes.

"Sorry."

"No, you're right." I shrug. "Lead the way."

Back in lockstep, we creep into the main office. Two officers sit at a desk, drinking coffee and gossiping about something that won't matter in two minutes. Viv drops my hand, sliding a second blade out from behind her back. A small beep chirps and we freeze.

"Ah, top of the hour," the closest guard says. "Time to radio the patrol. Grab the walkie, will ya, Yuri?"

Yuri stretches his arm toward a transmitter, straining to reach. "Patrols, count off please."

Multiple voices sound over the line. *Division one clear. Division two clear. Division three clear...*

"Division four?" Yuri calls. "Come in, four."

A coffee mug falls to the floor, porcelain shattering as brown liquid spills onto the carpet. The closest guard doesn't have time to warn Yuri as a hilt protrudes from his spine, and he slumps in his chair. A second knife glints in the air as it spins, impaling itself through Yuri's palm into his radio. He screams in pain, yanking the steel from his hand. His eyes catch on Viv, and bloodlust fills his features.

"You're going to die for that, bitch," he says in a tone that is much too calm for my comfort. I ready my pistol as Vivianna stands, confidently approaching.

"Put that away, Mr. Marano." She smirks. "This will be over in a second."

I don't know how the fuck she knew I pulled my gun, but I wasn't about to put it away. Yuri clutches Viv's knife in his uninjured hand, prepared to use it. Unless she has a third knife concealed somewhere or decides to use her guns, she's going in unarmed.

"Don't you know it's rude to use a girl's blade against her?" She taunts, raising her fists. Oh god.

Yuri roars and swings twice in quick succession. Viv grunts as she jumps back, arching her body out of his reach, though not by much.

"Try that again," she challenges, her voice icy and aggravated. "I dare you."

Yuri, the idiot that he is, does. He lashes out and Viv catches his wrist in one hand, using the other to push his palm back. The weapon falls as his wrist snaps, bone breaking in an unsettling crack. Viv catches the blade midair, swiping up in a fluid motion to slice through his midsection. Blood spurts across Vivianna's face before his heart stops, and he goes limp.

"Oh, come on," she groans, nose wrinkled in disgust. She wipes her face on her sleeve as she goes to retrieve her other knife. "That's just nasty."

"I appreciate your sacrifice," I tease as I jump onto the computer, navigating to the application I need.

"Yeah, yeah." She rubs her collarbone as she rolls her neck. "Hurry, we're going to have company."

Mr. Marano, Tony's voice sounds in our ears. *Bomb is set. We're outside at the rendezvous point. Let us know when you're clear for detonation.*

"Hold on that, Tony," Viv responds. "We're in the main security office now. Leaving as soon as we can."

Roger that.

"Are you sore from yesterday?" I ask, opening the emergency systems menu.

"I'm fine," she says tersely, dropping her hand to her side.

"That's clear, you took down a guy double your size." I scan the screen until I find the setting I'm looking for. "Maybe when we get back to the compound you should put a heating pad on your shoulder."

"Sure, whatever." She doesn't sound amused. "Can you just do the thing so we can leave?"

"Just did." I stand and wave her over. "Let's kick it."

We jog out the way we came, but halt when overlapping footsteps grow louder.

"Change of plans, this way." Viv pushes me down an alternative hallway. We cling to the wall as the assembled guards run into the main room, shouting as the bodies are discovered. "Fuck!"

She sheathes her knives and pulls out one of her pistols. As her hand slides beneath her blazer, I notice a slit in the fabric.

"What happened to your jacket?"

"We really need to work on your prioritization skills," Viv grumbles as she drags me down the hallway.

A group of guards cross our path and Viv fires rapidly, dropping three of them in a blink. We duck into a random room as more funnel toward us. Viv slams the door closed and I shove a bench in front of it as a makeshift barricade.

Her eyes scan the locker room, taking stock of our options. Several lockers and cubbies line the walls. There are no other exits, besides a few windows toward the ceiling that are too high to reach. Dead end.

"I'd love to hear a plan if you have one," I say, not having one of my own.

Viv walks over to a bench and drives her heel into the wooden slats. The wood snaps, and she pries the board free. She hefts it in her hand, feeling the weight.

"We're leaving via window," she announces.

"You're crazy." I look between her and the ten-foot jump.

"Probably, but I don't hear you suggesting anything better." Fair point.

Together, we push one of the cubbies against the wall. After clamoring on top, the gap is closer to six or seven feet. I duck as Viv rams the wooden rod into the window, sending crystalline shards of glass cascading down. She whips off her jacket with a wince, flinging it over the windowpane to cover the few remaining jagged fragments.

"I'll give you a boost." She squats by the wall and interlocks her fingers to form a foothold.

"You should go first." I glance at the doorway, seeing the door rattle as the guards try to break it down.

"Mr. Marano, you're wasting time," Viv snaps, frustrated. "Get your ass up and climb out the window."

"This is such a bad plan." I shake my head, but step into her hands. With her help, I am easily able to pull myself up to the windowsill where I perch and extend a hand down. "Come on, I'll pull you up."

"You're not supposed to wait for me," she groans. "Has Vinny taught you nothing?"

Regardless, she jumps up and I grab her wrist. Viv grunts with effort as her muscles flex, climbing up my arm to join me on the ledge. A flash of her tan skin shows through a rip in her shirt, but there's no time to investigate further as the wooden door cracks.

We hang off the ledge and drop to the grass. The shouts from those attempting to follow us draw the attention of a few men guarding the outside.

"Blow it up!" I yell into my microphone as Viv fires. "We're coming in hot!"

A few seconds later, a bright fireball explodes from inside the building we evacuated. Alarms ring out as smoke billows into the sky. The burning inferno emits beacons of light, thoroughly removing any cover the night had allowed us.

"Move!" Viv spurs me faster as more pursuers join the chase.

Motorcycle engines rev as the rest of the team drives into the clearing, providing cover fire for our escape. We get to my bike and Viv jumps on behind me, one hand squeezing my belt as the other stays wrapped around the grip of her pistol, locked on nearing hostiles.

My bike swerves into the clearing and the squad regroups, falling back in formation as we make our escape. I can feel Viv looking backward, waiting for the guards to try and follow, but she relaxes as the crew merges onto the highway. She tucks her pistol away and wraps one arm around my waist.

"Both hands," I correct, reaching behind me to grab the one that's dangling by her thigh. She tenses, sucking air through her teeth as I pull it around front. "Viv, what's wrong?"

"Nothing, just drive."

"Are you okay?" I can't turn to look at her, I have to focus on the winding road. All I can do is listen to the inflection in her voice, feel how her right hand is holding on tighter than her left.

"Just peachy." Her tone is terse and clipped. I replay the events of the past hour. She didn't get shot, right? Couldn't have. I would have noticed her stumble from the bullet's impact.

"Viv—"

"I'm fine!" She huffs. "Why are you hounding me all of a sudden?"

"Maybe because you're not giving me an answer I believe," I grumble.

"Just drive," she repeats softly.

So I do.

A hand subconsciously drifts from the handlebars to cover one of hers, holding her securely as I speed up, zooming down the nearly empty highway. I feel her chest rise as fall against my back, her breathing steady and relaxed. My fingers wrap around her wrist, her pulse strong.

Maybe I'm overanalyzing her. I've never been able to read her as clearly as I would like, so now I'm convinced that something's wrong. She's probably just tired, stressed, any combination thereof. But still, I can't shake the feeling that she's not being entirely truthful either.

My hand stays around hers until I park the bike in the garage. Viv hops off immediately, discarding her helmet on the rack and walking inside. She didn't return her other gear. Maybe she didn't want to change in front of the guys. It's a reasonable explanation, but I can't help but follow her.

She turns the corner and walks into the med bay. It's late, so our on-site medic is asleep, but she doesn't seem bothered, flicking on the lights and rummaging for gauze on the shelf. I stand outside in the hallway, unsure of whether or not to go in. But then she winces as she unbuttons her shirt, cursing under her breath as she lifts the hem over her head, and I'm by her side in seconds.

"I was wondering how long you were going to stand out there," she jokes as she grits her teeth. "It was getting a bit weird."

A thin red line trickles blood from her collarbone, a clean slice through the strap of her body armor. She yanks the other straps to release the vest, dropping it next to her discarded shirt. Viv doesn't balk at me seeing her in her bra, though I guess I've seen it all before.

"You lied to me." Averting my eyes, I grab a cleansing wipe and rip open the wrapper, swiping the damp cloth over the cut.

"No, I didn't." She doesn't react at the sting of the alcohol, except for her fists clenching the edge of the table she's sitting on. "It's just a graze. I really am fine."

"That's some semantical bullshit." My eyes flick to hers, anger leaking through. "You are my Ombra. I need to know if you get hurt so I can take care of you."

"And I need to keep you focused in the field," Viv counters, scrunching her eyebrows together. "You can't be worried about a little cut when there are a million other threats that take priority. I won't apologize for doing my job. This is what I was trained to do."

Viv slides off the table and turns away from me. She fumbles with the bag of gauze, trying to open it one-handed. I take it from her and pat the table, motioning for her to sit back down. She sighs and jumps back on, allowing me to carefully place the dressing over her laceration and tape it down.

"All done," I say, as I clean the last trace of blood from her chest.

"Good, now you can stop mother-henning me." She smiles as she teases me, slipping her shirt back on. With the white gauze underneath, I can now clearly see the gash in the black silk, and I internally curse myself for missing it earlier.

"I can take your gear back to the garage," I offer, unbuckling her watch from her wrist.

"Stop acting like I'm on my deathbed," she groans. "I can put my own shit away."

"I would prefer you use that time to shower." I nudge her good arm. "You have some of Yuri's blood smeared on your cheek."

"Still?" Viv licks her thumb and aggressively rubs at her skin. "Damn it."

"Go shower, Viv." I carefully take out her earpiece and grab her vest. "I've got to return my gear too."

"Thank you," she acquiesces, fiddling with the cuff of her shirt.

"It's the least I can do." I shrug. "You were crazy out there today. I've never seen anything like it."

"I'm good at what I do," she says, and I've lost her again, lost her to that damn wall she hides behind. I just want to take a sledgehammer and bang it down, but I can't. All I can do is smile and hope that revealing more of me reveals more of her.

"Goodnight, Viv."

CHAPTER 5
VIVIANNA

"*Damian Marano, where is he?*" *The voice cuts through the air, and my hands shake against the rough brick wall.*

"*Never met him.*" *I hold my chin high, pretending that I'm not terrified, pretending to be brave. The lights flicker and I feel so small, surrounded by hulking giants. Steel glints as it swings toward me, and I scream, ducking from the path of the blade.*

I'm not afraid to die. I'm not afraid to die.

Suddenly, the wall disappears. I'm straining against coarse ropes, which dig into my wrists as I jerk against a wooden chair.

"*Answer the question, Vivianna.*" *My father squats in front of me. "Where is he? Tell us now.*"

"*I don't know who you're talking about.*" *Tears stream down my face. My voice is raspy, hoarse from hours of pleading and wailing. A second man lunges at me, his fist whipping my head to the side.*

"*This could all be over now, sweetie.*" *Dad lifts my chin and I look anywhere but in his eyes. "Just give him up.*"

"*Who?*" *My words don't match the waver of my voice, more brazen than I look. Battered, bruised, bloody. "I don't think I can help you.*"

"*Stop being such a stubborn brat!*" *The second man yells. "You're wasting our time.*"

"Go to hell!" I struggle in my restraints. "Untie me and I'll send you there myself!" That earns me another blow, and I spit blood onto the floor, shaking in my chair.

I'm not afraid to die. I'm not afraid to die.

A hand pushes my chair back and I fall through the floor, landing in a heap.

I stagger to my feet in a brightly lit hallway, sterile and white. A man raises a gun, and I hurl my knife. It's not enough. I'm too late.

The gun fires before the blade can pierce his heart, and I watch as the bullet flies over my shoulder. I whip around, watching the patch of red grow on Damian's chest.

"No, no, no!" I scream. He collapses on the tile, and I put pressure on his wound, helpless as the liquid seeps through my fingers. "Damian, no!"

"You were supposed to save me, Viv," he whispers, running his fingers through my hair. "I believed in you."

"I'm disappointed in you, Vivianna." My dad shakes his head as the voice from the brick wall cackles.

"No, he's not dead," I beg and plead, praying to whatever gods may be listening. "I can still save him. He's not dead. He can't be."

"Viv..." Damian's voice fades as his hand falls limply to the ground.

I wasn't strong enough, wasn't fast enough, wasn't good enough. I failed, just like my father. I failed. Damian is dead.

The door is busted in, and a swarm of security guards pour inside. I don't try to move as their guns fire. Bullets thud into my chest, knocking me to the ground. My eyes lock onto Damian's, lifeless amber eyes staring into nowhere.

I'm not afraid to die.

I wake with a start, drawing the gun from under my pillow as my eyes frantically search for my assailants.

My chest heaves as I slowly take stock of my surroundings. Knives sheathed by my dresser, sheets rumpled at the foot of my bed, moonlight filtering through the curtains over my window. Gingerly, I engage the safety, though I'm hesitant to put down the pistol entirely.

It has been a few days since the mission. Damian's been laying low, biding his time as we prepare for a response from the Russians.

I've been spending my days training with whoever isn't busy, whether it's against Tony's brute strength, Vinny's precise attacks, or Marco's punishing aggression. Sebastian is the only one who always turns down my invitations to spar, apprehensively watching when I roll my shoulders back and lift my chin. It's no matter, there are always drills with a punching bag.

But every night, demons have haunted my nightmares, reminding me that I'm not good enough, that I'll never be enough. Vinny was right, our dad wouldn't be proud of me. My technique has been sloppy, my form has been weak.

If Dad knew the thoughts I've had about Damian. The way that my core tightens when he walks in the room, the way butterflies dance in my stomach when his eyes follow me…

His eyes. The breath is knocked from my lungs as I picture my nightmare again. His eyes. Dull. Vacant. Lifeless. Dead.

I bury my head between my knees, trying to still my shaking limbs. He's safe. He's alive. Damian is sleeping peacefully upstairs. I know this, but it doesn't stop the panic encircling my chest, squeezing tighter and tighter.

My bare feet quietly pad up the staircase until I'm standing outside of Damian's bedroom.

No one goes in. The rule was made crystal clear when I first moved in. Damian won't go in our rooms, and we won't go in his. A hard boundary splitting business and privacy. It makes sense, especially since he has an open-door policy for his office, but I don't need to go in to keep him safe.

I lean my back against the hallway wall and slide down to the floor, holding my 9mm loosely in my lap. *Damian is safe.* I repeat the words over and over in my mind. *He's sleeping peacefully. Damian is safe.* No matter how many times I try to assure myself, I can't seem to walk back down the stairs.

I will protect Damian. I will keep him safe. I will not fail.

The door opens and I'm startled when Damian walks out. His navy-blue pajama pants hang loosely around his hips as he tugs a cotton V-neck over his head, yawning and rubbing the sleep from his eyes. He takes several steps towards the stairs before he stops and does a double take, noticing me sitting on the floor.

"Viv?" His voice is groggy as confusion twists his facial features.

"Yeah?" I try to sound nonchalant and normal, like it's not creepy to sit in the hallway with a gun in my lap.

"Whatcha doin'?" Damian blinks a few times, trying to see with only the moon illuminating the hallway.

"Protecting you." There's a beat of silence.

"Okay then." Damian turns and walks to the top of the steps before stopping again. "Are you going to guard my empty room or are you coming with me?"

"I suppose I could tag along." I shrug. He chuckles as we walk down the stairs into the kitchen. Damian grabs two bowls and two spoons, setting them on the kitchen island.

"Mint chip sound good to you?" He murmurs, pulling out a carton of ice cream. When I don't answer, he scoops some into each bowl and places them in front of the barstools. He plops down on one and digs in. "Sit down, Viv. Eat the ice cream, that's an order."

I slide onto a stool and curl my leg beneath myself. My 9mm rests on the counter as I trade it out for a spoon. The mint chip tastes fine, but Damian beams as he delights in another mouthful.

"Guilty pleasure," he talks through the lump in his mouth. "Midnight ice cream run. Nothing beats it."

"Mm-hmm." I nod, taking another bite.

"Is there some new threat I'm unaware of that calls for overnight protection in the compound?" He turns to face me, gesturing with his spoon at my PJ's. There's an air of levity in his voice, but it doesn't mask the concern in his eyes.

"No, Mr. Marano." He flinches at my response.

"Damian, please," he corrects. "I know Marco insists, but when it's just you and me, I'd really rather drop the formalities. Call me Damian."

"Okay."

"Any particular reason you were sitting outside my door with a 9 mil?"

"Do I need one?" I shrug, stirring my melting ice cream with my spoon.

"Hypothetically, no. As my Ombra, you have pretty much free reign over the estate." Damian scrutinizes my body language as he speaks. "But realistically, I feel like there is a reason."

"It's my job." My defensiveness catches me off guard.

"Viv, talk to me." He leans over and confiscates my ice cream bowl. "Are you having problems sleeping or something?"

"Yeah," I confess, tucking a strand of hair behind my ear. "But that's nothing new."

"How can I help?" Damian asks softly.

"It's nothing." My hands wrap around the grip of my gun as I eject the magazine, checking for the millionth time that it fully loaded before clicking it back into place.

"I learned everything I know about the Ombra from my dad." Damian leans back in his stool. "I'll admit, Enzo and I... we're not a true Ombra pairing. Sure, we did the vows and all that, but we never clicked. We don't trust each other. We don't talk to each other. We don't even particularly like each other."

That much has always been obvious. Watching them through the window, Vinny bemoaned every playdate, every game of tag. Meanwhile, I was left setting the table and polishing the silverware.

"Viv, I think you and I have the foundation for something real here, but it starts in moments like these," he continues. "Our fathers would talk about everything — their fears, their hopes, their nightmares. When they leaned on each other, it made them stronger."

"Do you think your dad would be proud of you?" My voice cracks. I feel weak, vulnerable. I hate it.

"Oof." Damian returns my ice cream to me as he takes another bite of his. "That's a heavy question."

He sighs and smooths the fabric of his t-shirt.

"Yeah, I think so." The clink of his spoon resting in his bowl reverberates in the heavy silence. "He would definitely tell me things I'm doing wrong, criticize pretty much the whole operation I have going, but I think he would respect how hard I'm trying." He glances at me, hunched over my bowl in shame. "Is that what's bothering you? Your dad?"

"I was never supposed to be in the Ombra," I state blandly as Damian absentmindedly plays with his ice cream. "It was always Vinny. The only reason I was trained was to give him someone to compete against, but Vinny, he was all they cared about. My dad would be ashamed of me."

"What?" Damian drops his spoon in surprise. "That's not true! He would be so proud of you."

"It is though." I shrug my shoulders. "Even Vinny said so."

"No, Viv, it's not." Damian grabs my arm, and I force myself to face him. His gaze pierces through the weak points in my internal walls. "He talked about you all the time. You were his pride and joy."

"You knew him?" I stammer, pushing my ice cream away to give Damian my full attention.

"Of course I did." He tilts his head to the side. "He was here almost every day. Your dad was practically my uncle. He couldn't stop gushing about you. He tried to convince my father about a million times that you should be in my Ombra. If he found out you made it, my god, you would hear his cheers across the state."

A laugh escapes my lips picturing my stoic father whooping like a madman. I wish he told me. I wish he shared this with me. I wish he were still alive.

I scrunch my eyes closed as a wave of grief rocks my body. No, Vivianna, push it down. Now's not the time. Inhale. Rebuild my walls. Exhale—

"No!" Damian shakes my shoulder, and my eyes whip to his in alarm. "Stop! Stop it, Viv! It's just you and me here, stop hiding yourself. Grieve. Mourn. Just— argh!"

He yanks me into his chest, hugging me with all of his frustration. One hand holds me tightly while the other strokes my hair. I freeze, every instinct telling me to push him away while every intrusive thought begs me to give in and collapse into his embrace.

After a moment, I compromise with myself, wrapping my arms around him. I won't break, but that doesn't mean I can't allow him to provide me with this small comfort. My nails trace the muscles in his back as I press my cheek against his shoulder. I close my eyes again, clutching the back of his shirt in my fists.

"I've got you, Viv," he whispers.

Before we pull apart and retreat to our separate bedrooms, one thought crosses my mind.

Is this what it's like to feel safe?

Damian gives me the next day off, ordering me to catch up on sleep.

"You can't protect me if you're nodding off," he teases. After seeing him in his rumpled PJ's last night, his pristine exterior takes my breath away. Gelled hair, crisp dress pants, smoothly knotted necktie. If I know only one thing to be true, Damian was born to wear a suit.

He buttons his jacket and looks at me, allowing me to see past his defenses to his jovial nature. "Besides, I promised Enzo that we would have some fun. Can't do that with his little sis hanging around."

"Since when do you two have fun together?" I question, crossing my arms over my chest.

"First time for everything." He shrugs. "Just enjoy yourself tonight, Viv. Maybe pick up a hobby, paint your nails, something nice."

"And if I insist on coming?" I challenge, stepping closer to him. "I don't like this."

"Everything will be alright." Damian squeezes my shoulder as I sigh.

He snaps back into Mr. Marano as he steps out of his office. I stand in the doorway as he gives a fist bump to an unenthused Vinny. Seems the Palazzo twins are in agreement on this issue. They disappear together into the elevator, and I am left to wrestle with the nagging pit of my gut alone.

I do try to follow his advice. I do. But my bedsheets tangle around my legs as I toss and turn. But I smudge my polish within seconds of painting my nails. But even as I throw blade after blade into my mannequin, I can't find anything to soothe my unease.

I throw my hair into a messy bun, blowing the loose flyaways out of my face. The nail polish bottle taunts me, mocking my failed attempt at femininity. I can be girly and kick ass. At my old job, I was a highly sought-after dancer. Painting my nails? This is something I can do. I curl up on my bed, laying my hand on my nightstand. Each stroke is precise, exact, until all ten fingers have a matching sheen. Now to keep still until it dries.

Knock. Knock. Knock.

I frown at the door. The sense of impending doom rears its ugly head as I creep forward, carefully twisting the knob to avoid wrecking my fresh manicure. Sebastian and Tony stand there, nervously looking at each other. My stomach drops.

"Where's Mr. Marano?" If jumping to conclusions was an Olympic sport, I would win gold. The two men whisper between each other before Tony shoves Sebastian forward, electing him as the speaker of the group.

"It could be nothing…" he stammers.

"What?" I press, and Sebastian fidgets under my intense gaze.

"You see, Tony was nervous." Sebastian gestures over his shoulder.

"No, you were!" Tony defends himself as my patience grows thin.

"Where's Mr. Marano?" I repeat myself as I step over the threshold into the hallway.

"Neither of them will answer their phones." Sebastian swallows uncomfortably. "Enzo or Mr. Marano."

"Which would be fine," Tony cuts in, "except that the last text we got from Enzo was that he was clocking out for the night."

Damian's alone.

"Where's Damian?!" I grab Sebastian by the lapel and shove him against the wall. The deep red of my polish smears like blood over the black fabric of his suit. "Answer me!"

"Nightclub!" His eyes go wide as Tony tries to pull me off. "Il Locale Notturno. 32nd and Park Boulevard."

"Get out of my way!" I blow past Tony, sprinting down the stairs to the parking subfloor.

I straddle a bike, not bothering to grab a helmet before I peel out of the garage. The accelerator is maxed out, the engine whines in protest as I weave through the cars on the road. Bitter wind rips at my skin and hair. My hair tie is a casualty of my mania, snatched away by a particularly strong gust. The strands of my hair fall free of its bun and swirl around my face.

He's alone. He's vulnerable. I can think of a million different ways to kill someone at a nightclub, each one causing the vise around my stomach to tighten. Fuck, fuck, fuck!

Fear, panic, and dread all ripple through my chest. This is it. I'm going to be too late. I'm going to get there and he's going to be lying in a pool of his own blood, his hand reaching out for me.

The bike wheels are still spinning as I jump off, sprinting into the nightclub. The strobe lights are blinding as I wade through the crowds of people, scanning for a needle in a pile of needles. Hands grab at my t-shirt, whether trying to catch a feel or beg for a dance I don't care. Damian. Where. Is. Damian?

"Vivianna!" A slurred greeting as a hand plants itself on my shoulder. I whip around to find him — drunk and surrounded by handsy women. "Is that you? Crazy coincidence!"

"Are you okay?" I shout over the loudspeaker. "Where's Vincenzo?"

"I sent him away." Damian rolls his eyes. "He was cramping my vibe. Wait, why are you here?"

"You, dumbass." The thudding bass helps my heartbeat to slow, syncing in time to the music now that I know Damian is safe. "You weren't answering your phone."

"Were you worried about me?" He smirks, eyes twinkling mischievously. "Worried enough that you didn't change into your uniform?"

I cross my arms over my oversized t-shirt. I'm just glad I'm wearing leggings instead of my normal PJ shorts.

"Don't mock me," I seethe. "Not when I spent the entire ride here thinking you were dead."

"Aw, come on, Viv." He slings an arm over my shoulder. "Don't be like that. Tonight is about having fun. Letting loose. What do you want to drink? I'll buy."

"Fuck off, Damian." I back away from him, making no effort to conceal the hurt on my face. "Enjoy your night."

"Wait, no." Damian reaches for me, but I slink into the crowd, hiding among the masses. "Vivianna!"

No matter how pissed I am, I can't leave him here alone. So I take the name Ombra literally, becoming a shadow silently circling the club, watching, guarding. Several men come up to me over the course of the night — asking to dance, buy me a drink, take me home. I turn each of them down, keeping my eyes locked on Damian.

After I left, he meandered his way to the bar, leaning against the sticky wood as he waited for the bartender to bring him a new glass of whiskey. Damian throws it back immediately, and the bartender refills it before walking away to serve other customers. For a moment, I feel bad, watching Damian look so dejected on his own. But then a blonde and a brunette each run a hand over his chest, and he smiles. I lose all sympathy as his lips connect with the blonde's, his tongue running along her teeth. He can go to hell. Jerk. Asshole.

An hour passes. Then two. He spends the time cycling through women, grinding his hips along theirs. They weave their fingers through his perfect hair as they dance, tousling what he took such effort to style. His tie falls askew, his suit rumples, his eyes glaze over as he takes another sip of whiskey. A man normally so put together, now a drunken mess.

Damian's body stiffens and he waves off the women dancing around him. The women fawning over him depart, confusion and disappointment written on their faces. I tilt my head as he seems to sober up in a moment, his glass trembling in his hands. His eyes frantically scan the crowd around him, searching for something or someone.

This isn't right. He stumbles forward a step, the liquor sploshing onto his suit. Then I see the man whispering in his ear. He gives Damian another nudge, and they start to maneuver toward the back exit.

I shove my way through the crowd, taking stock of the situation. In my foolish hurry to get here as fast as possible, I didn't grab any weapons. Not my knives, not my pistols, nothing. Fuck.

I sneak out the back door as quietly as I can, relying on my stealth to assess the situation. Damian cries out down the alley, and my feet run toward his pained groans. I turn the corner and see him holding his stomach, propping himself up against a wall with his other arm.

"My, how the mighty have fallen," the mystery man croons, the metal of his gun flashing in the streetlight. "Mr. Marano in the flesh. You were supposed to be difficult to kill, but this is almost embarrassingly easy." He grips the back of Damian's neck and throws him to the ground. "Your precious honor guard can't save you now. Kneel and accept your death like a man."

"You know nothing about my Ombra," Damian sneers, trying to retain what's left of his composure.

"Your Ombra?" The assassin crouches as he yanks a fistful of Damian's hair, wrenching his head back. Damian's throat bobs as fear flashes briefly in his eyes, but then it too is hidden behind his crumbling defenses. I search the area for anything I could use as a weapon, maybe a broken chair leg or a discarded pocketknife. "The Palazzo family used to be the stuff of nightmares, but now? They're nowhere to be seen, and here you are, defenseless and alone."

"If I were you, I wouldn't speak so lowly of my Ombra," Damian warns. My fingers curl around a hefty brick as I creep closer.

"Oh, yeah?"

The butt of the pistol whips down, connecting with Damian's temple. My vision tinges red. Not because of the insults to my family, I've heard all of those before. It's the blood dripping down Damian's forehead as he forces himself to rise to his knees. That is enough to drive me into a murderous frenzy.

"If I were you, I would get on my knees and beg for mercy," Damian pants, rolling his shoulders back. The assailant laughs, but it dies in his throat when he sees Damian staring past him. "But I can see in her eyes there will be none."

He doesn't have time to react before my brick connects with the back of his skull. The gun skids across the concrete, but I don't pay it a second thought. The assassin crumples to the ground and I am on top of him, wailing down with my brick until nothing remains of his skull except jagged fragments of bone and mush. I would keep going, but one sound cuts through my rage.

"Viv..." A plea, laced with pain.

Damian is bent over, his hand pressed against his abdomen. I drop my brick as he crumples, rolling onto his back.

"You came back," he whispers, rubbing his thumb over my forearm.

"I never left, dumbass." My eyes tear up as I rip open his shirt, frantically looking for the source of his pain. "Where does it hurt, Damian?"

"Here."

"There?" I touch the spot and he bites his lip, trying to silence his howl. "You're kidding, right?"

"How bad is it, Viv?" His voice shakes. "Am I dying?"

"No."

"What?" He strains to look. "But it hurts and I'm bleeding."

"It's a minor cut, man." I run my hands through my hair as relief washes over me. "God, you really scared me."

"But..." Damian tries to sit up but I push him back down.

"Lay down for a bit." I look around the alley, trying to find something I can use to clean up the small amount of blood.

"I'm sorry," Damian grunts through the pain. "I was stupid, and an ass, and I should be dead right now. Worse than that though, I hurt you."

"You were stupid," I agree, my shoulders droop slightly as I kneel next to him again. "But no matter how stupid you are, I'll still be there."

"Vivianna." He grips my forearm tightly. "Asking you to be in my Ombra was the best decision I've ever made, and even if I would have died tonight, I wouldn't regret a moment."

"You are so dramatic." I roll my eyes as I smile. "I'd hate to hear your actual death bed speech. What's next? Asking me to kiss your boo-boo?"

"I don't know how you fought after you injured your shoulder," he murmurs. "This hurts so bad."

"Let me stop the bleeding, your royal highness," I tease. There's no clean fabric anywhere, so I whip off my shirt, using it to apply pressure.

CHAPTER 6
DAMIAN

Tits. Oh god. Tits.

Viv presses her shirt onto my cut, the motion pushing her lace-clad chest forward. Now it's hard to breathe for a different reason. I turn away, forcing my eyes to look anywhere else.

"You okay?" The back of her hand brushes my forehead.

"Yeah." I glance at her but fall back into the trap of her perfect breasts. She doesn't notice my ogling, her attention returned to my abdomen. I pray she doesn't look any further down, or else she would find a clear sign of my lust in my pants.

I flinch as a raindrop plops on my cheek. Then another lands on her shoulder. A third on the pavement. Viv holds out her hand as the sprinkles accelerate. Within seconds, we are caught in a downpour.

Her long black hair becomes soaked instantly, clinging to her back. She shivers as the cold drops run down her skin, which glistens beautifully beneath the streetlights. The chill must be getting to her, since I notice her nipples pebbling in her bra. I want to run the pads of my thumbs over them, twisting until I hear her gasp above me. I want to swirl my tongue around the buds, feeling her writhe in my lap. And when she's close, I want to graze them with my teeth, hearing her cry my name as she unravels in my arms. I reach toward her, diverting at the last moment to grab her bicep.

"We need to go," I say, partially concerned about her but mostly afraid of how the whiskey is diluting the control I have over my body. Viv gently lifts up her shirt, checking the status of my wound. She pulls it back over her head, a small red blotch staining the front of it.

"You're all good, let's kick it."

I'm not all good, but she doesn't have to know that. She helps me to my feet, and the alcohol rushes to my head. Viv catches me as I stumble.

"This better not be some lame trick to get me to carry you again," she threatens, though I can tell that she's making fun of me.

"I can walk." My words slur as they leave my mouth, and I'm becoming less sure of their accuracy.

Viv slips my arm over her shoulders, propping me up as I stagger down the alley. She shivers again, her hair dripping water onto the concrete below. Her shirt is sopping wet, the fibers turning transparent and showing everything they are supposed to keep hidden. The material clings to the curves of her breasts, and my cock twitches in my pants. Goddamn, Viv.

We make it to the bike, and I slide off my suit jacket.

"Oh god, please tell me you don't strip when you're drunk." Viv panics as she forces the material up again.

"You're cold." I shrug it back off my shoulders.

"I'll be fine." She dismisses my concern, but I feel a possessiveness rise within me.

"No, Vivianna. You will put it on." I order, my voice snapping as heat flashes in my eyes. "Anyone who looks at you can see everything, and I mean everything. I will not have complete strangers driving by staring at you. Put it on, now."

Viv doesn't say anything as she takes the jacket from my hands, sliding her arms through the sleeves. My tense body relaxes as I breathe a sigh of relief. I look up toward the sky, closing my eyes as the rain cools my fervor.

Viv straddles the bike and I scoot behind her slowly, not used to being on this side of the seat. Her fingers deftly braid her hair, tying the end into a makeshift knot to secure the strands before tucking it under her collar.

"That's not going to hold worth shit," I chuckle.

"I know," she sighs. "I lost my elastic on the way over. It's the best I can do. Sorry in advance."

"I'll manage."

My hands brush her sides as I wrap them around her waist. She shifts as her foot flicks the kickstand, and her hips rub against me. This is going to be a long drive.

As I predicted, her hair is already starting to unravel by the time we get up to speed on the interstate. I lean forward, nuzzling my face in her neck to avoid the whiplash of the strands. Her scent is intoxicating — the warm aroma of vanilla and the subtle spice of cinnamon. Mixed with the smell of the whiskey I spilled on my jacket, it creates a sinful fantasy.

There's a voice in the back of my mind, screaming at me. *She's your Ombra.* Yes, she's mine. *You can't think about her like that!*

Like what? Like how I wish I could peel those leggings from her ass and bend her over this bike? I can picture it so clearly. She would spread her legs wide, taking all of me like such a good girl. She seems like the type to like a little pain with her pleasure, and I would oblige, digging my nails into her back or pulling her hair as I thrust into her. I can hear her calling my name.

"Damian!" I am roused from my daydreams as she shakes my arm, still ensnared around her waist. "We're here. You can let go now."

I moan into her neck as I drag my hands along the edge of my jacket. Viv mistakes my actions for me wanting my coat back, and she slips free of the fabric as she gets up. She drapes it over my shoulders as she helps me stand, the alcohol fully drowning my senses. We stumble together to the infirmary, and she guides me to sit on one of the exam tables. She grabs a bandage before she unbuttons my shirt, knowing I'm too drunk to do it myself.

"Now what did we learn today?" Viv teases as she opens the bandage wrapper.

"To not go out without my Ombra," I groan as her fingers carefully smooth the dressing over my cut. Her touch leaves a trail of fire in its wake.

"And?" She taunts, enjoying laying into me. I would enjoy if she did lay on me, right here and now.

"To not take you for granted." This answer earns me a smile.

"Anything else?" Viv goes to throw away the wrapper, and I slide off the table to follow her.

She didn't hear me approach, so she gasps when my hands grab her hips, spinning her around and pulling her flush to me. Her hands land on my bare chest as she catches herself. A growl escapes my throat as I lean in, smelling the lingering vanilla on her neck.

"You're drunk," she says softly. Her hands leave my skin, hovering in the air.

"I'd still want you if I was sober," I murmur into her ear as my fingers inch underneath the hem of her shirt.

"Damian." Her voice is firm, and it feels like a bucket of ice water is splashed into my face.

I jerk away, the nagging voice in my head reclaiming the forefront of my thoughts. Viv's face holds no expression, no one walking by could see how much I just fucked up. I stare at my hands in horror as I backpedal, putting space between the two of us. My hips ram against the exam table, and I fall to the ground.

"No!" I yank away as she tries to catch me. She stands there stunned, hands empty though still extended in the shape of my body.

"No," I whisper. "What did I just do? You're my Ombra and I tried to touch you."

"Nothing happened, Damian." Viv kneels next to me. "Your emotions are high, you're drunk, and you had a horde of women teasing you all night. I know that wasn't real."

But it was. Oh god, it was.

But I don't tell her that. Not as she drags me to my feet and leads me to the elevator to the main floor. Not as she struggles to get me up the stairs to my room. Tony and Sebastian find us, halfway up the staircase and Viv swearing every curse she knows. They run up, each taking an arm from her to easily carry me the rest of the way up. I pull away from them as we make it to my room, staggering inside and shutting the door. Their whispered voices are muffled, and I press my ear to the wall to hear.

"Thank you for getting me earlier, guys." That's Viv. "Sorry if I got a little... overzealous."

"You're surprisingly strong," Sebastian says apprehensively. "Next time, Tony is delivering the message. You ruined my jacket."

"No way." I can hear Tony laughing. "I'm not delivering bad news to her ever again. Maybe next time we'll use a pigeon or smoke signals."

"Ha ha," Viv says dryly. "Very funny."

"Is he okay though?" Sebastian asks, lowering his voice. "I saw the gauze on his abdomen and the bruise forming on his forehead."

"He will be," Viv sighs. "Thanks to you two."

"Are you okay?" Tony cuts in. "There's blood on your shirt."

"It's not mine." I can imagine Viv tossing her hair over her shoulder in that nonchalant style she has. "Anyway, you guys can go tuck in for the night. I'm going to stay here for a while, just in case Dam— Mr. Marano needs something."

The trio bids each other goodnight, and I hear Viv slide down the wall, reclining in her familiar spot. She sighs.

"Get your shit together, Vivianna," she curses under her breath. "How could you be so stupid?"

As I slump onto my bed, I tell myself the same thing.

◇ ◆ ◆ ◆ ◇

The floodgates have opened, and I can't figure out how to close them. All that runs through my mind is images of her. The way her skin glistens in the rain. Her lips as she says my name.

Or now, when her long hair whips around her face as she kicks the shit out of a new recruit dumb enough to spar with her.

I stand at the entrance of the gym. It's not unusual for me to be here lifting weights or running on the treadmill, but I've never been to the sparring ring before. The assassination attempt the other day revealed a weakness I've ignored for years, and it's time to address it. Or it will be when I can find the strength to tear my eyes away from her.

Enzo, her brother, enters the ring with a smirk, and the recruit practically jumps at the chance to leave, nursing a bloody lip. A deadly glint twinkles in Viv's eyes as she raises her fists. She'll fight anyone who will step in the ring — Marco, Tony, literally anyone — but Enzo is the only person who can give her a run for her money. The twins circle each other before turning into a blur of limbs striking and blocking faster than I can follow. Enzo eventually gains the upper hand, wrangling Viv into a headlock, but she sweeps his legs out from under him, rolling free of his hold.

"Sloppy execution." Marco shakes his head as he comes up next to me, joining me in spectating the match.

"You trained the Palazzos, right?" I ask. For some reason, their backgrounds were never fully explained to me, and I never thought to ask.

"Primarily their father and I did, yes." He raises an eyebrow slyly. "Why? Any complaints?"

"No, none at all," I respond, unsettled by how casually he discusses them. "I was actually wondering if you could train me."

"You don't need to know how to fight," Marco dismisses, repeating the party line my father always said. "That's what the Ombra is for."

When in danger, run to your Ombra. It's been forced into my head my whole life. *Your Ombra will protect you. Find them and get out of their way.*

Well, that mentality almost got me killed. When I felt the nuzzle of the gun press into my back, I had no idea what to do. Enzo was gone. Viv was gone, or at least I thought she was. I simply did what he said, walking submissively toward my death. I need to learn to take care of myself, take some of the pressure off Viv's shoulders.

"I'm not trying to do anything crazy here." I grimace as Enzo catches Viv with his elbow, but she laughs, dodging his next blow. "Just the basics."

"If you insist." He shrugs and we walk over to a punching bag.

Marco helps me set up my stance, adjusting the spacing of my legs and how I hold my arms. He guides my fist into the bag, showing how my whole body is used in a single punch.

"What are you doing?" A hard voice bites out, dripping with vitriol.

I whip around to find Viv standing there, fists clenched at her sides. Her ire isn't directed at me, instead her death glare is targeted at Marco.

"Teaching him how to throw a punch." Marco smiles, but his insincerity is clear. "If you did your job right then I wouldn't have to, but here we are." She bristles at his insult.

"Hold on!" I interject. "That is not at all why I asked for help."

"You aren't going to train him." Viv doesn't react to me, her attention solely on Marco. "If he wants to learn how to fight, then I'll take care of it."

"Honey, I'm the best around." He steps closer, looking her up and down. "I made you, didn't I?"

"You aren't going to train him!" She repeats herself, raising the volume of her voice.

"It's okay," I assure her. "It doesn't mean anything, it's harmless."

"Ignore her." Marco turns back toward me. "Face the bag again."

As soon as his fingertips brush my bicep, Viv is between us. She shoves Marco away, caging me behind her back with her arms. She blocks me with her body and doesn't shirk from Marco's glare.

"What the hell is going on?" I try to step around, but Viv clamps her hand around my wrist, yanking me back.

"The Palazzos protect the Maranos," she answers. "I won't let him hurt you."

"You've gotten weak, Vivianna," Marco sneers. "Maybe we should have a few sessions later, give you a refresher."

"Name the time and place." She raises her chin defiantly, and Marco narrows his eyes. He slowly walks forward until the two are chest to chest.

Marco leans down and whispers something in her ear. Her whole demeanor shifts in an instant. She recoils as the breath is stolen from her lungs, blood draining from her face.

"I might need to borrow Vivianna for a few days." Marco picks a piece of lint from his shirt as he addresses me. "She'll be a little banged up when I return her to you, but nothing she can't handle."

"Marco, back off," I order. I knew Marco and the Palazzo twins have some bad blood between the two of them, but this? I don't know what's going on, but this isn't some petty jealousy from Viv. This is fear. "Vivianna does not report to you, as such, you have no authority over her. You're dismissed."

"She needs to be properly trained," Marco pushes back. "This is standard procedure."

"I said, you're dismissed." I stand tall, placing a hand on Viv's shoulder protectively. "Now leave."

"Fine." He glances at Viv. "Next time, Vivianna."

Marco looks at me with disgust before turning and storming out of the gym. Viv doesn't lower her arms from around me until the doors close behind him.

Once he is gone, she takes a shaky breath and scrunches her eyes shut for just a moment.

"Hey, you're okay." I squeeze her gently, unsure of how to help. "I'm right here."

"Don't train with him," she whispers. "Please. I'll teach you anything you want to know, I promise. I can't watch him break you."

"Viv, what did he do?" I scan her, looking for clues to the questions circling in my head, but she throws up her walls before I can find anything.

"I'm fine," she states, shrugging me off. "Now show me your stance."

"You can't expect me to believe that."

"Arms up." Viv turns me to face the bag. "Widen your legs, right foot back. Find your center. You should be sturdy, unmovable yet mobile." Translation — end of discussion.

An hour later, my arms are jelly, and I have a whole new respect for Viv's skill in fighting. She stays back in the gym to run drills at her caliber as I trudge upstairs to shower.

The hot water trickles down my back, following the ridges of my muscles. Normally, showers clear my thoughts and give me fifteen minutes of serenity, but I'd be damned if I get fifteen minutes without Vivianna on my mind.

My dick stands at attention, stubbornly demanding my assistance. Viv is my Ombra, I can't just... It's not... Well...

Maybe once is all I need. Maybe just once will be enough and scratch my itch, clearing her from my mind. She wouldn't mind. She doesn't have to know.

I spit in my hand before it ventures south, tenderly wrapping around my shaft. My eyes close as I lean against the wall, letting the shower stream massage my spine. In my mind, another hand is the one touching me. A softer one with smudged nail polish. She seems to glow as the steam leaves dew drops on her skin. Her hair is draped across her chest before I run my fingers through it, pulling her head back to look deep into her eyes. She smiles before her tongue darts out, glancing off the tip of my dick.

My nails dig into the grout of my tile as I imagine her soft lips opening, her tongue swirling around my shaft as it sinks into her mouth. She licks her lips as she leans in, taking my cock all the way to the hilt and gagging on its length. She keeps her eyes on me the whole time, the warm brown melting me. Her sweat mixes with the smell of vanilla and cinnamon and... and... oh god.

I moan her name as I find my release, resting my head on the cold wall. My breath comes in short pants as my heartbeat slows. I dunk my head under the water, hoping to fix my haywire brain, but it doesn't work. Nothing works. Vivianna has taken hold of me, and I can't find a way to let her go.

The shower water trickles to a stop, and I step out, dragging a towel over my hair before wrapping it around my hips. My hands grip the edge of my sink as I hang my head, unable to look myself in the eyes.

How dare I? Viv's put her life on the line for me countless times, and I repay her by picturing her naked and sucking my cock. Fuck me.

My closet is full of endless copies of the same thing. Black shirt. Black trousers. Black jacket. The uniform provides a sense of camaraderie among the men, as well as intimidates our enemies. It can make me feel so powerful, but now it just feels fake. Regardless, I pull a set off their hangers.

Composure, control, competence. My dad's mantra. He always said that it starts with your appearance. Back in the bathroom, I check in the mirror to ensure my shirt is tucked cleanly into my trousers, no weird pleats or wrinkles. Cufflinks on. I slide open my drawer of ties, a few different options — all varying designs of black and gray. My fingers deftly maneuver the strip of fabric into a full Windsor knot. I don't need a mirror, I've done the knot thousands of times now, but I check my reflection anyway. Symmetrical, tight, perfect. My hair is still damp, so I give it a quick blow dry before combing it back, running my fingers through it with a touch of gel to hold it in place.

On my counter is a grocery bag with supplies I had Sebastian arrange to be delivered. I was low on a few hygiene products, but I also had a new ask — hair elastics. The cardboard sheet has a dozen or so black hair ties. I don't know if they're good quality or not, but I slip one onto my wrist. It's hidden beneath my sleeve so I won't get any strange looks, but now I can assure Viv will never be without one.

The man staring back at me in the mirror has been carefully crafted, twenty-six years of meticulous details. Only show what makes me stronger, hide my emotions, my weaknesses. Run the mafia with an iron fist, no mercy for our enemies. My shoulders droop as I meet my own eyes.

What the fuck am I doing? The Russians are banging on our door, sending assassin after assassin. My Ombra is comprised of two members — one that gives no shits about me and one that I can't stop thinking about. My dad would turn over in his grave if he knew I let Viv in the Ombra, much less wanted to fuck her.

The stairs creak as I walk down. Somehow Viv can always pass through silently. Just another thing she excels at.

I hear her laugh across the room. She's sitting on the couch with Enzo. This close together, the twin resemblance is clear. Same nose, same cheek bones, same brows. He throws a handful of popcorn at her, and she laughs again. Loudly. Freely. It rings through the room joyfully, radiating warmth. I've never seen her this happy.

Viv eats a spoonful of strawberry ice cream before she feels my gaze on her. Quickly, I cover my choked desolation, replacing it with my charismatic grin, but not fast enough. Her smile fades and concern leaks through for just a moment before another kernel of popcorn pelts her cheek and she slowly turns her head away.

"Move." Marco appears behind me and shoves me toward my office. "Not here, Damian."

Marco escorts me to my office, quickly pulling the blinds shut.

"She's off-limits." Straight to the point.

"I don't know what you mean." I sit in my chair and glance over the top sheet of paper on my desk. Simple invoice. Signed. Placed in a stack to be sent to the operations team. Next paper.

"Cut the shit," Marco rips the sheet from my hand. "I've known you since you were in diapers. The Palazzo girl is off-limits, and it's disturbing that I have to tell you that."

"We haven't done anything, Marco." I take back the sheet he stole from me, signing it without looking. I don't even know if I wrote my name in the right place, but it hardly matters. "There's nothing for you to worry about."

"Really?" He scoffs. "So I've just been imagining you looking at her all doe-eyed the past week? It won't be long until Enzo notices, and he won't take it nearly as well as I am."

"You're overstepping your bounds, Marco," I warn, setting my pen on my desk firmly. "And not that it's any of your business, but We. Haven't. Done. Anything."

"Yet." Marco lets the word hang in the air, and I struggle to swallow past the lump in my throat. "Get her out of your system or send her away. Those are your options."

"Don't you think I've tried?" My voice cracks as I meet Marco's disapproving stare. "I can't."

"Then I'm getting rid of her." He steps toward the door, before I stand.

"Absolutely not." I force all of my dwindling authority into my voice. "Her work as my Ombra is invaluable. I'm vulnerable without her."

"You have Enzo," Marco protests.

"Yippee." I twirl my finger sarcastically. "We all know the best bodyguards have obvious disdain for their protectees."

"Then at least find some whore to fuck until you forget about her."

"I tried!" The stack of papers crashes to the floor as I swat them off my desk. A few loose pages float through the air before joining their fallen comrades. That's why I took Enzo to the club, why I couldn't bring Viv. Girls threw themselves at me all night, and I threw myself right back, hoping that one might be able to take her place in my mind. Then she saved my life yet again and made everything so much worse.

"Figure it out, Damian!" He roars. "I don't care what it takes. You are the Don of this mafia. There are expectations for your position, ideals to live up to, legacies to protect."

"You don't think I know that?" I yank on my tie, loosening it so I can breathe. There's a quiet knock on the door.

"Go away!" Marco thunders as I call out, "One second!"

"We're still discussing this," Marco seethes as I fix my tie, securing the knot tightly against my shirt collar.

"I don't need your lectures to know where I'm fucking up," I whisper pointedly, keeping my voice low so the person at the door can't hear. "Trust me, I'm aware."

I fling the door open, the picture of suave confidence. Tony and Sebastian stand a polite distance away, obviously trying not to eavesdrop. The soundproofing on my office is good, but fuck, there's only so much it can do.

I glance across the way, Viv and Enzo are still chatting on the sofa. Good, they couldn't hear. Marco clears his throat as he follows my gaze, but I ignore him, waving my two lieutenants inside.

"How can I help you two?" I sit back in my chair, ignoring the scattered papers beneath my desk.

"The Russians have responded to our latest assault," Sebastian says calmly. "They hijacked one of our shipments, and we lost the entire batch of imported firearms. Several of our men were killed. Good men."

"They also left a message," Tony adds. "They said, 'Enjoy your spaghetti, you Italian fucks. With hatred, Bruno.' This was next to two boxes of pasta. Not to split hairs, but it was macaroni, not spaghetti. And it was the cheap, processed kind, not even name brand."

"Tony, I don't think Mr. Marano needed to know all of that." Sebastian rolls his eyes.

"It's insulting," Tony defends, throwing his hands in the air. "The name of the pasta is right on the box. Are they illiterate or just stupid? Or was it intentional? It's relevant."

"Thank you," I sigh, rubbing my brow.

"We have to deal with the Petrov family," Marco slams his hand on my desk. I would jump at the noise, but frankly, he does it too often. "They are getting too comfortable, bolder than I've seen them in years. They haven't acted like this since..."

His voice trails off. Neither Tony nor Sebastian is ballsy enough to finish his sentence.

"Since they killed my father." Marco's silence is all the confirmation I need. I grab a sticky note and take notes, reminders to be actioned later. "We'll need to increase security around the compound — Tony, I'd love your contributions here. I'll need to speak with the Ombra about raising threat assessments. Fuck me, Enzo is going to hate this. Sebastian, take a look at our operations and see what's vulnerable. We might need to tighten some processes or divert resources."

"We need a show of power," Marco's voice booms with righteousness, like a propaganda piece from the '40s. "Put the fear of god into those potato-drinking motherfuckers."

"That has literally never worked," I argue, annoyed with the migraine threatening to take hold of my brain. At least I'm not thinking about Viv anymore… Fuck. Deep breath. "The Petrov family, especially Bruno, has always been hot-headed. Violence only escalates with them. Despite that, they're also cowards. If we call their bluff, they'll back off."

"Let's force a meeting," Sebastian poses his idea. "We'll send you in with a small army of suits, intimidate them into standing down."

"That's not how they roll." I shake my head. "They only meet with rival families in their clubs. One person in, one person out. I could arrange a meeting, but I'd be going in alone."

"Well that's obviously not going to happen," Tony groans. "What's to stop them from killing you the second you walk in?"

"Jesus, Tony," Sebastian gasps.

"I'm just saying!"

"It's true," I sigh, leaning back in my chair. "The Bratva isn't exactly known for their integrity."

"We need a way to get someone on the inside," Sebastian mulls aloud. "If we could get Enzo or Vivianna in there undercover, I would feel less terrible about this."

"It's obvious, isn't it?" Marco scoffs. "Send in Vivianna. She's already got the skillset to be a whore."

"You get my sister's name out of your mouth!" Enzo busts through the door, which apparently was not shut all the way. He points at Marco with a violent fury.

"I'm just calling it like I see it, kiddo," Marco jeers. "Once a whore, always a whore."

Enzo jumps Marco, fists flying. Marco grabs him by the collar, shoving him into my bookshelf. Hardcovers fall off the wall, painful projectiles for those below. Sebastian and Tony shove their way into the fray, trying and failing to separate the two.

I turn back to the door and Viv is just… standing there. Her eyes are locked onto mine, but she's otherwise motionless as my office erupts into chaos.

I've watched her long enough I've started to understand her tells. The small twitch in her mouth means she's sad, the clench in her fists points to anger, the flash in her eyes means she's happy. But none of those are there, she's completely blank. That means one thing — she's very, very upset.

"Everybody out!" I yell, booming over the other screams in the room. I stand abruptly, knocking my chair to the floor. "Vincenzo, Marco, go cool off!"

They grumble unhappily as they shove away from each other, Marco nursing what will become a black eye.

I sigh and stare at the ceiling, before speaking in a calmer voice.

"Tony, go with Enzo. Sebastian, go with Marco. Try not to let them kill each other. The six of us will meet in the conference room in ten minutes. My office is too damn small for this." I wave my hand to dismiss them. "Viv, please step inside and shut the door behind you."

"No way!" Enzo shouts. "You stay away from her."

"You're just pissed that I'm right!" Marco can't resist getting in another dig.

"Knock it off!" I slam my hand on the desk, and unlike Marco's attempt earlier, this one cuts through the tension in the room. "She gets a say. All of you are arguing about her, but not one of you even bothered to ask her. Get a grip, for fuck's sake. She gets a say."

There's a beat of silence as four grown men stare at me.

"Now get out. Conference room, ten minutes, go."

I don't know if they listen to me. I don't care. All I know is Vivianna steps inside my office and closes the door, and I have some serious groveling to do.

"It goes without saying that none of that was meant to leave this room," I sigh, sitting on my desk. "How much did you hear?"

"Enough to know that this is the same family that killed your father." The bluntness of her words doesn't help to abate the sting. "Not that you care about my opinion, but I agree. If you go in alone, you won't come back out."

"I do care about your opinion," I protest. "That was a first draft plan. They always suck."

"If you say so, Mr. Marano."

"Viv, come on." Somehow, that hurts worse than the fear of my impending death. "That's not fair."

"You don't get to tell me about fair!" Her voice cracks. "You don't even know what you're asking me to do."

"I'm not asking anything!"

"But you are!" Her facade shatters as she crumples into one of the armchairs in the room. "I can't let you go in alone, but Damian, this is a Russian club we're talking about. They're not like yours."

"What does that mean?" My heart races and I feel my skin go pale. She hangs her head, crestfallen. "Viv, what does that mean?"

"You don't know what you're asking," she repeats quieter.

"Then it's settled." I stand and walk behind my desk. "I'm going in alone."

"Absolutely not!" Viv whips her head up in a panic, her hand clutching the scar snaking down the side of her face. She drops her hand when she notices my hardened stare. "You're not going in without me."

"Then help me come up with a new plan," I beg, sitting in the armchair next to her. "Help me figure something else out."

We brainstorm for the rest of our ten minutes. Then ten minutes turns to twenty, to thirty, and we have nothing. Her eyes meet mine, desperately racking for a better idea, but this isn't what she was trained to do. Her expertise is in defense, not strategy. This is my problem.

"Come on, Viv." I hold out my hand. "Let's not keep them waiting any longer."

The short walk to the conference room feels like a death march. I know what our decision is. Viv walks in a step behind me, taking a seat by her brother near the foot of the table, I stand at the head.

"Please tell me one of you has come up with a better plan." I keep my composure on a tight leash, faking my confidence when no one answers me. "No one?"

"Alright then." I straighten out my sleeves, feeling the hair tie hidden on my wrist. "I've come to a decision. This decision is mine, and it is final. I'm going in—"

"I'll do it." Viv stands, interrupting me. Enzo grabs her wrist to yank her back down, but she is unshaken, looking only at me. "I'll do it."

"No," I negate her consent. "It's off the table. I won't allow it."

"It's not your choice, it's mine." The corner of her mouth twitches down, just barely enough for me to notice. "What's the name of the club?"

"No!" I interject, feeling my heart drop in my stomach.

"The Nesting Dolls," Marco says.

Viv nods and backs away from the table.

"Vivianna…" A clear warning in my voice. She holds my gaze, saying everything while saying nothing at all. Then she bolts. "Vivianna!"

I run after her, but her bedroom doors slams before I can catch up. The lock engages and I shake the doorknob, pounding on the wood.

"Open this door right now!"

"You're not going in alone!" She screams back. I hear movement inside. My pulse races in my ears, accelerating as I lose my grip on my panic.

"Vivianna, you open this door, or I will break it down!" I've always made it a point to stay out of the barracks, wanting to keep this a sacred space for my men. Well fuck that and fuck this door.

I take a step back and kick the wood.

THUD.

A few splinters appear, and I make a note to buy sturdier doors.

THUD.

Another kick, and wooden shards fall to the floor.

At this point, I've drawn a crowd. I don't care. Marco and Enzo scream in the hallway behind me, Tony trying desperately to keep the two separate.

"Mr. Marano," Sebastian grabs my arm. "Maybe we should take a second to—"

I shove him off. Nothing is stopping me from getting inside.

CRACK!

One final kick and the door folds.

I shoulder my way through the remaining splinters, but Viv isn't there. Her uniform is strewn on the floor, hangers are discarded on the bed, her makeup kit is upended on her dresser. The curtains billow softly, and I pull them aside, revealing an open window. I dive through in a heartbeat, running into the clearing searching for any sign of her. There is none. I silently fall to my knees, accepting the truth.

Viv is gone.

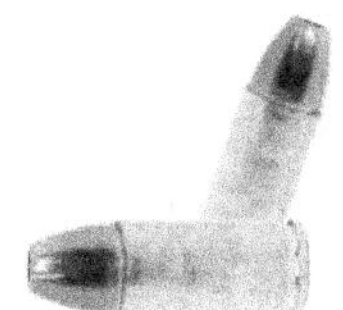

CHAPTER 7
VIVIANNA

The Nesting Doll hired me almost instantly. They were low on staff, especially ones with any skill. I'm not excited to find out why.

All eyes turn to me as I step through the doors of the compound. I raise my chin as I walk toward my room, refusing to feel shame from those who don't understand the sacrifice I'm making. I'd refuse to feel shame even if they did.

My steps falter as I enter the barracks, seeing the wooden shards that litter the hallway. A few men stand in my doorway, power tools whirring as they replace my doorframe. I duck around them and make my way to Vinny's room. He opens on the second knock and pulls me inside, tousling my hair. He doesn't yell at me, doesn't scream that I'm losing my mind or being stupid. Instead, we sit on his bed, and he holds me as I cry.

I don't see Damian the rest of the day, in fact, I don't see him the rest of the week. I avoid him, holing up in my room whenever possible. It's not as hard as it sounds since I now work nights, leaving me to try and catch up on sleep during the day.

The lights are always off when I get home, the only sign of life is the increased security patrolling the perimeter. They nod to me as I walk past. I pretend that I don't exist.

My feet know how to avoid every creak in the stairs, silently creeping up in the dark through brute muscle memory. I sit by his door through the wee hours of the night, holding my vigil as he sleeps. The Russians can't hurt him, I won't let them.

The Palazzos protect the Maranos.

I'll be strong, even as I put concealer over my scar each afternoon, hiding any proof that I'm not Gemma, the Italian Jewel. I dance on the stage, though the cigar smoke seeps into my clothing and follows me home. I won't complain, even when the clients get drunk and rough, leaving bruises in the shape of their fingerprints on my skin. I won't scream, even when the management does the same.

The Palazzos protect the Maranos.

I focus on what I can control. I can turn the shower as hot as it will go, replacing the feeling of their hands with the sting of the water. I can hide the marks with strategically placed garters and bracelets. I can hold back my tears until I'm on the bus, sobbing into the sleeves of my sweatshirt. I can use the short walk from the bus stop to the mansion to pull myself back together, and repeat the cycle, stepping into the scalding water.

The Palazzos protect the Maranos.

So I sit by his door every morning in the few hours before the sun decides to rise, leaning against the wall with damp hair and baggy sweats. But the stress is taking its toll, invading my nightmares. Metal poles spinning on a stage, metal blades pressed against my cheek, metal guns pointed at Damian. I'm tired. So tired. So, so tired.

The Palazzos…

Oxfords click softly on the hardwood, and I stir awake.

"Shh," a warm voice murmurs. "Go to sleep. You're okay."

"Vinny?" I mumble, lingering in my sluggish haze. A hand brushes my hair behind my ears. "I have to protect Damian. Not safe."

"He's safe, Vivianna." An arm gently pulls me against his chest while another slides beneath my legs, lifting me from the floor. The scent of pine settles over me. "You can rest. He's safe."

"Safe." I relax, hearing a steady heartbeat through his suit jacket. "He's safe."

"Go to sleep." His voice is so soothing. It feels like home.

"Vinny?" I nuzzle in deeper, my fingers drawing little circles on his tie.

"Mmm?" He shifts me in his arms, turning the doorknob to my bedroom.

"Don't let Damian see me like this." The mattress cradles my body as I am laid carefully onto my bed. "It'll hurt him too much."

"Don't worry about him." A shaky breath sounds by my side, though tender hands drape the sheets up and tuck me in. "Just rest."

"He's safe." The words drift from my mouth as sleep tugs me back down. "He's safe."

"Goodnight, Viv." A warm glow spreads through my chest at his words. He strokes my hair, combing it free of my face. His hands falter for a moment before a hesitant kiss brushes my hairline. The door clicks shut as he leaves, and no nightmares haunt my dreams as I fall into a peaceful sleep.

The manager's backhand stings as it cuts across my face, knocking me to the floor. I don't resist. It would raise questions if a girl could fight back, questions I can't answer without putting my cover at risk. I have to protect Damian, and that means taking the blow.

"Why am I hearing complaints about you from Igor?" Lev snaps, his thick accent making his speech hard to decipher. "He paid a lot of money for your time."

"I don't speak Russian." I keep my gaze fixed on the dingy carpet floor. "I can't understand him."

"Well I can't understand why we hired Italian trash when there are plenty of Russian beauties available." It's because no one wants to work here, asshole. As if he could hear my internal dig, he lashes out, landing a strong kick on my ribs.

I take the blow. I duck my head and kiss the proverbial rings. But I don't scream, won't scream. No matter how much I know they want me to. It's the one bit of power I let myself have. Instead, I grunt and dig my fingers into the frayed fibers on the ground.

Lev yanks me to my feet, a bruising grip on my wrist. I grimace as he pulls me closer into his arms. It's all I can do to not gag at the smell of stale peanuts, vodka, and cigar smoke.

"You might want to pick up a Russian dictionary," he threatens, shaking his cigar at me. I flinch as the warm ash stings my skin, burning holes through the lace of my bra. "It might make your employment here more pleasurable."

"Yes, sir."

He drops my hand, turning away from me without a second thought. I scurry away to the dressing rooms to grab my things. He's kept me late today, so I need to hustle or I'll miss my bus. All I want to do is get home. Waiting thirty minutes for the next one is not on my agenda.

I throw my sweatpants and a baggy sweatshirt over my lingerie then trudge through the pouring rain to the waiting bus. My fingers rifle through the bills I pulled from my garter earlier, depositing my fare into the collection box. The driver looks at me with pity, surmising enough about my night from the dead murkiness of my eyes. The only other passenger raises an eyebrow, before tightening her cardigan and returning to her crossword puzzle.

The closest bus stop is a mile away from the compound. From there, it's a quarter mile up the driveway. I don't dare take one of the motorcycles to the club or take a taxi, too afraid that someone will follow me or find out that Gemma isn't who she says she is.

The rain pelts me with every step through the cold, and my clothes drip onto the hardwood as I step over the threshold. I wait until I'm securely in my bedroom before I peel my soggy clothes from my frame, chucking them angrily in the hamper.

Black suits line my closet, taunting me. I grab a fistful of the fabric as my chest constricts. Soon Vivianna, I'll wear them again soon. I shove the hangers aside to pull out leggings and a new sweatshirt, ensuring the sleeves are long enough to hide all of my fading and developing bruises.

This time, I notice small lights lining the staircase. Motion-activated, they cast a dim glow over the stairs and hallway like a landing strip. Those are new. I discreetly climb to the landing, pausing when I see a form sitting in my spot.

Damian's head is resting against the drywall, his eyes closed as he sleeps. His breathing is deep and peaceful, despite his rumpled tie and wrinkled trousers. It's clear he'd been sitting there for a while before nodding off. He knew I was coming. He was waiting for me.

I hurriedly take a step back. I can't be here. He can't see me. But in my rush, I make a wrong step onto one of the spots I should have known to avoid. The wood creaks under my weight, and Damian yawns, stretching as he wakes.

"Viv?" He rubs the sleep from his eyes. I freeze, hoping that maybe he'll drift back asleep or that the lights will turn off, but I'm not lucky enough for either. "Damn, how do you sit here every night? I need to get you a chair or a cushion or something."

"The floor is fine."

I stand there awkwardly for a moment as Damian rubs his aching neck, then I turn to walk back down the stairs.

"Wait, Viv, please!" The desperation in his voice makes me pause, one hand on the handrail. "I never see you anymore. I don't know if you're okay. I…"

I glance over my shoulder to see him on his knees, pain written clearly on his face. Something in me breaks. Everything I've done, everything I've let happen to me was to protect him. He knows this. Hiding in my room was supposed to shield him, prevent him from seeing the impact of my decision. I'm beginning to think it made this worse, sending his mind spiraling down the worst hypotheticals imaginable.

"Please, stop running from me," he begs. "I'm not fast enough to catch you."

One conversation. I can hold myself together for one conversation. Ignore the bruising on my skin, bottle up my emotions, convince him that I'm okay. I sigh.

"Ice cream?" I offer.

The rigidity leaves his body as Damian exhales, rising to his feet. We walk together to the kitchen where I gather bowls and spoons. Damian rustles in the freezer for a quart of mint chip. A scoop in each bowl, and then we sit. Damian slowly eats his ice cream, I push mine around in my bowl, loosely feigning interest.

After a minute, Damian stands and returns to the freezer. He plops down a half-empty quart of strawberry ice cream in front of me. He grabs my spoon from my hand, wipes it on his shirt, and jabs it into the container. I stare at him, surprised when he doesn't find a towel to dab at the smudge on his shirt. He stares back, trying to read my mind.

"I don't care about my shirt right now," Damian says softly. As if he could feel me not believe him, he yanks it free of his trousers, leaving it untucked and wrinkled. He tugs at his tie, loosening it until it hangs askew. "I don't care about my clothes, Viv. I care about you."

I turn away, digging at the strawberry ice cream with my spoon. His gaze doesn't leave me as tears prick at the corners of my eyes, though I try to blink them back. My plan is already going to shit. I close my eyes as I eat the hunk of strawberry ice cream, savoring the chill as it melts in my mouth. God, I love strawberry ice cream.

"What'd I miss?" I wipe away a stray tear as I go back for a second spoonful. "Have you been keeping up with your training?"

"Not really." He shrugs, retaking his seat. "Sebastian and Tony both learned to fight on the streets. I figured you would kill me if I picked up any bad habits from them." He's correct, their technique is awful. "Marco offered to help—"

"No." I clench my spoon hard enough to turn my knuckles white.

"I turned him down," he assures. "Enzo stepped in then and gave me some pointers, but he wasn't really thrilled about it. I think he only did it because of the beef between the two of you and Marco."

"Probably." I nod. "That sounds like him."

"Viv, what happened?" He whispers his question, tiptoeing on uncertain ground.

"Marco did what he had to do." I glance up at Damian. "I wouldn't be able to protect you if he hadn't, but I don't have to forgive him for it."

"Did he—" Damian falls silent as I hold up my hand.

"I'm done talking about it. Move on."

Damian doesn't say anything, doesn't move. I expected at least some push back.

I look up at him to find his gaze locked squarely on the purple handprint wrapped around my wrist.

"Don't." My voice is quiet as I pull my sleeve down, lowering my hands under the countertop. "I'm fine."

"Vivianna, you're not going back there." He tries to sound firm, but I can hear the plea in his voice.

"It's just one more day." I wrap my arms around my stomach. "The meeting is tomorrow. I can do one more day."

"Why are you doing this?" He stands and paces behind the counter. "I don't want you to. I never asked you to."

"That's why." I brush my hair back out of my face.

"What?"

"You told me that if I joined your Ombra, you would ask everything of me." I toss the empty ice cream container in the trash and drop my spoon in the sink. "You haven't. Everyone else here has asked more of me than you."

"Is this some power play then?" Damian throws his hands in the air. "Are you trying to prove to Sebastian or Tony that you deserve to be here? Are you trying to show your strength to Marco?"

"God, Damian, do you even hear yourself?" I explode, the last brick in my wall crumbling to dust. He stumbles as I push him against the wall, but I catch his lapel, pinning him to the drywall. "I don't give a damn about anyone else! Fuck them. I'm doing this for you!" My voice cracks as I repeat myself. "I'm doing this for you."

He should be scared. He should try to shove me away, squirm out of my grasp. It's not like I'm gripping him tightly. If the roles were switched, I could break the hold in a second. But Damian didn't even flinch, his trust in me that strong. He rests his hands on top of mine, rubbing my knuckles with his thumbs.

"God, Damian." I pull away and run my fingers through my hair, holding it off my neck.

"Here." A ponytail appears in his hand. I take it, too tired to care where he found it.

"Thanks," I mumble, twisting my hair into a bun, before I let it fall back down over my shoulders. "You know what? No. Get your ass in the gym."

"I'll go change."

"No, now." I grab his arm. "You think that the Petrovs will wait for you to put on workout clothes? Fat chance. Practice in the worst conditions, and you'll always be prepared. Why do you think I spar with my hair down? Shit happens, and you can't let it be an excuse."

I shoo him to a punching bag.

"Tomorrow, anything could happen." I force my voice to stay level. "I can't promise I'll be able to keep you safe. You are going to need to watch out for yourself."

"I'll be okay," he whispers.

"You will be, because I will accept nothing less." I pull his crooked tie free and shake out the knot. "You wear a full Windsor, correct?"

"Yeah?"

"Good, it's a self-release knot." I loop the strip behind his neck and weave it into a Windsor, thankful that I paid attention when my mom taught me the different ways to knot a tie. "First lesson, if someone controls your tie, they control you."

To demonstrate, I grab the knot and yank it. He steps forward to catch himself as his head jerks along with it.

"Wear a tie clip tomorrow to keep your ends close to you," I order. "Now, the key here is the skinny tail. If I can grab that, I can tighten your tie and strangle you. But slipping it out is the fastest way of getting it off, eliminating it as a threat. Do you understand?"

"Yes." He pales as I fix his tie, adjusting it to sit where he likes it.

"Now punch the bag." I step back, crossing my arms as I watch his form. His stance is fine, not where I'd like it to be, but I can fix that over the next few weeks. Tonight is a crash course, down and dirty. He swings and I grimace. "You're going to break your hand if you hit someone's face like that."

"If I break my hand, then maybe that will also break their face?" Damian shrugs optimistically.

"Sure, maybe. But not the second person who comes at you." I take his hand and form his fist. "Your strongest knuckle is this middle one. Plus, it's supported by the bones in your arm. Hit with that part. If you punch with your pinky, you won't go very far. Show me what I told you."

I have him drill that motion a few times, adjusting small things here and there.

"What percentage of your strength would you say that you are using?" I ask, eyeing him.

"I dunno, maybe sixty or seventy."

"Show me one hundred." I scrutinize the movement of his body as he connects with the bag again.

"You're not using your hips nearly enough." I step behind him and place my hands on his hips, guiding the motion I want to see. Damian tenses at my touch, but I push through the awkwardness. "You're leaving all of this power on the table. This could be the difference between conscious and unconscious."

Damian swings again, grunting with the effort as his fist makes a pleasant smack on the bag. I nod, happier with the results. We continue like that for another twenty minutes, until I make him stop.

"That's going to have to be enough practice." We sit on the mats as the air grows still around us. "I don't want to wear you out too much."

"Gee, thanks," he pants, wiping the sweat from his face.

"What's your plan for the meeting?" I grab his hand and massage his knuckles and wrist, knowing how sore they can get. "What do you need from me?"

"I don't really have a plan," he admits. "Go in there, lay down the law, don't get killed. The team will be waiting about a block away in case we need back-up. Otherwise, just wing it."

"We are so fucked."

He gives a slight chuckle. "Why do you think I don't want you there?"

"Why do you think I'm going?" I squeeze his hand before taking a deep breath. "I talked to some of the girls who've been at the club a little longer. Bruno will likely pick out a girl for you tomorrow. That's not unusual. But if he sends her to set up a private room for you, that means he's about to make a move. If that happens tomorrow, run. Get out. No matter whether or not I'm with you. Promise me."

"What about you?" Damian sits up straighter. "I can't just leave you."

"Promise me," I beg. "I know how they work, I've seen the inside. I can get myself out as Gemma, but if I think you're in trouble, I'll blow my cover in a second to save you. If you feel like anything's wrong, the safest thing you can do for both of us is run. Promise me you'll run."

"I promise."

I stare into his eyes, not believing him for a second. He doesn't even try to hide his crossed fingers.

"Fucking hell," I curse under my breath. "Look if you're going to be stupid, you've got to commit to it, alright? One hundred percent in. The first punch sets the tone of the fight. Throw the first punch, throw it hard. Then. You. Run."

"I've got this, Viv." He straightens his tie. "I've been taught by the best."

"Your dad?"

"No." Damian smiles. "You."

CHAPTER 8
DAMIAN

I was going to try and convince Viv one last time to not go tonight, but she had already left by the time I knocked on her door. Guess we're doing this then.

The clock ticks slower and slower, dragging as I look myself over in the mirror one last time. There's a bit more gel in my hair than normal to keep every strand exactly where I've placed it. A thin layer of body armor is concealed below my dress shirt, unnoticeable to those who aren't overly familiar with the shape of my chest. My watch is fastened securely around my wrist, my panic button hidden in plain sight. Next to it is a new hair elastic, straight off the cardboard packaging. Viv won't need it, but after wearing one the past week, it felt wrong to leave it off.

The only catch was the tie clip. I hate tie clips. They look fucking pretentious, so I've never worn one. However, I trust Viv's safety advice over my fashion taste, so tie clip it is.

The door to my father's bedroom complains as I push it open, the hinges rusted from disuse. A thick layer of dust coats the room, and I leave a trail of footprints in my wake. The room is just how he left it. I've had no reason to come in here and pack up his things, so I haven't. A book sits on the nightstand, a bookmark shoved a third of the way through the novel. The hamper is half-full. A bulletproof vest lies abandoned near the dresser. Ironically, it wouldn't have changed anything if he wore it. Body armor doesn't help against headshots.

I step into the closet, coughing as a plume of dust billows from the clothes. A small box sits on a shelf. The lid creaks open to show my dad's collection of cufflinks and tie clips. I remember most of them.

He wore these monogrammed ones during the first strategy session he let me watch. I was so excited to sit at his left hand, Marco on his right. He led the room with such confidence, I was in awe of him for days after.

He wore these silver ones the day I had the first attempt on my life. I'd snuck out of the compound to go to the Palazzo's house. Vivianna had smiled at me the day before, watching Enzo and me play tag on the lawn through her bedroom window. I was hoping I could get her to smile again, but I never made it to her house. The car appeared out of nowhere. I don't know how my dad and Mr. Palazzo found me, but they did. I was thirteen.

He wore these gold ones the day my mom fled to Italy, scared of the rising tension between the rival families. They screamed at each other for days before she had someone drive her to the airport. My dad said she was being dramatic, good riddance and all that. Though he wouldn't let me see, I heard him crying as he signed the divorce papers. That was only a few months before he died. Seems she was right to leave.

A knock on the door draws my attention away from my melancholy walk through memory lane.

"One minute," I call out, running my fingers over the trinkets in the box until I select the tie clip I hate the least. The cuff links I'm wearing are replaced by the matching set of his. If I'm going to die today, at least I'll have a piece of him with me. Fuck, that's a morbid thought.

My reflection catches my eye from the full-sized mirror at the end of the closet. The glass has a hazy film over it, and it almost looks as though my father is standing in my shoes. A second figure appears next to him, and I feel a hand on my shoulder.

"You're going to be fine," Marco reassures me. It isn't hard to guess what I'm thinking about.

"I said I'd be out in a minute." My tone is gruffer than I intend to be, but Marco doesn't take any offense.

"It's time to go." He wipes a piece of dust from my shoulder. "The tie clip is a nice touch. You look like him."

"Thanks." Maybe I'll die like him.

I step around Marco, and we make our way into a waiting SUV. The pistol concealed in the small of my back digs into the seat behind me, reminding me of the danger I'm walking into. That Viv's already in.

Marco reclines casually in the seat next to me. It's his fault she's in danger, and he couldn't give two shits about her. This was his idea. She shouldn't be there. I should've stood up for her, should've been right there next to Enzo screaming at him for even suggesting it. Goddamn it!

My fist lashes out and I angrily pound the divider in front of me. Marco jumps at my sudden movement, but a second later, I've regained my external illusion of self-assurance. Composure, control, competence. I have to keep my shit together, if only for Viv's sake.

Our fates are tied together. If I don't talk my way through this and convince the Bratva to back down, then I might not make it out of there alive. And if Viv senses that, there's no telling what she'd do. The Ombra is a two-way relationship. She protects me, and I protect her.

My SUV veers off from the convoy as they go to find a spot to lay in wait. Marco rubs his hands together as we stop in front of the Nesting Doll.

"You've got this, Damian." I don't want to hear his tainted pep talk. "Go get 'em. Vivianna's in there. She'll watch your back."

"Go to hell, Marco."

His face falls as I yank open the car door, stepping out with the air of a politician or prince of a foreign nation. Two armed guards intercept me as I stroll toward the door.

"Hello gentlemen." I smirk. "I have an appointment with Sergei and his son, Bruno."

"Hand over your weapons." The guard is unfazed by my charm. "Now."

"I was instructed to come unarmed." I shrug, opening my jacket so they can tell I'm not wearing a piece on my hip or side. I rebutton the coat before they can check further. "If you could please step aside, my time is valuable."

They both scoff and roll their eyes, but I really couldn't give two shits. One stays behind while the other escorts me through the seating area. I pick an imaginary piece of lint off my sleeve as I subtly take stock of my surroundings.

Viv was right, this club is nothing like mine. Grime coats all surfaces, water rings mar the tables. The walls certainly used to be white, though the heavy cigar smoke has stained it a greasy yellow. Burn holes dot the mismatched furniture. I conceal a grimace while thinking about the last time they were cleaned.

More worrisome than having to burn my suit later, I don't see Viv. A few dancers mull about. Their hair is ratted, and bruises swallow their thin bodies. Track marks are visible on some of their arms, scars on others. I kept my chin held high, pretending that it isn't killing me that Viv is here somewhere.

"Little Damian!" Bruno claps me between my shoulders once I am delivered to his section. I'm taller than him.

"Bruno, what a pleasure." He gestures for me to sit, so I do, ignoring the hopefully bleach stains on the seat. "Is Sergei running late?"

"Oh, he won't be able to make it today." Bruno grins, and I narrow my eyes at the insult. He has the gall to not show?

"Shame." My smile matches Bruno's. "It's been so long since we've been able to catch up. Please pass along my regards."

"Of course." He gestures toward the stage where a few dancers twirl on poles. "May I interest you in someone to warm your lap?"

"Perhaps after we chat." I wink, playing along. Viv still isn't here. Where is she? "I prefer to keep business and pleasure separate. It makes a woman's touch feel much softer."

"Later then." Bruno raises an eyebrow. "That's surprising to hear from you though. With the number of clubs your family owns, I imagined you would be more... pleasure focused."

"What can I say?" I shrug, holding his stare. "The clubs are more fun to manage than our sizable import business."

"How can I help you today, Damian?" Bruno folds his hands in his lap. "I doubt you came all this way to gloat about your father's accomplishments."

"I came to remind you about the delicate balance between our families." My tone darkens, and I allow the slightest bit of ire free of my contained emotions. "This peace we have is hanging on by little more than a frayed thread, it has been for years."

I take a sip of my whiskey with a hardened glare his direction.

"Your squabbling ends now," I continue. "We don't have to be friends. I really couldn't give two shits what you think of me. But our families need to come to an understanding before this escalates further."

"Do you have a proposition for me or do you just want to spout nonsense?" Bruno narrows his eyes but appears to keep a somewhat open mind, at least more open than I was expecting, which was a bullet.

"I don't see why we have to interact at all." I glance up as a man walks behind Bruno, whispering in his ear. "We can have a straight split. I don't bother you, you don't bother me. Our business interests barely intersect as it is."

"I suppose there is value in never seeing you again." Bruno rubs his chin and I roll my eyes. "I planned a surprise for your visit. Consider it a parting gift."

I sit straighter in my chair, alert to whatever Bruno has up his sleeve.

"We typically only hire a certain type of dancer, but when this one walked through our doors, we had to snap her up. They call her the Italian Jewel."

Tattooed hands wrap around her shoulders, pushing her onto the stage. She stumbles, falling to her hands and knees. She plays it off, seductively swaying her hips as she crawls down the stage. Her hands wrap around the pole as she stands. Despite the poor excuse for a spotlight, her skin glimmers in the glow.

Viv.

"I personally picked out Gemma's outfit for tonight," Bruno continues. "Do you like it?"

Rhinestones drip down her body in a display of brilliance. They line her cheeks, her breasts, her hipbones, accentuating every curve of her body. On anybody else, the gauche display would look tacky, but somehow, she exudes elegance. It's obvious that this was supposed to be insulting to both me and her, but the cheap peel-and-stick gemstones aren't what has me struggling to keep my mask in place.

It's the bruises.

Thick bangles with plastic jewels aren't enough to conceal the handprints circling her wrists. Fingerprints peek out from underneath a bedazzled garter. Torn fishnets come up to her knees, and the only thought that comes to mind is that Bruno better pray they came pre-ripped.

"It's sparkly" is all I say. Much more appropriate than "I will kill you and your whole motherfucking family."

Viv catches my eye for a split second as she whips onto the pole, glancing just long enough to make sure I was okay before diverting her attention away. I understand why she can't look, needing to pretend she doesn't know me, but it kills me to have to sit back and watch.

"Can we have some peanuts over here?" Bruno yells out to no one in particular, yet a bowl appears on the table between us. "Damian, you're going to love this." He grins before hollering at Viv. "Do a trick! Go on, whore!"

She flinches as Bruno hurls a handful of shells onto the stage, a few shards pelting her. Regardless, a second later she is hanging from one arm, posing with her legs bent in the air.

"Damian, have a go," Bruno urges, holding out the bowl. "It's fun."

"I'll let you enjoy it." He doesn't notice my icy tone.

"I wonder if she speaks Italian." He shoves a handful of nuts into his mouth. "What's Italian for 'whore?'"

"*Bellissima*," I lie smoothly.

"Show some ass, you *bellissima!*" He screams, throwing more shells her direction.

Viv whips to face Bruno, confused by his words. She laughs when she sees my mischievous grin, her long black hair flowing gently down her back.

"What?" Bruno looks between us. "What just happened?"

"She speaks Italian," I state, shelling a peanut. The inside nut is discolored, so I gingerly discard it and wipe my hand on the chair. "You don't."

Bruno's skin flushes red and he stands, storming up to the stage.

"Wait!" I stand panicked. "What are you doing?"

Bruno rips her from the pole, and she slams into the floor with a pained groan. Before she can recover, Bruno lands a kick in her stomach. I run a few steps forward before I see Viv raise her hand, glancing up to make eye contact with me. To Bruno, it looks like she's trying to crawl away, but to me, it's a clear message. *No. Stop. I'm fine.* But I'm bad at listening.

"Bruno!" I shout, forcing as much authority into my voice as I can muster to get his attention. He pauses with his hand gripping her scalp. "I made the joke, not her. Let her go."

"She laughed," he growls.

"Of course, she did." I don't back down, no matter how much she pleads with her eyes. "You called her beautiful. She was accepting your compliment."

Bruno hesitates, and I see my chance to cinch the deal.

"I haven't gotten my gift yet." Come on, Bruno. Stop being stubborn. "Let's shake on our new arrangement so we can enjoy the rest of our evening."

"Fine." He drags Viv off the stage and throws her at my feet. "You can have her."

"Come here, *bellissima.*" I help her stand. "Tonight's a night for celebration."

"Gemma, go tell Lev to set up a private room for Mr. Marano here," Bruno orders with a roll of his eyes. "The two of you have some 'celebrating' to do."

I can hear Viv's breath catch in her chest, almost imperceptibly quiet. Her eyes slowly meet mine, a flurry of thoughts and emotions. Fear. Regret. Acceptance. She knows something, something more than what she shared yesterday.

"I'll see you soon." Her mouth smiles, but no one told that to her eyes. One of her hands grabs mine, moving it to cradle the back of her head as she leans in to nuzzle my neck. Hidden by the strands of her hair, Viv presses my panic button and leans in close to my ear. *"Corra." Run.*

With that, she sashays across the room. Her back muscles tense in a way I know all too well. She's primed for a fight.

I expect her to turn around at the last second, pulling out a concealed knife to fling into Bruno's throat.

But she doesn't.

Instead, she takes a breath and disappears backstage.

"I'm really glad we could work this out, Bruno." I smile, fully alert as I feel the walls closing around me.

She's in trouble. I don't know what or how, but I know that something is happening behind-the-scenes. I can't just walk away. I can't lose someone else to these Russian bastards.

"Any excuse to not deal with you Italian fucks." Bruno smirks as he glances down at his watch.

"The feeling is mutual." I keep my tone crisp and clear, though my thoughts growl in my chest.

"It's just a shame our little rivalry has to come to an end." He munches on the stale peanuts.

"I'm sure you can find someone else to antagonize." I roll my eyes and he laughs, tossing his empty shells on the floor. He glances at his watch again, tapping on the glass. "In a hurry?"

"Not at all." Bruno stretches his arms above his head as he stands. "I'm more surprised. Gemma is supposed to be screaming by now."

"Excuse me?" I rise to my feet calmly.

"Yeah, it's normally this big dramatic moment, but I guess we'll have to skip it." He shrugs. "Anyway, I decline your offer. Simply, I'm not interested. You're not leaving here tonight."

If you're going to be stupid, you've got to commit to it, alright? Viv's voice echoes in my head. *One hundred percent in.*

Oh, I'm in.

A bloodcurdling scream sounds from the back, but it's not a woman, it's a man.

Bruno whips around and I see my moment. Middle knuckle, hips, one hundred percent. He turns back to face me, and my fist connects straight with his nose. Bruno cries out as I follow him to the ground, shoving my pistol under his chin.

All hell breaks loose.

My men pour into the building, jumping through windows and breaking down doors. I duck as gunfire sounds around me, but the sound I hear next scares me more than any number of bullets.

"Damian!"

Viv.

A small herd of Russians pour out from the back room, most of them looking worse for wear with scratches across their face and blood dripping onto their clothes. A few of them limp or cradle their arms to their chest, but they're walking away. She wouldn't let them walk away. Something's happened.

"Get outta here!" Tony crouches beside me, providing cover fire. "Go!"

I look at him then look at the door to the back. One hundred percent stupid.

"Drop your weapons!" I yell, yanking Bruno to his feet. My 9mm is pressed firmly against his temple. "Drop them or I kill him!"

"Do what he says!" Bruno raises his hands, terrified.

My team swarms as the hostiles surrender, restraining them with zip ties and confiscating their firearms. I push Bruno into Tony's arms, running like a madman toward the scream I heard backstage.

"No, no, no!" Tears stream down her face as she yanks against her handcuffs, which are looped around a metal bar bolted into the wall. Blood drips down her wrists as the metal bites into her skin. She's missing a heel. Vivianna.

After a final tug, the drywall cracks and the bar is released from the wall. Viv falls to the ground but quickly staggers to her feet, kicking off the lone platform heel. She's running toward the door before she can even turn to look up, crashing into my arms. Alas, her first reaction to running into a mystery person in a hostile environment is to punch. Unfortunately for me, she's had years of coaching compared to my one week.

"Ow! Goddamn it, Viv!" I curse and sink to my knees, dazed and disoriented. "It's me."

"Damian?" She kneels beside me. "Are you okay?"

"No! You just punched me, so I'm not okay." I cradle my eye. "I was fine before that."

"Why are you here?" She growls as she grabs my arm, yanking me to my feet.

"There's no way I was going to leave you," I state pointedly.

"You were supposed to run!" Viv yells, furious.

"I did! I ran toward you."

"That is not what I meant and you know it!" Her hands shake, and if she wasn't handcuffed, I'm not too sure she wouldn't try to strangle me. Scratch that, she could definitely do that handcuffed.

"You screamed!" I raise my hands as I defend myself. "I panicked."

"I screamed after the gunshots. I thought you were dead!" She rolls her eyes. "God, I even pressed your panic button for you. Do I have to hold your hand through everything?"

"Yes," I tease with a small smile. "You're my Ombra."

"Arghh!"

Up close in the fluorescent lighting, I can get a clear view of the bruises dappled across her body. Angry purples and blues, some raised into welts. I slip out of my jacket and drape it over her shoulders, keeping only a flimsy grasp on my temper.

"Vivianna." My tone is deathly serious. "I need you to be honest with me."

"Yeah, what?" She's distracted, sliding the ripped stocking off of her legs.

"Who has the keys to your handcuffs?"

"Lev." She doesn't even look up.

"Good." I nod. "Now I need you to point him out, as well as every single fucking person who touched you."

"I'm fine, Damian." Her voice is just barely more than a whisper as she stares at the floor.

"Vivianna, this is an order." I stand, ignoring the throbbing in my eye. "No one hurts my Ombra without consequences."

"I don't need you to fight my battles."

"Oh Viv, we're at war." I smirk. "And I'm about to send a message."

I gently place my arm around her shoulders, holding the door open for her. By this point, every assailant has been lined up, their hands bound behind their back. I chamber a round in my pistol as I walk up to the first asshole.

"Yes or no?" I stare at Viv who refuses to answer. "Did. He. Touch. You?" She looks away. I huff and step to the second person. "Fine, what about this guy?"

She glances up, curt shake of her head. "No."

"No you're being stubborn or no he didn't touch you?"

"He never touched me." She stares into my eyes.

I step back to Asshole Number One. "Yes or no?" No answer. "Works for me."

Bang! Viv's eyes widen slightly as Asshole Number One drops to the floor. I step to Asshole Number Three, looking back at her. Same question. No reply. *Bang!*

Viv sticks to her silence or one word response for every person except for one.

"Yes or no?" I ask, and fury slips out from behind her impartial gaze.

"He has the key." No emotion can be heard in her words, but her message is clear. I nod.

"Tony, Sebastian, get him up," I order, and the man quivers on the floor.

Now standing, I search his pockets, pulling out a small key and unlocking Viv's cuffs. Viv rubs her wrists as she glares daggers at the man. She takes my gun from my hand and stalks toward Lev.

"I would like to tender my resignation, effective immediately," she spits. "My employment here has not been pleasurable."

"Please, Gemma," he whimpers. "You don't understand—"

She doesn't listen. Her hand raises from the floor slightly, and she enforces my HR policy. He screams as Tony and Sebastian hold him up, blood dripping from between his legs. She keeps her eyes locked on him, refusing to look at me, refusing to show any weakness.

"Tony, take him to the Pit," I instruct. "I'm going to take a bit longer with him." Tony nods and drags him away. Viv passes me back the pistol and I step back.

Bruno waits at the end of the line. Someone had the good sense to gag him, a small blessing in an otherwise hellish day. I crouch next to him, ignoring the warm blood splatter on my cheek.

"I don't even need to ask with you." A wicked smile grows as I use his shirt to polish my pistol. He tries so hard to keep from shaking, it's almost cute. "No, I saw you touch her. I saw you throw her to the ground and abuse her, and for what? Because I made her laugh? What a poor excuse for a man."

My anger has taken root in my chest, growing and entangling through my body with every passing second. I slide my gun into its holster, and Bruno mistakenly relaxes. He doesn't deserve a quick death, I won't give him one.

My heel connects with his sternum, knocking him to the ground. The vision of him hurting Vivianna overruns my thoughts, and I can't stop. I kick him again as his muffled screams cut through his gag, and again as I hear something crack inside. I yank a fistful of his hair, dragging him to Viv's feet and unholstering my gun.

"Grovel," I command. "Beg for her forgiveness, or I'll kill you right here."

It's hard to grovel with your hands tied behind your back, but he figures it out. Viv isn't impressed, her lip curling like I left a rotten fish on her doorstep.

"Can we go?" She addresses me, not even acknowledging the sniveling human in front of her.

"A few more minutes," I promise, with a curt nod. "I'll wrap things up."

She sighs and steps over Bruno, walking to lounge in one of the cleaner-looking chairs. I follow her with my eyes, fixated by the way she exudes dignity and elegance though she's covered in press-on gems and other people's blood. My shoulders relax as she sits, returning her gaze to me to keep watch from afar. I'm safe, surrounded by a legion of armed men, but they mean nothing compared to her. And she's wearing my jacket. *My* jacket.

Bruno squirms on the floor, and I catch him watching me, studying the look on my face. There's nothing to see. Nothing happened.

But as realization dawns on his face, I know that he sees through the lies I tell myself. I force myself to put on a cocky face, crouching down to whisper in his ear. "What are you going to do about it? Huh?"

Tony returns to the club and I motion for him to come over.

"I have a message for you to deliver to Sergei," I say to Bruno. "If it's war he wants, it's war he'll get. Just remember this moment when I grind your empire into dust. I tried to be the bigger man,

I tried to rise above, but I am more than willing to put my manners aside to protect what's mine."

"My friend here wanted to give you a gift, as thanks for the one you left for us." I nod and Tony pulls out a carrot from his inside jacket pocket.

"Thanks for the *spaghetti*," he sneers, throwing it on the ground next to Bruno. "Enjoy your *potato*." He raises his hand for a high five, but I just stare blankly at him.

"Really man? That's the 'epic burn' you begged to say?"

"That was hilarious." Tony smiles, still holding up his hand. Sebastian pulls him away as I shake my head embarrassed.

"The only reason you're leaving here alive is because I don't believe you're a threat." I lean in close so only he can hear the words I'm saying. "You are weak. You are helpless. And when your father's kingdom crumbles around you, know that you never could have stopped it."

He tries to yell at me through the gag, but I don't care. I've grown tired of his company and my Ombra is waiting on me. While he curses me and my family, I'm focused on the girl wearing my jacket.

"Let's head out, men."

I extend a hand to help her to her feet, but don't let go once she stands. I don't let go the entire car ride home.

We sit in silence, each needing the drive to process the shitshow that plan was. Her free hand plucks the gemstones from her skin, dropping them in the cup holder with a plunk. I watch her for a moment then tear my eyes away to stare out the window.

The gravity of the situation starts to sink in. We're at war. This meeting was supposed to deescalate the conflict, but instead the stakes have risen to their highest peaks yet. I wish my dad were here to tell me what to do. My fingers rub the tie clip I borrowed. My father would know what to do. He would call a meeting with his underbosses, devise a clever yet simple strategy, and win.

My eyes glance back to Vivianna and the bruises marring her tan skin. She's my Ombra. The more danger I'm in, the more danger she's in. I have a responsibility to keep us safe.

The driver pulls into the garage, and I release Viv's hand, wiping mine on my trousers. She leaves hers dangling on the hump seat between us.

"Thank you for being there for me tonight," I whisper, staring out the window. "I promise, I don't take your sacrifices lightly."

"You're welcome." I don't look at her, can't bear to see her face portraying her quiet acceptance, or pained sadness, or worse — nothing at all.

I jerk the car door open, striding through the unloading convoy. High fives surround me as they celebrate the victory over Bruno, how we showed them who's boss. They don't realize that the gloves are now off, and trouble is brewing. It's all my fault. Marco tries to intercept me, but I shoulder my way past him, not in the mood to celebrate with the guys or be lectured by him. I don't stop until the door to my office is shut and locked behind me, the blinds drawn tightly over the windows.

It is only then that I allow myself to fall apart. I scream until my throat burns with the sting of my anger and frustration. My tie clip skids across the hardwood as I yank my tie from my neck, flinging it to the floor. It's not enough. I want to throw something else, something bigger, heavier. My fingers clutch a hardcover from my bookshelf, hurling it to the other wall. The text thunks against the drywall, opening to a random page as it plonks onto the floor. Another book joins it, and another, until the bookshelf is nearly empty.

Knock. Knock. Knock.

My head whips toward the door, then I scan the disarray I've strewn through the room. Aw fuck. There's no way I can begin to hide this in an unsuspicious amount of time. I run my fingers through my hair, trying to at least make myself presentable. I pull open the door, dreading whoever is on the other side.

"Hey." Viv stands there, holding a bowl of ice cream in each hand. She's changed into pajamas, though a shadow of her stage makeup remains. "I don't think you should be alone right now."

"I'm not good company at the moment," I warn sullenly, my voice hoarse from misuse.

"Move aside or I'll break down the door," she threatens. "It's only fair, you broke mine."

I cringe, but step back, letting her in. She takes a moment to assess the state of the room before nodding.

"What?" I snap, then instantly kick myself. I'm not angry at her, just at the world.

"I'm not judging." She shrugs, passing my bowl to me. "You throw books, I throw knives. At least your vice isn't sharp."

"This isn't something I normally do." The ice cream soothes my raw throat, through my rage simmers below the surface, still looking for a vent.

"Are you okay?" Her eyes soften, and I hate how worried she is about me.

"I should be asking you that."

"I didn't just trash a room." There's no malice in her voice, but I flinch anyway, ashamed that I lost control, even if I did so in private. "Damian, talk to me."

"There's nothing to say." I jab my spoon into my ice cream. It gives way unsatisfyingly under my thrust. Viv's knives seem more appealing by the second.

"Try anyway." She curls into an armchair, listening intently.

"How do you think I am, Viv!" My bowl thuds against my desk as I jerk to my feet. "I just started a blood war, a fucking war! This isn't going to end until all of the Maranos or the Petrovs are dead. Luckily for them, they already killed my dad. It's just me now."

"They'd have to go through me first." Viv growls defensively, sitting up in her seat.

"And I hate that!" My heartbeat thuds in my ears as I pace across the room. "You think I like seeing you hurt, putting you in danger every time I go outside? I can't keep you safe, Viv!"

"Damian, I can take care of myself." She stands, setting her bowl aside.

"Do you know how scared I was today?" I grab an overlooked book from the shelf and heave it towards the wall. It dents the drywall from the impact. "I couldn't find you, and all of these scenarios, these nightmares took hold of me. I... I..."

"Shh." Viv steps in front of me, blocking me from the bookshelf and any further projectiles. She takes my hand and presses it against her pulse point. "I'm okay, Damian. I'm alive, I'm safe, I'm right here."

"I couldn't do anything." My voice wavers as her scream replays in my mind. "Everything was out of my control. I was powerless."

"Control me," she whispers.

"What?"

"Control me," she repeats desperately, moving my hand to wrap around her neck. "I can take your pain away. Use me. Control me."

"I won't do that to you, I can't be another person that hurts you." I try to step away, but Viv pulls me back in by my belt.

"You can't hurt me, Damian," she pleads. "Whatever you need, however you want it, take it. It's yours. You could never hurt me."

"No, Vivianna!" I step back more forcefully, and she lets me go with tears in her eyes.

"What am I supposed to do?" Her hand clutches her stomach. "I hate seeing you like this. I'm supposed to protect you."

"Ice cream is a start." I slump on the floor, leaning against my desk. "I'll have to get back to you with the rest of the list."

"I must be the worst Ombra in history." She flops down next to me.

"How could you think that?" Doesn't she see how much she does for me, how much I need her? "You're more than I deserve. I let you sell yourself, and it ended up being all for nothing. I failed."

"It wasn't for nothing." Her eyes find mine. "And if I remember correctly, you did everything you could to stop me."

"They hurt you, Vivianna."

"And you killed them for it."

A beat passes in silence. Then another.

"You knew, didn't you?" I say.

"What?"

"That they were going to try to kill you backstage." I stare into her eyes, daring her to lie to me. She doesn't.

"Yes." She runs her fingers through her hair. "My plan was to not let them. Take care of them and then go from there. I didn't realize there would be so many of them waiting. I was winning though, until they heard Bruno scream. Then they handcuffed me to the wall and ran to help."

"To think, Vivianna Palazzo almost bested ten men at once," I brag on her behalf.

"Almost." She smiles. "And it was thirteen."

"Please don't do that again," I whisper. "Don't hide things from me, don't take on the world by yourself, any of it. If I lost you... I can't lose you."

"Palazzos don't go down easily," she promises, her hand squeezes mine.

I shift to my knees, knowing the one thing she can do to help me, to soothe the desolate thoughts in my head. I hug her close, burying my head in her neck. My eyes close as I parse out the cigar smoke and sweat from her skin, ignoring the metallic blood and the pine of my cologne.

Faintly, I find it. Vanilla and cinnamon. I breathe deeply as her arms wrap around me, clinging on as tight as she can. She scoots closer, straddling my lap so our bodies are flush together, our hearts beating as one. Suddenly, I understand why my father didn't approve of Viv. The relationship between Ombra and protectee feels an awful lot like love.

CHAPTER 9
VIVIANNA

"No excuses, Vivianna!" He circles me in the ring. I would say a sheen of sweat glistened on my skin, but that's giving myself too much credit. I'm dripping. My shirt is drenched and my hair clings to my neck. "You have a job to do! Failure is not an option."

I've gotten weak, lax in my training. That can't happen. Damian is in more danger now than ever. I owe it to him to be stronger, faster. My body is a machine, and it must be lethal. I have to protect Damian, so I turned to the one person I knew would mercilessly whip me back into shape.

"Is that the best you can do?" Marco sneers as I dodge his latest bout of assaults. My hands are zip-tied behind my back, but he has full use of his limbs. He's right though. He's kicking my ass, and he shouldn't be. "What kind of a Palazzo are you?"

Marco's trying to rile me up, make me sloppy. It won't work. I duck under his next punch, driving my shoulder into his chest. He stumbles back a step and I use the space to whip out a roundhouse kick. Too slow. Marco catches my ankle and yanks, knocking me off balance. The ring is cushioned, but that doesn't stop me from hitting the floor hard. My head slams onto the ground, but I force myself to roll to my feet before Marco can take advantage of my vulnerable position.

"What's going on here?" Damian calls in the distance.

I glance over my shoulder, taking stock as he jogs over toward the ring. A sharp pain rips through my scalp as Marco tugs on my hair.

"I didn't say stop," he scolds, throwing me on the ground and backing up to reset. "You get one pass. One. The next time I won't let you off as easily."

I grit my teeth as I stand, not excited to have Damian in the audience as Marco humiliates me. Deep breath in. Deep breath out. Roll my shoulders back. Let's go.

Fake to the left, spin to the right. Elbow out, catching Marco in the ribs.

"No elbows!" Marco shouts, clutching his side.

"Elbows are totally allowed," I argue. "You said no hands!"

"Always looking for a shortcut, huh?" Marco laughs. "No wonder you've gone soft."

"You've got this, Viv," Damian encourages from the side, sensing my growing frustration. "You're doing great."

"Remind me, Vivianna," Marco provokes. "Wasn't Sergei Petrov the one who gave you that scar?"

"Watch it, Marco." I narrow my eyes as a warning, but it only encourages him to dig deeper.

"If you keep taking these shortcuts, maybe he'll give you a matching one on the other side." Marco shrugs.

I'm done listening to him talk.

I jump forward, catching him square in the gut with my heel. He keels over and I take the opportunity to stomp on his foot before knocking him to the ground. I follow him down, but he slips away before I can pin him against the floor.

"Do you think Sergei even remembers you?" Marco circles me again. My fists clench behind my back as my nostrils flare.

"Back off, Marco," Damian cautions, but the world outside the ring doesn't exist. It's just Marco and me.

"You're weak, pathetic," Marco sneers. "With you as Damian's Ombra, nothing will stop Sergei from carving into Damian. I bet he'll even use your knife."

Something snaps within me, and I charge. Marco swings, but I weave around his attack, returning to offense with a kick to his jaw. We exchange blow for blow. He pulls my hair, I knee his ribs. His fist catches my hip, my shoulder strikes his sternum. I finally have some momentum, until I come crashing down, slipping on a puddle of sweat. Marco pounces, pinning me beneath his hips while his hands encircle my throat and squeeze.

"Escape, Vivianna!" He roars. I buck my hips, trying to shake his foundation, but he doesn't waver. "No tapping out! Save yourself!"

I'm trying! If my arms were free, I'd be out in a heartbeat. I struggle harder as the edges of my vision fade. My lungs are burning, my heart is pounding. I gasp for air, but there is none. There's screaming in the background, and I see a silhouette jump the ropes, pulling Marco off my torso. My shoulders heave as I roll onto my knees, greedily gulping for air. I'm still swaying as I stagger to my feet, stumbling as I try to get my bearings.

Damian is screaming at Marco, the cufflinks of his suit catching the light as he gestures wildly. Marco is having none of it, rolling his eyes in annoyance. They're drawing a crowd, but they're outside the ring. They don't exist.

Wait. Damian.

He's inside the ring.

Marco catches my eye, smirking as he raises an eyebrow and pulls back his fist. I act on instinct, shouldering Damian out of the way and taking the blow myself. He falls to the ground, but I can't worry about him right now. Marco circles me, trying to sneak past my guard to get to Damian, but there is no way in hell he's beating me.

He lunges, but I'm faster, throwing myself at his feet and knocking him down. My legs wrap around his chest, pining his arms to his torso.

"Finally!" Marco cackles. "Some decent fucking technique!"

"Damian, leave the ring." My voice is firm, though I'm panting harder than I have in weeks. "Everything in the ring is fair game."

"No, you're both done!" Damian shouts. "This crossed like fifteen lines. Marco, you went too far!"

"Damian, leave!" My grip on Marco weakens as he squirms.

Holy hell, I don't know if I can do another round with Damian in play. Maybe an hour ago, but certainly not now.

Damian storms up to me and grabs my shoulder, roughly dragging me across the floor and out of the sparring ring.

"Oh thank god." I slump to the ground as fatigue overtakes my muscles.

"She's not done!" Marco stands and glares at Damian.

"Take a walk!" Damian points to the far side of the gym.

"Do you want him to die?" Marco redirects his abuses to me. "Right now, all I see is a quitter. Who will be there to protect him if you're this useless in training?"

I jump to my feet, but Damian wraps his arms around me before I can give Marco a piece of my mind.

"Let me go!" I struggle, restrained by both Damian and the zip ties now. "I'm going to kick his ass!"

Someone else beats me to it. Vinny jumps into the ring, sucker punching Marco while his attention was focused on me. Marco falls to the ground and Vinny kneels on his chest, grabbing his shirt and socking him in the jaw.

At this point, several men clamor into the ring to pull Marco and Vinny apart. I don't get to see what happens next as Damian tows me out of the gym.

After a quick snip with a pair of kitchen shears, I have use of my hands again. I groan as my shoulders relax, sore from the intense training.

"What the fuck, Viv?" Damian seethes.

"Why are you mad at me?" I pant, filling a glass of water. "He's the one who swung at you."

"He almost killed you!"

"He would've stopped," I say, less sure than I'd like to be. "Aren't you glad I didn't let him train you?"

"Do you mean to tell me that happens often?" His voice lowers to a growl as he cages me against the counter.

"It used to. Lots of things used to." Memories lash through my mind but I shake them away, taking a sip of my water. "It happens less often now. This exercise was new though. I need to practice before we do it again."

"You're *not* doing that again." Damian takes my glass from me. "In fact, you're not training with him ever again. I forbid it."

I open my mouth and close it again. "Can you… can you do that?" His eyes darken at my question, and he leans forward until I can feel his breath on my neck.

"I just did." His voice is just loud enough for me to hear, and goosebumps riddle my skin. "Do you have a problem with that?"

"I need him." The words taste bitter coming out of my mouth. "He pushes me. I can't let up, not now."

"He 'pushes' you?" He shakes his head. "No, Viv. No more. End of discussion."

Damian stares down at me until I nod in agreement. He retreats with a smile, tossing me an apple from the fruit bowl. I take a bite and offer it back to him, but he holds up his hand, content.

"Do you have any plans the next few days?" He asks, leaning against the fridge.

"Plans?" I joke. "What are those?"

"I don't know." Damian shrugs. "Lunch with Enzo, a date, tickets to a knife symposium?"

"Oh yeah, I do have a date tomorrow." I take another bite of apple. "Dinner and a movie, then I was planning on going back to his place after."

"Really?" He stands up straighter, losing his casual air.

"No." I cross my arms over my chest as I analyze his strange reaction. "Would you have a problem if I did?"

"Of course not." He smirks, and I can sense his demeanor shift. "I was just wondering if you would be available to take a weekend trip with me. My family has a hunting cabin a few hours north, and I was looking forward to a change of scenery."

"I don't know if you could afford my overtime rate," I tease, tossing the apple core into the trash.

"Please, Viv?" His eyes light up as he smiles. "Fresh air, hunting, falling asleep to the sounds of nature. I would take Enzo, but he would throttle me before we finish the drive up."

"What's in it for me?" I cock my head. "This sounds like a lot of work on my end and a fun joyride for you."

"Fresh venison for dinner?"

"Sold."

"Go shower." Damian claps his hands together. "We leave as soon as you're packed."

"Viv, wake up. We're here."

"I'm awake," I mumble, snuggling deeper into my seat.

"Viv..." Damian sings gently, nudging my shoulder.

I gasp as I shoot up.

Shit, I fell asleep.

"Why didn't you wake me earlier?" I scold, running my hands through my hair. We haven't even stepped outside the truck, and I already fucked up.

"I think I am more than capable of driving without my bodyguard." Damian rolls his eyes. "Besides, you looked like you needed some rest."

He's probably right. He doesn't know this, but this weekend is going to be hell for me. At least at the compound, I can relax, trust in the security in place. Out here, I'm all Damian has. I won't be getting much sleep.

I unbuckle my seatbelt and slide out of the truck, pulling my 9mm free. Damian is unamused as I sneak up to the cabin, peering through the windows, but he's in my care this weekend, so he can suck it up.

The door creaks as I swing it open. After a quick sweep of the one room cabin, I can confidently say there are no hostiles there.

He takes his bags inside as I inspect the outhouse. I jump back when something leaps out at me.

"Ah!" I squeeze the trigger, firing a round at my assailant. My aim is true, direct shot to the head.

"Vivianna!" Damian screams, bolting out of the cabin. I clutch a hand to my chest as I try to calm my racing heartbeat.

"Raccoon," I gulp. "We startled each other. I'm okay. New rule, don't go to the bathroom unarmed."

Damian blinks at me slowly before turning dramatically and walking back into the cabin. I grab my two duffels, grunting under the weight as I bring them inside.

"Did you really need to bring all of that?" He gestures at my luggage. "You really only need a few changes of clothes."

"That's what is in this one." I toss him the lighter bag and heft the other one onto the table. "The other is all for work."

I unzip it and unpack my emergency supplies. First aid kit complete with blood-clotting bandages for gunshot wounds, rifle for long-distance defense, ammunition for the rifle and my pistols, a few rations of nonperishable food, several other odds and ends. I inspect my rifle before setting it in a stand by the front door. I repack what we don't need right now, stowing it away to save space in the tight quarters.

My mind is whirling as I go down my mental checklist, ensuring I'm not forgetting any of the warnings my dad taught me so long ago. I run my hands through my hair, lifting it off the back of my neck.

"Do you need a ponytail?" Damian asks.

"Eh, I threw a few in my bag before we left." I drop my hair. "I'll find one later."

"I have one here." He pulls up the sleeve of his sweatshirt and slides an elastic off his wrist.

"Why do you have a hair tie on your wrist?" I throw my hair up into a quick bun, not concerned with how it looks.

"In case you need one," Damian answers plainly, as if I asked him why he keeps his license in his wallet.

"Huh. Well, thanks."

"No problem." Damian casually pulls off his sweatshirt, and his t-shirt rises to reveal a glimpse of his abs before he adjusts it.

I sweep out the inside of the cabin as he chops wood outside. It never occurred to me to ask whether or not there was electricity here, but the answer is nothing beyond a fridge and a few dim lights. There is a water pump, but no other plumbing. Even the stove is wood burning. At least it's not a tent.

"I think we've got enough wood for the rest of the day." Damian wipes the back of his hand across his forehead, flicking away his sweat. "I'm going to go find some dinner."

"Wait for me, I'll be right there."

"Leave the pistols." He calls as he walks toward the door.

"Why would I do that?" I check to ensure they're loaded, before reholstering them.

"Viv, no one is around for miles," he laughs. "Relax, take a breath, enjoy the wilderness. Leave the pistols."

"I think I'll bring them." I tighten my bun. "They're good against malicious raccoons."

Damian saunters toward me and I back up until I run into the wall of the cabin. He smirks and fiddles with the collar of my flannel. I swear my heart is about to beat out of my chest as his fingertips brush my skin. He moves my collar out of the way and nimbly unbuckles my chest holster, dropping my pistols on the table.

"Leave those there and I'll let you bring your knives." His voice is smooth and rich as he makes fun of me. He stands there, close enough I can feel his chest move as he breathes. I realize he's waiting for a witty retort, but I can't find one.

"I'm bringing the rifle," I stammer.

"Of course you are," he teases. "I'm bringing one too. We're going hunting."

We hike through the forest in a comfortable silence. I've never seen Damian like this, completely relaxed and at peace. The past few days have been hard on him. Though from what I can tell, he hasn't thrown any more books since that first night. But now, he whistles back to the birds with a cheerful lilt. His rifle is slung across his back lackadaisically.

I'm not quite as relaxed as him, though I try to be. I rest my firearm on my shoulder, fighting the urge to draw it as twigs snap in the underbrush from the wild fauna — not hidden assassins lying in wait.

Damian insisted that we leave the suits behind. Fair. Traipsing through the woods in Oxfords and jackets would be miserable. Boots and jeans are much more appropriate for the terrain and weather. I unbutton my flannel, pulling it back to allow the breeze to cool my midriff. It's probably unprofessional to be hiking in a sports bra with my boss, but he's seen it all before. Honestly, he's seen much more. My sports bra is prudish in comparison.

I've never thought about it before, but I wonder if the suits are as much an emotional armor for him as they are for me. We really only have to wear the suits when we're actively on-duty, though I tend to wear mine any time I'm not in the gym. Thinking back on it, I don't know if I've ever seen Damian not wearing his — except when we sneak down to the kitchen in the middle of the night. Every day, all day, same suit. But not today.

His t-shirt is tight on his chest, concealing none of the ridges of his muscular torso. It has the logo of some band I've never heard of. Maybe we can listen to them on the drive back to the compound. The worn denim of his jeans encases his thighs, his ass.

Goddamn, Damian.

My core clenches as his eyes pierce through me, stripping my defenses down to nothing. I freeze in his gaze as his hands slip beneath my flannel, brushing against my bare skin until they settle on the small of my back.

Then as if a switch was flipped, he slams me against a tree trunk, lifting me to wrap my legs around his back. His lips taste of mint as he claims mine, moaning as I grind against his hips.

My hair catches on the rough bark, but I don't care, not when he's whipping his shirt to the forest floor so my hands can trace every line on his chest. Not when he's unbuttoning my jeans, feeling how damp I am between my legs. Not when his fingers slide—

"We're here," Damian announces, fully-clothed, and I clear my throat as I blink my fantasy away. His grin doesn't leave his face as he turns to me. "Lost you for a minute there. Where'd you go to?"

"Nowhere," I lie, mentally kicking myself for allowing myself to get distracted, especially in that way. "It won't happen again."

"It's all good, Viv," he assures unbothered. "Relax, this is supposed to be a vacation for you too."

"Next vacation we're going to a private island in the middle of the ocean." I pause as visions of pirates and hurricanes and sharks flash through my mind. "Actually no, I still wouldn't relax there."

"You must be a ton of fun on a road trip," Damian teases, heading toward the ladder to his childhood tree house.

"I am actually." I gently steer him out of the way as I sling my rifle strap over my back. Who knows the last time someone was in that treehouse? There could be a pack of feral squirrels inside. He's not going up first. I test out a metal rung embedded into the side of the tree before I start to climb. "Road trips allow for more adaptability. It's easier to adjust course if things go wrong. Plus, I have great taste in snacks and junk—"

One of the rungs gives out beneath my feet, and I gasp as I lose my footing. My fingers clench around my handholds as I fall, tensing for the jerk of my weight on my shoulders.

Damian jumps forward to catch me, clutching my hips above his head. He shifts to get a more secure grip, propping me up with his hands on my ass. He holds me steady until I regain my footing and shift my weight back on to the rungs.

"You good?" He calls up, though he doesn't remove his hands.

"Yeah." I'm a bit flustered, but not from my near fall. "Don't trust that rung."

Damian stays directly under me, hands in the air, as I continue my ascent. I move slower than my first stretch, now checking each step before I commit to it. All of the other hand and footholds seem stable enough. I push open the trapdoor into the treehouse and hoist myself inside. No feral squirrels, no malicious raccoons, and no murderers. Seems good.

Damian doesn't even wait for my okay before climbing up himself, and I extend a hand down to help haul him up the last stretch.

"Damn." He leans on one of the windowsills and looks out at the forest around. "What a view."

I sling my rifle free and look down the scope, carefully scanning the surrounding landscape for anything suspicious. All clear.

"Get shooting, Damian." I lean back in a canvas chair and set my rifle against the wall. "I'm hungry and we're losing daylight."

"You're not helping?" He raises an eyebrow as his eyes twinkle with laughter.

"I could, but I didn't walk all this way to go back in thirty seconds," I taunt playfully. "Besides, I shoot things all the time. It's your turn to be useful."

"Wow." Damian chuckles. "Your trash talk is a little strong for someone who can't climb a ladder."

"I revealed a safety hazard," I gasp dramatically, clutching my imaginary pearls. "I saved your life."

Damian shakes his head, a wide grin stretching from ear to ear. He straddles a chair and props his rifle against the windowsill, scanning for dinner. I scoot my chair closer to him, kicking my feet up on some wooden toy crate I found.

I can just picture a little Damian playing with his action figures as his father sat where Damian is now, looking out the window as the breeze ruffles his hair.

The jet-black strands are normally coiffed so particularly, a precise imperfection, but the way it falls now is truly effortless and just as suave. Part of me wants to run my fingers through it and feel how soft it must be, but the other part would hate to ruin it. He glances up from his scope, catching me staring.

"Planning on shooting anything?" I ask. Oh god, I hope I'm not blushing.

"I'm working on it." He rolls his eyes. "Nothing yummy has walked by."

"Maybe I'll order a pizza so you can shoot the box." I lean back against the wall. "I'm thinking stuffed crust, pepperoni. Ooh, garlic bread."

The grin falls from his face as I shift, his eyes widening as he grabs my thigh. The next second I am standing, guarding him with my knife outstretched.

I search for the threat, my eyes scanning the surrounding for a concealed rifle barrel or a pack of rabid squirrels, but there's nothing. Yet his grip on me tightens.

"Help me out, Damian," I murmur lowly, not sure if the threat knows Damian has spotted them. "What am I looking for?"

"Spider." His voice shakes. "Big one. Giant. Huge."

"Seriously?" I slide my knife back in the sheath as I spot the average-sized offender. "A spider? Damn it, Damian."

"Kill it, Vivianna." He's squeezing my thigh hard enough it might leave a bruise. "Do your Ombra thing. Kill it."

"I thought I was on vacation. Killing things is hardly relaxing."

"Please, Viv." He gives me a nudge toward the small creature. I should probably stop torturing the man. Besides, protecting Damian's emotional health is part of my job description, so this kinda counts? Maybe? Whatever.

"Alright." I crouch down and untie the laces of my boot, yanking it off. A deadly weapon. "Close your eyes."

For once he actually listens to me. I dispatch the threat quickly and painlessly, searching for any of its compatriots before shoving my foot back inside my shoe. "All clear."

"You sure?"

"Damian, don't insult me." I yank the laces tightly and flick my pant leg over my boot. "I can take out a spider."

"Thank you, Viv." Damian wipes his palms on his jeans, though his eyes cautiously peer behind me.

"So the Don of the Italian mafia is afraid of spiders?" Since I'm already standing, I grab my rifle and do another security check through the windows.

"It doesn't come up that often." He shrugs awkwardly.

"Can't fight. Can't be in a room with spiders." I elbow him in the ribs. "Any other weaknesses I need to know about?"

He looks up at me, and there is a flicker of profound sadness in his eyes. He opens his mouth but closes it without a response.

"Damian?"

He wrenches his eyes away from me and picks up his rifle. A smile is forced across his face and he chuckles.

"Just my inability to hunt dinner apparently."

I hesitate for a moment, wondering whether I should pry deeper, but then I let the subject shift. There's plenty of darkness at the mansion, it won't hurt to let him enjoy whatever light we can find here.

"You could start by looking down the scope," I jest, looking down my own rifle. "There's a buck right there."

"What? No way!" Damian groans. "How did you find one so quickly? I've been watching forever."

"Stop talking and shoot it," I scold, tracking the buck in my own crosshairs. I hear Damian breathing beside me, then a long, slow exhale. His round flies through and through, a clean kill. "Nice shot. We've found a strength of yours."

"One of the few things I'm better at than Enzo." His eyes have a playful gleam.

We sling the rifles over our shoulders and carefully climb down the ladder rungs to retrieve our hunt and take it back to the cabin. Damian makes quick work of the butchering as I start a campfire on his request.

"There's a stove inside," I comment idly. "I don't mind cooking it if you want."

"Nah, we're going to eat like cavemen," he laughs giddily. "Just us, the fresh kill, the fire. We can eat with dignity in the morning."

"You are such a child," I say, as if that idea doesn't sound fun as shit.

His nose crinkles as he looks up at me, and I know he can see through my superior exterior. Damian places the tenderloin onto a grill rack as I drag a thick log over. We sit on the ground shoulder-to-shoulder, resting our backs against the wood as the aroma of fresh game fills the air.

The sun has begun to tickle the horizon, revealing glittering stars against the darkening sky. Soon, the only light is the orange glow of the fire, flickering against the sharp profile of Damian's face.

"Pass me one of your knives." He holds out his hand as the hilt is placed in his palm.

"If you get grease on the handle, I am going to make you clean and polish that," I threaten, though I wouldn't follow through on it. Not many people get to touch my knives and live, and even fewer get to care for them.

"First bite goes to you." He ignores my threat, slicing into the center of the loin to cut a chunk out.

"Nah, you're the warrior who fell the beast," I say dramatically, leaning into the caveman atmosphere. "Enjoy the first bite."

"I couldn't have done it without my trusted defender who slayed the monster lurking in the corner," Damian joshes me back, but then his voice softens as he holds out the morsel. "Open your mouth, Viv."

I don't know if my mouth falls open in obedience or in shock, but it doesn't seem to matter as Damian gingerly places the piece of venison on my tongue. His eyes reflect the firelight as he stares at my lips, leisurely sucking the juice from his thumb.

"How is it?" He doesn't even blink.

"Perfect," I whisper. It's definitely the heat from the fire making my cheeks flush.

He smirks cockily as he returns to the slab of meat, carving a bite for himself. He closes his eyes as he chews.

"Oh, fuck me," he moans. I want to. Oh god, I want to.

But instead, I take back my knife and distract myself by cutting the next inch or so of the venison log into a thick dice. His thigh presses against mine as he reaches over to grab a cube. I swallow arduously as I feel his attention shift back to me.

"Thirsty?" He asks, and his voice sends shivers down my spine.

"I'm fine." I can't think of anything else besides his eyes watching me.

"If my Vivianna dictionary is accurate, that means you're damn near death's door." He stands, wiping his hands on his jeans. "Stay there. I'll be right back."

"I'm okay," I protest. "Really, just sit down."

"It's a life-threatening emergency?" He winks at me. "I'll hurry."

"Damian..." I groan, but he's already gone.

He jogs back out of the cabin a few minutes later, a bottle of water in his hand. He kneels next to me and twists off the cap.

"We're losing her, we're losing her!" Damian holds the bottle to my lips. "Hurry!"

I'm laughing so hard, we end up spilling a good third of the water on my shirt. Eventually I wrangle it from his grasp and take a sip, trying not to waste all of it.

"Just in case that doesn't sate your thirst, I brought something a little more fun too." He slips a wine bottle from behind his back and admires the label. "A Chianti, fine vintage — about twelve years. Great year for Tuscan wines. Care for a sip?"

"I wouldn't appreciate it as much as you." I wave him off. "Enjoy it. I'm happy with what's left of my water."

"Nonsense." Damian expertly manipulates the corkscrew, easily opening the bottle and taking a sniff. "Wine is best enjoyed with others."

"Then why didn't you bring any glasses?" I tease.

"If we're not using forks, why would I bother with glasses?" Damian takes a slow sip of the wine, exhaling happily before extending the bottle to me. "Besides, I'm not afraid of cooties."

"I'm good, thanks." He raises an eyebrow at my refusal. "I can't drink. I'm working."

"We're on vacation," he reminds me. "You're not on duty."

"I don't know." I lean back against the log. "An evil spider could pop out at any moment. I need to be ready."

"A little bit of wine is not going to affect your arachnid-slaying capabilities." Damian rolls his eyes. "Take a sip, Viv."

"Is that an order?" A laugh slips from my mouth but fades quickly as Damian's eyes darken.

"Would it make a difference if it was?" There's no humor in his voice, only a grave seriousness that steals my breath away.

"Only one way to find out." Please. Please use that tone again, the one that has me hanging on every word. I'll do anything you say.

He shifts to a crouch, every movement precise and deliberate, dominating the space. His arm connects with the log behind me, forming an immovable wall of muscle and control. My heart races faster as he leans down, closing the distance between us.

"Drink the damn wine, Vivianna." I'd do anything to keep his eyes on me.

"Just a sip?" My hands brush his as I take the bottle, sending a jolt of electricity to my core. I have to stay alert, have to keep him safe, but one sip is fine, right? Just a small little sip?

"Just a sip," he promises.

Just one sip.

The bottle falls to the dirt as Damian finishes it off. I'm twirling around the embers of the fire pit, not even noticing the evening chill due to the warmth in my chest. My hair whips around me, my elastic long since lost to the tipsy euphoria flushing my cheeks.

Damian takes my hand, spinning me into his chest. We both laugh as I thud into him abruptly, the wine diluting my coordination. His laugh is perfect, warm and free, ringing into the open air with reckless abandon.

"Thanks for coming with me," he whispers. "I needed this. Fresh air, good company, no one expecting everything from me all the time."

"My pleasure." The smile on my face is real. They used to be so rare, kept locked away, but they've become more commonplace recently.

"We should probably think about heading to bed, unless you want me to crack open the Prosecco I saw in one of the cupboards."

"Whatever you want," I murmur, resting my head on his chest. The smell of campfire smoke sticks to his t-shirt.

"Come on, Viv." He wraps his arm around me and guides me back to the cabin. I can walk fine on my own, but I'm certainly not going to push him away. "I'll take the air mattress, you can take the bed."

"I don't mind an air mattress," I offer. "Really."

"Knowing you, Viv, you sleep with your knives," he jests as we step through the doorway. "I don't think the air mattress is the smartest idea."

"Excuse me, I am a lady!" I say with mock offense. "I sleep with a gun, thank you very much."

"My apologies, madam." Damian rummages through a closet before pulling out the air mattress. I unzip my duffel and rummage for my PJ's, turning away from him as I strip. "Aw, fuck."

"What?" I look over my shoulder to see a long slash in the casing. "Oh, no worries then. We can share the bed."

"Are you sure? I wouldn't want to make—" Damian glances up at me and his voice cuts out. His eyes linger on the bare skin of my back before he rips them away, stammering as he continues, "To make you uncomfortable."

"Can you keep your hands to yourself?" I'd be okay even if he couldn't. I smooth the soft fabric of my shirt down and step into my cotton shorts.

"Of course." He seems appalled that I would even ask.

"Then we're fine." Damn it.

He changes his clothes as I check my pistol, but I hesitate. Sleeping with a loaded firearm is not exactly the safest thing I do on a day-to-day basis. I can live with the slight chance of it going off in the night when it's just my life at risk, but with Damian in the same bed?

I remove the magazine and eject the chambered round, setting those on the nightstand as I slide the empty pistol under my pillow, ensuring the barrel is pointed away from his side of the bed — just in case.

Damian curls up under the blankets and I flick off the light, but I don't go to bed quite yet. Instead, I rummage through my equipment bag for the small set of bells I packed. I wrap the cable around the door handle, ensuring that any unexpected visitors would accidentally announce their presence as they enter.

I pace the perimeter of the cabin, checking that all of the windows are locked securely, but it's not enough. It will never be enough. I can't shake the feeling of dread settling in my stomach.

You're weak, pathetic. Marco's insults encircle my thoughts, latching onto my deepest fears. *With you as Damian's Ombra, nothing will stop Sergei from carving into Damian. I bet he'll even use your knife.*

Damian's breathing slows as he falls into a peaceful slumber. He trusts me. He's a fool. I'm going to get him killed. I can't protect him. I'm not enough.

Why do I keep letting him down? For fuck's sake, I drank half a bottle of wine tonight. My father would have my head if he knew. I'm an embarrassment, a scar on the family legacy. Sergei knew who I was, he marked me so the rest of the world would know too.

Ashamed, I crawl into bed beside Damian. I'll do better tomorrow. I'll be better. I'll keep him safe.

Sergei's evil smile leers down at me condescendingly.

"Did you really think you were strong enough to save him?" He snickers. The dim light casts shadows across his face, but it's not enough to obscure his monstrous expression. "Sorry, little girl. You're not."

"I won't tell you anything." My voice sounds so small and weak compared to his sinister bass. It doesn't matter. I can't let him win. I can't.

"That's where you're mistaken, I don't need you anymore." His gaze leaves me and I follow it, the blood draining from my face as I see Damian, struggling against the far wall. He has his own set of goons pinning him to the brick.

"No," I gasp. I failed. Oh god, I failed.

"Let's go see what he has to say." A knife appears in his hand, dangling lackadaisically between his fingers.

"No!" I scream as Damian cowers in fear. "No! Come back, please! Don't touch him!"

"You had your chance to talk!" He growls.

"Let him go!" I plead desperately. "Damian, I'm sorry! I'm so sorry!"

"Quiet!" Sergei whips back to me, brandishing his knife. I don't stop begging, although he only grows angrier. "I said, be quiet!"

He swings, and the blade of his knife comes away with a coat of red. Blood. My blood. I wail in agony, doubling over as warm liquid dribbles down my cheek.

"Vivianna, wake up!" Damian yells from across the room, panic in his eyes.

But I can't wake up. I can't accept my failure. Damian, I'm sorry. I'm so sorry.

The blade flashes again.

I shriek as I open my eyes, clawing at my face, thrashing in the covers. Someone is straddling me in the dark, struggling to restrain my wrists.

"Vivianna, stop!" The man grunts. "You'll hurt yourself!"

"Let him go! Let him go!"

"Viv, I'm right here!" As my eyes adjust to the dim starlight, I can see the outline of his jaw, his cheekbone, his hair falling into his face. Damian.

I cave, surrendering as he pins me to the mattress.

"I'm okay," he whispers, rubbing his thumb along the inside of my wrists. "It's just a nightmare, that's all it is."

My sobs rack my body as he pants above me, catching his breath. After he's sure that I've woken up, Damian slides onto the mattress and pulls me into his arms. He strokes my hair as I wring my fists into his t-shirt, quickly growing damp from my tears.

"It was just a bad dream," he assures, holding me tightly. "We're safe."

"No," I whimper, my breaths coming in shallow gasps. "We'll never be safe. Never. I have to protect you. I have to be ready."

"We're safe, Viv," he repeats persistently. Damian's voice is soft and soothing, and I can feel my fears melting away. "Nothing bad will happen to you in my arms, I promise. Just let me hold you."

His words smother my lingering anxieties as I burrow into him. He embraces me, patiently waiting until the last shudder leaves my body. His hands cradle me tenderly before I pull back, wiping the lingering tears from my cheeks. I stand and turn away, hanging my head as I wrap my arms around my torso.

"Sorry I woke you," I whisper, my voice hoarse from screaming. "Go back to sleep."

"You have nothing to apologize for." He watches me carefully. "Are you okay?"

"I'm fine." My voice cracks, and even I don't believe myself. "I'll be back to bed in a minute. I won't wake you again."

Translation — I'm not going back to bed.

Damian gets up and turns on the light like the stubborn jackass he is.

"I don't have any ice cream," he mulls, standing in front of the fridge. "Would you take a bottle of water in these trying times?"

"Whatever you want." I shrug indifferently, trying to regain some of my composure.

"I want you to talk to me." Two bottles of water are placed on the table. Damian leans back in a chair, opening one for himself. "Let me help you. What was your dream about?"

"I don't remember," I lie. I slink into the chair across from him, holding the second bottle in my lap.

"Maybe I can jog your memory." Damian tries to catch my eyes, but I refuse to look at him. "It sounded like I was in trouble. Is that right?"

"You don't have to worry about it." My hands shake as I set my water bottle back on the table. "I'll take care of you."

"When I woke up, you were clawing at your eye... Wait, no." He tilts his head as his eyebrows furrow. "Your scar. You were clawing at your scar."

"So?" Deep breath in. Deep breath out. "That doesn't mean anything."

"What Marco said this morning, was that true?" Damian asks quietly. "Did Sergei Petrov give you the scar?"

"No." My chair screeches on the floor as I push myself away from the table suddenly.

"You're lying." He sounds hurt.

"Why did you bother asking if you knew the answer?" I grab my pistol from beneath my pillow, inserting the magazine.

"Because I don't know anything," Damian huffs. "As much as I've wanted to, I haven't asked Enzo or anyone else what happened. I know it's not my place, but I was just hoping that one day you would open up to me."

"I can't." My voice is strained as I eject the magazine again, setting my 9mm back on the nightstand.

"Yes, you can," he urges.

"No, I can't!" I lose the feeble grip I had on the string of my self-control, turning back to him angrily. "I can't, Damian, because I won't hurt you like that!"

"I don't understand." He runs his fingers through his hair in frustration. "Why would it hurt me? I wasn't there! It's not like I—" His face pales as he locks eyes with mine. "Oh god. It was my fault, wasn't it? I did something…" He scrunches his eyes shut as he thinks. "What did I do? How?"

"Stop, please." I kneel by his feet. "Don't do this to yourself."

"How do you know the Russians?" He mumbles, ignoring my pleas. "You have no reason to know them. I've only met them a few times myself…"

"Fine!" I grab his hands and he looks into my eyes, vulnerable and scared. I bite my lip, hesitating before I force myself to continue. "I'll tell you."

I lower my head, resigned to sharing the one secret I promised to always keep from him. He squeezes my hands, and I look back up.

"It was the night of your dad's assassination." I regret saying it immediately.

"No..." Damian gasps, the pieces falling into place in his mind, but I keep going and tell the whole story.

"I dragged you into the cellar, and you didn't want to leave me behind, but I made you. I had to buy you time to get away, no matter what..."

"Palazzos don't go down easily," I whisper. Footsteps pound down the staircase and Damian's breath catches in his throat. "Go! Now!"

He pulls me into an anguished hug, and for only a moment, I allow myself to absorb the slight comfort, but then I push him off into the corridor and close the wall behind him.

Focus, Vivianna. I might not be in the Ombra, but I can still protect Damian, if only for a few more seconds. I steel my nerves as I turn to face the approaching intruders.

Run, Damian. Run.

The silhouettes of men are barely visible through the wine racks. I crouch down, hiding behind a barrel.

"Spread out, men!" A gravelly voice with a thick Russian accent commands. "The little twerp must be down here somewhere."

Whether it's the musty air of the cellar or fear settling in my bones, my lungs struggle to fill. My fingers wrap around the neck of a wine bottle, and I lift my makeshift club as I crawl to the end of the shelf to peer around the corner. Four men split up and walk through the aisles, each carrying a pistol outstretched in front of them. I wipe my sweaty palms on my dress to better grasp the wine bottle as I slink behind one of the men. I count down in my head. Three. Two. One. Swing!

A crack rings through the cellar as his skull connects with the bottle and he drops to the ground. Unfortunately, the distant gunshots are not enough to cover up the noise. The remaining three men whirl around, but I am already running away.

"After her!"

Fuck. Fuck. Fuck. I sprint around a shelving unit but one of the men takes a shortcut to cut me off. Another man blocks the exit behind me. I'm trapped. They prowl closer, laughing as I raise the bottle defensively.

"How cute." The leader of the group steps out of the shadows, jeering in my direction. "A little girl all by herself. Must be scary down here in the dark with no one to hold your hand. Let's make this easy, shall we? Tell me where the boy went, and no one will harm you."

"I don't know who you're talking about," I grit through my teeth.

"Damian Marano," the leader spits. "Where is he?"

"Never met him." The boss narrows his eyes at my denial, and it takes everything in me to not let my hands tremble.

"Grab her."

I throw my bottle at the nearest assailant, and as he ducks, I ram my shoulder into him to knock him over. His hand darts out to snatch my ankle as I bolt past him, and I land on the floor in a heap.

Blood from my skinned palms mixes with the remnants smeared earlier from Damian's hand. I guess this is as close as I'm getting to taking my own blood oath.

The two men seize my arms and pin me against the wall. The leader of the group unsheathes a knife and taps it derisively on my nose.

"Sweetie, I don't think you know what's going on here," he mocks, dragging the flat of the blade down my cheek. "We're going to find him, and we're going to kill him. This doesn't have to be hard, but if you don't tell me where he is, then this will not be a pleasant experience for you. Where. Is. He?"

I try to choke back a laugh, but the cackle flies free from my lips. If only he knew the wall I was held against, the one I was protecting with my body, was the very one that Damian had just escaped through. The boss's backhand stings as it whips my head to the side, cutting off my hysterics.

"I am the head of the Russian Bratva!" He roars. "I will not be disrespected by some lowly Italian brat!"

"I am Vivianna Palazzo," I spit, straining against the men holding me. "I will die to protect the Maranos."

"Oh yeah?" He creeps closer, brandishing the knife in the dim cellar light. "Let's see how brave you really are."

His hand grips my scalp, forcing my head back against the rough bricks as he brings the knife to my face. My agonized scream echoes through the room as he drags the blade from my brow to my cheek. My vision tinges red as blood trickles into my eye.

"Where is he?!" The monster yells in my face as I writhe in my captors' arms.

"You'll never find him," I taunt, though my bravado is forced. My voice wavers as the left side of the world blurs.

Stay strong, Vivianna. The pain doesn't matter. My eye doesn't matter. He's going to kill me. I can't let him kill Damian too.

"Where should I cut next, boys?" He wipes the knife against the fabric of my dress, cleaning the blade. "Do you think we should start carving?"

"Go to hell!" I curse, lashing out with my legs. My foot connects with his shin, and he drops the knife. It clatters on the floor.

Keep fighting, Vivianna. Every second spent with you is another second for Damian to get away. God, please let him get away.

A wicked smile crosses the leader's face as he leans in close.

"I'm going to enjoy killing you." He rubs his thumb across my chin. "The feisty ones are always the most fun."

I have one simple answer for that. My forehead slams into his nose, and the Russian staggers back, spewing profanities as he clutches his injury. Blood spills from his fingers.

"That's it. I'm going to show you what the Russian Bratva does to—"

"Stay away from my sister!"

A gunshot thunders through the cellar and the leader lurches to the side as a patch of red grows through his shoulder. Vinny fires again, killing one of the men pinning my shoulders to the wall.

I fall to the floor as the other reaches for his weapon. My hands fumble for the discarded knife, which I impale into his thigh and rip through his muscle. His screams fill the air, but I don't stop stabbing until Vinny pulls me off of the limp corpse.

Frantic footfalls fade in the distance as Sergei flees. We should follow, put him down before he can try to hurt Damian again, but as Vinny holds me, I allow myself to be a scared teenager.

"I can't see," I sob hysterically into his shirt. "I can't see, Vinny. I can't see!"

"Shhh." He tilts my chin up, looking at my wound. The rough fabric of his sleeve is gently dabbed over my eye, clearing some of the blood. "You're okay, Anna. He didn't cut your eye. There's just blood in the way. Got it, Vivianna? You're okay."

"Vincenzo? Vivianna?" My father calls as he scrambles down the stairs, dark stains marring his black suit. He sees my twin and I curled up on the floor and kneels next to us, enveloping us in his arms. "Where's Damian?"

"He's safe." My voice cracks. "I got him to the passage before the Russians caught up to us."

"I'm so proud of you both." His pride doesn't reach his voice. Instead he sounds broken, gutted. Where I succeeded, my dad failed. Mr. Marano is dead.

"I should have pursued Sergei," I chastise myself as tears drip onto the floor. "I let him get away. It's my fault. I'm sorry."

"No," Damian chokes out, kneeling next to me. "Don't ever say that again, don't even think that. You risked everything for me. You… God, Vivianna, we were children."

"I was born to protect you," I seethe bitterly. "My whole life, I was raised with the one goal of keeping you safe, and when it came down to it—"

"When it came down to it, you got me out of there." Damian grabs my chin, lifting my face until I meet his gaze. "And I'll never be able to repay you for it, for any of this."

"I don't want anything from you." The words fall from my mouth in a desperate outpour. "I just want to sleep. I'm so tired. I'm exhausted. But every time I close my eyes, I only see you beaten or tortured or dying. It's killing me."

"Come here," he whispers, pulling me back toward the bed.

"No." I shake my head. "I can't watch you die again tonight."

"Do you trust me?" The question hangs in the air until I acquiesce, allowing him to guide me under the covers.

Damian wraps his arms around me, holding me tightly against his chest. I lay my head on his shoulder, his heartbeat a steady pulse in my ear.

Slowly, I allow myself to relax, molding my body against his. My leg drapes over his hips, and he rubs his thumb into the muscle of my thigh. Finally, I let my eyes flutter closed and dream of midnight ice cream adventures.

Turns out, Damian does not know how to cook.

Grill? Sure. Cook? Not really.

I scrounge through the groceries he packed the next morning. He didn't bring much, and what he did bring doesn't quite make sense. But my mother raised a homemaker, so I take control of our lunch.

The pasta dough has rested, so I steal one of Damian's wine bottles to use as a rolling pin. I've never liked to use pasta machines, much preferring the labor of love. I swear you can taste the difference. Not that the cabin has a pasta machine anyway. I blow at a strand of my hair dangling in my eyes.

"Need a hair tie?" Damian sneaks up on me, back from chopping wood for the stove.

"Too late." I hold up my floury hands. "I'm committed."

"Nonsense." He gently combs my hair back with his fingers and secures it in a low ponytail. "There. Better?"

"Thank you." I return to my rolling. "I really appreciate that."

"Anything you need, I'm right here." He winks as he walks to his duffel and slips a new elastic onto his wrist. It's only then Damian notices what I'm making. "Pasta? Oh fuck yes. What shape are you thinking?"

"Depends how hungry you are." I can't help but smile at his enthusiasm. "I can cut this into tagliatelle in like two seconds if you're starving, but I was planning on making farfalle. Making shapes is a bit more fun than cutting ribbons."

"Then farfalle it is."

Damian takes a seat at the table as I cut the sheet into small squares, carefully folding little bowties. I get through a row before I stop and tilt my head.

"Actually, I lied. These aren't farfalle." I shrug and keep going. "Farfalle has ridges on the edges. These are… strichetti? I think that's what they're called."

"How dare you?" Damian fakes a gasp. "I can't believe it! This changes everything."

"You laugh, but some people really care about those nuances." I scrunch my nose. "My mom is such a stickler for pasta names. She wonders why I stopped cooking with her."

"The two of you aren't close?" He asks.

"God no," I laugh at the notion. "Oh god no. She wanted a girly girl who she could marry off, real traditional values. It's ironic really, Vinny and I would have gladly swapped places growing up. He wanted the white-picket-fence, two and a half kids with a dog. All I ever wanted was you."

"Viv," Damian hesitates before he continues, "what would you do if you weren't in my Ombra?" I pause and look at him, confused.

"… strip."

"No, no, no." He shakes his head. "Like if you weren't a Palazzo."

"Oh, that's easy." I crimp another bowtie. "My mom would marry me off to a high-ranking mafia man to elevate the family name. She tried to do that anyway, but—"

"Forget the mafia," Damian groans. "The mafia is gone, doesn't exist. What would *you* want to do?"

"Why are you asking me these questions?" I look at him suspiciously, abandoning my pasta dough. "I'm a Palazzo. I was born with the sole purpose of protecting you. It's who I am. I like to think I'm not doing too shitty of a job, and the company isn't too bad." I smirk at him as I finish my sentence.

Damian sighs and picks up a small square of dough, trying to replicate the shapes I was folding. He fumbles clumsily. I walk around the table and drape my arms over his, gently guiding his hands in the correct pattern. We make a few together until he gets the hang of it, and his pasta looks somewhat like bowties.

"I want you to be more than just my Ombra," he says after a moment. "I want you to have hobbies, passions, things that make you happy."

"I am happy." I sit back down in my chair, continuing my rhythm of shaping the farfalle or strichetti or whatever.

"Are you?" He pushes back, dropping the piece of dough he was folding.

"Yes," I insist. "I am."

"Name one thing," Damian challenges. "One thing in your life right now that makes you happy."

"My best friend does." I finish folding all of the pasta dough, so I reach over to fix some of his misshapen defects.

"Who's that?" He sits up in his chair, a flash of jealousy in his eyes.

"I think you've met him." I smirk. "He spends way too much time in front of a mirror, super stubborn, doesn't listen to me at all…"

"He sounds like a real ass," he grumbles.

"A dumbass." I roll my eyes, dumping the pasta into the water boiling on the stovetop. "Damian, it's you."

"Oh." He instantly relaxes, a tinge of blush coloring his cheeks. "You need to get better friends."

"I don't want better friends," I chuckle as I check on the venison in the oven. "I like eating ice cream at midnight and having you give me crap for literally everything, apparently now that includes not hating you. Figures."

"I'm your boss," he protests. "You should hang out with people who aren't me."

"But it's always been you, Damian," I blurt out. The butter in my pan sizzles as I struggle to find the right words. "I've always been the background character, the female twin. My whole life, Vinny was the important one, I was told to stand back and smile. All of the work I put in, all of the training, was only for his benefit, to make him stronger. I was discarded without a second thought as soon as Vinny left the room. So I closed myself off, let everyone ignore me."

"That sounds lonely." Damian rubs my back softly.

"It was what it was." My all-too-familiar sad smile takes its place. "Except it wasn't. You were the only person who managed to catch glimpses of me, carefully watching for something — I don't know what. But you always said hi, waved at me from across the lawn, thanked me for the biscotti. I felt real. I was alive, if only for a moment."

"And now, we talk every day." I shrug my shoulders as I strain the pasta, spooning it onto two plates. "We talk, we laugh, we cry, we yell, but we talk." A ladle of sauce. "So you ask me if I'm happy?" A venison steak. "I'm the happiest I've ever been."

I wipe my hands on my jeans as lunch is served, strichetti with a brown butter sauce and venison. *Buon appetito.*

I start eating, but Damian sits there for a minute, digesting my words. After a while, he lifts his fork and picks up a few bowties.

"Your smile."

"What?"

"What I was watching for," he says. "All those years ago, I just wanted to see you smile. I still do."

"You've got to earn it." I smirk. The corners of my mouth try to twitch up, and I struggle to keep from grinning.

"Hmm." Damian scrunches his eyebrows as he thinks. "Okay, I've got something. What kind of deer make great weather forecasters?"

"Please no, not the dad jokes."

"Rain-deer." His eyes twinkle playfully. I hide behind my hands, pretending to be mortified.

"Oh my god," I groan. But Damian is insistent, leaning over the table.

"What did the deer say when he saw the hunters? 'I've got to hoof it.'" He grabs my hands, prying them away.

"I can't be seen with you ever again." I relent, laughing freely.

"How do you let a deer know you like her?" He takes in every inch of my smile, of the brightness in my eyes. "You fawn over her."

Damian keeps making horrible puns the rest of lunch, until my cheeks are streaked with tears and my abs cramp from laughing. He insists on washing the dishes afterward since I put so much work into the homemade meal. I would argue, at least dry the dishes, but he gives me a firm look that dares me to try him.

So instead, I sit and watch, trying not to stare as he rolls up his sleeves, exposing his strong forearms. I try not to study his ass, so perfect beneath the denim of his jeans. Try not to gawk at his firm grip on the plates, wishing his fingers were around my neck instead. I don't know how much longer I can last in this cabin, alone with him and those intense amber eyes, meticulously learning all of my tells. All of them, except arousal.

Hopefully.

Oh please god.

"Something about a good meal and a warm cross-breeze makes me crave a nap." Damian yawns as he hangs up his dish towel. "You game?"

"Nah." I pull the elastic from my ponytail, letting my hair fall around my shoulders. "I'm good."

"Come to bed with me, Viv," Damian murmurs, his voice low and husky. I think my heart skips a beat, but I know for certain that my underwear is now damp. He must have heard the way that sounded because he awkwardly clears his throat. "For a nap. Please."

"Okay." As if I could say no to the mental picture that was firmly thrust upon my mind.

Damian lays on top of the quilt, reclining with one arm casually beneath his head. I slide onto my half of the mattress, acutely aware of how close we are to touching. His breath tickles my skin, and goosebumps appear in its wake.

"Go to sleep, Vivianna," he whispers. His words sound like melted caramel, dripping across my subconscious with a warm viscosity. I didn't think I was tired before, but with his urging, I drift away in seconds.

In my dreams, he's there.

His fingers trail down my neck before reaching my flannel. He moves painstakingly slow, methodically undoing every single button. Then, and only then, does he slide the fabric aside to gaze upon my chest. I shrug the shirt off my shoulders, throwing it to the floor, but then he grabs my hands and presses them into the mattress.

"We're going to take this slow, Vivianna," he growls, a low rumbling deep in his throat. "And you're going to enjoy it."

"Oh, Damian," I mumble, his name falling through my lips like I was born to say it. Maybe I was.

"Just like that," he praises, a feral gleam in his eye. "Keep saying my name just like that."

He returns to my body, running his hands over the lace concealing my breasts.

"Now, this just won't do." He shakes his head roguishly.

The lace rips easily in his fingers. Immediately, his tongue surrounds an erect nipple, eliciting a gasp from my lips. His sly smirk sends a shiver down my spine. He knows what he does to me. Worse, he knows I like it.

"Fuck, Damian," I groan.

My eyes flutter closed as he continues his relentless teasing, swirling and sucking, swirling and sucking. Oh god.

"Damian, please," I beg. I don't know what I'm asking for, but whatever it is, I crave it desperately.

His hands softly stroke my cheek before gripping the nape of my neck and claiming me as his own. Mint dances through my senses as I weave my fingers into his hair. How can a kiss be both soft and possessive at the same time? How can I need it this badly?

His fingertips dance down the waistband of my jeans, unbuttoning the material without looking away from my eyes. They travel down further and further, slipping in between my legs. I arc my back as he circles my clit, sending pleasure through my entire body.

"God yes, Damian," I moan. "Don't stop. Please, Damian."

His thumb continues its orbit while his other fingers focus on a different mission. He thrusts inside of me mercilessly. My fists clench the bedsheets as I grind on his hand, every motion building a pit in my stomach until I climax, screaming his name.

"Damian!"

My shoulders heave as I open my eyes, back in cold reality. I jerk to sit up as I notice a pair of amber eyes locked onto mine. Damian.

"Did I wake you?" I stutter, my heart still racing a mile a minute.

"No," he replies.

"Good." I force myself to relax, still coming down from the high of my dream. "I feel a bit warm. I'm, uh, going to step outside for a minute."

Damian nods, adjusting to lean against the headboard. I run my fingers through my hair as I stride to the door, but I pause before I can pass through the doorframe.

"I didn't say anything while I was asleep, did I?" Does my voice sound calm?

"If you did, I didn't notice."

"Good. Good." Thank fucking god.

CHAPTER 10
DAMIAN

My name. Her lips. Over and over and over.

The truth is, I wasn't tired, but I knew she was. The small amount of peaceful sleep Viv got last night was not nearly enough, but she would never admit it to me. So I lied, but I knew it was the right call when she passed out as soon as her back hit the mattress.

I lay next to her attentively, terrified that she was going to slip into a nightmare. I won't let it happen. Viv was going to have a good dream for once. She deserved it. I'm not sure what I could do about it, but damn it, I am going to figure something out.

For about thirty minutes, everything is fine. She seems content, peaceful. In essence, I'm crushing it. Then a soft mumble slips through her lips.

What did she say? I didn't quite catch it, but it sounded like my name.

Alarm bells sound in my mind as I lean closer, trying to hear her better. It's not a good sign if I'm in her dream. Viv gasps, and my heart sinks into my chest.

Shit. I've got to wake her up. My hand reaches out toward her shoulder, only inches away when—

"Fuck, Damian."

Oh.

Good news — not a nightmare. More good news — that was definitely my name. If her moans are anything to go by, it sounds like I'm doing a good job.

A cocky smile spreads across my face as I picture what "I'm" doing to her. God, I would love to, but this is just a dream. It isn't real, it can't happen. She's my Ombra.

I shake my head as I move to stand. She deserves privacy, I shouldn't be here for this.

"Damian, please." Her voice is a direct hit to my gut. I try to reason with myself. Viv's sleeping, she doesn't even know I'm here, but still, the desperation in her voice has me laying back down.

What does she want? What should I do?

I hesitate as I reach out, barely brushing my knuckles down her cheek, hoping it's enough for her to feel but not enough to wake her. She responds to my touch instantly, leaning her head back into her pillow. I do it once more, savoring the softness of her skin, how my name sounds falling from her lips.

"God yes, Damian," she moans, and my cock twitches within my jeans. "Don't stop. Please, Damian."

I don't know much, but I am definitely not stroking her cheek in her dream. Every part of me wants to wake her up and rip her clothes off, but I force myself to be thankful that I can give her some form of release, even if it's just the idea of me.

"Damian!"

I yank my arm back as she sits up with a start, her shoulders heaving as she gets her bearings. Good job, imaginary me. Viv startles slightly when she sees me, instantly throwing up the emotional walls she defaults to.

"Did I wake you?" Her cheeks are flushed, the light shade of pink the only thing betraying the sensual dream she had.

"No." My voice is strained, breathless, as I clench my fists. Deep breath, I need to stay in control. She doesn't seem to notice my internal struggle to stay casual.

"Good," Viv says, though her mind is elsewhere. "I feel a bit warm. I'm going to step outside for a minute."

I nod, trying to look like I was doing something the past half hour besides watching her like a creep. Maybe look out the window? Sure, let's do that.

"I didn't say anything while I was asleep, did I?" There's a nervous lilt to her voice. Play it cool, Damian.

"If you did, I didn't notice," I lie, not moving my gaze from the bird outside. If I looked at her, I'm not sure she wouldn't see the deception on my face.

My name. Her lips. Over and over and over.

"Good. Good." She turns away, accepting my falsehoods.

Thank fucking god.

As soon as the door closes behind her, I lay back on the bed, holding a pillow over my face.

Holy fuck, that woman is going to be the death of me. Her soft skin, her muscular curves, her silky hair. She could raise her gun to my temple and pull the trigger, but as long as she moans my name first, staring deep into my eyes, I would die happy.

I wait what feels like an appropriate amount of time before I head outside, finding Viv sitting on a boulder staring toward the horizon.

"Hey," she greets me, sensing my approach.

"Hey," I echo, standing next to her with my hands in my pockets. "Do you want to go on a hike or something?"

"Cool with me." She shrugs, popping back in the house to grab her rifle. I force myself to avoid rolling my eyes. It makes her feel more secure, and we would be up shit creek without it if there was any danger, but still.

The birdsong carries across the valley as we amble downward, following a deer trail deeper into the forest. It must be new, I don't remember walking this way as a youth. The leaves of the trees grow denser, filtering the rays of sunlight into a pleasant glow. Viv's hair shines in the light, fluttering ever so slightly in the mild breeze. I would offer her the elastic on my wrist, but it looks so beautiful, and she doesn't seem to mind. I slow just a bit to saunter behind her, admiring her in secret.

The tree cover fades, and we step into a secluded clearing. A large lake glistens, the blue water appearing tantalizingly cool and refreshing. Smooth boulders line the side closest to the mountain forming a perfect cannon ball platform, whereas the rest of the lake is encircled by plush green grass.

"Let's go over there!" I grab Viv's hand excitedly, dragging her to the lake as she giggles behind me.

"Why are we running?" She pretends to complain but jogs easily beside me.

"Because it's fun!" I hurdle over a fallen log, not breaking my stride.

"You are such a child!" She teases. I stick out my tongue at her and get to hear her laugh again.

I pull her all the way to the edge of the water. The water is beautiful to look at, but the sparkle in Viv's eyes is even more breathtaking.

"Is this what your playdates with Vinny were like?" She asks, smiling from ear to ear.

"No." I shake my head, panting lightly from our run. "This is better. So much better."

"Where to now?" Her nose crinkles happily as she looks around.

"In the water. Duh!"

My hands peel my shirt from my chest, and I throw it onto the ground. The rest of my clothes follow suit quickly, leaving me standing in just my briefs. I climb onto one of the boulders and crouch there. It occurs to me that this is the most skin I've shown around Viv, but I brush the thought from my mind quickly. I've seen her in lingerie plenty of times now, it only seems fair that she sees me in my underwear.

I dive into the water, a small splash in my wake. The water is exhilarating, just cold enough to awaken my senses without sapping the heat from my body. I crest the surface and look back up at the boulder, waiting for Viv to jump in too.

Except… she's not there. I blink a few times before I find her lounging on the shore, her rifle propped up next to her. She's not coming?

I swim back to land, dripping water as I step onto the grass.

"What are you doing?" She asks, shading her eyes from the sun as she looks up at me.

"I could ask you the same question." I try not to let the hurt into my voice. Her frown says I'm not successful.

"I…" She sighs as she glances at her rifle. "I have to stay here."

"Please," I beg. "Come swim with me."

She hesitates, close to giving in. I pick my next words carefully.

"You don't have to watch from the window anymore, Viv." Her gaze whips up to mine. "It's okay. You can play tag."

"If you say so." She fiddles with her hands as she stands, walking a few paces away nervously. Suddenly, she glances over her shoulder, mischief glinting vividly in her eyes. "Then you're it."

Viv takes off, running through the grass cackling.

"You little bitch!" I smirk as I chase after her.

Viv might have more endurance than me, but I'm faster on a sprint. She weaves through the clearing, zigging and zagging, just out of reach. Her laugh is full of childlike glee as she races away. She slips and it's barely enough for me to leap forward and tackle her, pinning her to the ground. Viv squeals as water drips on her from my scraggly hair.

If I would have known she would be this happy to play tag, I would have dragged her from her room twenty years ago, no matter what her parents said. I wish I had. I won't make the same mistake again.

As the victor, I claim my prize, heaving her over my shoulder and striding toward the lake. Viv playfully pounds on my back with her fists, kicking and screaming.

"Put me down, you ass!" She's laughing so hard she can barely get the words out. "Damian!"

I can't tell if I prefer her screaming or moaning my name. Actually, that's wrong. Moaning is obviously better. Screaming is a solid contender though.

"Okay, actually put me down though." She stops playing so I know she's serious now. "Please."

"Vivianna, just go swimming with me." I put her down because I'm not a complete dick, but I am annoyed. "If you say some bullshit about Ombra this or that, I am going to take your rifle and chuck it in the lake and—"

The words get stuck in my mouth as Viv's fingers undo the top button of her flannel, moving slowly down until she shrugs it to the grass.

"What were you saying?" She teases as she wriggles out of her jeans. "Something about my rifle?"

"I was saying that I am so very sorry for being a dick." Stay cool, Damian. Don't stare at her tits. "And that you are the best Ombra in the history of Ombras."

"Mmmhmm." She rolls her eyes before she raises her arms over her head, waiting for me to throw her over my shoulder again.

Instead, I delicately lift her bridal-style, carrying her carefully up to the makeshift jumping platform, her feet kicking absentmindedly. The wind picks up slightly, billowing her hair behind her. My breath catches in my chest as I look down at her in my arms. Her eyes widen slightly as she stares back at me, and I can feel her heart beat a bit faster as I stand over the lip to the water below.

"Are you nervous?" I chuckle. "Wait, you know how to swim, right?"

"Wouldn't you like to know?" She bats her eyelashes coyly.

"That wasn't an answer." I take a step back, cradling her against my chest tighter.

"Nuh-uh," Viv taunts. "I lost. You have to throw me in."

"You know how to swim though, right?" I ask again.

"Do you really think I would let you throw me in if I didn't?"

"Yes," I say honestly. "You have a terrible sense of self-preservation."

Viv throws her head back laughing at my response. Slowly, I walk back to the edge of the boulder, watching her reaction closely. She seems relaxed, calm. I decide to trust her.

She squeals as she flies over the edge, splashing into the lake below. I dive in right after her, just in case she is stupid enough to bluff. My arms wrap around her as we surface together, pulling her back securely against my chest.

"Calm down, Damian," she chuckles. "I know how to swim."

"Too bad." I hitch her legs around my hips as I tread water. "I am now responsible for you, thus, you're staying right here."

"Is that so?" She gets that mischievous look in her eyes again.

"Whatever you're thinking, no."

Viv splashes me and tries to slip out of my arms — probably looking for a second round of tag — but I dig my nails into her hips, tugging her tightly against me. She continues squirming, giggling in my arms. My palms clutch her ass, and I'm sure she can feel my growing erection between her legs. It takes everything in me not to fuck her right here, right now. As an alternative, I lift her up and toss her away from me, yelling that this time, she was it.

We swim around and splash each other for what feels like hours. Once our limbs are completely unusable, we drag ourselves onto the grass, laying there as we air dry.

"That cloud kinda looks like a monkey riding a unicycle." I point at one toward the right.

"Do we need to get your eyes checked?" She nudges my ribs. "That's obviously a beetle doing a cartwheel."

"No way." The back of my hand brushes hers, and I feel sparks tingle through my spine. "At least call it a lemur."

"I suppose we could compromise." Her fingers interlock with mine as though it means nothing.

To be fair, we've gotten much more comfortable with physical touch ever since my outburst in my office. Maybe this does mean nothing. Maybe this is normal. The lines are so blurry and intertwined. Where does Ombra end and Viv begin? How much of my feelings for her are colored by lust versus her saving my life time and time again versus... something I don't dare to give a name to.

"What about that one?" I point towards a separate one to the left.

"Easy. A ladybug holding a parasol."

"Okay." I roll my eyes. "Now you're just fucking with me."

"Maybe," she admits, her shoulders shaking from holding back her laughter.

The sun starts to droop in the sky. If we don't want to hike in the dark, we need to get going. Yet, I can't bring myself to let go of this moment, this perfect afternoon. Unfortunately, Viv is stronger than I am, and she shakes her hand free of mine. Instantly, I feel colder, missing her touch on my skin.

"Get dressed." She tosses my clothes pile to me with a smile. "We'll finish drying off at the cabin."

"I'm not worried." I shrug. "We could always cuddle in bed if you get cold." Shit, did I say that out loud?

"Touché," Viv laughs. Is she flirting or is this just friendly banter? She shimmies into her jeans, unintentionally taunting me as she tugs the tight fabric over her ass.

The air is light as we hike back. Wildflowers line the worn path, guiding us back to our private refuge.

We get to the cabin as soon as the sun kisses the horizon. Impulsively, I reach out and grab Viv's hand, yanking her to stand next to me. I don't say anything, just watch as the sky blurs together bands of purple, orange, and red. Her fingers weave between mine, squeezing gently. I sneak a glance. Her mouth is slightly agape as she is basked in the final rays of sunlight, seeming to glow in its radiance.

"*Bellissima.*" The word falls from my lips before I can stop it. She only nods, entranced by the fading colors, and soon we are left in darkness.

"Wow," she breathes. "Just wow."

She doesn't know the half of it.

We change into our PJ's and crawl into bed. Viv's asleep in a few minutes, her hair splayed over her pillow as she's curled into a tight ball. Her muscles are tense, primed to act.

"No," she gasps, her fists clenching.

I don't even take a moment to think. My arms wrap around her waist and jerk her to my chest, holding her body protectively.

"You're safe," I whisper. "Nothing bad will happen to you in my arms, I promise. I promise, Viv."

It takes a moment, but with every hushed reassurance, she relaxes a bit more. Soon, she's nestled into my shoulder, breathing softly. She's perfect, everything I could ever want. The one thing I can't have.

I lean forward ever so slowly, determined not to wake her. My kiss brushes her forehead tenderly. My *bellissima.*

◈　　◆　　◆　　◆　　◈

I wake before her the next morning. Untangling our limbs is a slow, delicate affair, done with utmost precision. In the end, she is undisturbed as I slink toward the door.

The bells on the handle are another issue. Viv thinks I didn't notice the little alarm system she installed, but I did. My hand cradles the spheres as I hold my breath, ever so carefully lifting them free of the handle and setting them aside. I open the door just enough to slip through, avoiding the wooden creaks. I don't dare to breathe again until I'm several steps away from the cabin.

The empty Chianti bottle is laying empty near our trash barrel. I grab it and wash it out using the water pump until the purple tinge is gone and it's filled with clear water. I make sure to stay within eyesight of the cabin as I wander into the forests, kneeling every once in a while to examine patches of wildflowers along the way. My inspections are intense, and only the finest flora meets my standards. I pluck the stems from the ground, dropping them into the neck of the wine bottle. After I have a good selection of flowers, I meticulously arrange them into a bouquet. There. Satisfied, I start the short trek back to the cabin.

"Damian!" The door flies open and Viv bursts through, a 9mm in her hands.

"Over here!" I wave to her. It only takes her a second to assess the situation and tuck the pistol into her waistband. It's enough time for me to close the distance and present her with the wine bottle. "Good morning. I picked these for you."

She smiles. Oh god, she smiles, and I can barely think.

"Those are gorgeous!" Viv's hands brush mine as she examines the bouquet. "Thank you."

"I'll carry them in for you," I say, feeling a sense of pride in my work.

They fit perfectly on the table, a centerpiece fit for a queen. Okay, maybe not that good, but it works. Viv reaches out subconsciously to turn the vase toward me, but I place a firm hand on the bottle. I want the best flowers to face her.

The ringing of our satellite phone disturbs our flower fight, and we lock eyes. There's only one reason someone would call us. Vacation's over. I answer the phone.

"Marano."

There's been an attack, Sebastian says grimly. *We need you back on base.*

"Start packing," I confirm to Viv, hating the hardened look that returns to her eyes. It had just left. She had just relaxed. Damn it! "What happened, Sebastian?"

The Petrovs stormed one of our clubs last night. His voice is firm, matter-of-fact.

"Any casualties?" I ask, fidgeting as I take in the information.

Yes. Sebastian seems to hesitate before continuing. *All of our of men are fine, some need medical care but will survive. But sir, they killed the dancers. Every one of them.*

"What?" My blood drains from my face as my eyes snap up to Viv. She glances over her shoulder at my tone, concerned when she sees my expression. "Hold on a moment, Sebastian." I briskly walk out the cabin until I'm sure I'm out of her earshot. "Just the dancers? No one else?"

I'm sorry, boss. The girls are innocent. They didn't do anything wrong. *Witnesses said it was quick, they didn't suffer.*

"Thank you for letting me know." I hate how easily I slip back into the role of Mr. Marano, but it's a necessary evil. "Vivianna and I will leave as soon as we can. Expect us in a few hours."

There's one more thing! Sebastian blurts out, trying to catch me before I hang up. *Bruno left something behind for you.*

"What?" I grit my teeth feeling my temper spike.

A note. I hope you don't mind, I read it. He wrote, "Say hi to her for me. I'll find her soon." There was also a small bag of plastic gems.

Viv. He's going after Viv.

"Who else knows about the message?" The malice is clear in my voice. This is not a threat I take lightly.

Just me.

"Keep it that way." I glance back at the cabin. "We don't need to scare her over nothing."

Vivianna will be okay, sir, Sebastian says with conviction. *We'll keep her safe.*

"Thank you," I breathe, a small amount of vulnerability. "I'll see you soon."

◈　◆　◆　◆　◈

I walk down the stairs onto the main floor of the compound, freshly showered and back in my suit. Marco is waiting for me, pouncing as soon as I step onto the hardwood.

"You took her to the cabin?" His tone is gruff and frustrated. "For three days? How many times did you two fuck? Huh?"

"Not that it is remotely appropriate for you to ask that, but the answer is none," I snap. "Get off my back, Marco."

"How many times did you want to fuck?" Constantly.

"Marco…" I growl. "What would you have me do? Go by myself and get assassinated?"

"May I remind you, Enzo is also an option."

"No, you may not." I try to step around him, but he blocks my path.

"You're in dangerous waters here, Damian." His tone is sharp, pointed into my psyche.

"Was that a threat?" The air grows heavy as I narrow my eyes, stepping chest-to-chest with Marco. "I must have misheard you, otherwise, we would have a very serious problem."

"My apologies." His voice doesn't match his words.

"You are not the Don, Marco. I am." I say calmly. "I won't remind you again."

With that, I force my way past him, not caring that I ram my shoulder into his. He follows me into the conference room, my other lieutenants already waiting.

They share their plan as I stare out the glass window into the living space. Enzo runs out of the gym, giving Viv a big hug. She laughs at a joke he says, and I wish I could hear the way it floats through the air. Instead, all I can hear is my team go over manpower and blueprints.

Threats on my life are one thing. They're expected. Half of the time they are meaningless posturing and bluffs. I'm used to it. But Bruno threatened *her.* I won't stand for it.

And so, I listen to my team, ask questions when needed, and generally try to keep my rage contained. Once we are all aligned, I dismiss them to assemble the troops. Payback is coming, and it's coming tonight.

I am the last person to step out of the conference room. Viv's eyes are locked onto me, as though she can feel the wrath biting at my skin. I take a tie clip out of my pocket and fasten my tie to my shirt, an unspoken statement. She nods and heads to the elevator, riding down with me.

"Take care of yourself tonight," I grumble, checking the magazine of my pistol. "We're going in hot."

"I could use a good fight." Viv smirks, cracking her knuckles.

"Then go punch Enzo," I snap. She recoils, her cocky grin fallen in shock.

The elevator doors open, and her walls are back up. The Viv I spent so long digging up has been buried, leaving only the hardened Ombra standing obediently beside me. She looks straight ahead, her hands resting on the small of her back. I sigh and give her shoulder a squeeze before walking out to grab my gear. Vest, earpiece, watch, the whole nine yards. Viv gets prepped, tightly braiding her hair. She has her own hair tie.

Sebastian shares the plan with the foot soldiers he called in. I can feel Viv standing just behind me, the perfect embodiment of the Ombra, a shadow lurking, watching, waiting. Sebastian notices her too, casting concerned looks her way every few minutes.

Two SUVs are loaded up — one with the footmen, and the other with my lieutenants and Enzo. I'm content to drive myself on my bike, Viv silently slipping behind me. She does a final pat down of her weapons before wrapping her arms around my waist. Visions of her sleeping form clinging to my chest run through my mind as I rev the engine. I have to protect her.

The motorcycle peels onto the interstate. I drive much too fast, much too recklessly, fueled by my anger. Cars honk crossly as I cut people off, weaving betwixt the bystanders going about their days.

Red brake lights catch me off guard and I swerve, wheels skidding as I take to the shoulder. Fingernails dig into my dress shirt as Viv braces for the inevitable crash. I regain control of the bike before that can happen, but my heart races faster than I thought possible. Fuck, that was close. Too close, I realize, as Viv keeps her nails dug painfully into me, her thighs clenched around my hips.

Immediately, I slow my motorcycle, merging back into the speed of normal traffic. Several minutes pass before Viv retracts her nails, though she doesn't fully relax. I take one hand off the handlebars and rub her thigh, a silent apology. She flicks my hand — hard — a silent fuck off. I deserve that. I am a model driver until we arrive at the rendezvous point near the distribution center.

Because of my "eager" driving, Viv and I got here quite early, but it gives us time to survey the scene. Based off of Sebastian's intel, I know that this is where the Russian's drug supply is repackaged for distribution. We're going to steal their product — the cocaine, the heroin, all of it. The Maranos don't deal with drugs normally — underlings tend to start sampling and things get messy too quickly. That being said, I don't mind finding some trash receptacle for all of this shit if it pisses off the Petrovs and hurts their bottom line.

"Those Russians are a mess," Viv comments. She scoots back on the seat, curling her legs in front of her as she sits on her little perch.

"You could say that again." Even in the short amount of time we've been watching, there's been nothing but chaos in the warehouse. People yelling and arguing over where things are supposed to go as they unload the two waiting semi-trucks. I think a fist fight even broke out between two of the workers.

"Why was Sebastian looking at me in the garage?" Her blunt question catches me off guard, without a prepared retort.

"What do you mean?" Maybe feign ignorance?

"Don't fuck with me," she bites, standing suddenly. "Something happened, didn't it? You've been in a pissy mood all afternoon."

"There was an attack on one of my businesses last night," I say slowly, choosing my words intentionally. "It hit close to home."

"Anything else I need to know?" She's unsatisfied, probably because I'm acting suspicious.

"I'm not in any more danger than usual, if that's what you're trying to ascertain." Not a lie, but definitely not a truthful answer to her question.

"Will Sebastian say the same thing if I ask him?" Viv narrows her eyes, seeing through my deception immediately.

"Yes." If he knows what's good for him.

"Fine." She pulls out one of her knives, twirling it in her hand as she plops down in the grass. "Then stop being such a dick."

We sit there in silence until the two SUVs pull up. Viv retakes her seat behind me and readies a pistol. It's go time.

The two SUVs rush in first, my men jumping out before the Russians have time to process their arrival. Their submachine guns pump out round after round, our enemies falling to the ground screaming. I hang back for just a moment to let the cavalry soften them up, Viv coiled like a spring behind me, ready to pounce at a moment's notice.

I rev the engine and she gives me a thumbs up. Then, the wheels are spinning as I drive in an arc around the fray, Viv's 9mm dropping target after target. The team pushes forward into the depot, so I pull over. Viv hops off immediately, a stray hostile locked in her crosshairs. He raises a gun. It doesn't end well for him.

Viv's head is on a swivel as she reloads, her magazine spent. Based on the gunshots coming from inside, I would say our recon was a little off. There are many more Russians here than we expected, but the element of surprise is enough for us to have the upper hand.

We crouch and enter the warehouse. It seems to be divided into two main sections.

The left is for storage, with pallets and shelving stacked to the ceiling. Parcels of white powder sit on forklifts, ready to be loaded or unloaded if the Russians ever got their shit together. Too late for that now.

The right side appears to be a repackaging area. Tables with scales, small baggies, and spilt drugs fill the space. Cook drugs in bulk, split it up for individual resale, profit. Good theory, until they decided to fuck with me.

I duck behind an abandoned forklift, popping out to fire when I can. Viv is a few feet away, darting from cover to cover with a seductive lethality. More hostiles pour out from the office spaces in the back, and I can see Viv curse under her breath as she switches pistols. She retreats closer to me. Her lips move silently as she counts each shot. Several of my men switch to fighting with fists, discarding their firearms. Slowly, their numbers start dwindling.

Two try to make a break for it and run away. I got them. Ready, aim… My gun clicks after a round drops the first. Empty. Damn it. Viv steps out behind me, her bullet flying true.

"Any spare magazines? Viv asks, her eyes scanning the room on high alert.

"No." I shake my head.

"Fuck, alright." She grimaces with an annoyed acceptance. "I'm low too. Hang back while we clear out the rest."

Her instructions turn out to be unnecessary as the team finishes off the last of the Russians. Corpses litter the room, blood spilling over the concrete floor.

"Let's move," I command, my voice bellowing over the lingering commotion. "We don't know how long until reinforcements come. Load up the drugs."

The foot soldiers and my lieutenants hustle, quickly jumping into forklifts and moving the palettes back onto the semis. In seconds, we have a better system than the one that was previously in place. Viv and Enzo treat the few who are wounded and load them into the vehicles. Nothing too bad, but they'll need medical attention once we get to the mansion.

While my men finish loading our stolen loot, I stroll to the back of the warehouse, lost in thought. There's a hallway lined with windows, and I can see a few office spaces through the glass. This was on the blueprints, no surprise there, but I'm intrigued by the fortified metal doors. What in an office would need protecting with such rigor?

"We don't have much ammo left." Viv's voice startles me. "It's your call if you want to go snooping, but we need to be quick."

I turn to find the crew ready and waiting for my next instructions. We have what we came for. We should go. But... taking a peek in their offices wouldn't hurt.

"Lieutenants and Ombra, on me," I order. "Everyone else, get the goods out of here and make sure the injured get seen by a medic. We'll regroup later." Nods and grunts of confirmation follow as the group splits.

"No trespassing," I read aloud from a sign bolted to a door. "Sounds like where we need to be."

Viv pushes me out of the way as she opens the door, gun raised. She and Enzo quickly clear the room before reporting it clear to enter. The rest of the group funnels in.

There's a stately wooden desk in the center of the room with a computer desktop and tower. A once grandiose, now bedraggled, rug lies over the concrete floor, desperately trying to cover the industrial aesthetic of the space. Vintage collectibles line a bookshelf — a ship in a bottle, a lantern, a cracked compass. Antique swords hang in mounts, their blades long rusted. Beyond that, the room is bare. Just four brick walls.

"Sebastian, see what you can find on the computer," I say. "Maybe they keep digital books or a list of their contacts."

"Sir, it's asking for a password." Sebastian opens the desk drawers and rifles through some papers. "I'm not seeing anything written down."

"Maybe it's 'one, two, three, four?'" Tony suggests. The team all looks to me as if I am the magical password guardian.

"Give it a shot." I shrug.

Sebastian types the four numbers and presses the enter key. Instantly, a screech peals through the warehouse, and I cover my ears, recoiling from the sound. Viv whirls around, gun aimed at the sky as though she could shoot the alarm. A resounding clank comes from the door. Marco tugs at the handle, but it won't budge, electronically locked. We're trapped.

"Boss!" Sebastian shouts as the alarm quiets, pointing at the screen. I run to his side as a message in Russian scrawls across the display. The red words flash on the screen, their meaning clear despite the language barrier.

Fuck, fuck, fuck!

CHAPTER 11
VIVIANNA

Okay, okay, okay. Problem solve. Deep breath in. Deep breath out.

"Unlock the door!" Damian yells as Sebastian frantically types on the keyboard, but it's no use, the screen won't navigate away from the creepy message. Sebastian is just as locked out of the computer as we are locked into this room.

Take stock of the situation. No windows. One door. Four brick walls. An unknown amount of time until very angry gunmen arrive to kill us. Oh, and I have one bullet left in my gun. That's great.

Tony and Marco struggle with the door, as though the two of them were strong enough to tear down a metal door. Actually, I would only be marginally surprised if Tony could, the wall of muscle he is, so maybe that's not a bad use of time.

Vinny stands in the corner, a dismayed acceptance on his face. He nervously ejects and reloads his magazine. It's empty, just like Damian's. Shit, do any of us have any fucking bullets? I take a second to check Marco's, Tony's, and Sebastian's. Tony is the only one with a useful number of rounds, but even still, it's not much.

Damian steps back from the computer, running his hands through his hair. He mutters under his breath before walking to me.

"We're going to have to fight our way out, aren't we?" He mumbles quietly.

"With what bullets?" I frown, leaning against the wall. "You and Vinny are both out, Marco, Sebastian, and I might as well be. Depending on how many reinforcements they bring, Vinny and I can try to brute force fight our way through, but realistically, not all of us would make it out."

I omit the detail that Vinny and I would be the first to die, holding the front line as long as we can. It's my job to die for Damian. It looks like he might be cashing that check today.

"Let's make that Plan C," Damian says, his face a grim line.

"Do you have an A or B?" He doesn't answer. I pull out my two twin blades, twirling them in my fingers. I've always preferred fighting with knives. At least they're how I'll make my final stand.

"We're not there yet." Damian puts a firm hand on my arm. "Put those away."

He's in denial. That's fine. We can pretend a little longer. I sheathe the knives if only to make him feel better.

No windows. One door. Four brick walls. One air vent. There's no way out.

Wait, hold up. One air vent.

"Give me a boost." I wave Damian over, and he hoists me to the ceiling.

The vent pops easily from the ceiling, and I toss it to the floor before pulling myself up to peer down the shaft. It's a tight fit around my shoulders. The tunnel goes straight for a bit before turning to the left. Every so often, there's a vent panel. I let myself dangle and Damian helps me down to the floor.

"I think I could crawl through the vents." I brush my suit off, straightening the sleeves. "But none of you would be able to fit. It's tight even for me."

"You could escape," Tony says. "No sense in you dying with us."

"Are you crazy?" Marco admonishes. "You want to send away our best fighter? No way!"

"Hold on!" I cut in. "I was eliminating it as an option, not suggesting it! I'm not leaving."

Tony frowns, but Marco practically glows with self-righteousness. Damian just stares up at the vent.

"Plan B," he whispers, just loud enough for me to hear. "Save yourself. Crawl in the vents and hide."

"We both know that's not going to happen," I snap, angry he would even suggest it.

"Please, Viv," he begs. "I—"

"Vents..." Sebastian's voice interrupts as he mulls something over aloud. "Wait, we're in the westernmost office, right?" Damian grabs the compass off the shelf, then nods. "Where's the sewer access?"

"What?" Damian widens his eyes as realization dawns on him. "The sewer access!"

"Yes!" Sebastian jumps up. "It was in my briefing. There's a sewer access in the center of the west wall of the office furthest to the west! I bet they just bricked it up, but if we could get to it, we're outta here!"

"We can't get through a brick wall." Marco rolls his eyes, annoyed at the suggestion.

"You can chisel out the bricks." My eyes lock with Sebastian's as I jump into the brainstorm. I grab one of the swords off the bookcase and toss it to him. "Try this."

The grout in the wall is old and crumbles easily as Sebastian digs the tip of the sword in.

"Tony!" Damian yells. "Grab a sword and help!"

He jumps into a frenzy, stabbing and scraping with the remaining sword. After a bit, Sebastian is able to pry the first brick out of the wall, revealing part of a rung. A few more bricks later, we can begin to see a dark tunnel leading down beneath the warehouse. I pace along the far side of the room as they work, counting the seconds. The work is going faster than one would think, but is it enough?

Eventually, they have just enough bricks removed for someone small to squeeze through.

"Proof of concept," Damian says. "We need to test to see if this actually goes somewhere." The group turns to me.

"I'm not leaving without Mr. Marano." I shake my head stubbornly. "Send Vincenzo. He's skinny."

"Thanks, Anna." Vinny rolls his eyes. "Of course, I'd love to go down the scary, dark hole first."

"Don't be a coward," I snipe back. "Take Tony's gun with you and secure the area."

Damian grabs the oil lantern from the shelf and Marco pulls out a lighter. A small flame sputters to life. Vinny scowls as he slings the strap of the gun over his shoulder and takes the lantern. Sebastian and Tony pause their digging just long enough for Vinny to shimmy through.

All clear. Vinny speaks over our earpieces. *There's a way out down here.*

We cheer and grin as Tony and Sebastian dig with a renowned vigor. It isn't but a few seconds later car doors slam outside. The atmosphere drops as quickly as it raised.

We are out of time. Even if we could all fit through the hole in the wall this second, the Russians would catch us in the tunnel. As it stands, we need at least another minute of digging, then single file climbing down the ladder… Marco catches my eye in the far corner of the room, and I walk over to him.

"We need more time." The words fall from my mouth, thick and bland.

"I know," is all he says.

"We need something to slow them down." My stomach drops into my gut.

"Do your job, Vivianna." For possibly the first time, Marco's voice isn't harsh or abrasive — it's soft and sympathetic. He places a hand on my shoulder, and I nod weakly before walking over to Damian.

"Hey," I say softly, passing him my 9mm. "Hold on to this for me. The magazine is empty, but there's one round in the chamber."

"Why do you need me to hold this?" He raises an eyebrow, confused. I shrug off my suit jacket and drape it over his arm. "Viv?"

My eyes drag up to his, and I can't help but throw myself into his arms. He stumbles back a step as I squeeze him tightly. I pull away before he can recover and hold me. I couldn't do what I need to do if he did.

"What's going on?" Damian growls, tucking my pistol into his waistband and passing my jacket to Marco. "Vivianna, whatever stupid ass thing you have planned, I order you to stand down. You are to stay right next to me. You hear me?"

My eyes flick over to Marco. A subtle nod, the closest thing I've ever gotten to approval from him.

"It's been an honor, Damian." I keep my voice steady, calm.

My sad smile is the last thing Damian sees before I turn and run, jumping up off the wall. The tips of my fingers barely catch the edge of the air duct.

"No!" He cries out as he puts together my plan. "Vivianna, come back!"

His hand brushes my ankle before it is torn away. Marco yells some bullshit about duty or whatever, but all I can hear is Damian's desperate pleas. I heave myself into the duct, ignoring the pain in his voice. He'll forgive me one day.

The Palazzos protect the Maranos. This is what I've trained for all my life. It's all I've ever wanted to do. *I'm not afraid to die.*

My dad would be proud of me. He would. I'm doing what he wasn't able to do. I'm saving Damian. I won't fail. *I'm not afraid to die.*

I peer through a vent and see a group of fifteen men strolling through the doors. Fifteen. My lungs constrict in my chest. I… I can't. It's too many. I…

Stop.

Focus.

I don't need to win. I don't need to kill them all. I just need to slow them down as much as possible, give Damian time to escape. Every dead Russian is one more that can't kill him. Every minute is one more for him to get away. *I'm not afraid to die.*

I pop off the vent cover and dangle from the duct before I drop to the ground.

Start with stealth. Knock off a few of their numbers before they know I'm here. The men are cocky, boisterous. They don't even look to the side as I creep along the wall, one knife already in my hand.

I walk behind the group, shadowing the person taking up the rear. No one hears his muffled cries as his neck is cut, his blood staining the gray concrete as I quietly lay him on the ground. The same goes for the second.

We're getting too close to the back of the warehouse. I need to turn them around. I slice the throat of the third, and shove his body into the horde, ducking behind a storage shelf as quickly as I can.

"Anton? Anton!" One of the Russians panics. "Anton's dead!

I skulk toward the other side of the group, using their confusion to my advantage. With their attention on their fallen comrades, I get the drop on a hostile on the other side. His neck slits just as easily as the others, though my luck doesn't last.

"There!" A finger points my direction. I dive out of the way and scramble for cover as bullets fly toward me. "After her!"

Four down, eleven still alive. And hey, I'm still alive too. Small victories.

I slide out my second knife, dual-wielding seems the best play from here on out. A man peeks around the corner. My blade darts out and he collapses in a heap, hands clamped on his chest where a new hole now exists.

"Come out little girlie," someone coos. "You have our attention now, let's play."

His goads don't bother me. If anything, they're helpful, allowing me to track his location, as well as those of his laughing companions. I crouch down, crawling around the shelving.

"I win," I hiss, sliding my blade between his ribs. He stops laughing.

The steel in my hands reflect the harsh fluorescent lighting. I wonder if Damian has made it into the tunnel yet, or if they're still carving at the grout. It doesn't matter, I have to hold the line, give them as much time as possible to run away.

Whispers float through both shelves on either side of me. I've got company.

I jump out from the shelving, ready to deal with the opponents on either side of me, but a flash of movement catches my eye. Two Russians, sprinting toward the offices.

"No!" My movement is practiced, rehearsed over and over in my bedroom. Hurl one knife, spin, fling the other. They thud into place exactly where I aimed, the two tripping with the hilts protruding from their necks.

I sense, more than see, the man step out behind me. I fling myself to the side as the gun fires once, twice, thrice. The first bullet rips open the side of my shirt, but luckily misses me. The same can't be said for his comrade, who sprung out at my cry. Patches of red grow in his chest.

What is that, nine down?

I don't have time to celebrate, already scrambling to my feet and running down the aisle, further bullets flying around me.

Yes, follow me! Don't go to the office. Please don't go to the office.

An arm darts out in front of me. The clothesline — a maneuver I haven't seen since I was a child, but effective nonetheless. The breath is knocked out of me as I crash to the ground. I roll out of the way as the wannabe defensive lineman tries to land a stomp on my chest. I kick the knee he's standing on, and he crashes down right next to me.

Before he can blink, I'm straddling him, punching down with my adrenaline-fueled determination. Rough hands grab at my shoulders, yanking me off of my prey. Doesn't matter, as they raise me up, my heel connects with his chin, and his eyes roll back unconscious.

The two men drag me back, as I writhe in their arms. I'm forced to my knees.

No, Damian needs more time. It can't end here. I can't give up. As if in response to my desperate struggle, Damian's voice comes over my earpiece.

Viv! We're cl—

A fist strikes my cheek, sending my earpiece skittering across the concrete. My shoulders heave from exhaustion as I take another blow, whipping my head back.

Clear? Close? Climbing back up because it was a dead end? I don't know what he said. I don't know what he needs. I don't know if there's anything more I can do. There's five men still alive. Five men. They can take five, right? I did enough?

Five men. Two holding my arms. One beating me. Two more… somewhere.

I raise my head, looking around. Two more walking back to the office spaces. Toward Damian. He needs more time. I can give him more time. I have to.

As my assaulter swings again, I jerk back. His momentum causes him to stumble when he misses, and I headbutt him. He staggers back, holding his nose. Moving quickly, I elbow one of my captors between the legs, and he falls down with a pained howl.

One hand free, I lash out at my last restrainer. He flinches just enough for me to wrest my arm free. They're not dead, not unconscious, but I can come back to them. I need to stop the other two.

They're nearly to the hallway when I catch up, pursued by the other three. I grab one by the collar of his shirt, slamming him against the metal window frame once, twice, a third time until I hear his skull crack.

Someone grabs me again, possibly trying to save the limp man in my grasp. I kick him off, feeling a rib give beneath my foot. As he falls back, another takes his place, lifting me by my shirt and throwing me through the hallway window.

The glass shatters as I tumble through the pane. I stagger to my hands and knees, wincing as the shards leave microscopic cuts in my skin.

We're getting too close to the office. I need to turn them around. Lead them away. Keep going, Vivianna. Damian needs me.

A bright red object catches my eye and I yank the fire extinguisher from the wall. The discarded pin skips down the hallway as I squeeze the handle, the white fog spewing into the crowd. They cough aggressively, choking on the hazardous fumes.

I take advantage of the haze, jumping back through the window and swinging my makeshift club as hard as I can. The Russian furthest to the left collapses with a satisfying thud. Another swing, another man down. The smoke dissipates and I take the chance to back toward the warehouse entrance, heckling as I go.

"What's wrong?" I sneer, dropping the now empty fire extinguisher. "Getting your asses kicked by one girl?" The two remaining men glare at me with daggers in their eyes. They step toward me forcefully, just barely out of arm's reach. Yes. Follow me away from the office. "I thought this was going to be a hard fight. This is barely a workout."

That's a lie. I'm exhausted and sore, my lungs screaming for a full breath of air that I can't seem to find. But I have enough in my tank to give Damian a few more seconds. Just a few more seconds. I lure them a bit further before I turn and run. I hear their curses as they chase after me. My eyes dart wildly around the warehouse, I don't have a plan. I don't have a weapon.

I yelp as I am tackled to the ground. I roll over, lashing out at the man grappling me. My fist connects with his throat, and he gives a strangled gasp as I crush his windpipe. I try to scoot away, but the last Russian is too fast, shoving his pistol in my neck as he pins me down.

"Try something," he threatens, his anger clear as his finger twitches. Blood trails down his nose, and I smile. I did that. "Give me a reason to pull the trigger."

Fourteen men down, one still alive. And hey, Damian's still alive too. Small victories.

I don't need to win. I don't need to kill them all. I just need to slow them down as much as possible, give Damian time to escape. And I did it. I gave Damian time. Even if this one guy catches up to them, Vinny can dispatch him easily, especially since I already gave him hell. I did it. *I'm not afraid to die.*

This is it. My body relaxes in the Russian's grasp, heartbeat slowing as I accept my fate. I close my eyes, raising my chin to give him a clean shot. All of the aching pains from my battered body subsides, replaced by one warm feeling. I did it. I really did it. *I'm not afraid to die.*

"Shame," the Russian taunts. "I would be impressed if it weren't so sad. You went through all of this work, and I'm about to walk through those doors and kill your boss regardless."

"You're too late," I chuckle grimly. "He's long gone by now. You failed."

"No," he sputters. "He's trapped. He's in the office."

"I was just the diversion." I shake my head. "I was never going to make it out alive. Just..." My voice wavers slightly. "Make it quick. Please." *I'm not afraid to die. I'm not afraid to die. I'm not afraid—*

"I'll find him." The barrel of his pistol jabs my chin as he leans closer. "I'll tell him how you screamed in your final moments, how you begged for your life. And then, I'll kill him too."

His boastful lies hurt more than the thought of my death, but I don't respond to his goads, don't let tears soil my dignity.

"Hey! Asshole!" The Russian jerks upright, whipping his face toward the shouts from the front door. Then he jerks again, this time as a bullet pierces his skull. "I'm right here."

His corpse falls to the side as I roll to my knees, staring in disbelief at the sight in front of me. Damian stands with my pistol outstretched, a look of pure wrath on his face. The rest of the crew stands behind him, gawking bewildered at the carnage strewn across the warehouse. I must look about as shitty as I feel, covered in the blood of a dozen men, more hair flying wildly around my face than in my braid, rips and slashes reducing my shirt to scraps.

"Are you hurt?" Damian asks gruffly, striding over to me.

"I don't know." I stare down at my red-stained hands, still reeling. I'm... alive? "I don't think so."

"Good. " He pulls me to my feet, looking me up and down for injuries. "Because I'm going to kill you."

I am shaken from my stupor as Damian grabs the straps of my bulletproof vest and shoves me against the wall.

"What the absolute fuck, Viv?!" He yells, but his anger doesn't scare me. I'm just relieved he's okay, able to give me a verbal lashing because he's alive. "Are you trying to get yourself killed? You ever, and I mean ever, disobey my orders again and I will shove my foot so far up your ass you'll taste the leather."

"This is my job, Damian." Fuck the Mr. Marano bullshit, I've earned the first-name basis for the next five minutes. "I don't care what you do or don't order me to do. My only concern is keeping you alive, no matter what that means for me. Out here, I'm in charge."

"You really think so?" His shouts turn to a growl, rumbling low in his chest.

He lets go of my vest to grip my throat. My hands wrap around his wrist, pulling him closer as the adrenaline in my veins gives me irrational courage. Can he feel my pulse racing in his hands?

Can he tell that my breathing is shallower when he touches me? His eyes fixate on mine, and I lose myself in the intensity of his gaze.

"Then let me rewrite your job description, Vivianna," Damian seethes, leaning in. I can feel the muscles in his forearms flexing through his suit jacket. "Your job is to *not* die. You are no longer allowed to trade your life for mine. No more jumping in front of guns, no more stopping assassination attempts without a single weapon on you, and absolutely no more final stands when I explicitly order you to stand down. No more!"

"You would never speak to my brother this way," I retort, feigning anger. The truth is I can't think past the way his breath kisses my skin, even if he doesn't.

"You're not Enzo," Damian spits the name as though it was a curse. I gasp as his grip tightens, restricting my breathing to shallow pants. "No more. Do you understand me?"

I say nothing, holding his glare.

"I said, do you understand me?" He repeats himself, slightly loosening his hold as if I didn't respond because he was cutting off my air. But the truth is, Damian Marano is everything to me. If he died… No. I have to protect him. I *will* protect him.

"I'm a Palazzo," I state stubbornly. "You're my Marano. The Palazzos protect the Maranos. Whatever it takes."

"Damn it, Viv." Damian slouches defeated, pulling me into his arms, fingers weaving in my hair. He cradles me gently, a stark contrast to the fervor of a moment prior. "No more. Please, no more."

Someone clears their throat, but Damian doesn't shy away from the intimate moment between us. He brushes a strand of hair out of my face.

"You're okay?" He asks quietly, as though he is scared of the answer, as though I'm hiding a mortal blow beneath my black suit.

"I'm okay," I promise, rubbing my thumb over his wrist, pulling away slightly so he can see me. He nods, swallowing with some effort.

"Let's go home."

Damian reaches for my hand, but I turn, walking further into the warehouse. I retrieve my two knives, wiping the gore onto the clothes of the corpses beneath them.

Once satisfied, I return to Damian, who wraps an arm around my shoulders and escorts me back to the motorcycle. He checks that my helmet is buckled securely and then pulls me tightly against his back.

The entire drive home, one of his hands is placed over mine. I notice he also drives well under the speed limit, nothing like his earlier recklessness. However, once he steps free of the bike in the garage, his frosty demeanor has returned.

"Marco. Vivianna." His voice is terse and clipped. "My office. Ten minutes. Vivianna, go shower. You have blood... everywhere."

Am I getting called to the principal's office? Well, shit. I run through the shower as fast as I can, scrubbing my skin until the water runs clear.

Nine minutes and a few seconds later, I shut the door to Damian's office behind me, damp hair and all. Damian is reclined in his chair behind his desk, though his body is tense and unrelaxed. Marco is leaning against the wall, arms crossed as he glares my direction.

"Sit down." There's a gravity to Damian's voice, and for the first time, I am intimidated by him. This isn't Damian. This is Mr. Marano. I quickly find my chair, anxiously waiting for him to continue, but his eyes are stuck on Marco. "Both of you."

Marco rolls his eyes and saunters over to a seat, as though this meeting was a complete waste of his time.

"It seems the two of you are both in need of a firm reminder of how things work in *my* mafia," Damian begins, and I gulp nervously. "What happened tonight was unacceptable. Disobedience will not be tolerated. This is your only warning."

"We would all be dead if we listened to you tonight," Marco scoffs. "Me stepping in saved your life."

"Really?" Damian is unimpressed with the claim. "Because my plan was to stall a different way, perhaps using the desk to barricade the door or — I don't know — not sending my Ombra to her death."

"Vivianna was raised to die for you." Marco sits up in his chair. "Forgive me for being the only one to acknowledge her role."

"Vivianna is not a lamb for the slaughter!" Damian snaps, set off by Marco's comments.

"Except she is!" I already know this to be true, a secret they never even pretended to hide, but I can't stop from flinching at Marco's words.

"Let's play your game." Damian lowers his voice, cold steel against Marco's flimsy tone. "Let's say your assertion is right. Then who would protect me next time?"

"What?"

"If Vivianna died tonight," Damian forces the words out as though they taste bitter in his mouth, "who would protect me against the next assassination attempt or mission gone wrong? There's no one else who could fill her role, unless you have more child soldier farms I haven't been informed of."

"I—" Marco falters, for the first time at a loss for words.

"I don't have the luxury of throwing out random orders when I feel like it," Damian continues. "I have to think about the entire team, about the organization. I expected you of all people to understand that, but it seems not."

"Now hold on, Damian—"

"Mr. Marano." With that one correction, I could feel something in the air snap.

"Dam—"

"You will address me as Mr. Marano or you will not address me at all." Damian stands, his authority filling the room. My face pales as he turns to me, a wall of stone. "And you."

Oh shit.

"You will never *ever* take Marco's orders over mine."

"I didn't," I stammer. Damian's eyes flare with ire.

"You did," he states, daring me to push back again. I don't, but Marco does.

"She was doing her duty—"

"One more word out of you and so help me god!" Damian whirls around, pointing a finger viciously at Marco. Wisely, he decides to take this opportunity to learn how to shut his mouth. Damian glares at Marco for a minute, ensuring his message sunk in before returning to me, taking a deep breath as he does so.

"I told you to stop, and you looked at him." His voice is strong, but there's a layer of hurt and betrayal just beneath the surface. "Vivianna, that will never happen again."

"It won't happen again, sir." I confirm and lower my head, staring at my hands folded submissively in my lap.

"To ensure it won't, you two are no longer allowed to interact with each other. No training, no talking…" Damian leans on his desk as he speaks. I sneak a glance at Marco out of the corner of my eye and Damian slams his hand on his desk. I quickly look back at my hands. "Unless I explicitly order it, you two don't so much as look at the other. Do I need to clarify what it sounds like when I order something?" He glares at me this time.

"No, sir." I shake my head, ashamed.

"Good." Damian stands, straightening the sleeves of his jacket. "Let's practice. Marco, you're going to go fuck off. Vivianna, you're going to escort me upstairs. Any questions?"

I stand slowly and Marco shoulder-checks me on his way out the door.

"Marco!" Damian shouts but doesn't chase after him.

"After you, sir." I hold open the door, not meeting Damian's eyes.

"You're allowed to look at *me*," Damian huffs, storming through the entryway.

I don't respond, meekly following behind until the door to the staircase closes after us.

As soon as the latch clicks, it's like a switch changes in Damian. He yanks me into his arms, burying his head in my hair. I step further into his embrace, and together, we sit on the bottom stair.

"Thank you." I barely hear the whisper leave his mouth.

"For what?"

"Everything you did today," he murmurs. "As angry as I am at you, I know you were just trying to save my life. I won't forget that. I promise."

"You're welcome." I relax as I lean against his shoulder. The scent of pine covers me like a warm blanket. We stay there for a few minutes, finding comfort in the arms of the other.

"Damian?" I ask hesitantly, half-convinced he'll correct me and insist on "Mr. Marano." Instead, he just rubs my back. My voice wavers slightly as I continue. "Why were you there? You were supposed to run. Why can't you ever run?"

"I did run." He grins like the cocky asshole he is. "I ran toward you. I'll always run toward you, Viv. No matter how stupid and reckless you are."

"Well… thanks, you know, for helping me out."

"You're welcome." He ruffles my hair. "Fifteen, right? That's gotta be a record."

"Almost fifteen." I pick at one of my cuticles.

"You would have finished him off without me," he promises. "I just sped things along." We both know he's lying, but I chose to accept his words.

"Fifteen." I nod my head. "Personal best."

"I'm still pissed at you though." Damian tries to appear tough but can't keep the smilc off his face.

"I can live with that," I chuckle, rising to my feet and extending a hand down to him.

He takes my hand and interlaces his fingers with mine. We walk side by side the rest of the staircase and down the hallway to his room.

Damian opens the door confidently and walks inside, forgetting to let go of my hand as he does.

I'll admit, I almost follow him in. Almost. But instead, I let his fingers slide out from between mine.

Damian walks a few slow steps further, looking down at his now empty hand. I reach over the threshold, carefully grabbing the doorknob and pulling the door closed. It latches with a heart-wrenching click.

I squeeze my eyes closed and hang my head as my hands grasp the doorframe, nails digging into the wood. I'm a Palazzo. He's a Marano. My place is on the outside of the door.

My exhale is shaky at best. Normally, I try to get a few hours of sleep before I keep vigil outside of Damian's door, however, I think I might just start there tonight.

Before I can move from my spot, the door flings open and I am yanked inside. Damian kicks the door closed, both hands busy clutching me. One tangles itself in the hair at the nape of my neck, while the other rests on my lower back, pulling my body flush with his. Mine are pressed onto his chest, catching myself as I stumble.

"Why are you being so goddamn stubborn, Vivianna?" His voice is husky and filled with need. A fluttering sensation instantly appears between my legs. "It's driving me crazy."

Damian walks me backward until I am pressed against the door. I gasp as his hand shifts, delicately encircling my throat.

"Tell me to stop." His mouth is only inches from mine. "Tell me you don't want this." Now only a centimeter. "Tell me that you haven't thought about how it would feel to be fucked by me, because I can't think of anything else besides the way your smart mouth would feel on my cock, the curves of your body beneath that suit you wear too well, or how, more than anything, I want to throw you onto my bed and hear you scream my name until your voice is hoarse."

His breath is warm against my skin as I stare into his fiery eyes, entranced by the burning within.

"Tell me to stop," he continues, flicking his gaze up from my lips. "Otherwise, I won't."

He waits for an agonizingly long moment, expecting an objection that's not coming. There is nothing on this earth that would cause me to make a single sound right now. Instead, I plead to him inside my mind. *Please. Please, Damian. Please.*

Damian answers my prayers, and his lips crash into mine. His hands cup my face, drinking me in deeper and deeper. My fingers trace the edge of his tie, too scared to do anything more as if I'd startle him and he'd back away. Damian comes up for air, smirking as he reaches down and rips off his tie clip, flinging it across the room.

"I really hate that thing," he chuckles. "But it getting in your way was the last straw."

With that, something snaps in me. His tie is wrapped around my hand as I yank him back down to me, my other hand weaving in his hair. He's kissed me before as Gemma, but this… This is something else entirely. A floodgate within him has burst, and something feral has been released.

A deep growl rumbles from his throat as he hitches my thighs around his back, carrying me to his bed as he flings his jacket to the floor. Our lips don't separate as we undress layer after layer. His cufflinks, our gun holsters, my knives.

"Goddamn, Viv," Damian whispers, glancing at the arsenal on the nightstand next to me. "All that and you still ran out of bullets?"

"I'd be happy to take you through a play by play of where each bullet went," I say as I slide my pants past my ankles, "or I could fuck you. Unfortunately, we only have time for one or the other."

"It takes that long to satisfy you?" Damian murmurs into my neck as he rubs my thighs.

"I did this for a living," I remind him as I slide his tie free of his neck. "The things I'm going to do to you…" He shivers in anticipation.

"In that case." He rips my shirt open, buttons flying everywhere.

"Hey!" I protest, but he quickly shushes me with another kiss.

"I'll order you a hundred new suits if it means I can get this one off you a little faster."

Good argument. The rest of our clothes fall off quickly under this new logic, until I am kneeling on the mattress in a sports bra and my underwear.

For a moment, I worry that Damian's going to be disappointed. I'm not Gemma. I'm not perfectly shaven wearing nothing but small strips of lacy lingerie. I'm Vivianna, with fresh cuts from getting thrown through a pane of glass and a supportive full-coverage bra that allows me to grapple men twice my size. Yet his eyes scan my body with nothing but reverence.

"Bellissima," Damian breathes, a catch in his throat. He lays me down on his silk sheets gently, his hands roaming the sides of my body. "My *bellissima.*"

"You don't have to keep flirting," I tease, trying not to blush. "I'm kind of a sure thing."

"I promised to never take you for granted, Vivianna." He leaves a trail of kisses from my neck down to my collarbone. I moan, shuddering beneath his touch. "I don't tend to break my promises."

My bra joins the pile of fabric on the floor, and Damian is nestled between my legs immediately, massaging my chest.

"Do you like pain with your pleasure or do you prefer an all-sweet variety of loving?" His fingers lightly tweak my nipples and goosebumps prick up under his gaze.

"Anything you want," I whisper, running my fingernails along his biceps.

"I have all night to unravel your secrets, Viv," he says, rolling a nipple between his thumb and forefinger. "But you can shorten my learning curve with some actual answers. What do you want?"

"I want to show you what you bought that first night in the Masquerade." I slide into my best sultry voice and wrap my legs around his waist, trying to flip our positions, but he resists. He furrows his brows as he brushes the hair out of my face, scrutinizing my expression. "What?"

"You've never had sex before," he utters, a surprised realization crossing his face.

"Excuse me?" My face is deadpan except for my raised eyebrow. "Damian, I was a whore. I used to have sex professionally. I'm kind of an expert in that department."

"Okay, semantics." He leans back on his heels. "You've never had sex you weren't paid for."

"What makes you say that?" Suddenly defensive, I sit up.

"You're not answering any of my questions, and you keep trying to pimp yourself to me." There's no judgment in Damian's voice, only curiosity. "I'm right, aren't I?"

"I can still make you happy," I purr as my fingers trail over his upper thighs, trying to salvage our night. "I was a girl at your best club for a reason."

"That's why you don't know what you want." He ignores my advances, tilting my chin up to meet him. I've never had a client this stubborn before. If he would just shut up, I would gladly fuck him. For free. Hell, I'd pay him at this point. "You've never had someone take the time to help you find what you like."

"Damian, you mansplaining sex to me is not going to get either of us off," I grumble, getting frustrated.

"Have you ever had someone finger you?" His blunt question catches me off guard, but he can see the answer on my shocked face. "Really? What about go down on you?"

"People pay to receive oral, not give it." I change tactics, running my finger on the inside of his waistband, hoping that's enough to refocus him. "If you ask nicely, I could be convinced to do some anal though."

"I would have paid to go down on you." The lustful tilt to his voice is back. "If I had known that was a menu item, I would have given you all the cash I had for just a taste."

"Relax, you don't have to pretend to like going down on girls." I roll my eyes. "I'm not going to judge you."

"Vivianna!" He gasps, and for a second, I think his horror is real. Wait, no. It is. This man is horrified by what I said. "I don't just like going down on girls, I *love* it. The way I make them come as their arousal drips down my chin, there's nothing like it. Any real man would agree with me."

"Come on, Damian!" I smack the mattress, losing my patience. "Lay down and let me fuck you!"

He grabs my waist and pulls me flush with his body, eyeing me greedily. Finally.

"Do you trust me?" He whispers. Oh, Jesus Christ, does this man not understand how sex works?

"Yeah, sure." I ignore him and start nibbling on his ear, my hands roaming further south. I'll jump-start his sex drive manually.

"Vivianna…" Damian grabs one of my hands in each of his, asking for my full attention. "Do you trust me?"

"Yes," I sigh.

He stands and searches through the pile of clothes.

Fuck, I'm not getting laid tonight. I thought I had this in the bag. How did I blow this? But then he comes back with his tie dangling lazily around his neck.

"Lay down, Viv," he commands with a husky drawl. "Hands together by the headboard."

"Bondage is extra," I tease, but I do what he says.

"Send me an invoice tomorrow." He grins, knotting the tie tightly around my wrists and tying me to the headboard. "Now, if we're going to do this, you have to be honest with me. If you don't like something, tell me and I'll adjust or stop doing it. If I begin to think that you're lying or faking, I'm kicking you out."

"And what if I do like something?" I taunt, testing the strength of my restraints.

"I'll know." A roguish glint flashes across his eyes, and my panties are soaked.

"Okay then." I lean back on the pillow with an exhale. "Do your worst."

Damian slowly crawls over my body, heat radiating from his skin. I reach out to caress his cheek, already forgetting my hands are bound above my head. He smirks when he sees me tugging. It hasn't even been five seconds.

"Careful," he scolds playfully. "You'll stretch out my tie."

Before I can counter, his lips connect with mine, silencing the sass I was about to dish out. This is different than the Damian of five minutes ago, all ferocity replaced with tenderness, though the underlying passion and desire is still there. He catches my bottom lip beneath his teeth, giving it a gentle tug.

I lean into his kiss as his hands explore my torso, running along my stomach and ribs, finding a place to rest on my breasts. He circles my nipples with his thumbs, and my eyes flutter closed.

This is about as far most of my clients get before all of the attention turns back to them. Men love tits, so I already know I love this. He gradually increases the pressure, switching to pinching and twisting. Ooh, I like this. I liked it even more as his tongue joined his hand, though I did miss his sweet kisses. He swirls the buds around as I take a shaky breath, leaning my head back. Then, he bites down on the sensitive skin.

"Ow!" I yelp. Damian sits up immediately, hands in the air, staring at me intently. I stare back, not knowing what to say besides, "That hurt."

"Sorry." He smirks. One hand goes back down to rub away the lingering sting. Serious again he asks, "Do you want less teeth or no teeth?"

"I can take it if you like that." I lean back with a deep breath.

"Got it, no teeth." Damian teases a nipple again.

"That's not what I said," I protest, squirming beneath him.

"Viv, there are a million things that I would like to do to your body," he purrs with a lick along the curve of my breast. "I won't miss a few things being crossed off the list."

"But—" I start to counter him, but the sensation of his fingernails scraping down my ribcage stops the words in my throat, turning them into a breathy moan.

"Oh, we really liked that," Damian chuckles, repeating the action as my eyes roll into the back of my head. I try to nod, but even that takes too much mental focus.

Damian starts to multitask, his mouth toying with a nipple, one hand grazing my ribs, and the other sliding down my body between my legs. He brushes over my folds, and I eagerly spread my legs. A cocky smile crosses Damian's face as he peels off my panties and slides a finger between my lips. A curse falls from my mouth as he circles my entrance, slowly at first, then gaining speed.

"Oh god," I groan, arching my back as he slips a finger inside me.

"That's a funny way of pronouncing my name." He abandons my tits to kiss my neck, his sensual whispers tickling my skin. "But I'll take it."

Damian adds a second finger to the fray, firmly stroking them against my inner walls. I struggle to stay still, to not buck my hips or grind against him, but I lose all control as his thumb brushes against my clit.

"Fuck, Damian!" I exclaim, writhing beneath him.

"Say my name again, Viv," he growls. "Tell me how good my hands feel in your pussy."

"Damian, you feel perfect." I strain against the tie binding my wrists to the headboard. "Oh god, Damian. I… Oh god."

"This image will be burned into my mind forever," he purrs. "You clenching around my fingers, desperately pulling at my tie, my name on your lips. It's taking everything in me not to slam my dick into your wet cunt right now."

"Do it," I beg. "Fuck me, please."

"Soon, Vivianna," he promises, his breath warming the skin of my neck. "There's just one thing I want to show you first."

Damian shifts to kneel between my legs, fondly massaging my thighs. He leans down, but I scoot out of his way.

"You don't have to," I blurt, angling my hips away. "We can skip straight to fucking."

"I know I don't *have* to." He pulls me back. "This isn't a chore, Viv. This is dessert."

"What?" I joke. "Are we out of ice cream downstairs?"

"I have a feeling you will taste so much better than ice cream." A mischievous glint flashes in his eyes, but it doesn't soothe my anxious nerves.

"You can't honestly believe that," I breathe.

"Then I'll prove it," Damian says defiantly.

Before I can ask how, he's dragging two fingers between my legs. His eyes don't leave mine as he brings them dripping to his lips, sucking them clean. A euphoric expression crosses his face though he tries to stay stoic, but then he caves, closing his eyes as he fists the sheets in his other hand.

"Damn it, Viv," he groans. "You taste even better than I imagined. Now let me enjoy my reward for making you so fucking wet."

He lowers himself between my thighs, and my heart nearly explodes in my chest. I scoot away but he just crawls closer. His breath on my exposed center sends shivers up my spine.

It's too much, it's too strong, I can't take it. His tongue flicks out, sending shockwaves through my system. I panic, shoving him away with the heel of my foot. Damian yelps as he tumbles off the bed.

Shit, that was so not an Ombra thing to do.

"Good thing I tied you up earlier," Damian jokes, rubbing his shoulder. "I'd hate to imagine what you would've done if your hands were free."

"I'm so sorry." I try to sit up, but obviously can't. "I don't know what happened. It was just so much and I—"

"Shhh, it's okay, Viv." Damian climbs back on the mattress with a sly smile. "I'll go slower this time."

"Wait!" I clench my legs together in alarm. "I can't!"

"Hey, I've got you." He sits next to me and brushes a thumb over my cheek. "I would never do anything to hurt you. I'm hearing that it was too intense, so I'll make sure we build up to it. It'll feel good, Viv."

I want to believe him, want to be vulnerable and give up control to him, but then I just remember the overwhelming sensation and I can't bring myself to move.

"I am going to be a massive hypocrite, so I will not blame you if you tell me to go to hell," Damian whispers, twirling a strand of my hair around his finger. "But I really want to do this for you. Give me thirty seconds, that's it. If you like it, we can keep going. If you don't, I'll drop it, full stop. But Vivianna, I really think you'll like it. Please. Thirty seconds."

Hesitantly, I spread my legs. The cheeky grin he has as he settles below me, goddamn, I would do anything he asked. His elbows pin down my thighs — a lesson from last time — and with a wink, he begins.

True to his word, he goes slower, flattening his tongue and dragging it across my opening. The same unusual shiver appears, this time starting at the tips of my toes. I hold my breath, waiting for it to drown me, but it doesn't.

Instead, a pink flush rises in my cheeks, and I feel a tingle creep through my arms. I squirm slightly, and Damian presses tightly against my legs, placing flirtatious kisses along my thighs. Once I still, he gradually shifts his focus to my clit, skirting around the bud with his tongue. He's so close but deliberately avoids the spot I want him the most.

My eyes flutter closed as I tilt my hips, craving the sensation of him. As if an answer to my silent prayers, I feel the softest flick against my clit. I gasp as the tingle inside me flares, washing me in an intoxicating high.

"Thirty seconds, as promised," Damian says, releasing his hold on me. He goes on to try and say something else but doesn't get the chance when my legs wrap around his neck and jerk him back down.

"More," I beg, desperately. "Please."

"Oh fuck yes."

Damian's nails dig into the flesh of my hips, pulling me ever closer as he passionately dives back into me. Steadily, the tingles in my limbs grow, matching the twisting knot in my gut. Every wall I've built tumbles down, leaving me exposed and vulnerable, delirious tears streaming down my cheeks. The feeling is so strong, constantly threatening to overwhelm my body, but Damian deftly toes the line, shifting techniques as soon as I feel it's too much. My fists clench as I arch my back, approaching my climax.

"Damian," I moan, barely able to speak. "I'm going to come. I... Oh god, Damian."

I try to squirm away, but Damian presses his forearm firmly into my pelvis, keeping me securely where he wants me. His tongue flicks at my clit with a renewed vigor, listening to the sounds of my choked sobs as he keeps me building toward release. I grab on to the headboard when I can't hold back any longer, crying out as I climax on his tongue. He doesn't let up, lapping up every bit of me as I lay shaking on the mattress. When he surfaces, his glistening lips are curved into an arrogant grin.

"Much better than ice cream," he taunts, licking his lips.

I roll my eyes, and a feral gleam flashes across Damian's eyes. He slowly crawls over me, each movement sinful and precise. His hand cradles the back of my neck before his mouth roughly collides with mine. I submit willingly, moaning as I feel his bare chest press against my torso. This kiss is different than the ones before, a subtle taste lingering on his tongue, slightly tangy with a hint of salt. It's kinda nice.

"Much better," Damian whispers, a hair's breadth away from kissing me again. "So much better."

"Is it my turn to find out how you taste?" I stare into his eyes as I feel his cock twitch against my hips.

"Next time." His voice is husky and deep with need. "I don't think I can wait another second to feel you around me."

"Mmm." I arch my back, pressing my chest into his. "That sounds like a fantastic idea."

"Let me untie you really quick." His hands trail up my arms.

"Wait!" I blurt, my fingers curling around the pegs of the headboard. Damian stills, his eyes scanning my hands and making their way down to my face.

"Vivianna Palazzo." He smirks with a soft chuckle. "You like being tied up, don't you?"

"It's fine," I stammer. His eyes darken at those words, those damn words that always betray my innermost thoughts. "You can untie me."

"You're right, I *can* untie you." Damian yanks my hips toward him until my wrists are taut against the bed frame. My breathing quickens as he slides out of his briefs, nestling between my legs. "But I think I like you where you are right now. Staring up at me with those fuck-me eyes, your flushed cheeks. Goddamn, Viv, you're not going anywhere."

I gasp as he digs his nails into my skin. He slides inside me and Oh. My. God. It's even better than I dreamed it would be. My eyes roll to the back of my head as he presses against my walls. A guttural groan escapes his mouth, so I know it's just as good for him. I wrap my legs around his back, pulling him flush against me, needing to feel all of him. His thrusts take my breath away, sending tremors through my body. I rock my hips, and Damian curses under his breath. He shifts his weight, propping himself up on a hand near my shoulder. His other hand caresses my body, leaving a blazing path in its wake.

"It's like you were made for me," Damian groans. "Your striking eyes, your addicting smile, your perfect cunt. There's not a part of you that I would change."

"You are an incorrigible flirt."

"Doesn't mean that I'm not telling the truth." He nips at my ear, and I laugh. His eyes twinkle, amused.

Tender kisses dot my neck, my collarbone. His movements quicken, and I can tell he's getting close. I clench my walls around him, and he sucks air through his teeth. His eyes dart to mine, utterly adoring him. I'm so busy staring that I miss his hand moving and jerk in surprise as his fingers rub my clit.

"We're going to come together," Damian orders, his firm circles matching the rhythm of his thrusts.

I'm not normally good at following orders, but there's a first time for everything.

Damian screams my name as he thrusts into me a final time, and I come undone beneath him. His eyes flash, something possessive taking over him, and he bites down on the side of my neck, sucking until a dark hickey forms. My pulse flutters at the feeling of his teeth on my skin mixed with my subsiding climax. His breathing slows as he comes down, and he slides the tie free of my wrists, giving each one a gentle kiss.

I nuzzle into his chest as Damian lays down, his hand pulls one of my legs across his hips. We lay there for a few minutes, mindlessly running our fingers over each other in a comfortable post-sex embrace. He chuckles and I glance up to him.

"What's funny?" I ask with a smile.

"Nothing." He shakes his head. I patiently stare at him, waiting. "Okay, so you know how until now you've never had sex with someone who wasn't paying you to?"

"If you keep making fun of me for that, I'll send you an invoice," I threaten, though my tone is light-hearted.

"I was just thinking how if you tilt your head and squint a little bit..." He does so, almost subconsciously. "It's kinda like I took your virginity."

"Oh fuck off." I groan and turn away, but Damian tugs me back to him.

"You didn't even squint," he jokes, running his fingers through my hair. "Tell me, in your professional experience, how do I compare?"

"Nuh-uh." I flick his chest. "Your ego wouldn't fit through the door if I told you."

"That good, huh?" He winks as I roll my eyes. "Kidding, I'm just kidding."

"Real funny guy you are." I lay my head back on his shoulder, and he pulls me closer. His heartbeat is steady, soothing, peaceful. "Remember my first day, how I stormed into your office?"

"Of course I do," he laughs, a warm sound that fills the room. "You made sure of it. That was one of the scariest moments of my life."

"Was not!" I protest.

"It so was!" He tousles my hair. "Picture this, you're in your office doing the most monotonous paperwork in the world and then a firecracker of a person is throwing shoes at you and screaming about respect before the door even fully closes. Mind you — this person had just bodied someone and pointed a gun at your top lieutenants a few days prior. I was fully expecting you to jump over my desk and throttle me, and I had no idea what I even did to piss you off."

"I would never hurt you," I whisper, concern drawing my eyebrows down.

"I know that now." Damian kisses my forehead. "I didn't know then. Anyways, you were saying?"

"I mentioned not being your little sex toy." I smile, remembering my tirade. "Since you wanted to revise my job description, I figured maybe we should add that in. There's been some persuasive arguments made in favor of that clause."

"I'd have to check with my HR rep." He smirks, rubbing my thigh. "She's real strict about our sexual harassment policies, and I would hate to have her enforce those on me."

"Did I or did I not just say I would never hurt you?" I trace the lines of his abs. "Fortunately, organizational policy does not supersede my duty as an Ombra."

"What about my orders?" His voice quiets as he brushes the hair from my face. "Does your Ombra code outweigh those?"

"Yes." The mood of the room shifts, tension lurking around the edges of the baseboards.

"Viv—"

"Don't do this," I beg, interrupting whatever spiel he was about to give. I force my gaze away from his hurt expression, looking at the dark hardwood floors or the gray paint on the walls or anywhere else in the room than at him. "Don't make me talk to Mr. Marano when I'm naked in your arms. You can lecture me tomorrow, and I'll yell right back at you, but I can't fight with you right now. Don't make me."

"That's fair," Damian sighs, stroking my hair. "I'm sorry."

I don't respond beyond sitting up, pulling my knees to my chest. Damian sits up too, rubbing my back.

"This doesn't have to change anything," he says softly, each word like a stab in my chest. "We can still be professional during the day and save whatever this is for when we're alone at night. You can be my Ombra and I can be your pain-in-the-ass. This doesn't have to change anything."

This… this doesn't mean anything to him, not like it does to me. He just wants to feel the warmth of my skin, feel the gentle kisses from my lips. I don't know what I expected him to say. What? *I love you, Viv. I have since we were children. Our parents could never keep us apart.* Don't be ridiculous, Vivianna.

"Are you okay?" He asks, spurring me from my trance of self-pity.

I almost say those two words. The ones that he's learned too well, that would reveal everything to him. My hurt. My heartbreak. But I know better now than to say, "I'm fine."

"I'm great." I bury my head in his neck as I straddle his lap, using kisses to hide the tears welling in my eyes. He's not mine forever, but he's mine for now. I'd rather have part of him than none of him. "Now, how about I show you what I can do when my hands are free?"

CHAPTER 12
DAMIAN

I am such a dumbass.

Really. For someone who is so proud of their observational skills, I am an absolute idiot. This whole fucking time, I've been studying Viv, trying to learn her tells. I noticed a trend — her heart racing, her eyes widening, her breath catching in her throat. I always thought she was nervous, anxious about a mission or whatever, but I was wrong, oh so wrong. It was never fear. It was *lust.* Her pressing against my back on the motorcycle, my hand wrapping around her throat, her clinging to me at the lake. Lust.

I am such a dumbass.

I could tell something was bothering her though. I didn't think about how she would feel about the lines between us blurring. She's my Ombra, and she's made it clear that is the most important thing in the world to her. So I told her nothing would change. She could be my Ombra during the day and my companion at night. What was I supposed to say? *Stop being my Ombra, Viv. Stop trying to die for me because you are what I live for every day. I love you, bellissima.* Don't be ridiculous. She would shoot me before she let me go.

So I promised her nothing would change, but that was a lie. My hands brush against hers at every opportunity, I stare out my office window every time she walks by, my heart stops when she looks at me. It's been over a week, and my appetite for her seems to be insatiable. During the day, I pretend she's just another one of the guys, but at night I taste her on my tongue, hold her body against mine, allow her to bring me pleasure I have no business feeling. She's my Ombra. She puts her life on the line for me every time I step outside. Yet I can't stop.

She's my Ombra. Enzo can go fuck himself, Vivianna is my Ombra. I haven't asked Enzo to escort me anywhere since the fiasco that was the distribution center. Not that he did anything particularly wrong, more so that Viv... I can't stand to be away from her.

"Mr. Marano, I really have no reason to get involved, one way or the other." Mr. O'Reilly shrugs. "I feel for you, I really do, but the Petrovs are assholes. I don't need them poking around my businesses."

Sebastian, Marco, and I are sitting at a conference table in the back of one of O'Reilly's pubs. He has a few of his men sitting around him, as well as one man standing against the wall next to Viv. Her long black hair is braided back out of her face, but today she's decided to wrap the end into a sleek bun. I don't know why she changed it, maybe trying to look more professional for the meeting today. I don't care. She looks gorgeous.

"Mr. O'Reilly, I don't think you see what's at stake here," I say, nursing my whiskey — the best part of a business meeting with the Irish. "The Petrovs are getting cocky, throwing their weight around. If they start thinking that's acceptable, they won't just stop with my organization. They'll push on you, on the Cubans, on the Japanese. The fragile balance of peace we've all worked so hard for will crumble."

"I don't know." He frowns, rubbing his thick red beard. "Have you talked to any of the other families yet?"

"You think I would go to them first?" I gasp, a playful amount of shock in my voice. "Mr. O'Reilly, our families have always been close. Don't tell me you didn't get the bottle of whiskey I sent over on St. Paddy's?"

"Aye, and the bottle on Christmas too." His green eyes twinkle.

It's a small gesture, but my father always gave the O'Reillys two bottles of nice Irish whiskey as a gift every year. I made sure we kept up the tradition after he passed. They return the favor with two fine bottles of Italian reds on Christmas and Easter. Mr. O'Reilly doesn't have to know we also send the Cubans rum and the Japanese sake.

I see a slight movement in my peripheral vision — Viv shifting her hands behind her back, shoulders tense, lips set in a firm line. My attention returns to the meeting at hand.

"Help us out, Mr. O'Reilly." I look him in the eyes. "Even just a public admonition. I'm not asking you to drop everything and go charging in, I'm asking for a show of friendship and support."

Mr. O'Reilly purses his lips, reclining in his chair. He leans toward his second, conferring quietly.

Another movement draws my attention. The Irish man on the wall. He's standing incredibly close to Viv, their shoulders practically touching. Viv takes a half-step to her left, and the gap is almost immediately closed by him. I lock eyes with Viv and lazily beckon her over to me with one finger.

I'm not Damian right now, I'm Mr. Marano, but I'm sure as hell going to take care of my girl. I just need to do it in a certain way to keep up appearances.

She strides to my chair, leaning over my shoulder. I take a slow sip of my drink before turning my head.

"Is that man bothering you?" I whisper in her ear, quietly enough that no one else can hear.

"No, sir." Her response is clipped, perfunctory, full Ombra mode. It's hard to read her when she's like this. Well, harder than normal.

"Are you sure?" Maybe I read into this too much, maybe she's all good.

"Yes, sir." Huh. Okay, then.

I dismiss her with a wave. She retreats to the back wall, eyes carefully watching the surroundings for the slightest sign of trouble.

Mr. O'Reilly returns his attention to the meeting, and I smile, shifting in my chair slightly. To him, it seems like I'm relaxing, more comfortable, but really, I'm adjusting to keep a better eye on Viv.

"You see, when my ancestors came over all those years ago, kinship was the only thing that got us through..." he starts to ramble. Goddamn it, not another Mr. O'Reilly story.

Having heard this upwards of twenty times before, I allow myself to zone out slightly. And that's when I see it.

A hand brushing her thigh.

Her face is expressionless, absolutely and utterly blank, and I know that can only mean one thing. She. Is. Pissed. I can feel my gaze darken. This asshole has the audacity to touch her? To touch my girl? Oh hell, no.

Viv clears her throat softly, and my eyes whip up to hers. A subtle shake of the head. *No.* How cute. She's trying to tell me what to do. But it's not up to Viv, is it?

"Excuse me." I'm sure I interrupted Mr. O'Reilly's story, but I don't give a damn. The whiskey burns my throat as I take another sip, walking to Viv. I can tell she is trying so hard not to roll her eyes, embarrassed by my concern. She can suck it up.

"Let me ask my earlier question in different terms," I murmur, close enough for my breath to kiss her skin. "Right now, you are a direct representation of me and my organization. How people treat you is a reflection of how they think of me, any insult to you therefore extends to me as well. Now, Vivianna, am I offended by this man to your right?"

"Yes, sir. You are." Her shoulders relax slightly at her confession.

"Thank you."

I step back and take a second to look at the offender in question. Early to mid-twenties. Typical enforcer type with big muscles and bruised fists. Quick to anger, slow to reasoning. Interesting.

"Have you met Vivianna before?" I ask, gesturing at her with my glass.

"No, sir." The "sir" is a nice touch, but it's a little too late for respect.

"She's really pretty, isn't she?" I smile, appearing light-hearted and casual. Just two guys chatting about a girl.

"Excuse me?" He furrows his eyebrows together, confused.

"Vivianna is pretty, yes?" My whiskey swirls in my glass, the ice clinking quietly.

"Yes, sir." He nods. "She is."

"That's not why I hired her." I place a hand in my pocket as I lean in, as though I was sharing a secret. "I hired her because she has an even prettier right hook."

"I don't know, sir." He finally smiles, relaxing into our conversation. "That's really saying something."

"Don't believe me?" A bitter laugh escapes my lips. "Maybe she'll get the chance to show you in a minute."

"I'm not worried about her, sir." The asshole leans back against the wall.

"Why not?" I look at Viv, who is just shy of glaring at me. "She looks pretty intimidating to me."

"For starters, she's a woman." He gestures at her disparagingly, oblivious to the anger brewing in my eyes. "Second, that nasty scar means she can't hold her own in a fight. Just be glad you're hanging with the O'Reillys. We'll keep you safe."

I glance over my shoulder at the conference table. The five men sitting there are quietly chatting among themselves, unaware of the rising tension by the back wall. I turn back to the man before me.

"Here's a little secret. Vivianna is the most skilled fighter I know. She could kill you, me, or anyone else in this room if she chose." My smirk drops to reveal a wrathful glare. "Apologize. Now."

"Excuse me?" His voice raises. I don't give a fuck.

"No, not like that," I snarl. "I was thinking more like 'I'm sorry I harassed you.' 'I'm sorry I'm a waste of space.' 'I'm sorry that I am an embarrassment—'"

I don't get to finish my last example as the asshole steps off the wall, fist raised by his cheek. He throws his punch, but I don't even flinch. Why? Because I know Viv's right there.

She catches his fist in her left hand, immediately clocking him with her right fist. He staggers back and this time, she's the one to close the gap, a solid kick to his chest knocking him to the floor. As if nothing happened, she retakes her spot on the wall, straightening out her suit as he is sprawled on the floor, cursing and holding his jaw.

"Did that feel good?" I smirk.

"Why yes, sir." A faint smile creeps onto her face, and she lets it stay. "It did."

"I'm glad."

"What do you think you're doing?" O'Reilly shouts at his henchman. "Why on God's green pasture would you raise a hand to a guest in my pub? Get out of here before he asks for your head. I have half a mind to give it to him!"

The now-recovered asshole takes several steps away before scrambling out of the room entirely. Viv relaxes, and now so do I, feeling her protective gaze lingering over me.

"Sorry for the interruption. Where were we?" I smile and pick up my whiskey glass, making unbothered eye contact with a ruffled Mr. O'Reilly. "You were telling a story?"

"For the life of me, I can't remember what I was saying," he mumbles. Thank god for small miracles.

"What a shame," I lie smoothly, finishing my drink. "Regardless, I'm sure you have other things to do with your evening, maybe watching a game of rugby with your men. I'd love to get out of your hair, but I really need an answer from you."

"Ah, that's what we were discussing." He nods as composes himself. "While we would prefer to avoid an all-out war, the Irish will back you politically. If you need anything, resources or weapons or the like, please send us a message. Perhaps we can provide some under-the-table assistance."

"We won't forget this, Mr. O'Reilly." I stand and shake his hand, a genuine smile on my face. "Thank you for your support."

"Best of luck, Mr. Marano."

With that, I summon Viv from her spot on the wall, and my entourage walks out from the pub. Two SUVs are waiting. I gesture for Marco and Sebastian to take one, while I guide Viv toward the other. Marco falters in his step. Normally we would ride together, debrief. He is my second after all. But there's someone — erm, some*thing* else I need to do first. The car door closes behind me, and I check to ensure the divider to the front seat is closed.

"You didn't have to do that," Viv sighs, grabbing her seatbelt. "I can handle a—"

I hold her head with both hands as I crash my lips into hers, kneeling over the cup holders. I don't pull away until my lungs are screaming for air, and even then, I wait as long as I can. Her chest is heaving as I lean back. My eyes don't leave hers as I grab her right hand, the one that so beautifully punched that asshole, and bring her knuckles to my mouth for a gentle kiss. The car turns onto the road.

"You should put on your seatbelt," she whispers.

I smirk, latching the buckle with a click. It isn't fair to hold this against her. Her wide eyes and flushed cheeks tell me she wants this, but we're not at the compound. She's on duty, and she's made it clear, Ombra comes first. But damn it, Viv. I just want to lay you back and eat you out until you scream my name loud enough for even that asshole at the pub to hear. But I'll click on my seatbelt obediently because I know it'll stress you out otherwise, and I'll hold your hand until I can hold you.

Viv leans her head on my shoulder, and I stroke her hair until the car parks in the garage. As soon as the wheels stop spinning, I take a breath and adjust my tie, slipping back into Mr. Marano. I've got paperwork to do.

Marco is waiting for me outside of my office, and I gesture for him to sit down, latching the door behind us.

"So we've got the Irish on our side," he mulls, rubbing his chin. "Are we thinking the Yakuza next?"

"I was going to play that by ear." I shrug. "I'm almost wondering if either family will approach me since the O'Reillys are committing."

"They really made us work for that though," he grumbles, leaning back in his chair. "I was expecting that to be more of a formality than an actual ask."

"Hey, we made it out of there with only half of a long-winded story." I pick up a pen and the top form of my pile, a sales report for one of the clubs. Sign. Move on. "I consider that a success."

"Speaking of which, what happened with the guard back there?" There's a slight edge to his voice, and I don't feel like that's the question he's actually asking.

"He insulted me." I sign another sales report, not even bothering to look up. "I took care of it."

"Insulted you or insulted her?"

"Does it matter?" My pen snaps back onto my desk. The sharp sound accentuating my annoyance. "An insult to my Ombra is an insult to me."

"You risked our relationship with the Irish over a childish crush," Marco spits. He unbuttons the top button of his shirt, pulling the fabric away from his neck. "You're lucky you didn't offend the O'Reillys. You could have fucked our plan entirely, all because you're pining over some girl."

"Careful, Marco," I warn, authority lacing my voice. "You're on thin ice."

"My apologies," he sneers. "I thought I couldn't talk to her, didn't realize I couldn't talk *about* her as well. Damian—"

"Mr. Marano."

"You can't be serious," Marco huffs. "I raised you, Damian."

"Mister. Marano." My stare is hardened, unwavering. "I've outgrown your tutelage. Thank you, but I no longer need a regent to help me rule my empire. *My* empire. You can continue to serve in the role of my second, within the parameters of that position."

"Don't you see what is happening?" Marco stands, leaning over my desk. "That harlot is weaving her way between your legs. She's trying to replace me, whispering in your ear until she can usurp your mafia and take control for herself. Don't let her convince you to push me away."

"The only person responsible for you getting 'pushed away' is you." I match his stance so we're face to face. "She doesn't talk about you at all. She is so unconcerned with your presence, while you seem to be obsessed with her. Why, Marco? Are you intimidated by her? Scared that I won't need you anymore?"

"Oh, you'll need me," he goads. "When you're on your knees and she's holding a knife to your throat. When you watch everything your family built crumble to the ground. I just have one question, is she worth it?"

I grip the edge of my desk tightly, but Marco doesn't falter.

"Have you fucked her yet or are you still pretending you haven't?" His voice lowers austerely. I'm not Damian, I'm Mr. Marano. I have to keep my shit together. I'm not Damian. "How long until you convince yourself that she loves you?"

I'm Mr. Marano. I'm Mr. Marano. I'm… Fuck it.

"I don't need her to love me," I whisper with a smirk. "I'm already obsessed with her. So if she wants your job, fine. She can have it. I wouldn't even think twice. I'd do anything she asks to keep her by my side."

I don't see his fist coming.

My head whips back, sending me stumbling. Marco jumps over the desk, yanking my tie to pull me to him. I try to push him away, but his grip is strong. He slams me against the wall hard enough to rattle the shelving.

"Do you know what I've sacrificed?" He roars as I struggle. "Everything I've done?"

"Don't pretend that anything you've done was for me!" I shout, thrashing in his grasp. I hear the door slam open as bystanders come to break up the fight. "You're loyal to my father, not me. Newsflash Marco, he's dead! You're the one who has to live with that guilt."

He gets one more punch in before Sebastian forces his way between us and Tony pulls Marco off. Several more men are needed to push him out the door.

I bend over to pick up papers that scattered onto the floor, slamming them onto my desk.

"Here." Sebastian passes me an ice pack, and I hiss as I hold it to my soon-to-be black eye. He closes the office door, shooing away the last stragglers. "You all good?"

"Just dandy," I snap.

"If you need me or Tony to intervene, we can." His tone is gentle.

I force myself to relax. Of everyone in my organization, Sebastian and Tony are the two I trust the most. They never worked for my dad, they have no allegiance to the mafia of old. They are loyal to me, and only me. That's why I made him my capo and Tony my lead enforcer.

"It's not necessary." I wave him off. He shrugs, picking up books and reshelving them. "I escalated the conversation. Marco will be fine once he cools off. Besides, I'm not the one he should be worried about."

"What do you mean?" Sebastian raises an eyebrow as he settles into a chair.

"What do you think Viv is going to do when she sees my black eye?" I smirk, and I swear he pales slightly.

"She's going to kill him," he mumbles. "Should we warn him? Send him to a safe house?"

"Nah." A small chuckle escapes my composed demeanor. "I'll just have to break the news gently."

"Doesn't she scare you?" Sebastian shifts in his seat. "The way she is so blasé about killing? She's so… cold."

"What do you mean?" Surely we can't be talking about the same person. Viv? The girl whose laughter I chase like a drug? Cold?

"Vivianna…" He shivers. "Sometimes I look at her, and there's nothing behind her eyes. Just a hollow, detached killing machine. Not even Enzo is like that."

"It's complicated." I frown, shifting the ice in my hand. "Life hasn't been easy for her, even more so than with Enzo. She feels everything, deeply and painfully, but keeps her emotions close to her chest. If you get to know her though, you'll find someone who will tear the world apart to protect those she cares about. And her smile…"

I clear my throat and sit up in my chair, realizing how soft my voice had gotten, how my frown had faded as I was picturing her face. I can't be Damian right now. I have to be Mr. Marano.

"Sir, hypothetically speaking..." Sebastian speaks quietly, his words hushed as though he was worried about someone overhearing them. "If someone perhaps was interested in developing a more intimate relationship with her, it might be best for them to act sooner rather than later."

"I beg your pardon?" I raise an eyebrow, though my walls are now carefully in place.

"All I'm saying is that I was in the gym with her the other day while she was training." He leans in, eyes locked onto mine. "There were some marks on her neck that looked suspiciously like hickeys. If someone was wanting to pursue something outside of a professional setting, they might have some competition to deal with. Hypothetically."

"Hypothetically." I nod as I lean back in my chair, doing everything I can to keep my mask from slipping. I know the marks he's referring to. I made them. Though I am a bit peeved he caught on to my interest in her. "Has anyone else brought up similar concerns or is this thought experiment contained to the two of us?"

"Hard to say, sir." Sebastian thinks for a moment. "As far as the interests of present company, no one has voiced any matters to me. I, myself, have only begun to suspect certain interests due to the message from Bruno, which I have not shared with a soul."

"I appreciate that." I pick up a pen and twirl it in my fingers. "Can I trust that your hypothesis will share the same discretion?"

"Of course!" He seems shocked I would even ask. To be fair, I have complete faith in his secret-keeping abilities. He wouldn't be my capo if I didn't.

"Thank you, Sebastian." I shift through some of the papers on my desk, sorting them into their correct piles.

"Any time, Mr. Marano." He takes the hint and stands, leaving my office with a friendly smile.

I really should take him and Tony out for dinner sometime, reward their hard work and dedication. I would ask someone to set that up for me, but ironically, that would be Sebastian. I'll have to do it myself.

I call the host of one of the restaurants I own and reserve a private booth, then text our driving team to arrange transport. When all is said and done, I send a calendar invite to Sebastian, Tony, Marco, and Viv. After a second thought, I add Enzo as well. If he doesn't come, things between Viv and me will be more suspicious than they already are.

The stack of unresolved paperwork glares at me as I close out of my calendar on my phone. I really, really don't feel like going through the pile today, but I've been putting it off too long. There is one person who could make the chore more tolerable though. My thumb hovers over her contact before pressing dial.

Damian? Her voice comes over the line slightly groggy. Fuck, what time is it? *Are you okay?*

"I'm safe, just in my office." I put the call on speakerphone and place it on my desk. "Where are you?"

My bedroom. She sounds much more awake now. *I'll be there in a minute.*

"No, stay there." I scan over an inventory report. "I need you to do something else for me."

Anything.

"I want to see how fast I can finish my paperwork while I hear your voice begging me to hurry so you can come." My voice lowers as I hear her gasp over the line. "Take off your clothes and lay on your bed."

What?

"Do not make me repeat myself, Vivianna," I scold, authority seeping into my voice. A beat passes.

Done. My cock twitches in my pants, picturing the sight of her naked and waiting. The inventory report is not nearly as enticing.

"Run your hands over your torso. Feel your beautiful curves for me."

Her soft breathing comes over the speaker, anticipatory and shallow. The numbers on the report aren't making sense. Our store of ammunition has practically halved in the past two weeks. I highlight the column and flag it to be reviewed again.

"Trail your fingers up to your tits." Her perfect, round tits. "Pinch your nipples."

She moans, but I'm not satisfied.

"Harder, Viv." A cry escapes her lips as she complies, and I loosen my tie, feeling my pulse race. Next paper — payroll. Everything seems in order at a cursory glance, good enough for me.

"Keep one hand there but use the other to drag your nails down your ribs, you know how you like it."

I can practically feel her skin beneath my fingers. How many fucking timecards need approved by me? Don't they know I have something better to hold than these nonsense papers?

"Is it just me or do I not hear you begging?" I taunt. "It's almost like you're content with only your hands touching you. Maybe I'll just work through the night and leave you to pleasure yourself without me."

No! Her protest is so sharp it startles me. *No, please. I want you to touch me, Damian.*

"Only a want?" I smirk, signing the timecards en masse. "How disappointing."

Need, she corrects. *I need you to touch me.*

"I would, but I have a pile of requisition forms to approve." I shrug. "It's going to be a minute."

I'll wait.

"That was never a question, *bellissima.*" Request to order more ammunition. Ah, there we go. Signed. "You're not allowed to come until I'm in the room with you."

Then perhaps I'll be waiting a little less patiently than before.

I chuckle as I review the next requisition form — a new semitruck for my gun-smuggling operations. Good news, we just stole two from the Russians. That division can have those. Denied purchase, with a note explaining my decision.

"How are you feeling, Vivianna?" I ask smoothly, as my pen signs my signature on a few approved purchases. "Are you ready to slide your hand between your thighs? Are you wet enough?"

Please, Damian. Oh god, please say I can.

"Since you said please." I smile, tapping my pen on my desk as I read over a contract. Seems we're trying out a new alcohol supplier for one of our clubs. "Go ahead, but just around your opening. Save your clit for me."

She groans in protest, but her complaint is quickly forgotten as her fingers venture south.

"And Viv? Keep working your nipples. I want them nice and sore when I get there."

Are you almost done? She whines. Oh, I should grab a bottle of wine for us to share after. *I need you to touch me.*

"Almost," I lie. But she doesn't have to know that quite yet.

Luckily the next chunk is papers I don't need to review, just sign so they can be sent to some bureaucratic office in some government agency. God, I hate the amount of paperwork involved in hiding crime from the feds. My hand cramps from the sheer number of times I sign my name.

Damian, please. I'm getting close.

"Wait for me, Vivianna," I order. "You do not get to come without me."

I don't know how much longer I can wait. Her desperate pleas have my dick straining against the fabric of my trousers.

"Not yet. Keep touching yourself."

I... Oh god... Damian, I can't hold it anymore. The way she says my name sends shivers up my spine. Is it possible it come just from hearing her voice?

"You're asking me to set aside my entire mafia just so you can climax?" I click my tongue disapprovingly. "You'll have to beg better than that."

Damian, I need you. I keep picturing your hands touching me instead of my own, and I can't stand another second of pretending. Please.

I look at the stack of papers I have left on my desk. It's dwindling, I could probably finish in a few minutes. But as if she could sense my hesitation, Viv's voice comes back through the speaker.

I'm wet, so wet. Don't you want a taste?

Fuck it.

"I'm on my way." I turn off speakerphone and shove the phone between my shoulder and my ear. "Vivianna, don't you dare come without me."

She moans again, a beautiful sound that has me speedwalking across the mansion. I duck into the barracks, slipping my cufflinks into my pocket and loosening my tie. As I reach for her door handle, I hear the sound of another door closing.

I look up and lock eyes with Sebastian, my tie slipping free from around my neck. He tilts his head when he recognizes me, taking a step forward to talk to me. Then he follows my arm to the doorknob and freezes. His eyebrows furrow as he looks at Viv's door, then back to me.

His eyes widen.

He looks at the door. Looks at me.

Looks at the tie, dangling from my fingers. Looks at the door. Looks at me.

His mouth opens, then closes. I wink and hold a finger to my mouth. *Shhh.* Sebastian eyes widen further at my confirmation before he holds his hand over his eyes and turns around. I smirk, then open the door to my waiting girl.

I flick off the lights as I shut the door behind me, cloaking the room in the soft glow of moonlight from her window. Vivianna squirms on her mattress, biting her lip as she struggles to not tumble into her orgasm. I'm kneeling by her side in two steps. One hand strokes her black hair cascading over the pillow. My other slides between her legs, rubbing her sensitive clit.

"I'm here, Vivianna," I whisper as she writhes in the sheets. "Come for me."

And she does, crying out as she convulses, her fist clutching the fabric of my shirt. My fingers keep circling until the last of the aftershocks cease, and Viv lays there panting. Slowly, I raise them to my mouth and suck them clean, savoring each drop of her I taste.

I give her a minute to collect herself before I unbutton my shirt, shedding it and my jacket at the same time. Viv so dutifully unbuckles my belt, and my pants fall to the floor. She's on her knees in a heartbeat, her tongue swirling around my aching dick.

A shudder runs through me as she takes me to the hilt, moaning happily. Jesus, how can one woman be this perfect? Her mouth is amazing, but I need to feel her right now. My hand weaves into her hair and tugs her head back. Her breathing is already quickened. I don't have to be able to see to know that she's grinning, eager for whatever I have planned next.

"Lay on the bed," I order, releasing her from my grasp.

I crouch down and find my discarded trousers, yanking my belt free of the loops. The mattress sinks as I nudge my way between Viv's legs, letting the tail of the leather hang from my hand and tickle her skin. My lips crash into hers, drinking in the taste of her. Her hands cup my face and glide up, a gentle caress that—

"Ow!" I jerk away as she brushes my eye socket, still throbbing from my bout with Marco earlier.

"Damian?" Viv sits up abruptly, reaching for the lamp on her bedside table. I grab her arm before she can flick on the light.

"I thought I told you to lay down." I lower my voice to a deep rumble, hoping to distract her. It's a long shot, but sex might be enough to make her lose focus.

"But—"

"Shh." I kiss her again, and her protests die in her throat. "Do you want me to fuck you or not?"

"Yes," she breathes.

The outline of her body reclines, and she holds her wrists together in the air, waiting submissively for me to tighten my belt around them. The leather is soft, but not nearly as soft as her skin. I lower her bound wrists over her head before moving my hands down to her perky nipples. She gasps as I just barely graze them, and I chuckle imagining the way she twisted and pinched them earlier. They must be so sore, so sensitive. I tease a bud, enjoying the way she writhes on the mattress.

This is the part where I would normally taunt her, providing the small tinge of pain she craves with her pleasure. I would normally yank her hair or drag my nails along her ribs, listening for her little gasps and whimpers.

But kneeling before her in the dark, I don't want to be rough. I don't want to scratch her or pull her hair. I don't want to. Instead, I want to hold her, embrace her. Touch her tenderly with warmth and... love.

I line up with her entrance and slide into her slowly, giving her time to adjust to my size. My lips kiss her shoulder, her collarbone, her neck, pausing right above her own. Her breath mixes with mine. I want to kiss her, but I hesitate. It's not like we haven't kissed before, plenty of times, but I don't want just another meaningless kiss. In the dark, I don't have to hide my expression. I close my eyes and allow myself to wish things were different. That Viv wasn't my Ombra, but that she was mine.

Viv's hands creep down to my cheek, gently pulling me down until our lips meet. Her touch shakes me free from my internal distraction, and I refocus on the woman waiting patiently in front of me. I slip the metal prong free of the frame, releasing the buckle of the belt and throwing the leather aside. I'm not fucking her tonight, not like that. She doesn't miss a beat, running her fingers through my hair and tracing the muscles of my chest. I expect her to scratch or dig her nails into me, but her touch is delicate. And so, I let myself believe that this time is different, that Viv is mine.

My hips rock, and I slide in and out of her with affectionate thrusts. Her lips taste sweet, indulgent. Her back arches as I find my rhythm, and I cradle her in my free hand. Viv wraps her arms around my neck, pulling herself closer to me. I kneel and bury my head in her neck, inhaling the vanilla and cinnamon scent that has become my drug of choice. She shifts without a word to straddle my lap, grinding with a smooth, relaxed cadence. Our bodies are flush together, our heartbeats synchronized. We silently cling to each other until we both find our release and lay on the bed, limbs tangled on top of the sheets. Eventually, I have to pull myself together and return to the role of Damian.

"Thank you for helping me finish my work." I smile as I lean my elbows on the bed, running my hand along the outline of her silhouette.

"My pleasure," she chuckles, reaching out for my cheek. I grab her hand before she can, smoothly bringing it to my mouth to kiss her knuckles.

"Did it hurt earlier?" I whisper. "When you punched that guy?"

"No, my nerves deadened years ago." Viv flexes her fingers. "Sometimes I get random spasms of pain, but they go away quickly enough."

I massage her muscles gently. In the dark, I can feel the small scars crisscrossing her fingers, instances where she maybe split her skin or broke a knuckle. It's strange to think about — my hand cramps from signing too many papers, hers from throwing too many punches.

"If I knew punching a guy would get me a hand massage, I would have done that ages ago," she teases with a lighthearted laugh. "Next time, I'm going to shoulder-check someone."

"How about we skip that step?" I drop her hand and guide Viv to lay on her stomach.

Do I know how to give a good massage? Not really, but I must be doing a good enough job since Viv groans quietly as I make my way across her back, neck, and shoulders. Her body goes limp, completely and utterly relaxed. That doesn't happen often. I make a note to do this again and frequently.

"Thank you," she sighs, patting my thigh. "I've been meaning to ask Vinny to work out some of those knots."

"Glad I could help." She'll never have to ask anyone else ever again. I'll take care of her.

I slide off of her back, leaning on my side. Her silhouette props itself up, her hair falling over one shoulder. I reach out on impulse, twirling a strand around my finger. It flows like silk as I let it slip away. I shouldn't be touching her like this. We had sex, there's no excuse for me to keep caressing her. She doesn't seem bothered by it, though whether she's humoring me or truly indifferent is hard to discern in the dim lighting. I roll onto my back with a sigh.

"Are you okay?" Viv scoots closer to me. "You seem distracted."

"I guess I am." The stars twinkle in the black sky outside the window. Visions of her eyes twinkling the same way cross through my mind. I shake my head, clearing the thoughts. "I'm sorry. It won't happen again."

"What were you thinking of?" Her finger draws little circles on my bicep, and even that small action sets my heart aflutter. "Anything you need to talk about?"

"It's nothing I can't handle." Does my voice sound like I'm smirking or do I sound as melancholy as I feel?

"Are you worried about the Russians?" Her voice darkens with a fierce tenacity. "I'll keep you safe from them, Damian. I promise."

"If there's only one thing in the world I know to be true, it's that the Russians stand no chance against you," I chuckle, pulling her into my side.

"So then what's bothering you?" She whispers, nuzzling closer.

"Absolutely nothing." I exhale, holding Viv in my arms. "I'm in the bed of a beautiful woman. What else could I ask for?"

"What a flirt." Her laugh tickles my ears before she kisses my neck, my cheek, my brow.

"Ah!" I hiss and jerk away.

"What's wrong?" Viv sits up, fumbling for the lamp. I grab her wrists, pinning her to the bed. She tentatively squirms beneath my grasp. "What are you doing? Let go of me."

"Just lay in the dark with me," I plead. "It's nice, isn't it? The dark?"

Viv stills underneath me. In a blink, she twists her wrists, effortlessly breaking my hold over her. I crumple onto the mattress as she rolls to the side, feeling blindly for the lamp switch.

"Wait!" The light flicks on before I can stop her, and I duck beneath my hands, shielding myself from the glare.

"Damian?" Viv kneels on the bed, tilting my head to get a better view of my black eye. Her concerned gaze scrutinizes the bruise as I wince. "What happened?"

"It's fine," I stammer, embarrassed and worried about her reaction. "I antagonized him, so it's like thirty percent my fault."

"I need a name." Her icy tone sends a shiver up my spine. There's no sparkle in her eyes, just a sinister rigidity.

"I took care of it already." I cup her cheek, but Viv swats my hand away.

"Name." She grips my jaw and leans down until she is inches away from me.

"I can't give it to you." I don't shy away from her anger. She won't hurt me.

"Why the fuck not?" She seethes, barely more than a whisper. "Someone dared to touch you. I need to correct that behavior, preferably with a knife, or a gun."

"Because you have a history of not following my orders," I snap. "And if I tell you who punched me, you'll go after them and I'll have to punish you." My tone softens as I continue. "Don't put me in that situation, please."

"It was Marco?!" Viv stands and yanks her sports bra over her head. "I'm going to kill him."

"Vivianna, please!" I grab her arm, but she shrugs me off. Her leggings slide over her legs and a gun is tucked into her waistband. Oh, shit. She might actually kill him.

"I don't feel safe!" I blurt, and she freezes, eyes intensely locking onto mine. "Don't leave me. I don't want to be alone."

It's a lie, and she knows it. There's probably no safer place in the entire mansion than in her bedroom, but if I need to stop the Ombra side of her, then I need to speak her language.

"You have to protect me," I assert, though I hate the words as they leave my mouth. The clear manipulation, taking advantage of the ideologies she holds dear. Her expression is unreadable, hardened, devoid of tells. "You swore you would protect me, Vivianna."

"Nobody touches you, Damian." Her voice sends a chill down my spine, deathly serious. "Certainly not while I'm in the same building. I have to respond. This is me protecting you."

"Stay with me," I whisper, holding my hand out. Her gaze softens slightly as she falters. "Keep me safe, Viv."

She looks back at the door before her fingers slide around mine. I gently pull her closer until she is back in my arms where she belongs. I confiscate her gun, setting it on the end table as we lay down, cuddling beneath the sheets. The light flicks off and we lay there in silent darkness, Viv's head on my shoulder.

I don't know how long I lie there awake, staring at the stars outside the window with one arm wrapped around Viv's waist. Certainly long enough that I'm surprised when she shifts, evidently also awake. I hold my breath and close my eyes as she inches closer, not wanting to startle her. Ever so softly, a kiss brushes my cheek before she rolls over.

She… kissed me.

No sex on the table, no heated make out session. Just a kiss.

I don't let myself dally on what it means, too afraid of getting an answer I don't want. Instead, I reach over and tilt her head toward me. She gasps quietly at my touch but doesn't shrink away. I cradle her cheek, tenderly pressing my lips to hers, pretending for only a moment that she feels the same way I do.

Screw indifference and casual hookups. It takes everything in me to pull away, especially as I fool myself into believing she leans into my kiss. I lie back on my pillow and wrap my arm back around her, hugging her to my body.

"Goodnight, Viv."

CHAPTER 13
VIVIANNA

Damian is gone when I wake, his clothes missing from the floor. All but a forgotten tie, lost beneath my bed, the only sign that he was here except for the faint smell of pine on the pillow.

I can't shake the guilt from my gut. The purple bruise marring his eye. Where was I? Why wasn't I there? I should have been there. I should have stopped it.

It won't happen again.

I get dressed with a cold fury, nearly snapping my shoelaces when I yank them too hard. Knives sheathed on my belt, guns holstered at my sides. I don't bother braiding my hair, instead quickly securing it in a ponytail.

There's a chill in the air as I walk into the common room. All eyes turn to me as though they can sense what I'm about to do. Maybe they can. Only one pair of eyes shifts away, averting his gaze as he hurries away.

"Hey, Sebastian." I follow him into a hallway, not caring when he flinches at the sound of my voice.

"Look, about yesterday, I didn't see anything," he stammers. "I promised Mr. Marano I wouldn't say anything and—"

"Where is he?" I cut him off to ask my question. God, Sebastian rambles so much when he's nervous.

"Mr. Marano?" Sebastian thinks for a moment. "I saw him go into his office about twenty minutes ago."

"No, not him." I step closer, my voice lowering to a growl. "Marco."

"Marco?" A flicker of confusion flashes across Sebastian's face before a glimpse of realization. "Oh, you're looking for Marco because he hit Mr. Marano."

"Are you in the habit of making me repeat my questions?" I raise an eyebrow, annoyed. It's not my fault he's scared of me. I apologized for my last interrogation. "Where is Marco?"

"I thought you two were…" Sebastian leans in and speaks in a hushed tone. "Marco is Mr. Marano's problem, not yours."

"Mr. Marano's problems are mine." I flex my fists as I step around him. "I'll find him without you."

"The gym," Sebastian sighs, pinching the bridge of his nose. "He's in the gym, probably waiting for you to do something rash. But I'm warning you, if you go after Marco, I have to tell Mr. Marano. I'm his capo, I can't lie to him."

"That's fine." I smirk. "I don't need long."

I stride toward the gym as Sebastian walks off. Men step aside, parting like the red sea from my murderous aura. I find Marco in the back, leaning against a squat rack talking to a group of guys. He doesn't see me approach, but his friends do, taking several steps back.

"Vivianna!" Damian shouts in the distance.

Marco turns toward the noise, not soon enough to avoid my fist. He stumbles back, cursing.

"You ever touch him again," I threaten, "and I will kill you."

"What?" Marco goads, stepping closer to me as he recovers. "Two little punches enough to break your fragile little Marano?"

"Two?" I bristle, gritting my teeth. "You hit him *twice?*"

"Easily," he mocks derisively. "Someone should have trained him to block better."

I don't listen to his insults or the growing crowd behind me. All I'm thinking about is how I'm still one punch below count. Someone grabs my arm, but I rip free, dodge Marco's moving fist, and deliver my second blow.

"And that's two." I hold up my hands, yielding to those pulling me back.

"What the absolute fuck, Vivianna?" Damian runs up to us, seething. "I explicitly told you to stand down. Am I not speaking clearly? Would you prefer Italian? Oh wait, 'no' in Italian is still fucking no!"

"Mr. Marano, she assaulted me, your second." Marco spits, clutching the side of his face which is already turning a beautiful shade of purple. "This behavior cannot be tolerated."

My eyes meet Damian's, and I see the struggle lurking beneath the surface. He begged me not to put him in this situation, but it needed to be done.

"Marco's right," I say, lowering myself to my knees. "I knowingly disobeyed a direct order, and worse, I would do it again. You warned me there would be consequences. Whatever punishment you see fit, I accept willingly."

"Hold her arms." A whispered command. I don't resist as two men step forward to restrain me. Damian averts his gaze, though I keep mine locked on him.

"Tony," he summons, and Tony steps forward apprehensively. "Two blows, closed fist. Same as she dealt to Marco."

"Four," I correct, hating how Damian flinches. "Two more for two counts of disobedience. Each was a separate decision."

"Four then," he confirms quietly and walks away a few steps, keeping his back toward me.

Look at me.

Damian, please. Just look at me.

I'm not fighting, I'm not resisting. I just want you to look at me.

"Boss, you can't be serious?" Tony hesitates, eyebrows scrunched together. "She's your Ombra."

Damian just nods, staring at the ground with his hands on his hips. No one in the audience makes a sound. No shifting feet, no coughs, nothing.

Tony turns to me morosely. A pit of dread sinks into my stomach as I take stock of the muscles straining beneath his suit. Six and a half feet of brawn, probably close to three hundred pounds of strength. And he is going to punch me. In the face. Four times.

"It's okay," I whisper, giving him a small smile. "I can take it. Four good ones. Don't break a knuckle on my account."

I will be okay. I will. I've felt worse pain. I've taken worse hits. But no one told that to my sweating palms or the lump in my throat.

"I'm sorry." Tony's voice cracks as he slides off his jacket, passing it to a random bystander.

I've changed my mind. I don't want Damian to look, don't want his comfort if it means he has to watch one of his closest friends beat me, one whose sole job it is to break bones and torture enemies.

I am Damian's fucking Ombra. He comes first, and now that means not being a little bitch. I won't scream. I won't make a single noise. I won't add to his pain, no matter how much I know this is going to hurt me.

Tony's eyes meet mine and I nod, urging him to approach me. He rolls up his sleeve and gently tilts my chin higher, angling my face to have a clean shot. My tongue presses against the roof of my mouth as my jaw clenches, my years of experience taking a punch subconsciously readying my body. His fist draws back.

I take a deep breath and close my eyes, bracing for the impact.

"Stop." Damian's command is jarring against the heavy silence. "Tony, stand down. Let her go."

Tony takes several steps back in relief. The two men release me immediately, but I don't move from my kneeling position.

"That's it?" Marco gripes. "She just gets off scot-free?"

"She was prepared to face the ramifications of her actions," Damian says coldly, turning to face him. "Getting beaten by my lead enforcer is hardly a light punishment, but she was willing to comply. She's shown obedience and deference to my authority. I'm satisfied."

"Well, I'm not!" Marco throws his hands in the air.

"Then I have marvelous news for you," Damian snaps, straightening the sleeves of his suit. "You're the second, not the Don. Your opinion on the matter isn't worth shit."

"Mr. Marano—"

"May I remind you why Vivianna felt the need to assault you?" Damian interjects, the sharpness of the voice enough to make half of the crowd flinch. "I believe I was lenient in your punishment as well."

"Then punish me!" Marco strides toward Damian. I jerk before Damian holds up a hand toward me. It takes every ounce of self-control I have to stay on my knees, though I don't bother to hide the scowl shooting daggers toward Marco. "I'll take four from Tony if that means the bitch gets them too."

"The punishment for assaulting a lieutenant and the Don are not the same," Damian says condescendingly. "Your sentence would be death. Unless you'd like me to reconsider keeping you alive, I would take the two blows you received and get out of my face."

Marco glares at Damian, clenching his fists by his side. My fingers slip behind my back, wrapping around the hilt of a knife in preparation. Someone rests a hand on my shoulder, and I shrug them off.

"Anna!" Vinny scolds under his breath, but I pay him no mind. All of my attention is on Damian.

"Careful," Damian threatens, coolly observing Marco's reaction. "I have an antsy Ombra who is determined to keep slipping her leash."

Marco glances at me, before scoffing and storming away.

"Enzo, take your sister somewhere to cool down," Damian orders, still not looking at me. "Maybe confiscate her knives too."

Vinny grabs my arm and practically drags me out of the gym. Past Damian, past Tony, past the crowd watching all of this unfold.

He keeps going, not stopping until we are out of the mansion and deep within the surrounding forest.

"On your knees," Vinny gripes, annoyed. "One hundred push-ups."

"You're kidding, right?" I roll my eyes.

"No, Anna, I'm not." He stands with his hands on his hips.

"One hundred push-ups is for sassing Dad," I protest. "I have been very unsassy today."

"My bad, Dad didn't pass down a punishment for being an insubordinate brat." Vinny points to the ground. "One hundred push-ups. I don't care if Mr. Marano let you off the hook. If you're going to be stupid, you have to pay the price."

I groan and lower myself to the grass. *One, two, three...*

"What were you thinking anyway?" Vinny admonishes. "Are you trying to piss off Marco?"

"Marco can go to hell," I grunt. *Seven, eight, nine.*

"Then why go through all of this fuss, Anna?" Vinny crouches down to make sure I'm getting close enough to the ground.

"He hit Mr. Marano." *Fourteen, fifteen, sixteen.* "Do you think maybe we could wait to have this conversation?"

"No." Vinny stands, ignoring the sweat beading on my brow. "The Ombra is supposed to protect against life-threatening danger, not a petty fight. Marco is not your concern."

"You and I remember the vows very differently," I retort. *Twenty-one, twenty-two, twenty-three.* Vinny puts his foot on my back, adding resistance as continue my push-ups. "You asshole."

"Sass me again and I'll sit on you." The threat is enough to curb my tongue, and I focus on continuing my push-ups despite the fatigue in my arms. *Twenty-six, twenty-seven, twenty-eight.* "Mr. Marano doesn't need you to fight his battles. All that does is upset the delicate politics within a mafia."

"I couldn't do nothing."

"Yes, you could have!" Vinny snaps. "You're in the Ombra. You have a distinct political weight, arguably more so than any of the lieutenants. They can be replaced, we can't. Mr. Marano has to treat you differently. That leads to bitterness, resentment, disgruntlement. Why do you think that Marco and Mr. Marano are fighting?"

"I don't know," I pant. *Thirty-five, thirty-six, thirty-seven.* "Any number of reasons."

"It's because you've threatened Marco's position." A squirrel chatters in the distance, laughing at me. "Mr. Marano has been spending more time with you and less with him. Marco thinks you have sway over Mr. Marano's decisions, or worse, that you're gunning for his job."

"That's not true." *Forty-one, forty-two, forty-three.* "I'm just keeping him safe."

"Optics matter, Anna," Vinny lectures, stepping off my back. I breathe a sigh of relief without the added weight. "That's why I keep to myself outside of when I'm needed. We were raised to handle threats, he was raised to handle politics. Stay away from him."

"I don't understand." The sweat now drips freely off my skin. *Forty-seven, forty-eight, forty-nine.* "Our dads were best friends. They said—"

"I know what they said." Vinny leans against a tree, dejected. "I've been doing this longer than you, sis. It's not fairy tales and rainbows. Being part of the Ombra is lonely and miserable."

"You're wrong." I shake my head. He has to be. Damian and I are friends, I can't just stand back, fade into the distance like a shadow...

Oh.

My arms falter as I struggle with my realization. The perfect Ombra, the perfect shadow. Silent, always a step behind.

"At least we have each other." Vinny tries to lighten the mood. "I'm happy to kick your ass in the ring anytime."

"You could try," I chuckle before pausing my push-ups. "Fuck."

"Lost count, didn't you?" He knows me too well.

"Yep."

"You know the rules."

Goddamn it. I shake out my arms before lowering myself to the grass again. *One, two, three...*

I lost count one more time after that, so Vinny took pity on me and counted the next set out loud. My arms are rubber by the time we finish and head back to the mansion.

Damian is speaking with Sebastian in his office when we pass by. His eyes catch mine, a myriad of emotions barely concealed below the surface. Regret, guilt, shame. I smile sadly as Vinny ushers me away to go shower.

Once I'm dry again, Vinny gives my shoulder a nudge and we go to hang out in my room. I subtly kick the discarded tie under my bed, hiding the evidence of my affair from my twin.

He lounges at the foot of my bed as I curl up by the window, staring at the clouds drifting by. I can't help but think of beetles doing cartwheels or ladybugs holding parasols. Our time at the cabin feels like it was so long ago, almost a different life.

Eventually, Sebastian comes to get us. I nearly forgot, there's some sort of dinner or something the lieutenants are going to. Vinny and I have to accompany them.

"No, I ordered two cars," Damian groans at the driver, who simply shrugs his shoulders. "Six passengers, two cars."

"Anna and I can take the bikes." Vinny passes me a helmet, shooing me away from the huddled group.

"I can drive too," Sebastian volunteers.

"No." Damian shakes his head. "I'm trying to reward you guys, not make you work for your dinner. The three of you take the car. I'll go with the Ombra."

The lieutenants shrug and load into the SUV as I grab a third helmet.

"We're okay, right?" Damian whispers quietly as he takes the helmet. "This morning—"

"Was not your fault," I interject, grabbing a set of keys. "I took my punishment, did my push-ups. Now, we move on."

"Viv, I—"

"Get on the motorcycle, Damian." I press the keys into his hand. "Please."

He wraps his fingers around the keys slowly, eyes never leaving my face. I turn away, pulling the helmet over my head and tightening the strap. Quick pat down — guns, knives. I'm good to go.

Damian straddles the bike and I take my spot behind him, holding on tightly as he revs the engine. He flicks the kickstand up, and we are off.

The restaurant is gorgeous. White tablecloths drape over tables with flickering candles as centerpieces. Soft string music plays over the speakers, adding to the elegant ambiance. Waiters move through the space in coordinated patterns. The hostess leads us to a private room in the back. Windows line the walls with two thick wooden French doors propped open. The men playfully jostle each other as they take their seats, Damian at the head and the others filling in around him.

"Guard the door," Vinny orders me. "I'll float around and keep an eye on the kitchen."

"Wait." Damian stands up. "You two aren't supposed to be working. Sit down, eat with us."

Vinny rolls his eyes, leaving without another word.

"Get us a to-go box." I shrug. "We can eat at home."

He goes to say something else, but a waiter comes in with a basket of garlic bread and the rest of the table cheers. I slip out during the commotion, taking my post by the door.

It's fairly boring as far as guard duty goes — waiters making the rounds in a pattern that I memorize with little effort, patrons eating and drinking quietly, but at least the music is nice. I catch glimpses of Vinny here and there, lurking in the shadows, ducking into employee-only zones. Maybe a bit overzealous, but I'm not going to complain, not when I give the waiter a stern warning glare every time he walks past me to enter the room. Bread. Drinks. Appetizers. More drinks. Entrees.

"Any interesting gossip?" Damian leans on the doorframe, nursing a glass of red wine. "That's got to be the best part of the gig, right? Eavesdropping on people?"

"Not tonight," I chuckle. "The tables are too far away for me to hear anything juicy."

"Damn." He smiles, taking a step closer. "You could come in with us. Sit down a bit, enjoy a glass of wine. We're safe here, Viv."

"There's no harm in being vigilant." No matter the fact that I can think of two separate times he was almost killed at a club he owns.

"Here." He holds out his glass of wine. "Have a sip, just one."

"I'm not falling for that again," I tease, lightly pushing his hand away. "Last time, one sip turned into half the bottle."

"Would that be so bad?" Damian frowns. "I'll stop drinking right now, I'm sober enough to drive us home. You can relax, let your hair down."

"Damian, stop," I warn, turning away from him.

"What about tonight?" He lowers his voice, ensuring no one can overhear us. "Will you drink with me tonight?"

"Is that a good idea?" Vinny's warnings creep into my mind. I'm his Ombra. Silent. Hidden. Invisible.

"We're so far past the boundary of a good idea," he whispers, leaning in closer. "Just say yes."

I bite my lip, hesitating.

"Look Viv, if you're upset with me, I understand," Damian sighs. "We can drink on opposite sides of my room or even at the kitchen island. It doesn't have to go any further."

"We'll see." I return my attention to the movements in the dining room. "You should get back in there before they realize you're missing."

Damian stands there a moment longer, watching me sorrowfully. He disappears as the waiter walks by again, a tray of tiramisu in his hands. I hear Tony celebrate as it is served. I'm glad they're enjoying their evening.

"Anna." Vinny runs up, out of breath. "I need your help."

"What's wrong?" My 9mm is in my hands instantly.

"Something strange is going on." Vinny looks over his shoulder and closes the French doors to the private room, shutting Damian and the others inside. Their loud conversation is quieted instantly, nearly silent in comparison. "There's two unmarked vans parked by the back doors. Could be nothing, could be something."

I catch Damian's eye through a window. He's the only one who noticed Vinny's rushed arrival, sitting up in his seat.

I'll be right back, I mouth. He nods uneasily, pushing his wine glass away.

"Let's go."

Vinny grabs my hand and leads me toward the front entrance. His grip on my wrist is strong, uncomfortably so. We make it almost all of the way outside before I hear a commotion behind us. Vinny yanks me forward, but I stop, turning to look as shrieks sound through the restaurant.

"Bomb!"

Damian. I wrest my wrist from Vinny and take off back inside. A crowd surges toward the exit, and I struggle to make my way upstream through the herd of people. Vinny screams my name, unable to reach me with the patrons pushing him backward. I keep elbowing and shoving, forcing my way deeper into the stampede.

Damian. I don't see Damian. I search every face I pass. Why isn't he here? That man can't run to save his life. I break through the throng of people, stumbling into the dining room.

Damian. He's pounding on the glass of one of the windows to the private room. We lock eyes, and I wave, gesturing for him to follow. He yells something, but the sound is lost. Then his eyes widen, and he screams something different. I barely make out the shape of the words. *Get down!*

I fall to the floor as a bullet whizzes past me, shattering an abandoned wine glass. My pistol is raised the next second, firing off two shots at the gunman sneaking up behind me. The second was redundant.

After a quick scan, it seems that he was the only hostile in the area, so I pop back up. Damian is still at the window, visibly relieved when he sees me unhurt. I wave at him, a bit more aggressively this time. He's mouthing something again. *Door.* Door? Yes, use the door please.

Tired of the charades, I dart through the tables, running to the private room.

Thuds sound from the door, rattling against the frame. I jiggle the handle, it doesn't budge. Motherfucker. Muffled voices shout from inside the room.

"Get out of the way!" I yell. Not waiting to see if they hear me, I drive my heel into the wood above the handle. Once. Twice. The wood begins to splinter. Thrice. The door cracks and they are able to force it open.

"Oh thank god," Sebastian wheezes, exhausted from trying to break it down against the hinges.

"Don't just stand there!" I shout, full Ombra mode. "Move!"

The three lieutenants run ahead as they crawl out. Damian is the last to squeeze through, grabbing onto my arm once he's free. I barely give him time to stand before I drag him behind.

"Gun!" Tony shouts up ahead, and a group of hostiles pour out of a hallway separating our two groups.

Luckily for them but unfortunately for us, the gunmen are much more concerned with Damian than the three lieutenants. Damian and I duck behind an overturned table for a shred of cover. He reaches under my jacket and pulls out my spare 9mm.

"Are you really not armed?" I groan, popping up to fire off a few shots.

"None of us are!" Damian snaps. "This was supposed to be a celebration, not an ambush."

Beep. Beep. Beep.

He leans around the table, dropping a few men himself. He gestures at the other crouched lieutenants to run. To their credit, they hesitate for a second, but they take off once I provide cover fire.

Beepbeep. Beepbeep. Beepbeep.

"We can't be here," I warn, but Damian already knows. I stand to fire again, but all of the gunmen have vanished. I don't question it, grabbing Damian and sprinting toward the back exit, away from where the shooters came from.

Beepbeepbeepbeepbeepbeep.

The beeping sounds like it's coming from everywhere, surrounding us with the piercing shrill. Are we running toward the bomb? Toward more gunmen?

Beeeeeeeeeep.

Damian tackles me to the ground, covering my body with his own. My gun skids across the floor.

Beep.

Damian clings to me as the blast detonates, sending a burst of wind ripping through the room. Glass shatters. Wood splinters. Sprinklers rain down as smoke billows toward the ceiling.

"Are you okay?" I cough, squirming my way out from underneath him.

"Yeah…" Damian sits up, shaking. A layer of dust coats his suit, slowly getting washed away by the sprinklers.

The private room is gone, decimated by the explosion. Flames lick at the remains. Soft footsteps grow louder, and I move to a crouch.

My gun, I lost my gun. I reach for my spare but find only an empty holster. Shit, Damian has it. We're doing this the hard way then.

I creep along the wall, pressing my back against the wood. Damian crawls after me, but I gesture for him to hide behind the hostess stand. He hesitates, but I can't worry about whether or not he listens as a submachine gun pokes through the doorway.

My hand grabs the barrel and pushes it toward the ceiling, lashing out with my elbow as I do so. I wrench the firearm away as the man falls unconscious, firing at his two companions behind him. My gun jams instantly. I dive around the corner as their guns don't.

"Russian piece of shit!" I curse, smacking the magazine to try and clear the round. I don't have time for this. Looks like I have a volatile club on my hands.

I jump up as the next gunman enters the room, bashing the butt of the rifle against his temple. He crumples to the ground. His comrade doesn't fall for the same trick, dodging out of the way as I swing toward him.

Thick hands wrap around my shoulders, yanking me closer. Both of our rifles fall to the floor, getting lost amidst the other debris. I knee him in the stomach, pushing against his chest, but his grip doesn't falter. He throws me into the hostess stand, the wood fracturing under my weight.

Damian? He's supposed to be here. Where is he?

The ground is slick from the sprinklers, puddles forming on the hardwood. I stagger to my feet in time for the assailant to be on me again, shoving me against the wall. My head whips back into a picture frame, the glass cracking into large shards.

The Russian slips on a puddle and falls to the floor, dragging me down with him. We grapple each other, both trying to get the upper position as we splash in the water. He gets on top for a second, but I slide out from underneath him, scooting back despite him clinging to my ankle.

He rises up, blood dripping from his hand as something glints in the light—

Bang!

Damian steps out from behind his cover, his bullet ripping through the man climbing above me. I watch as he brings his fist down in the final moments before the light leaves his eyes. Breath fills my lungs in a choked gasp.

Don't let the Maranos know if you get hurt. It was the first lesson my dad taught me. We would practice sparring without making a noise, no matter how hard the blows hit. *Don't scream. Don't cry. Keep it to yourself.* I've mastered the art of silence, taking the pain with only a grunt, hiding any injury until a private moment. *They will only panic. They won't think clearly. Your job is to keep them calm and get them out.* I'm good at what I do. I'm a fucking good Ombra. *Don't let them know you're hurt.*

But MOTHERFUCKER!

"The fire's spreading, Viv." Damian grabs my lost pistol as I grit my teeth. "The sprinklers aren't enough. We need to get out."

"I know, I know." My shoulders heave as I swallow the pain. I try to move my leg, but the muscles scream in agony. There's no way. "Take that hallway toward the back. Follow the emergency exit signs. I'll be right behind you."

"Are you stuck?" Damian eyes the man draped over my legs. "Let me help you."

"Go!" I protest, but it's too late.

Damian clears the body with a shove, revealing the jagged piece of glass impaled in my thigh. Rich blood has already begun to pool. Too much blood.

"No," Damian exhales, his skin paling. I hiss as he applies pressure, red liquid pouring over his fingers.

"You're going to have to get out of this one on your own, Damian," I say, hoping to keep any composure I have left.

"No way." He stubbornly rips away the fabric of my pant leg, getting a better look at my wound.

"I'll be fine," I lie. "But you need to go. The exit isn't far. I'll stop anyone who comes through here. Get outside and find Vinny, he'll get you home."

"I'm not leaving you behind." His voice cracks. "You'll… You'll…"

"I'm not afraid to die," I whisper, acknowledging the truth he can't bring himself to say. "I'll pass out before the smoke inhalation will kill me. There are worse ways to go. But Damian, you don't need to die with me. Run. For once, just listen to me and run."

"If it was me, what would you do?" Damian asks, his voice firm.

"Stop it!" I push him away. "Save yourself."

"Tourniquet, right?" He clenches his fists. "Like hide and seek?"

"Don't do this." My lip quivers. "Don't die trying to save me."

"Neither one of us is dying," Damian growls, grabbing a pen from the debris.

"Please." A tear escapes from the corner of my eye, then another. He takes the ripped fabric from my pants and wraps it around my thigh.

"You're not dying today, Viv," he reiterates. "I need you."

"Damian—"

"No, Vivianna!" Damian snaps, raising his voice. "You don't get to die. You don't get to give up. I love you! You don't get to die. So shut up and try to survive, goddamn it."

Damian tightens the tourniquet without warning, and this time, I can't stop my screams from crying out. I writhe on the ground as he pins me down, twisting the pen as a makeshift windlass.

"Take it off!" I wail as my nails dig into the floor. "Just let me die. Oh god, it hurts. Damian, it hurts."

"I'm going to get you out of here, Viv. I'll get you home, I promise." He ignores my desperate cries, securing the binding. "Just like hide and seek, right? It's just like hide and seek."

I cover my head with my arms, quiet sobs shaking my torso.

"Hey!" Damian yanks my arms down, gripping my jaw forcefully. "Vivianna Palazzo, you are not done! Do you hear me? You are not done. Do I look safe to you?"

I sniffle as I shake my head, staring into his eyes. The deep hues of amber don't flinch, don't falter.

"You're my Ombra," he continues. "You pledged your life to me. You're not dead yet, so your life is still mine. Now, pull yourself together, Palazzo." Damian shoves my gun into my hands. "Do your job."

He's right. I… I have to keep going. I have to protect him.

My sleeves wipe away my tears as I nod weakly. My fingers wrap around the handle of my pistol. He gently helps me to my feet, supporting my weight with his shoulder. The flames are spreading. We have to go.

I groan as Damian practically carries me, dragging me through the tables toward the exit.

"Anna!" I hear Vinny shout. He slips beneath my other arm, pulling it over his shoulder.

"No," I murmur. "Someone needs to be ready to shoot. It's not safe."

"I've got her, Enzo," Damian orders. "We can move faster if we're not worried about hostiles. Take care of it."

Vinny nods as Damian sweeps me off my feet, cradling me to his chest. Vinny scouts up ahead, firing off a shot here and there. I don't relax, focusing on keeping a feeble grip on my 9mm.

We burst through the door, coughing as we get a breath clear of smoke. Our trio hustles through the parking lot, nearly making it to our bikes before we hear shouts from the side. They found us.

I slide out of Damian's arms, shooting toward the Russian assholes as I sit backwards on the bike. Facing the rear, I can aim better at those bold enough to pursue us.

Damian peels out of the lot, Vinny following a beat behind, providing cover fire. The gunmen load into a van, leaning out the windows as they shoot at us. They're not worried about Vinny. Damian is their target.

Three bullets are fired in the next heartbeat. One hit the concrete beneath my feet. The second was from my gun, just high of the driver. The third…

The air is forced out of my lungs as I jerk back against Damian. Vinny screams my name, a feral war cry.

Something snaps within Vinny and something spectacular happens. His whole demeanor shifts into that of a cold-blooded killer. His pistol fires with a ferocity, murdering the gunman who brought out his rage.

After twenty-six years, he finally becomes an Ombra.

"What's going on?" Damian worriedly calls over his shoulder. My hands brush my stomach, coming back up dripping fresh red blood. "Viv?"

"I…" *Don't let them know you're hurt.* "I'm fine."

Damian weaves aggressively through traffic as my eyes grow heavy. We leave Vinny and the van of assassins in the dust, fading from my blurry view. The pistol falls from my fingers, clattering onto the concrete.

"Viv, give me an update." He taps on my hip.

"Safe." The one word is all I can muster as I slump against him.

"Viv!" His arm wraps around me before I can fall off the bike. He heaves me to his lap, leaning me against his shoulder.

"Safe." The taste of copper coats my tongue. I choke on each thick word. "Did my job."

"Stay with me," he begs, clutching me to his chest as he accelerates. "Please, stay with me."

"I…" The scent of pine cradles me as the world fades. "I lo…"

CHAPTER 14
DAMIAN

"Vivianna!" She doesn't open her eyes. She won't open her eyes. A droplet of blood trickles from her mouth, a ruby bead that takes her life with it. "No! No! No!"

I press my fingers into the side of her neck, praying to God to give her back to me. I'd do anything, just please, don't take Vivianna from me.

I know the protocol. Get back to the compound. Hospitals aren't secure, aren't safe. I'd be vulnerable, an easy target. But the medic at home is miles away. Miles Viv doesn't have.

A single pulse beats, soft and thready. She's still here. She's still in my arms, clinging to life. The interstate flies beneath my wheels. Straight goes home, the next exit goes to the hospital. The choice is obvious.

My motorcycle veers right, cutting off a soccer mom and her fleet of kids, but I don't give a single shit. All I can think about is the woman in my arms.

The wheels of my bike are still spinning as I jump off, holding her limp body against mine.

"Help!" I scream, my voice hoarse. "Save her, please. Don't let her die."

Hands lift her onto a gurney, sprinting away to who knows where. The warmth leaves my chest, her absence sinking in as my arms fall to my side. A nurse grabs my hands, asks me questions, but I can't hear her.

I'm a Marano. Composure, control, competence. I'm strong and confident. Authority leaching from every aspect of my appearance. Pressed suit, hair just so, crisp tie. Not now.

I fall to my knees in the middle of the lobby. Her blood stains my shirt. I've got soot smeared across my face and splinters of wood in my hair. My tie hangs loosely around my neck. I'm fine. I don't even have a scratch, yet she…

I'm a Marano. No one has ever seen me cry. I *don't* cry. But that doesn't stop the first tear. Or the second. Or any of the others that fall, turning black as they run through the ash on my cheeks.

My arms wrap around my stomach as I curl over my knees, sobbing inconsolably in front of a room full of strangers. Somehow the nurse steers me to a chair toward the back, away from pitying eyes.

My tears dry, leaving me numb and heartbroken. I don't want to live without her. The Petrovs could walk into the hospital right now, and I'd just sit here. Wouldn't even flinch as they pulled the trigger.

I look up every time a doctor walks through those doors, both hoping they're for me and dreading their news. Maybe luckily, maybe not, they never come to me.

Minutes turn to an hour, which turns to a lifetime. My phone rings in my pocket. I consider turning it off, throwing it across the room so it smashes into a million pieces, but I somehow remember how to answer it and bring it to my cheek.

"Marano." My voice croaks.

Damian, are you okay?! A frantic Marco panics over the line. *Where are you?*

"I'm at St. Mary's on 24th," I sniffle like a pathetic idiot.

A hospital? I can barely make out Sebastian and Tony in the background, also freaking out. *What's wrong?*

"It's Viv," I choke out, the tears prickling at my eyes threatening to spill. "I think she's dying." I lose it again, weeping into the phone as the line goes silent. "Oh god, she's going to die."

Are you hurt? My chest feels like it's being squeezed in a vise, but I don't think that's what Marco is worried about.

"No." I shake my head, struggling to catch my breath. "I'm fine."

Then she did her job, he says softly. That one sentence feels like a dagger through my heart.

"Don't say that," I beg. "She was a person, she was my friend, she…" She was the love of my life.

She knew the risks. Marco's voice hardens, admonishing my vulnerability. *The sooner you can accept that, the sooner we can respond to this blatant attack.*

"I don't fucking care, Marco," I snap, clinging to my grief with both hands. "Aren't you listening to me?"

You don't get to be a blubbering child, Marco snaps. *How many men have you lost to the Russians? If a member of your Ombra is added to the count, that is all the more reason to pull yourself together and avenge them.*

"Vivianna saved your life today!" I scream, not caring when every pair of eyes in the room turns to me. "Does that mean nothing to you?"

Vivianna gave her life so that the four of us could live.

"Yeah?" I scoff. "I wish I was the one dying instead."

I chuck my phone at the nearest wall, not bothering to gather the shattered pieces of it or my heart. My shoulders hunch as I collapse back in my chair.

Others come and go, but I stay here, anxiously running my hands through my hair. I've long since abandoned my cufflinks and tie, shoving them into my pockets. My jacket is draped over the back of the chair, my shirt sleeves rolled up to my elbows. A few people glance at Viv's 9mm tucked in the back of my waistband, but wisely choose to give me a wide berth.

"Is my sister here?!" A frantic man in a black suit rushes up to the front desk. "Black hair, gunshot wound to the abdomen?"

"Vincenzo." I stand and his gaze whips to me.

"You," he seethes, stalking toward me. "This is all your fault. She was safe! She was nearly outside, but she ran back in for you!"

"I know." My voice is hollow.

"You don't deserve her!" Enzo grabs the collar of my shirt, slamming me against the wall. I don't fight back, don't even hold his angry stare. "You should be the one dying instead of her!"

"I know."

Staff members run up and pull him away from me, but I just stand there, hanging my head in shame.

"If she dies, I'll never forgive you!"

I'll never forgive myself either.

Threats levied and aggression dealt, Enzo eventually calms down, holding his own vigil on the other side of the waiting room. He glares at me every once in a while, but I'm too busy delving into my self-pity to notice.

This is my fault. If I had never asked Viv to be my Ombra, she wouldn't have bled in my arms. If I hadn't been so selfish, so captivated by her smile, she could have been safely at home.

"Is anyone here named Damian?" A disheveled nurse bolts into the room. "I need a Damian."

"Me!" I jump up, closely followed by Enzo. "Please tell me Viv's okay."

"She won't stop pulling out her IV," he pants, propping himself up on his knees. "We can't get her to calm down."

"Where is she?" She's alive? She's awake? I hear her voice faintly in the distance, and I shove past the nurse, running down the hallway toward her distressed screams.

"Let me go!" Three nurses circle her bed, trying to force her into restraints despite her thrashing. "He's not safe! I have to protect Damian! Where is he? Damian!"

I shove through the nurses, wrapping her in my arms. She relaxes as she buries her head in my neck.

"I'm right here, Viv," I whisper, unashamed of the fresh tears soaking into her hair. "Let the nurses help."

"It's not safe here," she murmurs. "You need to go."

"I'm perfectly fine where I'm at." I stroke her hair before pushing her back against the mattress.

Viv stops fighting, but I still hold down her arms as the nurses swoop back in to reinsert the IV. There's a tiredness in her eyes, but whatever is in the IV is seeming to take away her pain. She exhales, sinking against the mattress.

"There you go," I soothe as the nurses leave the room. "Just rest."

"Okay, you had your turn." Enzo nudges me aside. "Get out of my way."

"Vinny!" Viv lights up when she sees her twin. "Dude, I saw the way you went after that van. I'm so proud of you! Total highlight reel moment."

"Yeah, yeah, yeah." Vinny ruffles her hair as I sit in a chair against the wall. "I don't care about that, I care about you. How are you feeling?"

"Good," she chuckles. "Ready for round two."

"That's not funny, Anna." Enzo furrows his brow. "I was really worried about you."

"You shouldn't have been." Her eyes dart playfully over to me. "Palazzos don't go down easily."

"But they can still go down," I whisper, leaning onto my knees. Her smile falters, taking in my haggard appearance for the first time — the tear-streaked cheeks, the red stain on my hands, the hair falling into my eyes. "You went down."

"I did." Her goddamn sad smile appears, the one that knots the pit in the bottom of my stomach. "But you got me back up.

Now you both need to stop moping, or I'll have to break out some really bad puns to lighten the mood."

"Anna—"

"Knock it off, Vinny," she scolds. "Someone wise once told me that finding reasons to laugh is important in our line of work."

"Really?" Enzo rolls his eyes. "Who said that? Dad?"

"No, someone else." Enzo doesn't see the look she gives me, but I see the flash in her eyes, the flush in her cheeks.

"What do you call the ghost of a chicken?" I sigh, rubbing my eyebrows.

"What?" Viv's smile stretches ear to ear. It must be contagious because I find myself smirking a bit.

"A poultry-geist," I say. Viv giggles, and for the first time in hours, I feel the tenseness fade from my shoulders. "Okay, here's another one. I just found out that I'm color blind. The news came completely out of the yellow."

"Wow, how funny," Enzo gripes sarcastically.

I don't give a damn what he thinks. All of my attention is on Viv, who is clutching her stomach as she laughs.

"Ow. Maybe we should hold off on the puns for a day or two," she groans, still chuckling as she rubs her abs. She stretches her arms above her head and then nods. "Okay, I'm ready. Can someone pass me my bag?"

"Ready for what?" I ask, finding a plastic bag in the corner of the room.

"To leave." Viv riffles through and pulls out her clothes and knives. "Did I really lose my gun twice in one day? Damn it, Vivianna. That's rookie shit."

"Whoa, you're not leaving any time soon." Enzo takes the bag from her, but she yanks it back.

"Damian isn't safe here," she protests. "And since he always runs headfirst into danger, I need to make sure he gets home. Besides, we have pain meds and antibiotics at the compound. There's nothing keeping me here."

"Viv, don't worry about me." I pull the blankets back up to her shoulders. "Take a nap. I'll be right here when you wake."

"I want to go home, Damian." Her voice wavers slightly. "You promised. Take me home."

"There's no way I could convince you to stay?" I hold her hand as she shakes her head. Fuck. "Alright."

"Hold on, what?" Enzo grabs my shoulder, but I ignore him, helping her sit up.

Viv slowly pulls on what's left of her pants, one leg missing. Several buttons of her shirt are lost, presumably from when the medical staff ripped it open. I drape my jacket over her shoulders. Hers is right there in the bag, but I don't care. Mine doesn't have a bullet hole in it. And it's mine.

She takes a deep breath and yanks out her IV, wincing as she does. Enzo groans, finally admitting defeat. He gathers up the rest of her things and confiscates her knives. Viv struggles to reach the wheelchair parked by her bed, so I sweep her into my arms where she belongs. The chair is quickly abandoned as she leans her head on my chest.

"I can carry my sister," Enzo snaps. I shift Viv defensively.

"I promised her I would get her home," I growl. "She's staying with me."

Enzo glares at me — a look he's getting far too comfortable giving me — until Viv wraps her arms around my neck, nestling in contentedly. His face softens as he sees her relax, and he bites back whatever retort he had prepared.

"Whatever," he scoffs, holding the door open.

A few of the staff try to stop us from leaving, though they step aside when they catch sight of the two pistols beneath Enzo's blazer. I carefully set Viv in front of me as I straddle the bike, keeping her arms wrapped around my neck.

"This isn't where I go," she mumbles, struggling to keep her eyes open. "I sit behind you."

"Not this time, *bellissima*," I whisper softly, guiding her to lay on my shoulder. "You're going to take a nap, and when you wake, you will be in your bed."

"Will you be there?" Viv falls asleep as soon as the words leave her mouth, but it doesn't stop my response.

"There's nothing in the world that could keep me away."

The purr of the engine thankfully doesn't rouse her as I start the ignition. Enzo's bike follows alongside as I pull out of the parking lot, my arm cradling Viv's sleeping form. I curse every bump in the road, avoiding all that I can to avoid rousing her from slumber. The speed limit feels too high with such precious cargo wrapped around my chest, breathing peacefully. Enzo doesn't seem to mind my slow pace, glancing at Viv occasionally but mainly keeping an eye on the surrounding vehicles. Together, we make our way safely to the parking garage.

"Go wake the medic," I order Enzo as I lift Viv against my chest. "Let's get her back on an IV drip right away. I'll take her to her room so she can settle in."

I don't stick around for him to argue or throw a half-cocked insult my way. Someone else is more important right now.

I walk as steadily as I can, hoping to avoid jostling her as I enter her bedroom.

She sinks into the mattress as I set her down, but I can't just leave her like that — in the shredded clothes stained with her own blood. I rummage through her dresser and search for the pajamas I've seen her wear the most often, a pair of gray shorts and an oversized t-shirt. They're folded neatly in the bottom drawer. As gently as I can, I slip her free of the remnants of her suit, sliding the soft PJ's on in their place.

She smiles as I tuck her in, cozy and snug. My lips brush her forehead as I stroke her hair, kneeling by her bedside.

The medic comes in and I step aside, giving him space to work.

"You changed her clothes?" Enzo hisses under his breath.

"I wasn't about to let her wake up with such a visceral reminder of..." I shake my head. "Of course, I changed her clothes. It's not like I haven't seen her naked before."

"Excuse me?" he growls. Shit, bad choice of words.

"Gemma," I say, avoiding his eyes. Maybe he won't see the half-excuse for what it is. "If she's offended when she wakes, I'll apologize to her then, but I have a feeling she'll have other things on her mind."

"Thanks to you." The malice in his voice is clear and cuts deep to my core.

"I never wanted this," I whisper, feeling my chest tighten with each breath. "I tried to protect her. I tried to keep her safe. I never wanted her to get hurt."

"Yet she's the one who took a bullet." The accusation hangs in the air, suffocating me with guilt. The room is silent until he speaks again. "She's done."

"What?" I whip my gaze to him, but he remains steadfast, looking only at Viv.

"When Anna wakes up, she's done," he threatens. "She gave her life for you. She fulfilled her duty. She's done."

The ground shifts beneath my feet as I look at her. Done. A life not in my Ombra, a life without me. A life that's… safe. No guns, no knives, no bombs. She could move back home, find someone else to love, protect them from paper cuts and stubbed toes instead of assassination attempts and poisonings. She could be happy, smiling freely and openly, laughing at jokes better than mine. She could be safe.

I don't know what expression is on my face, and I don't care. Let Enzo see what he wants — heartbreak, grief, pain. I couldn't hide it if I tried.

"Now get out," he gripes, pushing me backward. "Get out!"

I stumble over the threshold, and he slams the door in my face, the echo reverberating through the barracks. I stagger up the stairs to my private wing, loneliness seeping through the empty rooms. All of my ghosts pulling at my skin. Rooms full of nothing but cobwebs, meant for my parents, grandparents, cousins, siblings, children… but it's just me. I'm the last Marano.

I used to dream of finding a wife, someone to share my life with. I gave up on that years ago after too many failed romances to count. For just a moment, I had a spark of hope that maybe, just maybe, I had found someone. Even if we couldn't be husband and wife, maybe Vivianna and I could have been companions, a rock for the other to lean on, someone warm to hold when the nights got cold.

Now I know that can't happen. Bullets will always be flying my direction. Someone will always want me dead. I can't sleep next to her wondering if each night will be the last I can hold her.

Maybe I'll send someone to check up on her once in a while, watch her from a distance. If I'm lucky, they'll return with a picture of her smile that I can hide under my pillow.

There will never be anyone else for me. No one to have or to hold. No one to comfort me in my darkest moments. I will never love anyone else. There will only ever be Vivianna Palazzo.

The shower pelts me with freezing droplets as I sit on the tile floor, the cold doing nothing to help the vise around my heart. I pull my knees to my chest, burying my head in my arms. The pinpricks of water numb my back but do nothing to numb my pain. I crawl out of the shower, dragging myself to the closet to throw on whatever PJs are on top of the pile.

My ceiling mocks me for the next hour. Vanilla haunts my sheets, lingering so painfully. The hair tie on my wrist is a cruel reminder I can't force myself to take off. Is this how she feels at night when she sits outside my door, keeping watch as though a boogeyman lurks around the corner?

I creep down the stairs.

Just one peek, just to make sure she's okay. Then I'll leave and trust Enzo to take care of her. Just one peek.

The doorknob turns slowly, and I step into Viv's bedroom.

There's just barely enough starlight to see her pained expression from the doorway. A soft whimper leaves her lips.

"Run," she murmurs. "Leave me here. Save yourself, Damian. Run away."

Fuck a quick peek. I am by her side in an instant, squeezing her hand in mine.

"You're safe, Viv." I flick the lamp on, illuminating the space in a faint glow. "Wake up, you're safe." Viv sits up with a start, eyes darting around her room. They land on me and widen in alarm. "Shh, you're okay. I'm okay. We're both okay."

Her shoulders heave as she fully awakens, taking slower and slower breaths. Viv leans back against her pillows with a long exhale, returning the squeeze of my hand.

"Sorry," she whispers. "Sometimes the nightmares are hard to shake off."

"You have nothing to apologize for." My heart splinters into another fragment. "Nothing at all."

She takes another deep breath, scrunching her eyes closed.

"Is there anything I can do for you?" I hold the back of my hand against her forehead, checking her temperature. "Water? Another pillow? I could go get Enzo?"

"I'm a bit hungry." Fuck! She missed dinner.

"What do you want?" I stand and pace anxiously. "Name it, I'll get it for you. Steak, soup, lobster, anything."

"I should get shot more often if lobster's on the table," she jokes. I recoil, feeling like a bullet went through my own chest at her words. "I'm kidding, Damian. Just kidding."

"Is that what you want?" I run my hands through my hair, rambling quickly. "I can place an order and have one here in thirty minutes. In the shell, out of the shell, either way. Or would you prefer it with pasta? One of my chefs has a lobster mac and cheese that is a crowd-pleaser, but I don't care if the crowds like it, I care if you do—"

"How about a bowl of ice cream?" Viv suggests, interrupting my blathering. "I think I saw some in the freezer this morning."

"I can do that." I nod, content with my marching orders.

A bowl of strawberry is in her hands within minutes.

"None for you?" She furrows her brows.

"I'm okay." The extra second it would take to grab myself a bowl would have taken too long. I needed to do this for her.

"If you're sure." Viv winces as she sits up, sucking air through her teeth.

"Are you in pain?" I'm standing again, supporting her back as I help her sit. "I'll go wake the medic, see if we can give you any more drugs."

"I'm fine." She shakes her head, but I'm not convinced.

"I'll be right back," I promise.

"Damian, sit your ass down!" Viv snaps. "Stop doting over me. I got shot. Of course it fucking hurts!"

Her words stab through my chest, driving home the fact I wish I could forget. I lean against the wall, pressing my forehead to the paint.

"You got shot."

The words sound hollow.

One second I was trying to slip her a sip of wine, the next she was running after Enzo. I tried to follow, but the doors, something happened to the doors. They wouldn't open. Everything else was a blur — shrieks about bombs, the shard of glass, driving away on the bike. I felt her jolt, I heard Enzo's scream, but I never thought...

"I got shot," she repeats, her voice cracking. I turn to see a single tear glistening on her cheek, her hand pressed against her stomach. "I got shot, Damian."

"I'm so sorry, Viv." I shouldn't have come inside. All I do is bring her pain. I'm the reason she's hurting. "I'm so sorry for everything."

"Will you hold me?" Her lip trembles as she pulls back her blanket. "Please."

I shouldn't. I definitely shouldn't, but I find myself laying in the bed next to her anyway. Viv curls into my arms as more tears fall, clinging to me like a security blanket. She looks up at me, and all I can see is the scar trailing down her face, yet another time she almost lost her life to protect me. This is why I need to let her go. I just don't know if I'm strong enough.

"You don't have to be strong in front of me," Viv hiccups, caressing my cheek. "I know you're hurting too."

"Don't worry about me." I tuck her hair behind her ear, forcing a weak smile to my face. "I'll be okay."

"Stop it," she whispers. "Just for tonight, don't be a Marano. Allow yourself to fall apart. Allow yourself to just be Damian."

"You got shot." My voice wavers. Her eyes meet mine, her beautiful brown eyes that have a way of trapping me inside them. She's alive, but I'm going to lose her in the morning. I crack, feeling the pain of my heartbreak. "Vivianna, you almost died, and it's my fault."

"Give me your hand." She presses my fingers firmly against her neck. Her heartbeat is steady. "Feel that, Damian? I'm alive. You saved me. *You* are the reason I'm still here."

A sob racks my chest, and I clutch her to my body, squeezing her as tight as I dare. Her tears mix with my own, flowing freely as we cry together. The two of us really were something — a true Ombra pair. She'll never forgive me for what I have to do, but at least she'll be alive to hate me.

"Did you mean what you said earlier?" Viv grabs my wrist. Her grip is weak compared to her normal strength, but I can feel the intensity in her gaze. "After the blast?"

"The Ombra stuff?" I wipe the tears from my cheeks. "Absolutely not. Not even a word. It was just a last-ditch effort to get through to you."

"No." Her voice trembles. "Before that."

My breath catches in my throat, remembering my panicked confession. What could I possibly say knowing that I will never allow myself to hold her again? Knowing this is our last night together? So I don't say anything. Instead, I lean in closer, gently pressing my lips to hers. When I pull away, my body is shaking with fresh sobs.

"I'm so sorry," I choke out.

"Damian?" She cradles my cheek with a worried expression. I slip out of the bed, turning away from her comfort. "Where are you going? What's wrong?"

I grab her slightly melted ice cream and place it back in her hands.

"Goodbye, Vivianna."

I do my best to avoid her after that night. Not strong enough to face her, unsure of how to let her go and break my heart. She recovers quickly from what I can tell. Sebastian and Tony each make time to sit by her bedside, taking shifts for Enzo. Sebastian gives me an update each time, subtly hinting at how lonely she is, how she would really like someone else to keep her company. I just thank him and nod. At least he's no longer scared of her.

She's on bed rest for the next few weeks. I think she's supposed to be for longer, but as usual, she's too stubborn to listen to anyone.

Then she's out and about on crutches, ditching them too after a couple of days.

Her limp gradually fades the following week, and the next, she's back in the gym, albeit training a bit slower than her normal all-out frenzy.

I see the way she looks at me as I leave the room every time she enters. She keeps her mask up, hiding her pain from everyone but me. I know her too well, know her tells. The slight furrow of her brow, the way her lips part just a hair. It just about kills me.

Viv comes to my room most nights now, knocking softly at my door. I don't answer, don't respond, don't give any indication I'm even there.

Damian, let me in. I can't.

Please, tell me what's wrong. Everything.

I brought some ice cream.

When she gives up on getting me to open the door, she slumps in her usual spot. She sits against the wall for hours, but little does she know, I sit right behind her, listening to her breathe with only drywall separating us. When I leave the next morning, there's always a bowl of melted mint chip waiting for me.

Luckily, paperwork waits for no man, so I bury myself in contracts and forms, checking every decimal point in a desperate attempt to distract myself. My life is a revolving door between my office and my bedroom. My lieutenants organize several missions, dismantling more of the Petrovs' drug trade. I don't go along. If I go, Enzo has to go, and he needs to take care of Viv. Someone has to. So paperwork it is, reviewing expense reports and requisition forms.

Our quartermaster submitted his recent expenses. It's a fairly standard list — mostly grocery items, uniforms, miscellaneous repairs around the compound. I scan some of the items: *Men's Dress Shirts — size XL (x54), Box of Dried Rigatoni (x20), Hand Soap (x33), Women's Blazers (x4).*

Women's blazers. Quantity four. Followed by four shirts, four slacks. He didn't need to list the size, we only order one size of women's clothing. There's only one person who wears it.

There are a million reasons why we need to replace uniforms. They wear out, they get stained. God, the number of jackets people set on a chair and lose. But Viv hasn't been around long enough to wear out her suits. No, hers are being replaced due to damage. The drug lab, the distribution center, the restaurant. Knife slash, windowpane, gunshot.

I slowly stand and close the blinds, shielding my office from view. The paper trembles in my hands.

Women's Blazers (x4)

Women's Dress Shirts (x4)

Women's Slacks (x4)

It's there in black and white. Proof. A life next to me is a life full of violence. Night terrors. Hypervigilance. Scars.

New suits.

It's time. I have to rip the band aid off. I owe it to her to at least tell her face-to-face. I tighten my tie and meander through the mansion, looking for her. She's not in any of her usual haunts — the gym, the living room, her room — but I hear her voice float down the hallway from Enzo's room.

I walk closer, noticing how the door sprung free from the latch. Whoever tried to close it didn't press hard enough. I'm near enough now to make out the words she's saying. She is pissed.

"You what?!" I've never heard Viv this angry. This is not the time to give her bad news. I turn to walk away and come back later but freeze when I hear my name. "What do you mean you talked to Damian? Goddamn it, Vincenzo! You should've stayed out of it! I'm fine!"

"You're fine this time, but what about the next?" Enzo matches her energy. I am all too aware there are two trained killers in that room, and a chill creeps down my spine at the tension seeping through the crack in the door.

"It's part of the job!" Viv bites. "You get shot, you dust yourself off, you move on."

"Oh yeah?" Enzo mocks. I cringe on his behalf, fearing the wrath of Viv. "Look at how Dad ended up. If Damian dies, are you going to kill yourself too?"

No. The answer is no. Vivianna, say no.

"He's not going to die!"

"I'll tell you what," Enzo yells. "If that prick eats lead for breakfast, I won't lose a wink of sleep over it!"

A crack splits the air, the sound of a palm striking a cheek.

"You watch your fucking mouth," Viv growls. "You are his Ombra."

"For how long?" His voice quiets, taking on a grave seriousness. "Am I going to get stabbed tomorrow? Next week?"

"This is what we signed up for, Vincenzo." Her whisper is firm, decisive.

"No! It's not!" A flip switches in Enzo, his screams borderline manic. "You signed up for this, I didn't! I never wanted this!"

"What are you saying?" I can't be here, I can't listen to this anymore. Viv's desperation, Enzo's bitter resentment.

"I'm not going to die for that man, and I won't let you die for him either! Anna—" I back away, the floorboards creaking beneath my feet. The conversation cuts out as the two realize they aren't alone. I turn and walk quickly down the hallway.

"Damian?" Viv's voice is uncertain, calling after me.

I make a mistake, I turn back towards her.

The twins stand together in the hallway. Enzo's skin pales in stark contrast to the red handprint on his cheek. But Viv? She looks good. Her color has returned to her face. She holds herself with her normal assured poise. Her baggy t-shirt and leggings show no sign that just a few weeks ago she was barely clinging to life. Then I catch her eyes. Dim, hurting, welling with tears.

"Listen to your brother, Vivianna." I force myself into the role of Mr. Marano. Composure, control, competence. Don't cry. Don't break down in front of her. "Go. Both of you. Find a better life to live."

With that, I force myself to tear my eyes away from hers and keep going down the hallway.

"Wait, Damian!"

I flinch at her voice but keep moving. I have to keep moving. If I don't…

Footsteps sound behind me. Fuck it. Fuck everything.

I take off, running up the stairs, running into my bedroom. I go to close the door, but she shoulders her way in.

"Is that all you have to say to me?" Her fury is now directed entirely at me, but I'm not scared of her. I could never be scared of her. "'Find a better life to live?' How pathetic."

"I know." My voice cracks as I stare out the window.

"You kissed me." The betrayal in her voice, the hurt.

"I did." I scrunch my eyes closed, leaning against the wall.

"You told me you loved me!" The raw emotion in her cry shatters the last bit of restraint I have.

"I do!" I whip to face her, my devastation clear through my tattered mask.

"Then why are you hiding from me?" Her fists clench at her sides. "Don't fucking say it's because of Vincenzo because I know that's full of shit!"

"It's *because* I love you." My admission does nothing to assuage her. "God, I love you so much."

"Get over yourself." Viv storms out, slamming my door behind her.

"Viv, let me explain," I beg, following her through the hallway.

"Fuck off!" She hurls the expletive callously.

"Viv!" I call after her as she strides through the common area. We're drawing a crowd, but I don't give a damn. "Just listen to me!"

She ignores me, tossing her hair over her shoulder. She doesn't want to listen? Fine. I'll make her.

I jog in front of her, pulling my pistol out from its holster. Her narrowed eyes follow me carefully as I abandon it on an end table, moving on without a care in the world.

"What are you doing?" Viv's tone is jagged.

"I'm going out," I say flippantly, not even bothering to look at her.

"Where?" One syllable. Clipped and terse, but it's enough. Enough to know she still cares.

"Don't know." I shrug as I turn around, walking backward toward the elevator. "Maybe to get a sandwich. Maybe to drink an entire bottle of whiskey. Maybe to kick Bruno Petrov in the nuts. Maybe all three. I'll figure it out on the way."

"Without your gun?" She crosses her arms over her chest, calling my bluff.

I keep going, facing forward now. Viv curses as she scoops my pistol off the table, jogging after me. She glares my way as she steps onto the elevator. The doors close and the car starts its slow descent before I flick the stop switch. The car shutters to a standstill.

"Oh, real fucking mature, Damian," Viv grumbles, reaching past me for the switch, but I press my back against it.

"Just give me five minutes, please," I beg quietly. "After that, you can use my own gun to shoot me, and I won't try to stop you. I'll deserve it."

"Careful," she warns, ice in her words. "Shooting you is sounding really good right now."

"Five minutes," I insist.

Viv nods begrudgingly, pulling the pistol free of her waistband.

"You almost died, Vivianna." I make it all of three words before my voice cracks and tears threaten to fall. "I was holding you in my arms, and your blood stained my clothes. I could feel your heartbeat slowing, and something inside me broke. If you would've died, nothing else would have mattered to me. I would've walked out on everything and everyone, holding vigil over your grave until I joined you in death."

"Dam—" Viv tries to interrupt, but I shush her.

"I still have four minutes," I say firmly, ignoring the wet streaks on my cheeks. She nods softly and steps back.

"I can't watch you die again." My eyes latch onto hers, sharing the heartbreak I've kept bottled inside the past few weeks. "There's no equation between us where you don't get hurt. I can't live with knowing that at any minute, you would throw yourself in front of a bullet for me, even though I would do anything to take it instead. I love you, Viv. I want you to live a long and happy life where you can let your guard down. Where you can sleep in the arms of someone who will protect you and won't put your life in danger every single second you're around them."

"If you think that's what I want from my life, then you don't know me at all," she spits angrily. She ejects and reloads the magazine of the pistol, ensuring that it's armed. "Two minutes."

"You couldn't be more wrong," I laugh sadly. "I know you better than I know myself. I know you hate mint chip ice cream, but you pretend to like it since it's my favorite. You will never eat more than a few spoonfuls of it but put a bowl of strawberry in front of you and it disappears."

Viv tries to interrupt again, but I don't stop, my words falling in rapid succession as I step toward her.

"I know you can't sit still long enough to paint your nails. Every time you try, you get antsy and the polish smudges on your fingers. I know you pull your hair back because it's more practical, but you feel more beautiful with it down, flowing over your shoulders. And I know that every single time you say, 'I'm fine,' you're lying through your teeth. All to protect me from your own pain, whether it be a wound to your body or heart. I know this, and I know that you're not going to stop lying no matter how much you get hurt, no matter if it ends in your death."

Viv's breath catches in her throat as she backs into the wall of the elevator.

"Viv," I whisper softly. "I know that being my Ombra is the most important thing in the world to you, because there is nothing in the world you look at the way you do strawberry ice cream. Nothing else besides me." I pause for a moment to let my words sink in. "Am I wrong?"

"Your five minutes are up." She chambers a round as a single tear slips down her cheek.

"That's why I can't look at you." My thumb brushes the tear away. "That's why I can't speak to you. Because all I want to do is hold your body against mine, but next to me is the most dangerous place for you to be. I have to let you go."

"Are you done yet?" Viv asks bluntly, but there's no malice in her words. I gently wrap my fingers around hers and guide the barrel of the pistol into my stomach.

"Yeah, I'm done." I tuck a strand of her hair behind her ear, distractedly. "Go ahead."

I expect her to make good on our deal and squeeze the trigger.

I don't expect her to yank me down by my tie, aggressively crashing her lips into mine.

"Fuck you, Damian," Viv seethes.

"Viv—"

"Shut up!" She snaps. "It's my turn! Fuck you for thinking you know best. Fuck you for trying to throw me away. Fuck you for being the dumbest man alive when the truth is right there in front of you!"

"What?" I stammer, overwhelmed by her sudden wrath and affection.

"Fuck you!" Viv kisses me again, full of passion and fire. "Damian, I have loved you since we were children. Why do you think I train so hard every day? Keeping you alive is the only way I can show you how much I care about you! So yes, I'm going to keep throwing myself in front of bullets and taking shards of glass to the thigh because I love you. I love you, Damian Marano. Get your head out of your ass and let me!"

Her chest heaves as she glares at me. I stand there for a moment, blinking in shock.

She… She loves me?

I hesitantly reach out and cradle the back of her neck, leaning down to tenderly brush my lips against hers. She deepens the kiss, pulling my hips flush against her body.

"Love me," she urges, staring up into my eyes as her anger fades.

"How do you want to be loved, Vivianna Palazzo?" I murmur, holding her close.

"Figure it out," she taunts, running her fingers along my tie.

I pop off the metal panel surrounding the elevator buttons, revealing a secret button for the second floor. The button lights up, and I replace the panel carefully.

"Did I really drag your drunk ass up a flight of stairs while this was an option?" Viv narrows her eyes.

"This is only for emergencies." My voice rumbles in my throat. "And getting you to my room as fast as possible is the biggest emergency I can think of."

The doors open to reveal a false wall. The hidden knob turns easily as we step out into the far side of the upstairs hallway. As soon as the false wall is closed, I lift Viv against my chest, greedily drinking in her lips as she wraps her legs around my back.

I carry her down the hallway, all the way to my bed. Her hands free my tie from my neck before working their way down the buttons of my shirt. I shrug off the offending fabric as I slide the cotton of her tee over her head.

"My *bellissima*." I breathe in the scent of the perfume she wears. Cinnamon. Vanilla. Goddamn, I'm addicted.

"Yours," she murmurs between kisses on my jaw. "Yours. I've always been yours."

A deliciously sinful look crosses her face as she kneels, unbuckling my belt and tugging my trousers down until my cock springs free. Her tongue slowly drags along my shaft, ending with a tantalizing flick at my tip.

"Vivianna, how many hands do you need for a blowjob?" I growl.

"Don't insult me." The corner of her mouth turns up in a sly grin. "None."

"That's what I thought." I shove her to the ground, pressing my knee against her back as I use my tie to bind her elbows behind her back. She pretends to squirm under me as I plant a myriad of kisses on her neck, combing her hair to the side. "God, I'm captivated by you."

Knock. Knock. Knock.

"Mr. Marano? It's Vincenzo." Fuck. "Do you have a minute?"

"Not now!" I shout back, before leaning down to whisper in Viv's ear. "He has never once knocked on my door. Not even once in ten years, and the one time he does, I'm about to rail his twin sister? Fucking hell."

"It's about Anna," he begs, knocking again. "I can't find her."
Fuck.

A laugh escapes from Viv's lips, and I quickly clamp my hand around her mouth to muffle the sound.

"Please, Damian, you know I wouldn't bother you if it wasn't important."

"Fine, I'm coming," I groan, hauling Viv to her feet. I tug my pants back up, cursing under my breath. Deep breath. I push Viv behind the door as I open it just a crack, keeping my hand firmly pressed over her mouth. "What do you need, Vincenzo?"

Enzo takes several steps back in shock at my appearance — disheveled hair, shirtless, unbuttoned pants. I don't think he's seen me in anything but a full suit in the past ten years. He can get over it.

"Enzo, what do you need?" I ask again, trying not to get annoyed.

"I can't find her anywhere." He rubs the back of his neck. "I've checked her room, the gym, the kitchen. She won't answer her phone. Do you know where she is?"

"Haven't seen her." I shrug. Someone licks my palm and I have to restrain the urge to glance at the perpetrator.

"You're the one who was with her last," Enzo claims. "What did you say to her? Where did she go afterward?"

"Look, Enzo." I exhale slowly. "Viv's probably just tied up somewhere." Not a lie. "I'm sure she'll call you back when her hands are free." This one's a lie. I'm not going to stop until Viv loses her voice from screaming my name over and over and over.

Enzo bites his lip, nodding as he accepts my reassurances. He looks back up at me, and uneasiness returns to his face.

"About what you overheard earlier—"

"Now's really not a good time," I interrupt. "Let's talk tomorrow, okay? You can have my full attention then." Viv's muffled laughter sounds again, and Enzo slides a hand under his jacket.

"Is someone in there with you?" He whispers, pulling out his pistol.

"Yes, Enzo." I feel my patience starting to wane. "A stripper."

"Oh."

"Anything else?" I grit my teeth with a fake smile.

"No, um, tomorrow." Enzo steps back awkwardly. "Good night, and um, enjoy?"

"Oh my god." I slam the door closed, holding Viv against my chest as I hear footsteps recede. "That was the worst conversation I've had in my life."

"Look at the bright side," she teases, wriggling in my arms. "There is a very eager stripper wanting nothing more than to suck your cock."

"Well then..." I release her and sit on the edge of my bed. "Who am I to refuse?"

Viv settles between my legs. Her mouth moves down the length of my shaft painstakingly slow. She hasn't even used her tongue, but I'm already groaning and tugging her hair. She knows what she's doing to me, a mischievous glint in her eyes.

Her gaze doesn't leave mine as she bobs up and down, saliva dripping down her chin. Oh fuck, oh fuck. Her tongue curls around my dick, and I can barely contain myself. Then, she winks.

She fucking winks at me.

Something snaps, and I need more than her sweet mouth on my cock. A growl rumbles in my chest as I yank her onto the mattress, pinning her down by her throat. Viv bites her lip as her eyes fill with desire. I lean close to her as I line myself up with her entrance. Her breathing shallows into anticipatory gasps as she wraps her legs around my back.

My lips crash into hers, swallowing her cry as I slam inside her. She moans into my mouth as I push against her walls, her thighs squeezing my hips with each thrust. I swear, this woman was made for me. Every glance, every breath, every touch. Perfect. Mine. My *bellissima*.

"Damian!" Her beautiful voice screaming my name is enough to send me over the edge, and we come together.

I release her wrists, discarding my tie over my shoulder. We're not done. I want to feel her nails digging into my skin, to feel her yank on my hair until my scalp burns. By the end of the night, I'm going to know the answer to the most important question of my life.

How many orgasms will it take for Vivianna Palazzo to lose her voice?

CHAPTER 15
VIVIANNA

Goddamn.

Last night Damian was insatiable. A delicious soreness throbs between my legs, even after several blissful hours of sleep. I haven't been fucked like that since… I don't think I've ever been fucked like that.

Deep red scratches stripe his back, his arm draped over my waist as he cuddles a pillow. I'll have to apologize for those in the morning, even though they drove him feral at the time. Orgasm after orgasm. Fingers, tongue, dick. Missionary, doggy, cowgirl. Damian didn't stop until we were both shaking, covered in sweat, voices raspy from screaming in pleasure. I practically collapsed after the last climax, not that I'm complaining. But still…

Goddamn.

I stretch through my toes, sighing drowsily as my muscles relax. I roll back over, content to resume my slumber.

Wait, what woke me up?

A soft scuffle sounds from the hallway, and I slowly sit up, pushing the comforter aside. My hand glides beneath my pillow. Nothing. My pistol is under the pillow back in my room. Shit!

A faint snore slips through Damian's lips as I inch out from under his arm. The doorknob is barely visible in the darkness, but I can see it turn from my crouched position. I duck as the door creaks open, hiding in the shadows as I creep toward the foot of the bed. A man dressed in all black tiptoes in. He's not wearing a suit. He's not one of ours.

Climbing a man is just like climbing a stripper pole, right? Right?

Impulsive decision made, I leap up, grabbing his arm and using the leverage to whip my legs around his throat. I channel the momentum to swing my torso down, flinging both of us to the ground as he screams. Damian jerks awake, flicking his bedside lamp on in a panic.

"Find a gun!" I shout at him, squeezing my thighs around the intruder's neck.

Damian fumbles for his phone, speed-dialing a number and shouting into the line. The assassin is finally getting over his surprise, flailing a dagger around. I trap his arm against my chest, hissing when the blade nicks my shoulder.

An alarm blares through the compound, startling me. The intruder takes advantage of my shock, slipping free of my hold. I jump to my feet, standing between him and Damian.

"Are you Gemma?" He smirks, licking his lips. "Bruno's been looking for you."

"I'm right here." I stalk closer, fingers itching for an opening.

"Maybe he'll let me take you for a spin after I deliver you to him," he flouts. "A finder's fee."

"Why wait?" I size him up, baiting him carefully. "I'm available now."

I take a step forward, a bra strap sliding off of my shoulder. His eyes flick down to my bra and panties, the only clothing I was able to put on last night before I collapsed under the covers. It's only a momentary distraction, but it's enough. I grab his wrist, twisting until it snaps. The knife falls from his grasp into my other hand. A quick spin and the intruder is wrapped in my arms, blade held to his throat.

"Stop!" Damian shouts, running forward. "Don't kill him!"

"Stay back," I order as the assassin squirms, trying and failing to break free. "I don't want you anywhere near this trash."

"Who you calling 'trash?'" The man spits. "You're nothing more than a whore!"

"Quiet!" I seethe, pressing the knife against his skin until a drop of blood trickles free.

At that moment, the door bursts open. The lieutenants and Vinny pour in with guns drawn and varying levels of pajamas. The intruder quickly realizes he's outnumbered and starts thrashing wildly, bucking against my hold.

"Vinny, help me!" I snap, feeling the fatigue in my muscles from my extended late-night dalliance.

Vinny steps forward, pistol-whipping the man who in turn slumps unconscious. I groan as I release him, finding Damian's belt and using that as a makeshift restraint for the time being.

Several pairs of eyes stare at me — taking in my very obviously just-fucked hair, my limited state of dress, my clothes scattered around the room. Damian scoops his shirt off the ground and covers me up, clearing his throat. Their attention shifts from me to the scratches lining his chest. Sebastian is the first to speak.

"Let's give them some privacy, guys." He tries to shoo them out, but Vinny's furious stare is locked onto Damian.

"The stripper you had over was my sister?!" My brother steps forward aggressively, and I subconsciously creep toward Damian. Vinny shoves me aside. "You mean when I came to your room yesterday, Anna was..." A nervous swallow from Damian confirms Vinny's suspicions. "You motherfucker. I'm going to kill you. I'm going to fucking kill you!"

I jump in front of Damian as Sebastian and Tony grab Vinny's arms, wrestling the gun from him. Marco leans against the wall, watching the fight with an amused grin. Asshole.

"I told you that you couldn't have her!" Vinny roars.

"It wasn't on purpose." Damian steps back nervously, raising his hands. "You can't control who you fall in love with."

"Try harder!"

"Vinny, back off!" I yell, caging Damian behind me. "You're part of the Ombra. Act like it!"

"Since when do Ombra duties include fucking?" He spits. "Huh, Anna?"

"That's it!" I push Damian away and stride toward Vinny. "One hundred push-ups!"

"You can't call push-ups on this!" Vinny shrugs off the two men holding him back, but I press my hand on his sternum and push him toward the exit.

"Watch me." The glare in my eyes silences his next retort as I shove him over the threshold, slamming the door in his face. I turn around, and once again, find several pairs of eyes staring at me. "If one more person even implies that I am a whore, I will start snapping necks."

Marco opens his mouth, but one look from me wisely convinces him to shut it silently.

"Tony," Damian speaks up, retaking control of the situation. "Take our new guest downstairs to the Pit. I expect you and Marco to get me answers. How did he get past our security?"

Tony heaves the man over his shoulders before Damian continues.

"One more thing, he referred to Viv as Gemma. Let's not correct him." His eyebrows are furrowed in thought. "Follow that trail. What did he want with Gemma?"

The two men duck out with our captive, leaving only Sebastian. He points two awkward finger guns at him before shuffling after the other two underbosses.

"Sebastian knew?" I raise an eyebrow, glancing back at Damian.

"Yeah, he saw me walk into your bedroom once, though he's suspected for a while." Damian sits on the bed, releasing a breath.

"That makes sense." I nod, curling up next to him. "He's been acting weird ever since we got back from the cabin."

Damian presses his lips into a thin line, rubbing the back of his neck. A nagging feeling tugs at my mind and I sit up.

"I never danced for him," I state, furrowing my brows.

"Hmm?" He avoids my gaze.

"The guy." I gesture toward the door. "How did he know my stage name? I've never seen him before."

The shadow over Damian's face darkens as he pulls me into his arms, stroking my hair.

"I won't let them hurt you," he murmurs, nearly too soft to hear. "I won't let them."

"What aren't you telling me?"

The only response I get is him squeezing me tighter, holding my body close to his. I pull away and grab my leggings, tugging them on underneath Damian's dress shirt.

"Where are you going?" He asks.

"To get answers." I glance over my shoulder. "You coming?"

He sighs before he walks over to his closet, picking out a fresh suit. He gets dressed quickly before ducking inside the bathroom.

The door stays open, so I cautiously follow. Hairbrush. Gel. I sit on the counter, dangling my legs as he puts himself together. One cufflink. Then the other. He leans over, clutching the edge of the sink.

"I don't know where is safe anymore." His voice is pained. Though quiet, it reverberates off the silent tile. "But I'll figure it out. I'll find somewhere, even if it's just the two of us."

"You'll be okay." I slide off the counter, hugging him from behind. "I won't let anything happen to you."

"But what about you? You were in my arms, in my bed, and he could have…"

"It sounds like I was exactly where I needed to be." I turn him around, brushing his cheek with my thumb.

Damian leans into my touch, closing his eyes. I pick a tie from his drawer, gently draping it around his neck and tying the knot snug against his collar. He rubs his palm along the fabric, subconsciously smoothing it against his chest. He buttons his suit jacket, instantly flipping a switch to turn into Mr. Marano.

But this time, it's different.

He interlocks his fingers with mine, a glimmer of softness beneath his hardened exterior. He strides down the stairs, pausing to hold the door open for me.

A few men give us looks as we pass by, evidently the truth of our relationship spread like lightning. Even if it hadn't, it's obvious when I'm wearing his shirt, holding his hand as I leave his room in the wee hours of the morning. Damian's confident gait doesn't falter, each step daring someone to say something. They would never, at least not to our faces.

We take the elevator down past the basement, to a floor I've never been to. The Pit. The harsh fluorescent light casts an artificial blue glow on the room, adding eeriness to an already unsettling space. Tools are hung from hooks on the wall — knives, drills, wrenches, and things I force myself to look away from. Some dark liquid is pooled by the drain in the corner, missed from an earlier hose down.

Tony is washing his hands in the sink, sleeves rolled up to his elbow. Sebastian sits in a folding chair off to the side, glancing grimly through a window. Vinny leans against the wall next to him, glaring at Damian but staying put.

"Hey, boss," Tony grunts. "We're still working on him, but we have a few things to report on."

"Go ahead." Damian releases my hand and walks closer to Tony.

I sneak a peek through the window, instantly wishing I hadn't. Marco stands over the captured man who is handcuffed to a chair. Brass knuckles gleam on his fist despite the blood dripping down his arm.

"He's admitted to having a man on the inside," Tony says, in a hushed voice. "We have a mole working with the Russians. That's how he knew the layout of the compound, our security…"

Tony continues on, but his voice fades from my mind. I can't look away as Marco's fist swings into the hostile's face, another bruise forming amid the several already blotched on his skin.

My head whipping to the side. A fist yanking my hair, forcing me back up.

"A fucking mole?!" Damian growls. "How could that happen?"

A firm grip on my jaw, leaving bruises in its wake.

"He can't see you," Sebastian whispers, rising from his seat to stand next to me. "It's one-way glass."

The sting of the whip, splitting my skin.

The screams don't make it through the glass, but I can hear them anyway. They sound like mine.

Answer me, Vivianna!

"Are you okay?" Sebastian's hand rests on my shoulder and I flinch, raising my arms defensively and ducking from the incoming blow.

The splash of ice cold water. A calloused hand holding my head under the surface.

Everyone's looking at me. I slowly lower my arms, taking a step back.

"Viv?" Damian tries to catch my eyes, but I stare blankly at Marco.

"Do you need me here or can I go?" My question is blunt and emotionless as I cling to whatever shards of my mask I can find.

"What's wrong?" He moves in close enough to whisper, hiding me with his body.

"Do you need me here or can I go?" I repeat myself with more intensity, feeling my heart pounding in my chest.

"Go, Anna," Vinny intervenes. "I'll stay here."

My twin doesn't even finish his sentence before I stride away, rapidly pressing the elevator button. It takes too long. Fuck this, I'm taking the stairs.

"Viv—"

"Let her go, Mr. Marano." Vinny's voice holds a warning. "Stop, Damian!"

I take the stairs two at a time, speedwalking through the compound until my bedroom door shuts behind me.

I fall to my knees as the flashbacks slam into me, stealing the breath from my lungs. The world around me blurs as tears spill free. I curl into a ball, trying to stop the wretched trembling of my body.

Blood dripping down my arms, pooling on the concrete floor.

The door latches quietly behind me. One footstep, then another.

"Go away," I whisper.

Chains clanking as I hang from the ceiling.

"I shouldn't have brought you down there." Damian kneels next to me. "I'm sorry."

"Get out," I choke on the words. "You were supposed to stay with Vinny."

Poor little Vivianna. Crying won't stop this.

"I think I'm where I need to be right now." He brushes a strand of hair out of my face, and suddenly I'm no longer in my room.

Concrete walls. Concrete floors. Flickering lights. Their hands yank my hair, forcing me to meet their gaze.

Days without sleep, days without food. Blood coats my throat, hoarse from screaming. I couldn't possibly scream anymore, yet the taser draws them out anyway.

I'm shrieking, pushing him away as I cower on the floor.

A backhand whips my face to the side. I strain against the coarse ropes digging into my wrists.

"Tell us what we need to know, Vivianna!"

"I don't know him!" I cry, burying my head in my arms. "I don't know him!"

"How do we find Damian Marano? Where is he?"

The taser sends shockwaves into my ribs. My body convulses, shaking against the chair. I won't break. I can't break.

"Vivianna?" A hand shakes my shoulder. "Vivianna, what's wrong?"

Sharp fingernails grip my scalp, holding my head back as a towel is placed over my face. Water streams through the fabric. I can't breathe. I'm drowning. The towel is ripped off.

"Give him up and we'll let you go. This doesn't have to last any longer."

I shake my head, tears streaming down my face. I gasp for air.

"Vivianna, look at me."

The towel. The water. Again. Again. Again.

"Vivianna! Look at me!"

Firm hands grasp my cheeks, forcibly turning my head to face him. It's not them. It's not them. It's not.

My eyes frantically scan my surroundings. Hardwood and drywall, not concrete. Natural light from a window, not a flickering light bulb. Damian's amber eyes, not theirs. He carefully watches me as I scoot back, still quivering.

"I told you to leave," I stutter.

"Where did you just go?" Damian places his hand on my shin, which I jerk away from him. "Is it Sergei?"

"No." I stand and wrap my arms around my stomach. My fear gradually subsides into bitterness. "Now get out."

"I'm not leaving until I know you're okay," Damian counters.

I stare at a chip in the paint on the wall, clenching my jaw. Damian just sits there, waiting, watching.

"Did they tell you I never gave you up?" I clench and unclench my fists by my side. "Not once, not a single time?"

"What do you mean?" Damian stands apprehensively. "It was just Sergei, just the one time, wasn't it?"

"Vinny was weak," I spit. "He gave you up within hours every goddamn time. Me? I lasted days. They never broke me, not even once. I've proved myself over and over again. So you don't get to come in here and mock me. You don't get to be offended when I need a fucking minute."

"Viv, what are you saying?" Devastation creeps into his voice.

"Watching Marco…" All of the air in the room seems to have vanished. I fight for a breath, unable to fill my lungs as I stagger against a wall. "I couldn't… I couldn't let them see."

I scrunch my eyes closed, digging my fingers into my scalp. *How do we find Damian Marano?* I don't know Damian Marano. *Where is he?* I don't know. *Answer me, Vivianna!* I don't know, I don't know, I don't know!

I grab a knife from my end table and hurl it at my mannequin, not even bothering to care where it ended up. My hands shake as I reach for the leather sheath, fastening it around my waist with the one remaining blade. Its familiar weight does nothing to soothe my frayed nerves.

"Are you saying you and Vincenzo were tortured?" Damian's face darkens, anger setting into his features.

"You didn't know?" I whisper, finally meeting his stare.

"How could you possibly think I would've let that happen if I did?" His wrath skims off him in waves.

"Once a year." I fall back to my knees, staring into space. "They would come at night, take us from our beds. They needed to make sure we were strong enough. No matter what, the Palazzos protect the Maranos. I never broke. Not even once. I'll never break."

"Who did this to you?" His growl sends a chill down my spine.

"My father. Your father." I blink, then force my eyes to look into his. "And Marco."

His nostrils flare as he takes a step back, nodding slowly. He pulls his pistol free of its holster, ejecting the magazine.

"Damian, what are you doing?" I force myself to my feet, but he ignores me. He walks out of my room, clicking the magazine back into place. "Damian!"

CHAPTER 16
DAMIAN

I hear her screaming my name. Her voice follows each step as I descend the stairs to the Pit, each heartbeat thudding in my ears, each breath trying to keep my rage at bay. My 9mm is pointed downward, but there's a bullet waiting in the chamber.

"I'll be able to crack him in the next few hours," Marco boasts to the other lieutenants, washing blood off his hands. "Right now, he's rethinking his life decisions."

He feels my presence before he sees me, his cocky stance shifting to one of concern when he takes in the look on my face, the way my finger is itching around the trigger of my pistol. I've never killed one of my own men before. I'm debating whether that will change today.

"Is it true?" The temperature of the room turns frigid. "Don't you dare lie to me. Did you torture the Palazzo children?"

There's a clamor from the side of the room as Tony drops the tools he was cleaning. I nearly forgot Marco and I had an audience, between the lieutenants and Vincenzo standing by.

"I was following orders." Marco wipes his hands on a towel. Residual blood streaks the fabric. "I've always been loyal to the family."

"Following orders?" I narrow my eyes. "That's your defense? For torturing children?"

"It was a necessary unpleasantry." He throws the towel over the edge of the sink. "Some sacrifices have to be made for the greater good, for the protection of the family."

"Children, Marco," I growl. "Children! You mean to tell me this was the only way?"

"It worked, didn't it?" He shrugs as he gestures toward Enzo against the wall. "Look at what I made. Two loyal soldiers who would step in front of a bullet for you. They would die with smiles on their faces if it meant you would survive another day."

"Vivianna was never supposed to be in the Ombra." My finger twitches against the trigger guard again.

"And?"

"She was never supposed to be my bodyguard." I take a distinct step forward. "Yet you abused her too!"

The silence in the room only seems to grow, the only sound that of the dripping faucet.

"Tell me that was for my benefit." My lungs struggle to fill with each breath. "Tell me that the man who raised me condoned that. Tell me her own father volunteered her for that 'privilege.' Tell me how you could do something like that and still look at yourself in the mirror!"

"She…" Marco swallows. "She was a mistake. If we would have known what she would grow into, we never would have allowed her to train."

"You're a monster." I grit my teeth. "What other inexcusable things have you done? What other secrets are you hiding from me?"

"I was following orders!" His voice snaps with acid. "Call me a monster. Call me whatever you want. It was your father who gave the command."

"Then it's a good thing he's dead."

"The former Mr. Marano was a greater Don than you'll ever be," he seethes. "He knew when to make the tough decisions. You think he would allow the Russians to bite at his ankles if he was still alive? You say you're fully grown, but you still have much to learn."

"Go to hell, Marco." My fingers tighten around the handle of my pistol. "Tell my father hi when you get there. The two of you can struggle with your consciences together."

"There's nothing for me to struggle with." He crosses his arms over his chest and leans casually against the counter. "The weight of that guilt is passed down to you, one of the many perks of being Don. Like I said, I was only following orders."

"No." My body tenses in disgust. "The sin isn't mine. I didn't give the order. I was just a kid myself. I didn't know."

"Are you truly saying you didn't suspect anything?" Marco prowls forward with a self-righteous smirk on his face. "All those years. You saw Vincenzo how often? Weekly? Sometimes more? And you really had no clue?"

The air is knocked out of my chest.

My eyes drift across the room until they lock onto Enzo's. His white knuckles are angrily crushing his water bottle, the liquid spilt over his hand and onto the floor. The flashes of rage, the aloofness, the apathy all make sense now.

"Enzo," I plead breathlessly. "Please, I didn't know. I would have never let anyone do that to you or your sister."

"Sure," Vincenzo spits, throwing the bottle onto the ground. "You're innocent as long as you play the victim card, but I'm still here, aren't I? Good thing your daddy's morals were dark enough for you to benefit from without getting your hands dirty."

"You're right." I clench my fist, an acrid taste building in my mouth. "And I'm sorry. Being oblivious is not an excuse, but my eyes are open now, and things will change."

"Yeah," he scoffs. "Of course they will."

I ignore his barb and turn to face Marco.

"I can't trust you anymore," I state coldly. "We might be made men, but we've always had standards, the bare fucking minimum. It would be one thing if you showed even a modicum of remorse for what you did, but you can't be bothered to feel shame."

"It's because I'm not ashamed!" Marco takes several agitated steps forward. "I did what I had to do for the Marano family. I'll always put the family first."

"The Marano name belongs to me." My voice rumbles through my chest. "Marano has to mean something. Honor. Integrity. Decency. If it means nothing, then it is not worth protecting. Starting today, starting with me, it *will* mean something."

Marco goes to speak again, but I hold up my hand, silencing him.

"You clearly don't share these principles, so until you do…" I take a breath and steel my nerves. "You won't be my second any longer."

"Excuse me?" Marco stammers angrily. "You can't just fire me! I have served this family for decades."

"The only reason you're alive is because of your service." My threat cuts through the air as my grip tightens on my pistol. "If you want to prove yourself worthy of being one of my lieutenants, you'll have to earn it. You can work your way through the ranks back to a leadership position, but for now, you're little more than an initiate."

"You can't do this to me, Damian," he growls, fingers clenching at his sides.

"I just did." My voice lowers to match his tone. "Get out of my sight."

Everyone waits with bated breath for his response.

He takes one slow step closer, then another, and then turns to leave, brushing past me with a hostile air. Vincenzo's expression is hard to read, whereas my two remaining lieutenants stare at me with open shock.

I take a second to glance at the ceiling, take a breath, and calm myself. My gun slots back into its holster, safety on.

Composure, control, competence. Lessons learned through blood and tears. Lessons I won't soon forget.

"Sebastian," I say softly, "there seems to be a job position available. I need a second. It's yours if you want it."

"You're kidding?" He shakes his head. "I'm not qualified. I wouldn't even begin to know what to do."

"Eh, it's easy." I shrug and run a hand through my hair. "Marco mostly just lectured me and told me I was being stupid."

"You're being stupid now," Sebastian retorts.

"See?" A small smile curves at the corner of my mouth. "You're already doing great. Accept the promotion, Sebastian."

Tony gives him a gentle nudge and a nod. Sebastian looks between the two of us a few times before swallowing nervously.

"It would be an honor, sir."

"Great. Next item of business, the Ombra." I face Enzo directly. His suspicious glare hasn't shifted. "There's nothing I can do to erase the suffering your family has endured, but I can promise it ends today. I hereby release you and your future children from any familial duty to my own. There will be no more Ombra. Never again. You and your sister are both dismissed."

His jaw falls open in disbelief, but someone else fills the silence before he can speak.

"No!" Vivianna emerges from the shadows of the staircase and desperately runs into the room. Her brother intercepts her, locking an arm around her waist and holding her back. "Damian, you can't do this to us! I won't let you!"

"I'm sorry." My voice cracks as tears prick at the back of my eyes. "Vivianna, I am so sorry. I never meant to hurt you, I swear."

"Please," she begs, clawing at her twin's grip. "Please!"

"We can go home, Anna." Enzo tugs her toward the doorway, far, far away from me. "Let's go home. Just the two of us."

She falls to the floor with a heartbroken wail of utter devastation, her dark hair splayed over the ground. Her shoulders shake with each sob as her nails dig into the cement. Vincenzo tries to pull her away, but she is unmovable.

I approach slowly, holding eye contact with Enzo who begrudgingly backs up to let me try to soothe her.

"Go," I urge, kneeling beside her. "You're free. You can have anything you want."

"You're wrong," Viv whispers. "I just lost everything. Everything. How could you do this to me?"

"I love you, Vivianna, but I can't be the person holding the key to your cage." I brush a kiss on her temple as I stand. "I love you enough to want you to live the life you deserve. You could be happy, safe. What comes next is your choice, not mine. Yours."

"You!" She whips her head up, eyes locking onto me instantly. "I choose you!"

"Viv…"

Her earlier distress is gone, replaced by a disquieting serenity as she unshcathes the knife from her belt. She takes a deep breath and drags the blade down her palm.

"What are you doing?!" My voice raises in alarm as she grabs my hand, bowing her head submissively. I jerk my hand away before she can speak. "You don't want this!"

"Yes, I do!" She attests as drops of crimson splatter on the concrete. "I've never wanted anything else."

"Anna, think this through." Enzo inches toward her with his hands anxiously outstretched. "We can walk away right now, go home to mom, finally be a family again. Come on, Anna. It's time to go."

"I have to let you go, Viv. I have to." I take a step back, but Viv sharply grabs my wrist, pulling me close to her.

In a blink, she forces the blade into my hand and presses it against her throat.

"My life is yours," she dares, tilting her chin up. "If you don't want it anymore, at least put me out of my misery."

I try to tear my hand away or drop the knife, but Viv's grip is strong, insistent. All I accomplish is smearing more of her blood over my knuckles, over the hilt.

"Go ahead." Her breaths are shallow as she puts more pressure on her neck. "Nothing you do could ever hurt me. I love you."

Everyone else in the room fades, and it's just me and her. Her brown eyes, still and pleading, staring deep into mine. My resolve fades as my free hand brushes a strand of hair out of her face.

"Are you sure you want this?" The words catch in my throat. "Really want this?"

Her single nod reminds of that day all those months ago in the Masquerade. So confident, so determined. If I were to go back knowing what I know now, would I still make the same decision? Would I still ask her that one question, the one that set all of this into motion?

"Please," she whispers. "Damian, please. Let me stay. I want to stay."

"Don't," Enzo pleads softly, his face portraying his quiet agony.

"Please, Damian."

Vivianna squeezes my hand once more, and in this moment, I know that I can't bear to let her go.

"Let's make the vows together then." I kneel, lowering myself until I'm level with her. "To protect each other from whatever dangers lie out there. To love each other through it all. Fuck last names, fuck family curses. Just you and me, facing the world hand in hand. Together."

Viv's mouth falls slightly agape, but her grip loosens until I can ease my hand away. The knife is heavy, its weight a reminder of the oath I'm about to take, but I have no reservations. I love Vivianna. And if she wants this, truly wants this, then I will let myself want it too.

The thin red line draws a hiss from my mouth, and I clench my eyes closed as the pain hits me all at once. The knife clatters to the concrete.

"Breathe," Viv coaches, cradling my cheek with her uninjured hand. "Deep breaths in and out."

"God." I wince, flexing my fingers. "Who was the asshole that decided this was a blood oath?"

"Are you sure you want to do this?" Viv asks quietly.

I don't validate her question with a response. Instead, I grip her hand tightly with mine, our blood blending as we speak in perfect synchronicity, the Italian words flowing freely from our tongues.

For as long as I may live, I pledge myself to you.

You will feel no pain, for I will take it from you.

You will fear no bloodshed, for I will keep you safe from harm.

I shall be the shadow behind you, the shield on your arm, the sword at your side.

From this moment on, my life is yours.

The final words barely leave my mouth before I tug her into my chest, crashing my lips into hers. My palm cups her cheek, smudging crimson across her skin, painting her red with my love and devotion. She returns my embrace, her handprint stamped on the back of my neck as she deepens our kiss.

As we pull away, I can't tear my eyes away from the woman in my arms, radiant regardless of the blood streaked along her temple.

"*Bellissima,*" I breathe, unable to keep the smile off my face.

"Did they…" Tony whispers to Sebastian. "Did they just get married?"

"Not yet." Though I answer Tony's question, each word is a promise to Vivianna, squeezing her hands as I hold her twinkling stare. "But soon. I'll book the biggest cathedral I can find, filling the pews so everyone can see my stunning bride. Time will stop as she steps through the doors, her beauty stealing the breath from our lungs. Everyone will know then that I am the luckiest man alive to have her for even a second, much less forever. My *bellissima*."

Claps sound from behind me, and I wrest my eyes away from Viv to see Tony and Sebastian beaming. Meanwhile Enzo just stands there, a look of horror covering his features. He quickly blinks it away, pretending to be an overjoyed brother. He'll come around eventually, or he won't. I really couldn't care less. Not when his sister is in my arms, positively glowing.

I lift her against my chest and carry her to the counter, grabbing the first aid kit off the shelf.

"I want to do this right," I say, gingerly wrapping her palm with gauze. "I want to give you the wedding you deserve. One where you can drink and dance and celebrate with me, without worrying about keeping me safe."

"I can't, not when—"

"Shh, I know," I soothe lowly, brushing a thumb over her brow. She takes the bandages from me, tightly encasing my own wound. "Wait for me. I'll give you the head of Sergei Petrov as a wedding present to show you how much I love you."

"Hmm." Viv smirks as she secures the gauze. "I suppose that would work for me, so long as I get to give you the head of Bruno Petrov."

"Anything you want," I promise. "You've got me wrapped around your finger, and I'll do whatever it takes to watch you walk down that aisle."

The title doesn't matter. Ombra. *Bellissima*. Fiancée. Mine. Vivianna Palazzo loves me, and I love her. Whatever happens, whatever comes next, we will face it together.

EXCITED FOR THE NEXT CHAPTER?

STAY TUNED FOR

AS LONG AS I MAY LIVE

COMING 2025

CHAPTER 1
DAMIAN

My entire life, one thing has been true. My Ombra will protect me. One statement. One fact. One certainty I've been able to trust time and time again. After lightning comes thunder. Where there's smoke, there's fire. A full Windsor is the only correct knot for neckties. My Ombra will protect me.

The past few months have taught me new facts, ones that resonate in my core. Wine tastes better on her lips. The scent of vanilla and cinnamon clings to her skin. She's going to be my bride. My Ombra. My *bellissima.* My everything.

Vivianna Palazzo.

The blades of her knives flash in the light as she spins, her long black braid whipping around her head. The idiots dumb enough to face her fall to the ground in a heap. Jesus Christ, she is stunning.

She doesn't falter as their blood sprays, dripping down her cheek. Instead, she leaps over a table, focused on the third hostile retreating toward the kitchen. I quickly swallow my last sip of wine before chasing after them, pulling my 9mm free of the holster in the small of my back.

"Viv, wait up!" I call out.

Unsurprisingly, she doesn't. Viv takes it personally when someone tries to kill me. It happens often. Such is life as the Don of the Italian mafia.

A sea of black suits seems to appear out of the woodwork. My men cut off the exits, leaving the would-be assassin spinning in the room, desperately searching for a way out. Viv twirls her blades in her hands, growing closer and closer with a look of pure hatred on her face.

"Mr. Marano, are you interested in interrogating this bastard or should I put him down like the dog he is?" Viv sneers.

Sensing his dwindling opportunity to escape, the attacker lunges at her, wrapping Viv in his arms and holding her wrist to press one of her own knives against her throat. Instantly, my gun and every other one in the building is trained on him. My vision flares red, but Viv is unbothered.

"I'm walking out of here or the girl dies!" The man screams, a bead of sweat dripping from his eyebrow.

"Mr. Marano, I'm still waiting on your answer." Her eyes are locked onto mine, calm yet alert.

"Kill him," I order, any mercy I might have had long gone. "Not too quickly though. Make him regret ever laying eyes on you."

"Put your guns down!" The attacker stammers uneasily. "I'm not bluffing."

"Are you forgetting this man tried to kill you?" Viv's mouth curves into a small smile. "That sounds like a much more severe transgression."

"We're leaving now!" The man shouts, tugging her a step toward the entrance. He forgot an important fact in his plan. Viv has two knives. "Get out of our— Ahh!"

Viv plunges her second knife into his thigh, simultaneously throwing her head back to smash into his. He stumbles back, holding his bloody nose as he drops his grip on her. Viv whirls around, slamming her foot into his chest. She follows him down to the ground and slides a blade between his ribs. Blood gurgles in his lungs as he chokes, dying much faster than the piece of shit deserves.

Viv stands slowly, stepping back as she resheathes her knives. I spin her around to face me, carefully dragging my sleeve over her neck to wipe away the blood splatter. I exhale when I find unbroken skin — no cut, no injury.

"I'm okay," she whispers tenderly, cradling my cheek with her hand. "I was in control the whole time. That idiot was never about to hurt me."

"You killed him too fast," I growl and pull her into my embrace. "He should have suffered."

"You know…" Her finger trails down my tie as she speaks just loudly enough for me to hear. "You're really sexy when you're overprotective."

"Excuse me?" I raise an eyebrow. "He held a knife to your throat. I am the correct amount of protective."

All I get from her is a coy smile, a slight twinkle in her eye. Then she's back to business, escorting me outside as she cautiously observes the staff and patrons with a stern look. The SUV is waiting, a driver holding the door open as I am ushered inside. My seatbelt buckle clicks, and gradually, my residual anger fades.

Why did I have Viv kill that man? He probably had information we could have used. We should have brought him in alive.

There's a mole in my syndicate. A goddamn mole leaking our secrets to the fucking Russians. Every person we bring in dies before they can confess who the source is. This time, it's my fault.

Viv curls into the seat next to me, resting her head on my shoulder. Vivianna. My fiancée. I want nothing more than to claim her in front of the world and change her last name, but I promised her the head of Sergei Petrov first. The head of the Russian Bratva. The man who killed my father and left her with the scar down the side of her face. Once he's dead, I'm whisking her to the nearest chapel.

My fingers brush a stray strand of hair out of her face as my lips brush her forehead. She lazily tilts her head up, and I eagerly comply, moving down to kiss her properly. My hand drifts down to unbuckle my seatbelt, but Viv catches it, tsking condescendingly.

"It isn't safe to be unbuckled in a moving vehicle, Damian." Mischief flashes in her eyes. "I must insist you remain buckled in."

"Really?" I taunt. "How disappointing. I was planning on kissing you until I forgot how to breathe on my own, but I suppose that will have to wait."

Viv's seatbelt is off in a second, her muscular thighs straddling mine as she crashes into me. I moan into her mouth as she grinds against my lap, rubbing my growing erection.

"What a hypocrite," I chuckle, cupping her ass in my hands.

"I'm your Ombra." She tugs my hair to get better access to my neck. Little kisses dot my veins. "It's my job to die for you, and fuck, this is the way I want to die."

"I took those vows too," I moan, feeling my eyes roll back in my head. "We're supposed to protect each other."

"Then tell me to get off," she dares. Her lips hover over my body, her breath tingles my skin, her fingers loosen in my hair. "Tell me to sit in my own seat and keep my hands to myself."

"It's not like you listen to my orders anyway." I dig my nails into the rough material of her pants, pulling her flush against my pelvis. Heat radiates from between her thighs, and I can feel my dick twitch beneath her.

"What are you going to do about it?" Her challenge lingers in the air for only a second before I answer, pressing my lips against hers.

Every breath I take comes from her mouth until the car parks, and Viv finally allows me to unbuckle my seatbelt. From there, it takes only minutes for me to escort her into our bedroom, barely able to keep my hands off of her as we hurry through the compound. No sooner does the door click shut than do I slam Viv against the wood, wrapping my fingers around her throat as I slide my tongue between her lips. Her pulse races at my touch. I bet I can make it go faster.

"We left the restaurant in a hurry, Vivianna," I scold with a playful tone. "I'm still hungry."

My hand stays around her neck as I slide the other between her legs. As she squirms against the door, I sweep a finger between her folds and suck it clean. Fuck, she tastes perfect. She steps out of her pants after I slide the fabric down her thighs. I kneel at her feet.

"Open your legs for me, *bellissima*," I croon.

Viv shivers when my breath glances against her core, but she widens her legs obediently. Funny how all of her listening problems go away when her pleasure is on the line. I lift one of her legs over my shoulder, giving myself even more access to my dessert.

"Good girl."

If she wasn't wet before, those two words would have done the trick. Regardless, she's practically dripping for me now. I run my tongue along her inner thigh, determined to not let a single drop of her arousal go to waste.

"Fuck," she curses as I lick her opening. Her hands grip my scalp for support as her shoulders press into the wood behind her. The muscles of her thigh clench around my head, pulling me closer to her center.

I'm not about to complain. There's not a single thing on this earth that could tear me away from her, from my meal of choice. Every part of Viv is exquisite, but damn, I could eat her out all day and still crave more. Always more.

I dive in deeper, relishing how her voice cries out with each lap of my tongue. Her clit is so sensitive, sending shockwaves up her spine as I nip and suck on the nub. It isn't long until Viv is shaking, digging her nails into the door behind her as her legs threaten to give out. I shift, carrying more of her weight onto my shoulders.

With that, she lets go, trusting me to support her as her orgasm shudders through her. I am all too happy to oblige, holding her securely against the wall until I finish drinking in the last of her salty arousal. Well-fed and happy, I stand, lifting Viv in my arms and walking toward the bed.

"I'm still covered in blood," Viv protests tiredly. "I need to shower."

"If you are able to stand, then I didn't do a good enough job," I tease, changing course to the bathroom.

I set her on the counter as I turn on the shower, letting the water heat up. Viv leans against the mirror, slowly slipping the buttons of her shirt free. The fabric pools on the floor, followed closely by my suit jacket, her bra, and then the rest of my clothes. I test the temperature of the water, then turn around to pick Viv back up, but she's standing, stepping into the stream on her own legs. Duly noted. I slide in behind her, watching as the red water eventually runs clear. Shampoo, conditioner, soap. She's clean. Time to dirty her up.

My arm snakes around her waist, pulling her shoulders against my chest. My other hand scrapes down her ribs, drawing the little gasps I know so well. It gradually inches lower and lower until it is nestled between her legs. Little circles. Big circles. Slow circles. Realllly slow circles. Viv leans her head back, closing her eyes in ecstasy.

"Damian…" Her voice trembles, already desperate for another climax. Her hand wraps around my shaft, gently pumping as I slip a finger inside her, then another. "Damian!"

Viv's legs buckle, but I catch her before she can fall. Instead, I turn her around, lifting her against the tile wall. Her legs wrap around my waist as my cock nudges her entrance, firmly sliding inside. I don't give her time to adjust, filling all of her at once. She can take it. Fingernails scrape my back, I'm sure leaving long, red scratches on my skin. I hiss at the sharp pain, but god, I love the way she marks me.

"Sorry." Her shaky apology comes between thrusts, her tits bouncing deliciously with each jerk.

"Do it again," I order, running a hand up her body.

"But it hurt you," she stammers.

"Again, Vivianna!" I tweak a nipple brutally, leaving no room for her concern.

My lips crash into hers, my contented groans melding with her gasps as she digs her nails into my muscles. I keep twisting and tugging, riding the fine line between pleasure and pain as my cock slams into her again and again. She screams as she tumbles over the edge of her release, clinging to me desperately. Her walls clench around me, and I can't help moaning her name as I join her.

"Vivianna." Each syllable is perfection. I am just obsessed with her. "Vivianna Marano."

"I'm still a Palazzo," she teases, brushing my sopping hair out of my forehead. "I haven't married you yet."

"You're mine," I growl, holding her against my chest possessively. "I don't care how long it takes. You are my fiancée, my bride, and one day, you will take my last name."

"Vivianna Marano," she whispers, dragging out each sound. Only she could make the name sound so sensual.

Fuck it. I throw her over my shoulder and step out of the shower. I grab a towel off the rack and lay it on the bed, tossing her on top of it. She laughs, trying to dry herself off, but I straddle her, dripping water everywhere.

"Say it again." The authority in my voice is immovable.

"Vivianna Marano." Light flickers in her eyes, playful and flirtatious.

"Don't stop."

My hand sends wave after wave of pleasure through her body as she repeats herself over and over and over again. This time when she comes, it's not my name she screams.

As the final aftershocks ripple through her body, I yield, content with knowing she has been thoroughly satisfied and is not about to stand anytime soon. With a fresh towel, I dry her off and tuck her under the sheets. Her soft snores float through the room as sleep takes her. *Bellissima.* My *bellissima.*

Quietly, I sneak back into the bathroom, gathering our clothes to toss into the hamper. Viv's discarded weapons are placed back where she likes them — knives on the dresser, one gun tucked into the bed frame, the other with mine in the safe.

I've tried to curb her hypervigilance with not much success. It took a week of begging to have her move her pistol from underneath her pillow to the bed frame. A week. Arguably a much safer location for us both, but Viv was worried about the extra second it would take to grab it if there was an intruder. She didn't appreciate the joke I made about setting up booby traps to catch them instead.

"Don't touch him." Her whispers pierce my heart as though they were bullets. Her fists clench the sheets with white knuckles. "Run, Damian. Save yourself." I dart over and wrap her sleeping form into my arms.

"Shhh," I hush, brushing her hair from her face. "I'm safe. You're safe. We're both safe."

"Damian," she mumbles, her eyes scrunching tighter closed.

"Damian's safe," I promise. "Relax, Vivianna. Rest easy. Damian loves you so much." Her breathing gradually slows, but I don't let her go. Instead, I stroke her hair, brush kisses along her cheek, squeeze her against my chest.

She has nightmares most nights. Normally, I can stop them before they get too bad, whispering sweet nothings until her muscles slacken. Sometimes I'm too late, and her screams wake me, her body thrashing in the sheets as she claws at her scar.

Those nights are rough for both of us. I pin her down as I try to rouse her, though sometimes she breaks free and gets a swipe on me before she fully wakes. Her sobs soak my shirt as I hold her, rubbing her back until her shuddering ceases. It kills me every time, knowing that I am at the center of each and every one of her night terrors. Bloodied. Beaten. Dead.

But tonight her dreams thankfully seem to sweeten without too much coaxing. I lean back on my pillow, adjusting her to curl against my shoulder.

The assassination attempts have become more frequent recently, but it didn't always used to be this bad. Once I kill the Russians, it will go back to normal. Viv could relax, let her guard down. Drink a glass of wine without feeling guilty and leave her firearms at home. We could go on dates where she is a gorgeous woman in a dress, not my bodyguard silently standing watch. Maybe I could find a way to show her and ease her fears. We're safe. We can close our eyes and sleep, dream of her walking toward me in a white dress.

Vivianna Marano.

Soon.

ABOUT THE AUTHOR

L. J. Wede has a guiding philosophy — write the book that you want to read. An avid lover of spicy romances, Wede has taken that to heart with her debut novel, *Igniting the Spark*.

Born in rural Iowa, Wede has always had a passion for books and for reading. While she originally worked in marketing, she would choose to unwind most nights with a book. It was out of this passion for literature that she began to write her first novel and fell in love with the craft.

Follow her on social media or subscribe to her newsletter at https://ljwede.com/newsletter/ to catch her latest release.

www.ingramcontent.com/pod-product-compliance
Lightning Source LLC
Chambersburg PA
CBHW060616300726

48975CB00005B/1581